WEREMONES

By

Buffi BeCraft-Woodall

Paranormal Romance

New Concepts   Georgia

Be sure to check out our website for the very best in fiction at fantastic prices!

When you visit our webpage, you can:
* Read excerpts of currently available books
* View cover art of upcoming books and current releases
* Find out more about the talented artists who capture the magic of the writer's imagination on the covers
* Order books from our backlist
* Find out the latest NCP and author news--including any upcoming book signings by your favorite NCP author
* Read author bios and reviews of our books
* Get NCP submission guidelines
* And so much more!

We offer a 20% discount on all new Trade Paperback releases ordered from our website!

Be sure to visit our webpage to find the best deals in e-books and paperbacks! To find out about our new releases as soon as they are available, please be sure to sign up for our newsletter (http://www.newconceptspublishing.com/newsletter.htm) or join our reader group (http://groups.yahoo.com/group/new_concepts_pub/join)!

The newsletter is available by double opt in only and our customer information is *never* shared!

Visit our webpage at:
www.newconceptspublishing.com

New Concepts Publishing, Inc.
5202 Humphreys Rd.
Lake Park, GA 31636

ISBN 978-1-58608-891-0
© 2006 Buffi BeCraft-Woodall
Cover art (c) copyright 2006 Jenny Dixon

NCP books are available at special quantity discounts for bulk purchases for sales promotions, premiums, fund raising, or educational use. For details, write, email, or phone New Concepts Publishing, Inc., 5202 Humphreys Rd., Lake Park, GA 31636; Ph. 229-257-0367, Fax 229-219-1097; orders@newconceptspublishing.com.

First NCP Trade Paperback Printing: March 2007

Dedication:

This book is for John and Shae for keeping the faith. And for Dad, for being all the kids' Papa.

Index of Terms

Alpha Canis/Pater Canis - The male leader of a wolven (shapeshifting wolf) pack

Alpha Matra/Matra Canis - The female leader of a wolven (shapeshifting wolf) pack

Change - The act of shifting forms from human to animal

Beta - The Alpha Canis's second in command. Often the wolven pack teacher/caretaker

Challenge - Contest or fight for a higher rank in the pack

Coyotemen - Shapeshifting male coyotes

Dragonkind - Dragons

Dueling Form - The half wolf/half man werewolf form used mainly for fighting

Duel of Ascendancy - Official challenge and fight to the death for leadership of a pack

Empath- A type of psychic who is has the ability to feel the emotions of those around him/her

Fairie - Pertaining to the fairy species

Fairy - Any of the species of elves, dryads, sprites, brownies, and so on, who are vulnerable to iron

Hell Hounds- Stray wolven running together without a territory of their own. Drifter werewolves

Pack - The wolven family unit. The family unit is made up of a male and female alpha leader pair and lesser member in a definite rank hierarchy.

Mate-bond - The magical/psychic marriage of a wolven or wolven/psychic couple. Only the female of the pair can perform this bonding.

Metaphysics/metaphysical - Supernatural or magical in nature

Normals - Term for normal humans with no supernatural or psychic gifts

Nul l- Less polite term for normal humans with no supernatural or psychic gifts

Omega - The lowest ranking in a wolven pack

Psychic - A type of magic user who does not need spells to perform their special magic.
Most psychics wrongly believe that their gifts are mental abilities.

Supernaturals - Inclusive term for all the magical species such as fairys, dragons, goblins, shapeshifters, witches, and so on

Territory - Wolven packs residing in the US define their boundaries by county or the same equivalent. Wolven Council law states that no less that two pack-free territories must separate those ruled by a wolven pack. Wolven packs are identified by county/state.

Warden - Protector of the Pack. Members of a pack whose job it is to protect and police the members.

Were[s] - A crude term used by the wolven (shapeshifting wolves) for all other animal species who can change forms

Werepanther - Shapeshifting panther

Wereraccoon - Shapeshifting raccoon

Werewolf - An outlaw shapeshifting wolf. A derogatory term for a shapeshifting wolf

Wolven - The proper term for a shapeshifting wolf

Wolven Council - Managing body of wolven (shapeshifting wolves) who make sure that no pack, wolven individual, or outsider endangers their species

Chapter One

Diana Ridley's lungs burned. Her feet tripped over another snarled root.

Behind her, the yip-yip of wild coyotes drowned out the crunch of dead leaves underfoot.

She stumbled, righted herself, and ran, before the snarling, snapping pack closed in.

Diana's world narrowed to two objectives. Running and breathing. One foot, breathe in, two foot, breathe out.

Stop and she would die. Horribly. Bloody images from a late night horror movie spurred her on.

If she didn't stop, her burning lungs would burst.

She scrambled over a deadfall tree. Wheezed for air. Halfway over, the break in the run brought her focus back to herself. Dirty khaki shorts and a fitted tee shirt were no protection from the biting thorny vines and dead brush in Dogwood Park.

Every bloody scratch on her bare arms and legs began to sting. Her limbs trembled. She gulped a breath.

A deadfall tree blocked her flight. Mid-scramble over the thigh-high obstacle, her shoestring lodged in the rough bark. Yip-yips and a chorus of coyote howls brought the terror back in an adrenaline filled rush. Diana jerked her foot loose. She stumbled, making the mistake of looking back.

No time to retie the shoestring. No time at all. Four coyotes crashed out of the brush behind Diana. Big, hungry coyotes. The animals growled, advancing in slow fits and starts. Eerie intelligence gleamed in their eyes. Foamy saliva from their exertion dotted their muzzles with white.

She was dog food. Dead. The excitement of the hunt washed over her, proving again that feeling others' emotions was not a gift, psychic or otherwise. It was a curse.

Her fear of being eaten crippled her mental shields, leaving her mind open to soak up all available emotion from those around her.

The animals' lust for blood incited a fresh wave of terror from her. The coyotes smelled her fear. The fear spiked their excitement, which scared her more. In her mind, she felt the slavering hunger.

They spread out for the kill. Diana lurched off of the downed tree trunk and fell. She scrambled to her feet and gasped. Her stomach somersaulted and dropped to the ground.

Two wolves, one black, one brown, jumped into Diana's path. They were huge animals, twice the size of the coyotes. The wolves' ears were pinned flat against their skulls. They bared the strong sharp teeth of healthy carnivores and growled. The newcomers' anger slapped into her mind, hot and possessive.

She never picked up on animal emotions. Only human's. Tonight was a fine night to learn a new skill set. The last thing she would feel would be how tasty she was when the coyotes and wolves ripped her to pieces.

The wolves bounded past her, tails high, clearing the fallen tree in a graceful leap. They descended on the coyotes, growling and barking.

Diana ran. Sounds of the vicious dogfight behind lent her speed.

There were coyotes *and* wolves in the park. The excess emotion and confusion cleared from Diana's mind with every bit of distance she put between her and the animals.

Teenagers. A new horror gripped its claws into her. Teenagers hung out here at night. Like her son, Matthew, who was stranded somewhere out here in the park.

She had to warn someone. Police, Animal Control.

Diana's new goal became her car and the cell phone in the glove box. She prayed that any teens parked out here had their windows up.

Not dogs, wild animals. She knew the difference. Matthew, her son, had written a term paper on them for graduation. Coyotes and wolves. Hungry ones. They weren't supposed to be in East Texas. At least the wolves weren't supposed to be here. Coyotes were a common nuisance, but weren't this big. The wolves too, were twice the size of normal animals.

Please God, she prayed, let Matthew's car have started. Let her son be safe. She had to find the spot where he and his girlfriend had broke down.

Diana changed her mind. She didn't want to put anyone else in danger.

The shadows of more animals materialized beside and behind her.

More wolves. They kept up easily and didn't immediately leap on her. She felt the animals' excitement. But unlike the coyotes, the wolves were not slavering for her blood. A psychic, she *felt* the difference in the animals emotions.

She wasn't stupid. She was no athlete, either. They were toying with her, wearing her down for an entertaining kill, she imagined.

The wolves could take her if they wanted.

Named for the copious spindly trees, Dogwood Park had few trees big enough to climb to safety. Without decent light, without time, she had no way to scope out a good climbing tree without first running headlong into it.

She wished for an oak or something equally tall and strong to smack into. A wolf snapped at her heels and barked impatiently. She wasn't running fast enough for its, *his* entertainment. Male emotions had a different flavor than female. The wolves were male.

The stitch in her side was unbearable. She stumbled and kept running. They wanted her to run. She felt their need in her mind. Chase the prey and take it down. Why didn't they take her?

A big one, black in the night, ran alongside her. A patch of hair was torn from his neck. He was one of the wolves that had fought off the coyotes. She didn't trust that saving her from being eaten before meant that she wasn't on the menu anymore.

The brush of the wolf's fur against her bare leg startled her into stumbling.

It barked at her.

Keep up. Run.

Diana felt the wolf's irritation. Irritated was bad. Where was the tree she needed?

She lunged forward blindly and smacked into something solid.

Diana rebounded, landing hard on her butt, arms and legs akimbo. She looked up and sucked in a breath.

Monster. She believed in monsters. Now.

His face was a horrific mask of animal and man. Anger boiled out of him, drowning out the wolves' excitement, scalding her psychic senses.

Red eyes shone in the dark. A muzzle full of teeth snarled down at her out of a furred half-man/half-wolf face. Powerful arms ended in sharp claws. His muscled body was covered in pale silvered fur and ... sweatpants?

Even his big, pale, furred feet were tipped with claws, weapons for rending and tearing.

Diana closed her eyes and gulped. She heard the quiet rustle as the pursuing wolves stopped. Time drew out as she waited for the attack.

Her head spun from lack of oxygen. Her mind whirled while imagination became reality.

A monster. A werewolf. She was going to die, eaten in Dogwood Park by a werewolf while her son necked nearby with his girlfriend.

She took a breath and forced her eyes open, daring to look her death in the face. Was she stupid or what?

When Diana looked back up, she doubted her own sanity as she gazed into the chiseled face of the best looking man she'd ever laid eyes on.

Monster? What monster? She was delusional from running. The man was gorgeous. The stitch in her side was barely noticeable. Her breath came in small pants.

She met his eyes, nearly colorless eyes in the night, and felt a jolt of connection. Magic, power, psychic energy, whatever it was called, flowed from the man in a live current. The energy flooded her senses, linking her directly into his emotional turmoil.

She tried to throw up a mental barrier. Wasted effort, she was too tired. Her defenses had been breached earlier and were useless. It was like trying to mop up a dam with a paper towel. The flood threatened to wash her away, taking her sanity with it.

"What the hell?"

The man's voice cut through her, breaking the enthrallment. Diana struggled against the surge of his power, trying to find the shreds of her mind somewhere in the chaos. Her fingertip hold on sanity turned into a tentative grasp. Attempting to strengthen her hold, she reached out with her psychic abilities. She made a connection.

What she found was a wild mental image of woods, earth, and running free. Diana was an empath. Her psychic gifts had never included visions before. Instinctively, she took the image, taking it for her own as a refuge against the man's overwhelming power and emotions.

Diana embraced the purely emotional and metaphysical thunderstorm that raged from the man. His anger, grief, and frustration filled her. Fumbling, she tried to use her empathic gift in reverse. She set aside the fear and reached for her hard won inner peace, pushing some of the peace she sensed he was searching for into him.

The sudden bark and whine reminded her of the danger. Diana snapped from her attempt to help. The sudden shift sending her back into panic mode.

Oh god. She remembered. The wolves. Coyotes. Matthew in the park.

Diana tried to climb to all fours, to warn the man. She had to get him to shut off the psychic and emotional connection between them. She was drowning.

A desperate wheeze escaped her. She swooned, giddy on exhaustion and overload. Her brain felt fried. A circuit board hit by lightning.

The man she'd mistaken for a monster reached down with one big hand and hauled her to her feet. The turmoil still churned inside him, but at a distance. As if one of them had finally put up a mental shield.

She had a glimpse of high cheekbones and moonlight hair as he scooped her high into his arms. The wide chiseled planes of his chest were hot against her skin. A distant part of her brain marveled at the ease that he held her. The rest of her wanted to pass out.

Wolves. She had to tell him about the wolves.

"Well? Explain. And it had better be good." His gravel toned voice brooked no disobedience.

"Wolves." She croaked into his chest. "Run. Get away."

The stupid man just stood still, holding her. A distant part of her mind screamed at him. *Run! It's not safe!*

Diana struggled to get down, to warn him. She was too weak to do more than wiggle.

The arms clenched around her, protective and immovable. She tried again to warn him but he shifted and pressed her face into his chest. The strong hand held her still.

Her mind ceased being buffeted by his confusing emotions. His amazing raw psychic energy was finally leashed and locked safely away under his control.

Diana inhaled the scent of man and forest. Her female instincts labeled him as the strong protector type. Her hands fisted against the crisp hair of his bare chest.

The steady beat of his heart drummed in her ears, lulling her. Exhaustion cast a haze on her senses, pulling her down toward blissful unconsciousness. She fought, knowing that if she lost, they would die.

"There were coyotes, Adam." A growly voice explained. "We took care of them. We brought her to you for safekeeping, Adam. I swear."

With her face pressed into the man's chest, she couldn't see. But she *felt* only the empathic presences of the man and the surrounding wolves. Surely the wolves weren't the ones talking? She was tired and mentally drained enough to believe. There was a familiarity to the voice that she couldn't place.

The edges of her awareness blurred.

"Damn it, Bradley. This is not acceptable behavior."

"But smell her. We couldn't let them have a psychic."

The man growled his displeasure, eliciting low canine whimpers from the wolves.

The leaves rustled. Diana wished she could see. She squirmed. The arms tightened to keep her still.

"No! Don't touch her." The man's sharp rebuke brought whimpers from the creatures. The emotion tugged at her, and her overloaded senses, but seemed to barely mollify the man. "All of you, Change and head home. You've done enough tonight."

The man's grip didn't lessen as she tried again to twist around. She managed a glimpse of several animal-men crouching at the man's feet.

Werewolves, her mind whispered. Not real wolves. They weren't animals. That was why she could feel their emotions.

A black haze crowded her vision. Then the blanket of darkness enveloped Diana's senses.

Chapter Two

Adam Weis waved his ride off and circled the psychic female's small blue car. He'd been too concerned last night about her health to worry about transportation, or what she might think waking up in his bed this morning. His pack had brought him a psychic female in need of protection. Her health and safety had been priority, and would continue to be now that he knew of her existence.

Damn werecoyotes. He really needed to do something about the other supernatural predators in his territory. He wasn't too worried about the werecoyotes or others of their ilk, just the inconvenience their presence caused. Most weres were disorganized and loyal only to themselves.

Pack Canis everywhere complained that you never knew what stupid thing a were would do next. No wonder it was policy to run the other supernaturals out of your territory as soon as possible.

Lately he didn't trust for his life not to go *fubar* all of a sudden. Weres and psychics were a temptation for fate to mess with him again. And kids, don't forget them and how they screwed with your personal life. His life was a chaotic mess.

Hell, yesterday morning he had promised that he'd oversee the clean-up of which of his boys were the culprits responsible for papering the middle school gymnasium bleachers with the words *Go Team!* The coach didn't appreciate real team loyalty when he saw it. Oh, well.

Adam sighed. Leaning against the car, he played one handed key toss. Being the boss had plenty of advantages. Calling the shots appealed to the dominant wolf in him. Adam truly liked working with his hands. The carpenter's life called to both sides of his nature.

Lobos Luna Construction had a reputation for good, fast work. On this beautiful Saturday morning, they'd been hard at work so that the first house in the subdivision he was building would be on schedule. He'd promised those folks they could move in the first week of July, and by God they would.

With a little hustling, and leaving his foreman Mack Spencer in charge, Adam had slipped away to retrieve the female's car.

Not everything about being the boss was daisy sweet. Not that he usually minded. Too much, that is.

Though today, Adam would cheerfully have strangled the idiot at the builder's supply. He'd never seen the like. Every two-by-four was warped, twisted, and full of knots the size of his fist. No exaggeration, the lumber had been that bad.

The delivery was dropped off after everyone had gone for the day. Thank God Mack had inspected the load first thing this morning. Had it been used, Adam would have rework instead, on top of dead time with men on pay. It would have been a hell of a mess.

Adam was later than he'd wanted to be getting the lady's car. There was no telling what was going on at the house in his absence. Last night, the boys had scared the wits out of Diana Ridley while rescuing her.

She'd seen and heard enough to think them all monster movie werewolves. Adam only hoped she blamed the fur-fest she'd seen last night on exhaustion and bad dreams. Maybe he could convince her it had all been a hallucination.

He wrestled with the seat adjustment on Diana Ridley's car, trying to fit his six-foot-four-inch frame into a space normally occupied by a petite, short-legged female. Not that he'd noticed her legs, or how her soft curves felt pressed close in his arms either.

Adam's pack consisted of five underage pups. No fighters. No wardens to stand with him against a threat. He didn't count the Mack, no matter how good the human was. He wanted Mack tucked away safe, but that wouldn't happen in a million years. The ex-soldier was too good at finding his own trouble.

In the confines of the car, Adam inhaled the woman's scent as he cranked and pulled out. A peculiar growl/whine slipped out of him. Her everyday use of it marked the vehicle as hers.

She smelled delicious. Woman/cookie/citrus was Diana Ridley, a tasty morsel that roused hungers in both the man and the wolf. ... No hint of the magical flavor psychics gave off when using their gifts lingered.

Apparently, he'd inherited his sire's human fetish, even if he wasn't in the market for procreation. Not a bad thing. At the end of the run, humans and shapeshifters shared the same DNA. Besides, humans had to be added in every couple generations for his line to stay fertile.

Halfway across town, his cell phone rang, pulling Adam from his musing. He glanced at the ID and pressed the button.

"Yeah?"

"Forget the lady's car, Adam. You better get back to the job site."

"Jesus, Mack. It's been what? Fifteen minutes?"

"Uh-huh. Just long enough for the crap to hit our doorstep. Hold up a sec." After a muffled bump, the line went silent. Mack had covered the receiver with one hand. Adam made an illegal u-turn and headed back across town.

"Adam? You still there?"

"Yeah. What's going on?"

"Sorry, that was the guy from Animal Control. We found a dead wolf in the dumpster."

A knot of apprehension tightened Adam's stomach. He'd had a few run-ins with animal control back in the Tarrant pack. Things were always touchy dealing with people who risked their lives handling wild and dangerous animals. People who occasionally ran into a changed wolven and captured them, thinking of keeping the human population safe from animal predators.

If they only knew.

The knot in Adam's stomach turned into a smoking lava rock as Mack continued.

"Animal Control is hauling it out now. I'm going to stall him as long as I can. But you'd better hurry if you want to take a look at it."

Damn, damn, damn.

Adam made a quick call to the house, checking heads as much as telling the boys to keep the woman there. His stomach eased while Mark rattled in his ear. There was nothing to eat in the house and the kid wanted this *awesome cool* skateboard with red and acid green flames for his birthday. Neither pronouncement was news to Adam. The boys ate everything they could pour ketchup on and the description of the skateboard was burned into Adam's memory from repetition.

Gee. Sarcasm laced Adam's thoughts. *I wonder what I'll get Mark for his birthday.*

* * * *

The world shifted. The gentle bounce of the mattress, the soft cocoon of blankets reassured Diana. Dreams and fantasies held no sway over the waking of day. With her eyes still closed, she drifted in a half asleep stage. The presence of another person near to her comforted her.

The dream had been awful. A lot of running and monsters trying to eat her.

No. Wolves. There'd been wolves and coyotes, but the monster had saved her. A monster that turned into a sexy hunk.

Yes, it had been a very bad dream. If she didn't do something about it now, she would be feeling everyone else's moods all day long. She'd wind up holed up in her bedroom with a migraine with a hot compress on her forehead, wrestling the child-proof cap off of a bottle of useless pain reliever.

As a natural empath, her first twenty-two years had been sheer hell, living a life bombarded by what others felt. Richard Ridley, her ex-husband had called Diana crazy. The truth was, her powers scared him. The divorce, emotionally devastating as it was, turned out to be Diana's salvation. When Karen's gifts manifested, Diana made sure her daughter had all the understanding and security she needed to develop.

This morning Diana's control over her own gifts was shaky. There was no one like her that she knew, no one to help her understand her abilities. She practiced a little yoga for control, to understand the energies that powered her psychic empathy. She had learned to build walls around herself, emotional and metaphysical.

The nightmare still felt so real. Her mental image of a fence and locked gate crumbled, leaving her mind open.

Diana felt drained, as if her energy was spread too thin, pulled outside her body over a distance. She sought her center, a nice seascape of peace and tranquility, but found a forest instead. A forest inhabited by wolves.

Her son, she assumed, settled on the bed and broke her scattered, sleep deprived, concentration with his insecurity. He *should* feel sorry.

If Matthew had needed a ride so badly last night, then he should have been at the Park entrance like he'd said he would. Sometimes he could be as thoughtless as his father. Diana pushed away the uncharitable thought. Matthew wasn't his father.

It was the dream. *Was* it a dream? Diana swallowed.

No, it was a dream. Otherwise …

Keep a low profile. You don't want the monsters to find you. Diana brushed off the stray admonition, obviously the result of too many internet chats with her favorite oddball computer whiz, Jax. She was going to have to get taller, less paranoid friends.

So close, his emotions resonated within her exhausted psyche, keeping her from sleep. She huffed and gave in to the inevitable. Digging under the comforter, Diana gave the lump behind her a pat and a light shove. He shifted, arm going over her legs. She wanted an apology, not this drawn out prelude to a drama.

"Matthew."

Not Matthew. The teen sitting next to her was not her son. And she *definitely* was not in her bedroom.

What exactly *had* happened last night?

Diana's heart thumped hard. She glanced around the room, checked her state of dress. Sudden fear dumped a jolt of adrenaline through her veins.

Her clean hand found her own dirty tee shirt. The underwire of her bra poked reassuringly into a breast. Her shorts were in a twisted wedgie.

Assured that she was relatively safe and unmolested, Diana forced herself to calm down. She focused on her visitor. Younger than her son, the boy was dressed in a ragged, oversize pair of jeans and an equally disreputable tee shirt that should have been thrown out by its first owner.

Familiar chocolate brown eyes watched her. The boy's prominent cheekbones and chin were all angles under the shaggy mess of rich, dark brown hair. The promise of a well-built man was there, needing only more weight and age to fulfill what nature had begun.

"Brandon Starr?"

He flushed and drew his knees up to his chin, wrapping his arms protectively around them. The boy's insecurity and underlying fear was a raucous noise inside her. This was familiar too.

Instinctively, she wanted to cuddle him and make it better. She pushed down the urge to mother everyone. Her own kids were nearly grown. Every day she was able to reclaim a little more time for herself. She didn't need to add someone else's to her list. She was almost home free from the awesome responsibility of parenting.

Brandon and his twin brother Bradley were from the pre-adolescent gang her daughter used to drag home for dinner. Over the years her, Karen had brought every kind of stray imaginable, human and animal, for Diana to mother. She'd been Room Mother, Club Den Mother, and neighborhood sitter.

Karen had a different dinner gang now--more giggling girls than the motley bunch of rough and tumble boys.

Of the twins, Brandon was a shy, sweet boy that often faded into the background. The others bossed him relentlessly until she pulled him into the kitchen to help with one thing or another. Diana didn't realize how much she missed Karen's old buddies, and almost thought of them as her own.

College was just a year away.

"Where am I?"

Diana tried not to sound harsh, she really did. Waking from starring as the prey in her very own werewolf flick in a strange man's bedroom set her on edge. The stack of Three Stooges videos on the bedside table were a dead give away.

She was physically exhausted. Nightmares tended to do that. *And* she had no memory of how she'd gotten here.

At any rate, her tone of voice fell short of friendly. Well within the range of a PMS moment. That state that every woman hits where simply existing was annoying. Warm and fuzzy memories weren't going to get poor Brandon off the hook.

Brandon, being male, and young and shy, did what any man with an ounce of self-preservation did. He froze.

"Well?" Diana raised her eyebrows, waiting for an answer.

He ducked and mumbled unintelligibly into his knees.

Oh, well. He wasn't forthcoming and she needed to find the bathroom. Diana slid off the edge of the bed.

"Don't mumble, hon. Which way is the--"

Her legs gave out. She gasped and crumpled into a surprised, painful, heap. She clutched at her calves as the muscles in both seized into rock-hard charlie horses.

"Are you okay, Miz Ridley?"

Diana glimpsed Brandon's head over the edge of the bed. Worry filled eyes peered down out of the shaggy mop that framed his face.

The bed moved, and then he was crouching down beside her. She closed her eyes against the agony in her calves and gritted her teeth.

"This is going to be weird." Brandon's insecurity threaded with a quiet confidence. "But pinch this little bit of skin between your nostrils."

A long forgotten Lamaze class floated in her memory. In the blink of an eye the boy turned from shy and intimidated to competent and nurturing. Like a pro, he massaged the hard knots out of her legs.

"That's better now, isn't it?"

One side of his mouth raised in a faint smile. His hand worked down her calf once more and dropped to pick fuzz balls out of the thick pile of navy carpet. Not one wear spot marred the plush surface. Not even a path to the door.

Diana eased out a breath, daring to let go of her nose. She could do without ever having to experience another charlie horse ever again.

"It is. Much better." She sighed, a little wary of the muscles knotting up again. "Tell me you're a licensed message therapist, because my old one, if I actually had one, is now fired. How did you know that?"

His hands were warm and steady as he helped her to sit back on the edge of the bed.

"The Discovery Channel. And I read a lot. You should wait and rest before you get up."

He squatted back down by where her feet dangled down from the high tester bed. If it were hers, she'd need a small stepladder to climb in, or maybe a wild scramble up.

She smiled a little at the thought. He took that for a good sign and smiled back, surprising Diana. She remembered that Brandon saved his smiles, like a priceless treasure sparingly doled out.

Handsome and sensitive. God, he'd be a lady killer when he grew up. His voice was soft, but sure.

"You should eat something. You need protein after physical stress."

"Something else you read?"

He made a little sound that could be taken either way. He touched her leg with the tip of a finger. For the first time, she noticed the mass of scratches and bruises covering her legs. Her arms looked the same.

Alarm flared through her and she leaned away, wary for the first time.

It was a dream. It had to be.

"What happened?"

She felt the spear of hurt from him. Why, she didn't know. She felt him simply fold away within himself, something she'd never experienced before. But that was not surprising since she'd devoted a great portion of her time to blocking out other people's emotions.

Brandon dropped his eyes and removed his hands to rest on his knees. The small space between them was a great chasm.

His answer was a mumble.

Well, *drat*. She felt guilty for weirding out and taking it out on the kid. It wasn't everyday you woke up in a strange man's bedroom, at least for her it wasn't.

She'd always had a soft spot for Karen's friends. She reached out to close the distance. Her fingers touched the silky softness of his hair.

Brandon sighed and closed his eyes as she finger combed through the messy locks. The look reminded her of a puppy getting its ears rubbed. She shoved that analogy away, hard. It touched too close to her nightmare.

It *was* a nightmare.

The emotional connection between them flared open again. She couldn't help but try to ease that need, the loneliness she felt inside him.

Vaguely, Diana remembered reading about the Starr boys' guardian dying in a fire last year. She felt bad for not paying attention to the events.

"How long since you last came to dinner? Two? Three years?"

Brandon leaned into her legs with a sigh.

"Two and a half years." He breathed.

"So, what happened?"

He tensed then peered up at her.

"Then or now?"

Diana ruffled through the silky mop again and smiled.

"How about last night? I had a strange nightmare and can't seem to get past that."

He went still, inside and out and looked away again.

"You fell."

Hmmm. It would certainly seem that she'd dove head first into something.

He spoke carefully, choosing his words. A nervous energy possessed him. Brandon pulled away while he was speaking and stuck his head under the bed. His voice rose so that she could hear.

"We found you at Dogwood Park. I think you rolled down a hill or something."

Diana's sleep and coffee deprived brain supplied the rest.

"Who's *we*?"

He popped up with her shoes and began to undo the laces.

"Bradley, Mark, Rick, Seth, and me. Oh, and Adam."

He stopped with the laces and added an after thought.

"Adam Weis. All of us live with him now. He's been our guardian since ..."

Diana felt like grimacing. No need to make the boy rehash all of that.

"I understand. Didn't you and your brother used to baby-sit the other three?"

Brandon nodded and slipped the tennis shoe over her bare foot. She decided not to worry about where her socks were. Diana slapped a palm against her forehead.

"Oh, no! Karen!"

She would have jumped up, but Brandon held her other foot in a firm grip. He was stronger than his appearance suggested. She fell back on the mattress with a bounce.

"Don't worry." He smoothed a hand over her calf. "We called Karen last night and told her what was up. Adam slept on the couch and the rest of us guys have rooms."

Diana felt the truth of his sincerity and massaged the point between her brows, hoping to stimulate thought processes. It didn't work. She needed coffee.

She studied the room for a moment trying to decipher what it told about the owner. Bold colors spoke of a dominating presence. There was a lingering of something that whispered to that part of her that read other people's emotions. She didn't delve into that.

Looney Toons poster prints and the Stooges movies told her that the man had a sense of humor. The furniture was golden and natural varnished in a simple blocky style. Overall, the room had an open-air feeling without the benefit of any windows.

"So. Where is this Adam? And why bring me here?"

Brandon didn't answer, so she gave his hair one last ruffle and decided to leave him to his silence.

"You really don't remember, do you?"

Disbelief and suspicion emanated from him. Bending down, Diana did what came naturally and placed a motherly kiss on the top of his head. If anyone needed one, Brandon Starr did.

* * * *

"Ah-hem."

Diana looked up, seeing a stronger, confident version of Brandon standing in the open doorway with his arms crossed over his chest.

This version looked more man than boy. He had a hint of rounded edges in his face and form that would finish filling out and harden in the years to come.

In his tight tee shirt and jeans, he looked young and tough, a brooding bad boy to set the girls' hearts, and hormones, aflutter.

His eyes were the exact shade of brown as his brother's, yet hard, as if they had seen the world and it had not been a nice place.

His dark brows pulled together as he watched her. She wasn't sure what he felt. Thankfully, his emotions were closed off to her from his end. She still didn't have enough strength of will to do it herself.

"Hello, Bradley."

"Miz Ridley." Bradley nodded, his eyes sizing her up.

Diana smiled, hoping for friendly instead of a grimace as she shifted to stand up. She really needed to find that bathroom. Her legs felt rubbery and sore.

Nightmare. It was a nightmare. Some delusions you had to repeat to keep them real.

Brandon stopped her with a warm hand on her arm. He directed his words at his brother.

"She's weak from last night." He gave a slight pause and glanced up at Diana. "She fell when she tried to stand up. I think she needs to eat."

Diana laughed at the mirrored concern in Bradley's face. The young tough strode across the room. His brother moved out of the way, climbing onto the bed, so that Bradley could stand in front of her.

She waved away their concern.

"I'm all right. A little rubber-legged, maybe. What I really need is to find the bathroom and head home."

She felt the warmth radiating from Brandon's body and reached out to brush a hand over his forehead. Diana frowned.

"You're running a temperature."

Brandon's eyes flicked to those of his brother. He leaned back, breaking contact.

"Ah," he mumbled. "I have a high body temperature. It's normal."

"Hey, Bradley! Adam called!"

A blond head with a smooth chili bowl haircut, shaved underneath, poked into the room. Bright blue eyes and a wide grin focused on Diana.

The boy bounced into the room in a flash of red and orange tank shorts. An equally blinding sleeveless tee completed the ensemble. The boy was a small dynamo, perpetual energy in motion.

"Hey Miz Ridley! You remember me? Mark?" He jumped onto the bed beside her. "Mark Cargill. You used to make cookies for me."

Diana made cookies for most of the kids that showed up at her house. But she didn't point that out. Mark's high energy and enthusiasm tended to make him stand out.

Her strongest memories were picking up the countless things Mark knocked over because he couldn't contain the energy he generated. He was sweet, if distracting.

"Mark, get off of Adam's bed. You're wearing shoes." Bradley scowled at the blond boy. "You're not supposed to be in here, anyway."

Mark flushed and ducked his head to stare at the bright red basketball shoes on his feet. Suddenly realizing where he was, the boy scrambled off of the bed. Bradley grabbed him by the neck of his shirt just as he started to dart out the door.

"What did Adam say when he called?"

Mark blinked then recalled the message. Diana could practically see the wheels turning in his head as he dredged up the information.

"He said that he was on his way with Miz Ridley's car. She's supposed to wait here 'till he gets back."

Bradley let him go and Mark dashed out. His blond head ducked back in.

"Hey, Miz Ridley?"

Diana choked down a laugh.

"Yes, Mark?"

"My birthday's in few weeks. I'll be twelve. Would you make my cake? No one here can cook for shit."

"Mark!" Bradley yelled and turned to Diana. "Sorry about that."

He shot another glare at Mark who ducked his head again.

"Would you?" The blond boy asked. *"Please?"*

"I suppose I could manage that."

"All right! I like chocolate."

Mark pumped a fist in the air and disappeared, feet pounding in the other direction. His voice came back into the room as he hollered.

"Hey, you butt-sniffers! Rick! Seth! Guess what? Miz Ridley's gonna make my birthday cake!"

* * * *

Adam pulled off the pavement onto the dirt road into the development he jokingly called a road. A billboard sign with Adam's distinctive Lobos Luna Construction howling wolf wearing shades silhouetted against the moon and his work cell phone number announced custom-built town homes in the Shady Path Home Development. The home of your dreams in a rural living area, minutes from the conveniences of town living. All with approved financing, of course.

He pulled into the muddy, rutted swath and parked in front of the shiny insulation and sheeting covering the outside of what would become the first of a neighborhood of expensive homes. This was his investment to put all of the boys through college. He hoped.

An institutional white truck sporting the official county animal control logo was parked among the colorful collection of rusted, beat-up pickup trucks. Adam's own red Ford had magnetic signs on each door, displaying his company's wolf and moon logo.

The air was devoid of normal construction sounds. No pounding of hammers or whine of a saw as it ripped through wood. Adam's sensitive ears picked up the sound of voices in the back of the structure where apparently his crew had gathered instead of working.

Scents washed over him in a blended muddle. Burnt-wood-building-material chemicals-new-concrete-hamburger-for-lunch sort of smell. Dead thing.

Adam raised his head, sorting through the odors as he angled around sawhorse tables set up on the side of the house in the driest spot in the yard. He insisted the men run the saws and orange extensions cords where there was no risk of electrocution by dragging through the mud. Besides, cleaning them up was messy business. He'd rather avoid overwork or injury by being neat in the first place.

Humans were a delicate lot. It took them weeks and weeks to recover from injuries that wolven would heal from in a few days. Especially saw cuts. Every now and then, Adam had to fire some guy who thought he was too smart for the safeties on his power tools.

He hooked his thumbs through his jeans belt loops as he strolled up behind the huddle of men.

Personally, he'd rather avoid dead things or get along with the disposal process, not stand around and stare at them. Intellectually, he understood the humans' fascination to be up close and personal with a wild animal. Especially, since there were no *known* wolves in the area.

Coyotes, yeah. Last night more than confirmed that werecoyotes were on the loose in Anderson County. By running Ms. Diana Ridley to him while he was partially changed pretty much gave away the wolven pack. How much she saw of the boys' Change he didn't know. Adam had tried to keep the female's face averted, but he was pretty sure she'd seen some of it before she passed out.

The human population at large was unaware of the supernatural population and he was determined to keep his part of that world under wraps. Just one more problem on his list of things to deal with.

* * * *

"Break time's over."

Everyone jumped, to a man, and stared at him. Adam met their gazes until the men turned away and mumbled excuses, hurrying back to their tasks.

Adam liked being the boss. The human workers fulfilled his alpha need to be in charge without all the pack politics crap.

Mack and the Animal Control guy, who smelled nervous, stayed behind. Underneath the harsh odor of chemical cleaner, Adam noticed that the man's scent was off. Not off as in psychic. A strange, *hey, I'm not quite human*, kind of way.

He smiled at the stranger, all white teeth and no warmth. His visitor went completely still, prey caught in the hunter's sight. The game filled Adam with dark amusement. The man was on *his* territory after all.

Mack cleared his throat, drawing both men's attention. The big foreman wisely looked at his boss somewhere around the nose, rather than meeting eyes.

Mack's gesture, though casual, held all the deference of introducing royalty to a commoner.

"Adam Weis, this is Jared Morgan. County Animal Control." Mack looked between them warily. His worry filled Adam's nose as much as the scent of psychic, which spiked as Mack tried to use his gift to keep the situation calm. One of Mack's minor gifts, Adam knew was interjecting his influence over others. Nothing major, the psychic had assured him, more the equivalent of easing a spooked animal. Anything more would give Mack the mother of all headaches.

"Mr. Morgan, Adam runs Lobos Luna Construction. The development belongs to him."

Jared Morgan was a smallish, wiry man who held himself with the upright confidence of a man in charge of himself and his surroundings. His shiny brown hair dropped below the crown of his white summer western hat, partially obscuring one lens of his glasses. The white oxford shirt, jeans and boots reminded Adam of a redneck nerd.

The dorky cowboy extended a hand, then seemed to think better of it and dropped it, treating Adam to a careful once over that never once made eye contact.

Adam's curiosity pricked. The wolf in him wanted to circle the oddity in front of him. Smell it. Taste it. Poke it to see if it would run. Maybe even roll in it to savor the scent at his leisure.

"Ah, Adam? Mr. Morgan mentioned that he wanted to get back soon."

Adam's gaze flicked to Mack, breaking the wolf's keen interest. Realizing he'd invaded Morgan's personal space, Adam frowned. He didn't remember moving so close. He was the guy in charge. Losing control of his baser instincts wasn't an option. He stepped back and allowed Morgan room to maneuver. The man stood rock still, barely breathing, his eyes fixed on the stalking predator.

Adam nodded. He ran a hand through the trailing strands of his hair while he got a grip on himself. Some perverse part of him still wanted to play. A small predatory smile escaped, lighting his eyes, snatching Morgan's breath again.

"Well, then I'll let you get back to your work, Mr. Morgan."

* * * *

Mack found Adam, neon orange tape measure in hand, double-checking what was destined to become a stairwell. It was a wasted effort. He sight-measured better than a survey team.

"So, now that you're finished marking you're territory, are you going to zip it back in?"

Adam let the tape recoil with a satisfying smack. The tension in the case vibrated against his palm, matching the hum in his body.

He ignored Mack's sarcasm and nodded, indicating that the foreman make his report. Adam respected the human, something that surprised them both.

An ex-Special Forces soldier, Mack Spencer had seen and done it all, including help take down a regime of very bad werewolves last year, making Adam the top alpha in town.

Mack was six-foot-six, taller and heavier than Adam. Yet the big man moved with startling grace and gentleness. Maybe Adam was projecting. After all, he had a vested interest in this particular human and a good deal of his attention was focused on Mack's safety.

Not that he believed that the human couldn't watch out for himself. Mack was the calmest man Adam had ever met, until angered. Then he was as deadly as any supernatural creature. Adam had experienced that firsthand, as had the werewolf bastards that Mack had taken out the night Adam became Canis of the pack.

In the short time he'd known Mack Spencer, the human had become something Adam had never had or wanted before. A friend. It was damned annoying.

Had he been wolven, Adam would have made him his beta, his second in command and a warden of the pack. The human had already given his protection to them. As it was, the psychic human was another temptation to keep under wraps, and not just from other shape shifters or a rival pack Canis.

The problem was that Adam *wanted* to make Mack wolven. The psychic was already bound to the pack, to him especially. One bite from a changed wolven and the human would be one of them, or die from the wolven venom in the saliva. That kept things in perspective for Adam. He'd find safer ways to increase his ranks.

He tossed the tape measure to Mack, who clipped it to his belt.

"I've got to get out of here. It's nearly noon."

Adam envisioned police cars showing up at his house to haul him off for kidnapping Ms. Diana Ridley. They could even tack on possession of a stolen car since he'd been riding around in it.

Feeling responsible for her well being, Adam made a mental note to fill up the tank on his way home and check the tires. He wondered when the last time was that the woman had checked her car fluids, too. Frowning, he ran a hand through his hair. He did not need to take care of her. His obligations were almost more than he could handle already. He just needed to make sure she was safe. There was a difference.

Mack walked him out, matching his pace with his employer and friend. He waited until they reached the little blue car to speak his mind.

"The wolf. Morgan said she was poisoned. She wasn't one of yours. You don't have any females in the pack."

Mack gave the statement a slight lilt, enough to make it a question, but not enough to pressure the wolven.

Adam drummed his fingers on the roof. He trusted Mack, yes. But he didn't want to involve the human in pack business. He'd done that once already against his better judgment and now the man thought he was one of them. Best to leave him out of it.

He shook his head, finding himself answering anyway.

"No, she wasn't mine. She was a *stray.*"

Mack raised his eyebrow at the pack leader's elitism. Too often he scolded Adam for his wolven ideology.

Adam let the look slide, telling himself that the human was only joking. In wolven society, the man would have already been on the ground, Adam's teeth at his throat, for questioning his judgment.

Damned nuisance friendship was. He hoped that didn't indicate a weakness in his leadership abilities.

"Do you think someone … another pack is looking for her?"

It was a valid question. Adam shook his head again.

"No. I don't know. She might have run with another pack, but it's more likely that she was a loner that ran into trouble. I'll sniff it out later." *Maybe.*

Adam's voice was low and thoughtful.

"Pack territory breaks up by county or the same equivalent. Most strays and weres stick to unoccupied territories."

Someone who'd chosen life outside pack law and protection would seek to avoid its enforcers, the Canis Pater and his wardens.

Mack choked back a laugh.

"You're wearing your King-Of-The-Weres expression. You wolven are so elitist, your noses stuck so high in the air, that you'd drown if it rained."

He grinned at Adam's painful wince at the word were, knowing that wolven hated to be called were.

"Did-ja think that maybe the girl was looking to join up with your pack?"

"No."

Adam didn't like to admit the truth out loud. Garrick, the old leader was a shameful stain on his reputation. He might have killed the bastard, but the old Canis' ghost haunted him still.

Adam had already queried a couple of wolven females for the alpha female spot. Strong females with charitable backgrounds who could help him build a solid future here. Both had very politely, very firmly, turned him down.

"No female in her right mind would place a paw in my county. Not after everything about Garrick came to light."

Adam had tried to keep the worst that Garrick Moser had done quiet, but it had been hard. You don't go into a territory and take over. There were laws, protocols to a challenge. All of that Adam had bypassed. Garrick might have been the nightmare monster that a wolven named werewolf. But no one knew that when Adam had killed him. It was murder.

Paul Sheppard, his Canis had done some heavy politics with the Wolven Council to keep Adam from being declared werewolf and hunted down. God only knew what fancy two-stepping Paul and Dom, the pack lawyer, had done to make the council recognize the fight as a legal challenge.

If Adam hadn't pressed for time, and gone ahead with and finished the mate-bond with his fiancée, Amanda, he would have known she was in trouble. He might even have found her before the Anderson pack had raped and brutalized her.

Wolven are hard to kill, even by other supernaturals. Stronger, faster, hardier. Among the supernatural pecking order, dragons, wolven, and vampires ranked deadliest. And those three took care not to cross paths. Garrick was supposed to have tossed the weres out on their butts, not gone into treatise with them.

Dragons retreated from the world, snacking on the unwary supernatural that ventured into its territory. Vampires lived in their own dark world of plots and intrigue. Wolven simply determined to stay at the top of the food chain in their territories by running out or outright killing their competitors. For the wolven, the same policy included potential threats to a Canis' rule.

All of which made Garrick stupid, on top of being the lowest of the low, a damned B-rated monster movie werewolf. The fool actively recruited strays to build up his pack. No application, no interview, no references. No blood bonding ceremony to metaphysically tie potential victims too close to the old leader.

It had been too easy for Adam to pose as a stray and infiltrate the Anderson Pack to find out what had happened to his fiancée, Amanda Delaney.

Everything Adam found added up to Garrick Moser being one dead werewolf by Adam's hand. To the victor went the spoils, and the pitiful remainder of the pack after he and Mack were finished.

And a year after the bastard's death, more crap floated to the top of the cesspool that had been Garrick's depraved existence.

Mack's question, louder for repetition, ended Adam's mental wandering. Adam stifled down a snarl for the dead werewolf.

"Do you think that Animal Control's going to find out anything *weird* with the body?" Mack's intense blue gaze was as predatory as any wolven. "It wouldn't take much to clean up. A couple of hours."

Adam shook his head, privately amused at how the human tried to take care of him. He wouldn't insult his friend by openly deriding his concern.

"No. He might do a few tests for disease and toxins, which will come up in spades. You have to pump enough poison to kill a couple of elephants to kill wolven. He'll think overkill and cremate the carcass."

And that was that, tidying up that little mess.

"Yeah. Isn't poison suspicious? Oh, and when did wolves stop being a protected species?"

"You need to find human friends, Mack. You're thinking like a supernatural. Dogs get poisoned all the time. Check the Internet. Official sources don't list wolves in this area. Don't borrow trouble where there isn't any." He warned, opening the car door.

Mack stopped him, persistently holding the door open.

"Adam."

Adam growled, his bared canines inches from Mack's face, biting off the human's words with sharp carnivorous teeth.

"I said leave it. She wasn't mine. Not my problem. Not yours, human."

Mack swallowed visibly. He met Adam's eyes with careful determination. His voice low and as unthreatening as possible.

"She belonged to someone, Adam. We both know that."

"Back off, Mack."

Adam got in and pulled the door shut. He cranked the car. When Mack showed no sign of turning around, he rolled down the window.

"I mean it." He warned. "Let it go."

Please. Adam begged silently. *Don't bring the Wolven Council's notice back to me. If you value your humanity, don't make me bite you to rein you in.*

* * * *

Mack Spencer stepped back two paces and watched the car drive away. He said a small prayer to fortify himself for the coming battle just as he used to do while still in the service.

Adam Weis might not want his help, or believe that the little dead wolf found in the dumpster would be his problem. Too bad.

Mack hadn't survived the secret, and not so secret hot spots, of the world to let a werewolf with baggage brush him off.

Mack believed in instinct and the foretelling. He had to. Both gifts had saved his life on more than one occasion. To be truthful, his gifts had saved his ass on a hell of a lot of occasions.

Now his gifts told him to stick closer to his werewolf buddy than a tick. So what if Adam didn't want any inferior *human* help! If Mack had listened to wolven rhetoric instead of his own gut instincts then Adam would have died in that fire instead of that mangy bastard Garrick. And the boys ….

That made him shudder. Night after night he'd had dreams of monsters right out of the movies. Never before had his gifts left him so raw. He'd wake from dream visions in the middle of the night, feeling helpless because he couldn't protect them before the monsters hurt them again.

When he'd finally had enough, Mack had resigned his place in the military, a job he loved. He'd tracked the nightmare to Palestine, a town he'd never heard of. He'd turned his back on his own people to travel to this place. Here he found something worth protecting.

He didn't care if Adam Weis, Canis Pater of the Anderson County wolven pack, got his tail in a bunch. Mack Spencer had given up everything and traveled halfway across the globe to protect those boys, and no one was going to get in his way.

Chapter Three

Diana Ridley sat and admired her hosts' kitchen, beautiful and airy with the latest in stainless steel appliances, while the boys plied her with coffee and junk food for breakfast. Underneath the table, two huge dogs explained her sudden nightmare about werewolves.

Nightmare. Right.

When asked what type they were, Bradley replied, "Mixed."

He exchanged an odd look with his brother, who refilled Diana's cup.

The dogs looked like some sort of husky-wolf mix. One was lean with coarse black hair. The other, a smaller, but by no means small, a reddish brown. Both animals' eyes were expressive and intelligent. She'd have sworn they were part of her nightmare, except these sweet animals parked themselves by her feet.

The black one lay with his head in her lap, half asleep while she stroked his sensitive ears. The other one confiscated her foot to lie on. Every so often he would give her bare ankle a doggie kiss.

Between the dogs, her hosts, and waiting for her car, Diana tried not to dwell on the fact that Matthew, her son, had decided this morning to pack a bag and stay at his dad's. Without contacting her. Karen, the younger sister, had reluctantly divulged the news to her mother when she called. Diana had no clue how to deal with the problem.

She smiled and refocused her attention on her young host's tale of skateboarding down Rollercoaster Road like he was the first one to discover the high hill. She remembered Rollercoaster Road from her own teenage years. She doubted anyone bothered to remember the street's real name.

"It was a wicked ride. Ya' know?"

His arms looped and waved, mimicking the wild ride while he sat atop the kitchen island, tennis shoes drumming against the golden beaded panel. Diana wanted to cringe at the abuse on the beautiful wood.

"I wouldn't a fell off that last time if Seth didn't chicken out by the cemetery. Everybody knows there ain't really ghosts there."

The black dog woofed. He sat up straight and stared at Mark. The blond boy stuck his hands under his armpits and clucked at the animal.

"Chicken-Boo! Chicken-Boo!"

Diana's mouth dropped as the dog barked at Mark.

"Cut it out." Bradley hollered over the noise.

"Scairdy Seth! Baaawk! Baaawk! Baaawk! Seth is a scairdy!"

"Bark! Bark! Bark!"

Diana watched in horror as the dog lunged for the boy. The dog's teeth bared. She screamed as the big dog hit the boy center chest.

Diana's adrenaline rushed as she dived for the melee. Strong arms wrapped around her, stopping her. Bradley held her tight while dog and boy rolled across the kitchen floor, knocking into a chair.

Heated emotions charged the air, the dog's anger and Mark's arrogance, burning past her nonexistent defenses.

"He's going to hurt him!"

Diana wiggled against the boy's iron grip. The growling, snarling combat went unseen behind the counter. A bright smear of blood on the floor pointed out the fight path in gruesome color.

"Hurt, yeah. Probably. Kill, no."

Bradley's answer shocked her. His voice bellowed into the kitchen.

"I said cut it out! *Now!*"

Silence reigned.

Behind the kitchen bar, a dark-skinned hand palmed the counter, braced to lift an equally dark face into sight. Short, curly hair was cut close to the boy's head in a wiry mat that he rubbed with the opposite hand. A smear of blood shone darker against his skin, a wet shine smeared from nose to cheek.

The boy's bare skinny chest was marred with deep bloody scratches.

Mark emerged equally bloody. He glared at the other boy, his face oddly distorted.

Realization set in. Diana gasped, drawing Mark's attention. Acceptance and horror coagulated in her stomach. She pulled free and stared around the room. Brandon sat under the table beside the other dog.

As she watched, the brown dog blurred, shifting into a naked brown-skinned Hispanic boy. He gave an all over body shake and winked. His brown eyes gleamed red.

"Hey, Miz Ridley. Are you really going to make Mark's birthday cake?"

Diana felt raw with emotion. She felt the sudden urge to get out of Dodge. Fast. She gave a hysterical little laugh and sidled to the little French kitchen door, wrenching it open. She aimed for the large wooden gate in the tall wood privacy fence.

Darting out, a solid wall of flesh and man blocked her escape. Strong, muscled arms steadied her.

Dazed, Diana stared up, mesmerized. He leaned closer, invading her personal space. His face was a study of square chiseled planes, honed to perfection. Thick, fringed, lashes, darker than his hair, framed his intense eyes. Husky colored eyes, blue with a dark ring around the iris, bored into her. His mouth was a strong, sensual slash. A stubborn cleft dented his chin. Pale blond hair brushed the tops of his shoulders.

The man of her dreams, ah, *nightmare*.

The big man's nostrils flared as he sniffed the air near her neck, carefully sidling his big body closer. Heat radiated from his body, warming her front.

His lingering aggravation and startled confusion at her running into him stirred inside her mind. He cocked his head and smiled.

Diana felt other, dark and lusty emotions stirring in him, as well. Or was that in her?

The corners of his incredible mouth tilted up in a very sure, male smile.

Licking her lips, she fought for a measure of control over her traitorous mind and body. The man focused on the movement, intent and hungry. Her entire body hummed in anticipation. She swayed into his hot, overheated frame.

When he met her eyes again, a predator stared out at her, more than a mere man. Diana blinked, confused. Her instincts screamed several conflicting orders.

Run. Hide. Stay. For God's sake--jump the man's bones!

The man appeared as mesmerized as she was. He didn't blink. He stared with those wild blue eyes. Slowly he cupped her cheek.

The rough pads of his fingers brushed down, following her cheekbone. Gently, he traced the line of her lips, chin and neck. His big hand found a home around the nape of her neck.

Diana stared transfixed. Would he kiss her? Should she let him?

The time was long past the part where Diana should panic. No man ever got this close. Not since divorcing Richard the Dick.

Her numb mind processed that this must be Adam. The growl/whine, he made as he leaned down, brought Diana to her senses.

Werewolf! Monster! Determination shot through her. She exploded into a fury of motion.

The man, creature, howled and doubled over, clutching his privates.

A knee to the groin could down even a werewolf. Processing that information, she snatched her keys from where they landed at his feet.

The blue Cavalier sat in the driveway, an invitation from God. She scrambled inside and slammed the door.

Her beautiful blue chariot cranked on the first try.

Jerking the gear into reverse, she gunned the engine, uncaring of the possibility of traffic. She yanked the wheel to the side, pulled onto the road, and shoved the gear into drive. She floored the gas pedal. Tires squealed and Diana was gone.

Chapter Four

In a pain-filled haze, Adam listened to the car race away.

That could have been handled better. God, what an understatement.

He suppressed the need to moan and cup his nuts. Tears pricked the back of his eyelids. He rose to his feet and sucked in a breath. Carefully, he made his way into the house.

Outside the door, he growled at Bradley. Speech was beyond him. The boy diverted his wide-eyed stare and moved out of the way. Inside, the rest of the boys waited in various states of bloody undress.

Adam fought the urge to lash out, or show his disappointment. This was one more disaster in a series of disasters. He should never have left the female with the boys. He hadn't planned on being gone for more than an hour. He'd trusted the oldest ones, Bradley and Brandon, to keep a level head.

The joke was on him to think that they'd be doing chores and homework. No doubt the younger boys had forced their chores on Brandon, the pack omega, in Adam's absence. He didn't agree that the lowest ranking wolf should be the one to get dumped on. But he was fighting a battle with nature and general teenage laziness. At times he despaired of teaching them any kind of responsibility at all.

A terrible nostalgia for his old pack and the freedom from his dubious parenting responsibilities gripped him. Sometimes, he felt like he had avenged his fiancée, Amanda and his reward was exile here in a small nothing town to parent a litter of unruly pups, not alpha to a pack of wolven.

He didn't understand why Paul wouldn't accept the pups into the Tarrant Pack. They needed help that Adam couldn't give them. They needed an alpha female. Or better yet, a pack mother, a Matra Canis.

Oh yeah, this was shaping up to be one hell of a day. Guilt at his selfishness hung like a monkey on his back, combining with the ache in his nuts.

In the kitchen, Adam found Mark bouncing on the toes of his basketball shoes. The blond boy's face was smeared with blood and tight with worry. Behind him, Seth, naked as the day he'd been birthed and probably just as bloody, mirrored Mark's expression. Looking for a snack to tide over a growing wolven's high metabolism, Rick's skinny bare butt stuck out of the open refrigerator. He looked up at Adam and shut the door, leaning against it with solemn expectancy.

Mingled scents of fear and guilt permeated the room.

Adam knew Brandon hid, silent and still as a mouse, under the table. He ignored the boy, knowing from experience that Brandon lived in terror of drawing his alpha's attention. Poor kid. Garrick, the former alpha, brutalized and molested the kid. Another very good reason that the bastard was dead by Adam's hand.

He didn't blame the boy for his fear. He wished he knew how to reach past the victim to the wolf inside. Adam had his own fear of doing more harm than good to the already damaged boy.

He felt every bit of the weight from those brown eyes today as he did that first time, finding Brandon bloody and broken in that locked basement after Garrick had done with him. The grisly trophy of Amanda's pelt was nailed to the wall. More than a year later, Adam still had trouble distancing from the images. It made him physically ill. Fury rolled into his gut and he wanted to kill the bastard again. A lot slower this time around.

Bradley crossed Adam's path to stand in front of and almost between the table and the two bloody boys. He faced his alpha with a healthy dose of subordinate respect and a tinge of fear. The fear, Adam would have happily done without.

Adam rubbed a hand over his face. He hated this. Instinct, to show no weakness to the others, had him channeling his own doubts into aggravation. And he was more than a little aggravated. At everything.

Pack members did not cringe in terror in front of his old Canis, Paul Sheppard, waiting for the alpha to tear into them with teeth and claws. Well, not without good reason. Over the years there had been a few occasions where heavy discipline was necessary. Yet within the Tarrant Pack, there was more love than fear for the Canis.

Adam pinned Bradley with a stern gaze.

"I left you in charge. Go wait in my office and we'll talk about what happened here."

The boy's shoulders wilted but straightened again. He turned and marched out of the kitchen, a condemned prisoner on his way to the electric chair.

Adam followed. He paused in the doorway. The scent of fear rising in the room, as the boys waited for him to blow his top, pissed him off more.

When would they get it? He wasn't their old Alpha. He didn't hurt children. Until they learned, though, Adam was going to pay for the sins of his predecessor.

Adam sighed. He leaned a forearm against the doorjamb without looking back.

"Brandon, get out from under the table. You're not a dog."

Ignoring the scramble of action behind his turned back, Adam straightened his shoulders and headed for his office to hear Bradley's confession.

* * * *

"Sooo, wha-da-ya think? Is Mr. Weis *hot* or what?"

Diana's reprieve was over once Karen slipped into the bathroom and closed the door behind her. She leaned against the robe draped door, fanning her face with a hand.

There was a law somewhere that automatically revoked a woman's privacy once she had a daughter, especially once that daughter turned into a teenager. Diana watched Karen slide down and park her butt on the floor. The teen's eyes glazed over with adulation.

Diana snorted and drew the curtain closed against Karen's chatty teasing. At least she hoped that was all her daughter's interest in Adam Weis entailed. Inverted Celtic shapes, fairies, unicorns, and other mythical creatures on a sky blue background blocked her view of Karen's expression.

"I wouldn't know. I didn't exactly stay long enough to ogle him."

Liar. She'd done plenty of ogling. Then she'd run like a scared rabbit.

Diana's stomach muscles tightened. Behind the shower curtain where Karen couldn't see, she ran a finger over the slight roll in her belly. Like a man, or a sexy were-hunk like Adam Weis, would be interested in a single mom nearing middle age with the ability to soak up other people's emotions like a sponge.

She'd gone stark raving loony when she'd bumped into her tall blond knight in sweatpants. By the time she'd pulled into her own driveway, Diana had decided she'd acted like an idiot. Whatever he was, he'd definitely rescued her last night.

She had a lot of the details muddled. But she clearly remembered the coyotes' bloodlust. Diana was reasonably sure those coyotes weren't normal. Then there were the two wolves that had leaped over her. Which two boys had interceded for her?

"You've met Adam Weis?"

Diana pulled back the curtain to look at her daughter. Her nerves skittered at the thought of her pretty, innocent daughter involved with a group of werewolves. Or was that a pack?

Okay, Diana was sure her daughter wasn't quite as innocent as she wanted to believe. But hey, sometimes a mom had to go with the fantasy or go insane with worry.

"Uh-huh." Karen nodded her head. "I see him in the school office sometimes. He's, like, a foster dad to the guys. Remember how they used to come over?"

Karen had the optimistic cheerfulness and sexy athleticism required of all cheerleaders her age. She bounced up gracefully to stand. Her curly ponytail danced with the motion.

"Yeah. Neat." Diana agreed in a flat voice. "I remember them."

Watching Rick change from a wolf to a boy wasn't something she was likely to forget anytime soon. She'd thought they were *dogs*? Diana frowned at her own naiveté. Pouring shower gel onto the squishy scrubber, she squeezed the thing until suds overflowed her hands.

"Bradley, Brandon, Mark, Seth, and Rick. You used to drag them home for dinner nearly every night. That's kind of hard to forget."

"Uh-huh." Karen's cheerful tone faltered. She picked backup her perky tone again. "The football coach says that he wishes he had those boys on the team."

"Which ones?"

"Bradley and Brandon." Karen picked up the nail pick from the silver vanity tray of colorful polishes and fingernail files. "Bradley, definitely. Our school would go all the way if he was team captain."

Diana didn't doubt it. Bradley Starr was one intense kid and the uncontested leader of the little group that had hung out at her house. She wondered how Adam Weis fit into the group dynamics. There was bound to be some friction between a new father figure in the house and a teenage boy feeling his way to manhood. That was something Diana knew a little about.

"So, why don't they play football? I imagine they'd be good."

Actually, the idea of a werewolf quarterback was kind of scary. Maybe it was a good thing the Starr twins had passed on sports.

Karen turned a noisy, distracted circle around the small bathroom. Diana retreated to use her scrubber in private.

"I don't know. Maybe they don't like sports."

Karen didn't sound convinced of her statement.

"They're usually in trouble about one thing or another. That's why Mr. Weis is in and out of the school office so much. "

Diana peeked around the curtain to see a secret smile hover around Karen's lips. Her eyes sparkled.

"Bradley's in my Chemistry class."

Chemistry. Oh, joy. This keeps getting better and better. Not Biology, please.

Diana frowned. Bradley, young and hunky, was definitely the focus of her daughter's fantasies.

Ouch. Diana didn't even want to go there.

"Mmm-hmmm"

Karen leaned back against the door again, oblivious to the robe she dislodged. It fell to the floor in a soft terry pile.

Diana didn't really want to talk about the boys. She needed to *think.* And she definitely had reservations about her daughter and a werewolf.

"They seem like nice enough kids." Diana kept her tone carefully light. "But you know, you don't really need any trouble."

"Well, they're not really bad--and it's usually just the younger ones. Bradley has the tortured, brooding hero aura mastered."

Karen wrapped her arms around herself and hugged tight. Her features took on a dreamy faraway stare.

"Got that whole Heathcliff thing going on, huh?" Diana asked.

Karen wrinkled her nose.

"Gah. Literature. Nope, more like Angel."

Diana glanced up from scrubbing her foot.

"Angel?"

"You know? Tall, pale, and sexy. The vampire detective."

Vampires? What vampires? There were vampires too?

Diana stared, clueless, sponge poised midair. Karen rolled her eyes.

"*David Boreanaz.* Jeez, Mom. Someday, you're going to have to cut loose and watch more TV than just the news. Go out on a date or something."

"Hey! I get out." Diana feigned outrage.

"Right. Work, the grocery store, various school functions featuring *moi.*"

Karen's chiding tone brightened. Mischief danced in her brown eyes.

"But things are looking up. You spent the night with Mr. Weis."

"Karen!" Diana poked her head around the shower curtain.

Her daughter sniggered.

"That's enough, young lady. Besides, I want you to be careful. Those boys aren't like us. They're *different*."

She pinned her daughter with a significant look, using the scrubber to make her meaning clear.

"Or Mr. Weis either."

The force of Karen's shock made Diana flush. Indignation rolled from her daughter. In the cooling water, Diana felt small, petty. Or was it her hot skin that suddenly made the water cooler?

Karen stood with her hand on the door, the picture of an outraged teen. Diana felt smaller still.

"Mother! I can't believe you said that. Like this house is *normal*."

Karen jerked the door open in a huff. Her ponytail swung madly. She stopped. Her eyes had a familiar vague look. Her voice was cool and distant with the gift of precognition.

"You might want to hurry up, Mom. Grandma Ridley is about to call."

Karen shut the door behind her and sure enough, the phone rang. Diana finished rinsing off, fortifying herself to talk to her ex-mother-in-law, who would no doubt be calling on Matthew's behalf, again. Richard's mother believed that Matthew should be living with his father, going to a university college in a bigger and better town. Not living with his strange mother and sister in a nothing town like Palestine and its community college annex.

Diana dismissed Mrs. Ridley from her thoughts. She'd always be at odds with that woman.

She focused on her newest pack of issues.

Karen was right, and not just with her psychic telephone predictions.

What right did Diana have to judge a household of werewolves, when she, an empath and her psychic daughter had their own weird set of problems?

She was an idiot all right. A paranoid, delusional idiot. That's what she got for getting what little information she had on supernatural creatures from Jax, the randy gnome and a witch that did magical home security systems. Those two had her jumping at shadows.

Thinking back on this morning, Diana realized that she'd gone off the deep end big time. She owed him and his boys a big apology.

Mr. Weis had played Good Samaritan and saved her a big emergency room bill when all she'd had were a few bruises and scratches. Okay, a lot of scratches. And not getting eaten by coyotes was a big bonus. Was there a such thing as werecoyotes?

So, the boys were werewolves and after she woke up, the monster movie footage had gone straight to comic relief. Boys fight. That was a fact of life. No biggie if one of them had been a wolf at the time? Well a decent sized biggie since there was more room for bloodshed.

Diana covered her face with her hands and sank lower into the water. Adam Weis. Oh, God. Had she actually kneed him in the … *nuts*? Water covered her head but she drowned in humiliation.

Dumb, dumb, dumb.

* * * *

Monday night Diana checked her watch and pulled into the Kal-Mart Supercenter parking lot for a quick round of after work Dash-Through-the-Store.

She would have had more time if the darned computers at the insurance office hadn't locked up. Diana didn't know a server from a modem, but if that thing didn't start working right, she was going to kick it right in its hard drive!

At least she didn't hate her job. When she was young, Diana had wanted to go into business for herself, doing something fabulous like opening a small, romantic restaurant. She'd taken a few cooking classes and fancied herself an up-and-coming chef. But then she'd met and married Richard and her plans took a backseat while he climbed the grocery store company ladder. He was a regional manager now and enjoyed the fruits of his labor.

For Diana, insurance wasn't a bad way to earn a paycheck. It was an interesting business. She met all kinds of interesting people. It certainly beat the heck out of bagging groceries and flipping hamburgers.

She didn't rely on anyone, especially her ex, The Dick, for help. He paid his dues for their two children. But sometimes

Diana felt like she suffered for every dime he forked over, Karen and Matthew being the only worthwhile things from that union.

Diana wheeled the basket past the snack food aisle. Hers was a healthy household. Despite her love of old fashioned comfort food, pre-packaged junk foods were on the forbidden list. They were full of preservatives and additives.

She bought exercise equipment periodically with every intention of working out. After a few weeks, some family crisis blew away all of her plans. After that, she could never muster up the same enthusiasm for exercise. Said equipment slowly got carried out to the garage.

Yet another destructive pattern in her life. At least Richard the Dick was no longer around to heckle her about her lack of will power.

She sighed and tried to push away thoughts of her telephone confrontation with her son. He'd left her to the wolves, *literally*, in the park then run off to his dad's without notice. Yes, he'd come home after she called. The apology for his lack of responsibility had been begrudging.

Too often of late, Richard's expressions flowed from her son. He was eighteen years old. Did she really have to know where he was every second of the day? He was legally a man. And he'd be gone to college soon. *Geesh Mom. Get a life.*

Diana had exploded and Matthew had driven off in an angry huff back to his dad's. Later Richard had called with his usual accusations and insults.

Was she too controlling?

Diana didn't know. In her house, she believed that her rules should be respected.

What was overbearing about that?

Should she ignore Matthew's actions? Write them off as a phase? Let him sow his wild oats?

Matthew *should* have called back and told her that he'd gotten his car to start the other night. He *should* have come home at the appointed time instead of staying out.

She didn't give a flying fig for his wild oats. If he wanted to stay at his dad's, then fine. She would stay firm even if she felt like Matthew had defected to the enemy and ripped her guts apart. Diana wanted her son back home, but not at the expense of her pride. Richard had taken that away from her once before. She wouldn't let him use her son to do it again.

* * * *

Adam tossed a box of sugared rice puff cereal in the basket. He considered his choices, then grabbed a couple of boxes of the cocoa puffs too. The fruit crispies were good and the marshmallow kind always went over well with the boys. He remembered that Brandon liked the Apple O's just as the scent of vanilla, citrus, and woman hit his olfactory and jolted through his body.

He usually ignored the bombardment of odors that came with a trip to the store. But that particular scent seemed to have burned itself into his sensory memory, waking the wolf. Primal instinct, beast, whatever, that part of him that ran wild rose to shimmer under his skin. The wolf demanded release, demanded a hunt. Adam could no more deny the instinct that gripped him that any other physical necessity.

He tossed two boxes of the Apple O's into the basket and followed the intriguing scent to its source. Because food was another necessity, the basket was not forgotten in his hunt.

There were all kinds of hunts. The hunt for food. Tracking for the adventure and curiosity. For play. Wolven did not need to kill in order to satisfy the need to hunt. Hunting was about using their senses, to track and find what was needed at that moment.

At that moment the wolf needed to find the woman. The one who smelled soft and delicious. The female had bested him. That was unacceptable to the wolf. The man found it intriguing. Both parts of him wanted a rematch.

He stopped, cocked his head to one side, and watched her reach for a jar on the top shelf. She was short enough that she had to stand on her toes to reach. Every sense focused, his eyes riveted on the way her pants snuggled tight to her lush ass. Soft, full breasts strained against her blouse as she stretched her limit.

Adam swallowed and tried to take in a breath. The scent of her filled his nose. His body swelled and hardened. Damn, he had to get a grip. She's just a woman. A human. Not his kind.

She was a psychic and female. That made her fair game. That she resided in Adam's territory made her his responsibility.

The wolf didn't care about politics. The wolf wanted closer.

"Here, let me." Adam reached up and grabbed a jar. He barely noticed the contents, olives.

She squeaked and bumped into him, giving him a chance to bury his nose in her hair. More soft female scent. Inside, the wolf howled in delight.

She turned, depriving him of her hair, but gracing him with the brush of her body. He could barely contain the wolf. With his quarry found, the wolf wanted to take her, like before, to his lair.

Remembering vividly what a mistake that had been, Adam stepped back. Inside, the wolf howled with frustration at the loss of her next to his skin. With a tentative smile, Adam held out the olives.

* * * *

"You."

Diana stared at him, eyes wide. She took a couple of steps back, regaining her personal space. It was him. What were the chances of running into him so soon after her debacle at his house? Pretty darn high considering the size of the town. Her cheeks pinkened.

"Ah … thank you." She took the jar he held out and gestured helplessly at the shelf. "Thank you. I'm, ah, a little short."

The intensity in his pale blue eyes was somewhat unnerving. Dear God, Karen was right. The man was absolutely gorgeous. His near white blond hair was longish and pulled back at his neck. Several strands escaped to tease around his high cheekbones. Tall and broadly muscled, he looked like he had stepped from the cover of a Viking romance novel. That much testosterone should both be illegal and go hand in hand with medieval weaponry.

"That's all right. I'm a little tall." His hesitant smile broadened a bit, showing a glimpse of white, white teeth. "Makes up for not having a ladder handy."

Oh. Something warm unfurled in Diana's belly. She reminded herself that men this good looking did not purposefully flirt with women like her.

She squared her shoulders, gathered her wits, and set the jar in the basket before looking back at him. No, men like him did not have an interest in plump thirty-eight year old divorcees. She didn't need to make a fool out of herself a second time.

Looking up, Diana met his direct gaze. He seemed to be waiting for something. She imagined she knew what.

"About the other day." Diana brushed a nervous hand through her short bangs. "I'm sorry about all that. The hysterics."

He cocked his head in that odd way she'd noticed. Like a dog. No, not a dog, he was all wolf. She imagined if he could, he'd have perked his ears forward. Her imagination brought a fresh flush of heat to her face.

"I mean … I don't know what came over me. I shouldn't have …."

He closed the distance swiftly, laid a gentle finger over her lips.

"Forgotten." He hesitated a moment. When he spoke again, his voice was a deep comfortable rumble. "Does what we are bother you?"

"N-no, Mr. Weis." She said against his finger. His presence mesmerized her. Heat seemed to roll off of him. She wanted to absorb the excess warmth, curl up next to him and stay there.

"Adam." He moved his finger over her lips, tracing them, his intense eyes memorizing the shape. Every part of her was earthy, womanly, and erotically delicious to his senses.

"Adam." Diana breathed against the digit. She noticed, with feminine pride, a shudder work its way from his arm to shoulder, and down his back.

Adam stepped back, the man regaining control. Ruthlessly, he pushed the wolf down. He leashed the instinct that pressed him to take the female, to drag her to his lair like a caveman and keep her there. *He* did not want a woman.

Yes, he did want her. But the wolf wanted more than sex, way more. Sex was all that the man was willing to give. He didn't want a mate, especially not a human one that would not be strong enough to hold her place in the pack.

Diana blinked away the fantasy and watched Adam distance himself. Oh, well. At least she had plenty of fuel for her dreams, because really, the man was way out of her league. She pasted on a bright smile. "Diana."

He drew his brows together, momentarily confused, and cocked his head again. He nodded when the proverbial light came on. His smile too, seemed more than it should be. He stepped over to his basket, taking possession of it.

"It has been a pleasure, Diana."

She nodded in agreement, realizing his hurry to get away. Must be those divorcee cooties. Maybe a neon sign labeled *desperate* over her head with an arrow pointing down.

"Yes. And again, I'm sorry about last time."

"Like I said, forgotten."

He started down the aisle, the frustrated wolf gnawing at his resolve. He focused on leaving the store a civilized creature. He nearly made it to the end of the aisle when she called out to him.

"Adam!"

No, no, no. He needed to get away. *He wanted to stay.* That part was the wolf. The wolf wanted to stay long enough to claim the female. Then they'd go to his lair. Oh, the things he would do to her there.

"Adam!"

He turned, his frustration and inner turmoil boiling to the surface.

"What?"

"You're leaking."

"Huh?" Her soft, full breasts bounced as she hurried toward him.

"Your milk is leaking."

He focused more intently on her full breasts. He would be able to smell her better with his nose buried between them, cushioning his cheeks.

"Milk?"

She brushed past him and leaned over his basket, giving him a better view of her heart-shaped ass. His mouth watered. His cock got harder.

He nearly choked when she reared back up and shoved a gallon of milk under his nose. The scent effectively obscured vanilla and citrus. He leaned away and refocused on the offending container. A small steady stream ran from the top, over the back of her hand, and dripped onto the floor. He had a sudden hankering for milk and woman *al dente.*

"Grab that box over there."

Numb with raging hormones, Adam removed the last can of something off of the shelf, he didn't care what, and handed Diana the box.

"Put it down there on the floor."

Yeah. The floor was a good place. He could spread her out and lick all that milk off of her sweet skin. She pointed and, finally understanding her intent, Adam set the box down on the floor near the shelf. His reward was another first class view as she bent to set the gallon in the box. Regret when she straightened.

"Ugh." She shook her hands of excess liquid. "I need to wash."

Adam could help her clean up. He liked milk. The wolf agreed with a howl. He realized he'd been caught staring again when she sidled away to the end of his basket.

"Interesting choices you have there."

What was wrong with his food?

Adam glanced at her basket. Mountains of vegetables, frozen and fresh, piled high. Lots of green leafy stuff. Yogurt and granola cereal peeked around various bags.

He looked down at his basket. Packages of steak and hamburger meat, frozen burritos, a dozen frozen pizzas, a case of hot dogs supported his cereal and Little Debbies. He had four different types chips, Gatorade, and about three more gallons of milk.

Did he need more bread? Was four loaves enough? Growing wolven ate a lot, about four or five meals a day. Snacks did not count.

Adam looked at her basket again, then at her expression of…disapproval?

He had a sudden urge to fling his body over the basket and growl, to warn her away from his food. Instead, he narrowed his eyes.

"What's wrong with it?"

Diana realized she'd been rude again. Why was she always sticking her foot in her mouth around him? Or her knee in other inappropriate parts?

"I'm sorry." She tried a smile and veered to more common ground to smooth things over. "I forgot that you have teenagers to feed, too. Sometimes they can be so picky, can't they?"

Her meaning went over his head, but he seemed to take it in stride. Obviously, the junk in his basket was intended for his stomach, as well.

No man had ever worn that kind of diet so well. So much for the body builder, protein drink, and steroid theory she'd begun to formulate about him. But then, he was more than just a man, she reminded herself.

Those cool blue eyes watched her as if she would grab his basket and run. She could tell he wanted to leave. So much for her grand finesse.

He nodded warily and she could see the bristling man slowly calm down. He surprised her by speaking instead of simply brushing her off and pushing his cart away.

"Yeah. Five teens eat a lot. I'm always running out of stuff."

Diana laughed. "I imagine so. Well, I guess I'll be seeing you around."

He nodded again, watching her go to her basket. His gaze bored into her back. Diana wondered that she didn't spontaneously combust. She waved once more as she wheeled out of the aisle and toward the cashier.

While stacking groceries in the trunk of her car, Diana replayed her reunion with Adam Weis and tried to regain control of her wayward female hormones. She tingled all over.

Good grief. She wasn't some teenybopper. She was thirty-eight. She needed to get a hold of herself.

It wasn't like the man had asked her on a date of anything. As if he would after she'd kneed him in the nuts the first time they'd met. This time around, she'd acted desperate, as if she couldn't bear to let him out of her sight.

Pathetic.

Diana shook her head, disgusted with herself. She slammed the trunk closed.

She slid behind the wheel and flipped down the visor. She looked okay for her age. In the mirror, her plain brown eyes stared back at her, fringed and long due to a fifteen dollar tube of mascara. Only tiny lines were starting to form around her eyes. Her lips weren't full enough, a vanity she hid by adding a hair more lipstick under her bottom lip line. Except for a strand or two, her short hair hadn't started going gray yet. Thank God for small blessings.

As if a man like that was going to take a second look at her.

Perhaps she should go out with Bob Benedict? He was more her speed.

Diana imagined kissing steady, dependable Bob. He was a little older that her. His salt and pepper hair might be thinning on top, but he wasn't fat. He wasn't built like a Greek god either. Behind his wire-rimmed glasses, the slightly myopic accountant didn't focus sharply on her with arctic blue eyes.

She'd call Bob and arrange to have dinner with him. She'd wear her best dress and heels. She pulled out of the parking lot and told herself firmly that she liked steady and dependable.

Really, she did.

Chapter Five

Adam strode through the door and tossed his keys in the direction of the TV. A hand shot up to catch them. Video game monsters growled and screamed their last breaths, subdued by artificial machine gun sounds. The mingled scents of popcorn, soda, and his laughing, sweaty pack permeated the house, a scene similar to his own teenage afternoons piled up with his half-brothers Dominick and Gavin. Here was pack unity, and he was the outsider.

"Unload the truck. Put up the groceries. I'll start dinner in an hour."

Adam didn't notice five pairs of eyes shift to glance at one another, or the sudden stillness of the room. He continued on to his room, oblivious to the fact that not one of the boys uttered a word of argument in the distribution of the chore. They simply filed out.

In his room, Adam dropped his clothes on the floor and stepped into the shower, closing the stall door behind. He turned the cold tap on all the way, letting the icy spray sluice down his body, shocking his libido into submission. When the ice finally infiltrated his veins, he shut off the water. He gave a full body shake and stepped out, grabbing one of the thick towels out of the cabinet.

Great.

Now he was cold on top of being in a bad mood. Since he was already in the right frame of mind, Adam decided he'd take care of the bills. He didn't feel like cleaning up, so he left his old clothes and the damp towel on the floor. The messy room fed his irritation in a dark and satisfying way.

He pulled a clean pair of jeans over his hips, buttoned up, and padded barefoot to his office. He grabbed the mail from the angled box fixed to the wall by the door before going in.

No one entered his domain here. The boys came and went pretty much everywhere in the house, but this room and his bedroom were off limits except by invitation. Or summoning. Their choice, not his.

Adam dropped the mail on his desk, then slouched into the leather chair behind his desk and glared at the dark computer.

He gave a canine snort. He could have almost any woman he wanted for sex. He'd had both wolven and human females. At least with his own kind, he didn't have to hold back. Humans were fragile creatures, their females more so.

He didn't need to get involved with a human female. He barely understood wolven females. Why would he want to try to understand a human?

To hell with it. What male, of any species, understood women?

Adam opened an email message. The formal Canis to Canis greeting made him stop. Fourteen months after Paul had exiled him here with those words, he still wasn't used to the title. A small thrill of pride warred with his sense of desertion.

Hail, Sire Adam,

Greetings, from Canis Tarrant.

Emotion engulfed Adam as he scanned the letter for news. *Damn,* he was about to become an uncle. His brother, Dominick, was going to be a father, a rare and happy occasion, since so few wolven females conceived or carried their babies to term. As a matter of superstition, wolven parents made no mention of the pregnancy until the last month. For their sakes, Adam hoped that Dominick and Valerie's child survived.

What other changes had happened in the Tarrant County pack in the year he'd been gone?

He missed his old pack. He missed the hunts with his half-brothers, Dominick and Gavin, working as a unit to bring down a deer. Playing hide and seek in the woods at midnight. The comfort of a warm pile of bodies, not for sex. A wolven pack needed the touch and reassurance of its members as much as they needed to hunt. Even strays preferred to travel in pairs for protection and someone to touch.

Adam was aware that he was in a raw sulk. It was a self-indulgence that neither of his fathers would approve.

Adam missed his wolven father and former pack leader. Paul had been there for him since after his first Change, guiding him, teaching him things that his human father could not.

Perversely, Adam was of two minds. He missed Paul and his guidance, but he didn't want Paul telling him what to do. He didn't want Paul's opinion anymore, though he was curious how the old wolf would handle the boys.

The boys were not Paul Sheppard's business. Adam didn't have to answer to him anymore.

Adam realized that he'd unconsciously bared teeth at the monitor. He gave a little shake and ran a hand over the back of his neck to smooth his hackles, then sat back to absorb his rioting thoughts and feelings.

He'd been so upset about what he'd lost, about having to start fresh here, that hadn't realized how he'd changed. He'd gone from pack Beta and warden chafing at his Canis' rules, to handing out rules in his own pack.

Maybe the boys hadn't fully accepted him because they sensed that he hadn't wanted to accept them. If Paul offered a place for them now, Adam would fight to keep all five of them right here in his house.

He propped his feet on the desk and crossed his arms over his chest, then tested a new truth.

The boys were not Paul Sheppard's business.

Adam frowned. True, but that didn't sound quite right. He rubbed his nose and re-crossed his arms. He tried again.

Sire Adam Weis of Canis Anderson.

Better.

To be Sire was to be the Alpha, the Pack Protector, Family Father.

The turmoil that had plagued Adam since last February melted, revealing the hard core that had been hidden from his sight, but not Paul's. Adam smiled and composed a short note to the other Canis.

Hail, Sire Paul,
Greetings, from Canis Anderson.
Send Dom my congratulations, Grampa.
Good Hunting,
Sire Adam.

After responding to his other messages, Adam grabbed the paper mail and flipped through the envelopes. A feeling of rightness settled into his gut. He tossed the junk mail. He set his bills aside. That left five small manila envelopes that had been tucked unobtrusively behind the mail. Bold black letters proclaimed the local middle and high school's addresses stamped on the appropriate envelopes. The boys' names and homeroom teachers' names were typed underneath.

Was it report card time again?

One by one, he pulled out each printout, read the expected news, and signed the bottom. Adam had been to enough parent/teacher conferences in the past months to know that Rick was only barely passing. Seth and Mark were failing. Seth didn't care one way or the other and Rick and Mark were driving the teachers nuts with their antics.

Mark especially. The kid was more than wired. Teachers called him at least once a week for one stunt or another. Complaints of Mark's daydreaming and failure to complete his work were written on progress reports. He had no idea how to keep the boy's attention focused or calm his behavior. Adam had grounded him, but had little hope of making an impression on the kid.

He'd heard enough lectures on helping the boys' reach their potential to make him want a beer, several beers in fact, with a chaser of school counselor's blood.

It wasn't that he did not respect the teachers. He did. God, they dealt with his kids every day, and some worse, and still managed to stay sane. Adam was simply at a loss of how to deal with the boys' needs, or how to get them on track academically.

He wasn't the boys' foster parent. His guardianship, obtained with the best wolven lawyers, was ironclad. He didn't worry that the boys would be taken from him, but he was concerned about their future.

Adam slid the printouts back into the envelopes and moved them aside to concentrate on the bills, most of which he paid electronically.

The report cards drew his attention once more. He stared at the neat manila squares on the edge of his desk.

Frowning, Adam pulled out the failing printouts again and scanned the contents. He tried to pin down exactly what bothered him. He set those aside and pulled out Bradley and Brandon's grades. Both were passing.

Bradley consistently brought in high A's. His little beta wolf should be in advanced classes. Nothing ever dropped below a ninety-five. Brandon was a steady middle of the road B. He carried an eighty-five in every class, every six weeks.

Adam glanced at the other report cards. Fluctuating C's and F's marked the other three. Mark might even have to go to summer school to make the next grade.

Adam picked up the twin's grades again, studied the averages. He set one down and stared at the other as an idea took hold.

He reached for his desk drawer that served as a filing cabinet, where he put the boys' school records and his guardianship papers. As a lawyer, his brother was nothing if not thorough. Dom had made sure that Adam had the boys' medical and school background, as well as documentation of his legal guardianship.

Adam flipped through folders until he came to the right set of grade printouts. He pulled them out and unclipped them, scanning the boy's averages over the years. All of the boys were smart and if they could be motivated would be college material. This particular one was brilliant. It was a near perfect plan.

Third grade, second six weeks, was when a nine-year-old child figured out how to stay unnoticed by becoming completely average. In Garrick's pack, a reward for your achievements wasn't a good thing. Failing grades would have been a bad idea because a call from the school would have irritated the boys' guardians.

Hell, his three underachievers had been barely passing when Adam took over. Maybe that was weird sign of trust in itself. That they trusted him *not* to hurt them if they messed up. You never knew with kids.

He felt like he'd discovered a key to the puzzle that was his pack. Adam laughed. Damn he was proud of that kid.

Potential. It was all about potential.

Adam ran a hand through his drying hair.

What kind of idiots missed the obvious? With these kind of fixed grades, he'd bet his tail that boy was the smartest of the litter. That kid would be hell in Vegas.

He put away all of the report cards but the one with the most potential. He still had to talk to the others about failing grades, assign punishments, and all that.

Excitement and pride thrummed through his veins. He nearly picked up the phone to call and brag, but he didn't know Diana Ridley's phone number. Mack would probably listen, but he didn't know if the man would understand. Adam put the phone down and decided he'd call his parents, his human parents, later.

But damn! An eighty-five in every subject since the third grade? What kind of planning did that take? The boy would have to have known how to take everyday work, homework, and final exams into account, and average them out accordingly. He'd have to plan out each paper ever turned in for the appropriate grade. Adam shook his head, amazed. Then walking to the door, Adam stuck his head out into the hall and bellowed.

"Brandon!"

The raw scent of fear reached the office before the boy. From behind his desk, Adam watched the door open, slowly, like a scene in a horror movie where the victim is brutally attacked. Brandon stood in the door, eyes down, waiting.

Geez. The boy was about to piss his pants. Adam wanted to kill that bastard Garrick again. This time he'd castrate him before strangling him with his own entrails. Death had been too easy for Garrick Moser.

Adam gestured at one of the chairs in front of his desk.

"Shut the door and sit down."

He leaned back, trying for casual. He hoped that his actions and mood would transmit to the boy and put him at ease.

It didn't.

Brandon sat, a silent ghost in the room. If the boy could control his fear scent, he'd be nearly invisible.

"Look at me, son."

In two jerky motions, the boy brought his eyes to Adam's chest.

"Good enough." He grunted. Better than the floor.

Adam leaned forward to put his arms on the desk. He hated the way the kid tensed. Adam sighed and ran a hand through his hair instead.

"Look kid, we can't keep going on this way. One of us is going to get an ulcer."

With no response forthcoming, Adam leaned forward. He didn't know how to get through.

"Dammit! Look at me. I'm not Garrick!"

Brandon paled. He looked as though he might be sick. He stared at Adam with wide eyes.

Not wolf eyes. No, the sick bastard had given the boy goddamn Bambi eyes.

That infuriated Adam.

He stalked around the desk, a red haze forming as the boy shrank away. Adam leaned over the chair, the sick scent of fear egging him on. The wolf wanted blood and pain for penance. Not this blood, though. This one was innocent.

The beast slipped under his skin. Sharp canines, upper and lower filled Adam's mouth. He gripped the armrests tight with hands that were more claw than human, caging the boy. He pressed his face close, his nose inches from Brandon's, so that all the boy would see, smell, and hear, was him, Adam Weis, no matter how he cringed or hid with his eyes shut.

"Who am I, Brandon?" He demanded. "Tell me."

"Alpha." The boy answered in a strangled whisper.

"Tell me."

Brandon whimpered. A knock on the door jerked Adam's attention from his prey. He snarled. A wise wolf would leave the door shut.

The door opened and Bradley slipped inside. He shut the door behind him and stood there.

Adam growled at the intrusion. Moving with preternatural speed, he pinned Bradley against the door. If they wouldn't see, he'd make them see. The boy's bared neck, barely mollified the wolf. Adam waited a second before accepting the offering, then dragged his tongue slowly over the heavy vein in Bradley's neck.

Adam released him and stepped back. He pointed at the door with one claw. His voice was harsher than he intended with the partial Change.

"You want to talk. We'll do it later."

He watched Bradley struggle inside himself, the need to protect his brother at odds with the desire to obey his alpha. Adam made the choice for him. He grabbed the pup by the scruff of the neck with one hand, careful of the sharp digits so close to tender skin. Pushing Bradley outside, he shut the door, locking it against another intrusion.

Adam turned around to size up his prey. Brandon sat huddled in the chair, literally quivering in fear of his leader. The only pack member the boy trusted was his blood brother. The wolf understood and reminded him. The pack was brotherhood. Blood bound them all. The blood of birth, blood shed in a hunt, it was all the same, shared blood between them.

"C'mere."

Adam watched Brandon slide out of the chair and begin to crawl toward him. He closed the distance and reached down, pulling the boy up against him.

"You're not a dog, son. Stand."

Adam cupped the boy's chin carefully between his clawed fingers and tilted his head up to meet his eyes.

"Look at me." He nodded when the boy finally complied.

"What do you see, boy?"

"I see you."

"Do you?" Adam stared deep, trying to find the psychic connection he had with his pack. "No. You don't. You see a monster."

Brandon closed his eyes tight. His breath came in short gasps.

"Look at me."

Adam gently feathered a deadly digit over the boy's cheek. The kid had amazing mental defenses. He pressed his mind closer, using Brandon's eyes as the window. Adam lowered his gravelly half-changed voice to lull the boy's defenses.

"Shhh. Look. At. Me."

Brandon relaxed against him. Adam caught him, careful not to hurt the boy and stared deep into the brown depths.

"What do you see?" He whispered.

"I see a forest. I've never seen one like it before."

Brandon sounded surprised and awed that he'd found The Forest, the psychic plane that connected all of their kind. Wolven were all a little psychic. It stood to reason that their connection to one another and the Earth would be too.

"And?"

Adam prodded, gently, lest he break the fragile bond he'd forged. If he failed here, he would fail with the rest.

"I see … everyone." Brandon closed his eyes and smiled faintly. He reached up to touch Adam's bare chest, laid a hand flat over his heart. "The Pack … all packs, running in the forest together. Hunting."

Carefully, he drew the boy close, and rubbed his chin over the top of Brandon's head, amazed at the feeling of possession that welled up inside.

His … boy, brother, pack, son. The words didn't matter only the meaning.

Mine. The wolf howled. Power filled him, driven by instinct. He staked his claim. *This is mine.* Let no one trespass on what I have claimed.

The wolf needed to seal the bond. In case the boy fought him, he shifted his hold so that he cradled the boy's head in one hand. With a quick slice of one claw, Adam opened a wound in his own chest near Brandon's mouth. Blood welled and ran down his chest.

Brandon blinked and jerked back, but Adam held tight guiding the pup to what it needed.

"Shhh. Drink." Words came, an ancient ritual that welled from deep inside Adam's soul. From his core.

"Blood to blood. Brother to brother. Hunt to hunt. Heart to heart. Run with me brother. My Heart, my Hunt, my Pack."

The pup, his pup, nuzzled at his chest. Adam threw back his head and howled, loud and long. He called his pack to him. He threw his power out, touching those he claimed as his own, demanding attendance.

Come! Now! Come All! Brothers! Attend Your Sire!

Adam opened his eyes. He looked down at Brandon, cradled in his arms. The boy's face was flushed pink with the power of the ritual and his Sire's blood. His eyes drooped and he rested quiet beside the wound on Adam's chest.

The rest of the boys lay in a pile at Adam's feet, each in a different state of Change. The office door was askew on its hinges where the boys had obeyed the compulsion to come. Bradley grinned up at Adam, flashing fangs. His eyes glowed feral in the room. Mark and Seth looked like the adolescent wolf-men they were. Rick the wolf lay on his side and panted, happy.

Adam lowered himself, and Brandon, to the floor. The rest of his small pack claimed their piece of their Sire. Soon, Adam was the center of a great sleepy pile on his office floor. He was a part of them and they, him. There was nothing obscene or perverse in their bond.

Distantly, the telephone rang. He ignored it, knowing instinctively who the caller was, because of past blood shared. He'd make peace later for the compulsion over a beer and pizza. All was as it should be.

Adam closed his eyes and felt for the faint psychic bonds that held him to each member of his pack. He scratched behind the ear of the wolf curled up next to his side and smiled. Time would make the pack bond strong. The Anderson Pack would live and grow strong.

Chapter Six

Diana woke up in her car. It was dark out and the motor was running. She didn't remember anything past doing the dishes after dinner.

Why was she out here? Where was she going?

She killed the engine and got out of the car on shaky legs. She still had the feeling that she should be somewhere important, but couldn't imagine where.

Inside, Diana set her keys on the counter. On second thought, she moved them to the top of the refrigerator, a place she never put them, and started toward her room. The clock in the living room said eight forty-five. Karen lay sprawled on the couch. Matthew had taken over the coffee table with his summer enrollment college applications.

"Mom?"

Karen watched her from across the room.

Matthew looked up, concern etched on his handsome young face, temporarily erasing his earlier sulk. Diana had re-established the curfew she'd lifted when he had graduated last year. He wasn't happy about that, but it was her house and her rules. Otherwise, he could get a job and his own apartment. Apparently, Matthew wanted to stay.

"Mom, you okay?"

Diana smiled and waved their worry away.

"I'm just tired. I think I'll go lie down."

She'd pray for no more dreams. No more wolves running through the forest. No more blood covering everything. No more calling to her, demanding her to come.

"Don't stay up too late," she called behind her and escaped to the dark sanctuary of her room.

* * * *

Diana sat outside on her patio lounger, enjoying the cheerful light of morning, her coffee, and two large banana muffins that would doubtless find a place on her hips.

All week she'd slept through the night without getting up, as evidenced by the latch she'd placed high on the door jam. If she had gotten up, then maybe the extra lock had sent her back to bed. That was the theory. Any dreams were peaceful and forgotten upon waking.

Yes, she was paranoid. Monday's excursion to the car had frightened her. Sleepwalking was one thing, but sleep driving would be like putting a drunk behind the wheel. She was trying to be a safe sleepwalker rather than sorry where she woke up.

This morning she was content to just be.

She closed her eyes, feeling the morning warm up. Somewhere above in the pecan tree, a squirrel argued with a woodpecker that had invaded his territory.

Ratt-tatt-tatt. Chatter-squeal-chatter. Ratt-tatt-tatt.

Soon summer would be here and the laughter and arguments of children would drift over her backyard all week long

Diana remembered her own children doing the same. She'd married Richard so young. Neither one of them had been ready for children. All Richard had wanted was to move up in the ranks of business and a pretty young wife to adore him.

Richard had gotten his promotions. The pretty young wife who'd supported him while he worked his way up the ranks had put on weight. A lot of weight.

And the children that he'd never really wanted in the first place had needs and demands that he couldn't fill. They were holding him back, so Richard Ridley left, moving in with his new girlfriend Laina the Lawyer.

Laina had been a much better lawyer than the one Diana could afford.

The Dick.

Well, these days the ex-wife was fifty pounds lighter. The kids were nearly grown and two months ago, Laina had left Richard for a younger, much prettier lady police officer, who, according to Matthew, was a hell of shot at the gun range.

All Diana had to say was: *You go girl!*

Diana grinned.

As sayings went, forget '*time heals all wounds*'. '*What goes around comes around*', felt really good about now.

A faint sound pulled Diana from her musing. She sat up and brushed crumbs from her tee shirt. She looked around. Not seeing anyone, she leaned back against the cushion.

The trashcan rattled and a dog yelped as it fell over. Diana jerked back up, staring at a large dark brown husky. A lighter brown and white pattern around his jowls and eyes gave him personality. The dog looked so affronted at the fallen can that she chuckled. The dog froze, its dark eyes focused on her, stilling her laughter. It—*he*—tensed as if to run away.

She stared and realized the dog wasn't a husky. He wasn't a dog either. She wondered which one he was.

"Hey, fella."

Diana didn't look him in the eyes. That was a bad thing to do.

She'd been checking up on wolves on the internet late at night. She found basic information on wolf packs, their social structure, and communication. Very informative stuff. So far, she was still confused on how to interpret what traits and instincts, human or wolf, would be dominant.

"Did you stop by for breakfast?" she crooned and carefully reached for the extra muffin balanced on one thigh. "I made muffins."

She broke it in half, scattering crumbs all over her lap. Diana held a muffin half out. Her sane half derided her as nine kinds of idiot. He was a werewolf. Was she insulting him by treating him like a skittish dog? She seemed to do that a lot.

And if he was insulted and bit her, would she be heading off to the emergency room for an anti-werewolf shot? Probably not. Diana only knew of one shy, skittish werewolf.

Brandon stretched out a dark muzzle and sniffed. He took a tentative step toward her.

Did a werewolf remember what he did as a wolf when he turned back into a man? It was much too early for that kind of convoluted thinking. She decided to go with the flow.

"You want it, don't you? Come on. You know that I make the best muffins."

He took several more steps toward her, each one bolder that the last.

A series of sharp barks halted the brown wolf. They both turned to look at the newcomer.

Another wolf, this one was huge and vibrantly healthy. She'd thought the brown was big. This newcomer was easily the size of a Great Dane. He was beautiful, all pale cream and silver with pale blue eyes. She didn't really have any doubts about who his alter ego was.

The pale wolf barked an order again at the brown. Brandon lowered his head and whined. If size difference and attitude hadn't already clued their identities, then the cream and silver wolf's authority pegged him as Adam Weis. That and the fur coloration.

"Hey, big guy. I've got another piece," she called.

She was already breaking rule number one for wild wolves by offering food. She reached out a hand, palm first to the pale wolf so that he could get her scent.

He had no reservations about approaching her. In fact, he nudged away her empty hand, going for the muffin. Just like a man. Food first, then everything else.

She stayed very still, riveted by the beauty of the creature.

The wolf's ringed blue eyes conveyed the man's intelligence and power. Gently, the he took the muffin from her palm, wolfing it down in one swallow. A swipe of his tongue over her palm conveyed thanks.

He barked at the brown wolf to come. Diana handed the muffin over to the skittish creature. She got a lick on the hand for that treat, as well.

Diana held her fingers out to the alpha wolf once more. He sniffed, and deigned to let her touch him. She curled her fingers into his thick fur.

"I've never been much for dogs. But you guys are amazing." She kept her voice low, but the care wasn't needed anymore.

Other than a growly wuff of protest at the dog remark, Adam trusted her.

Brandon, she noted was easy. For half of a muffin, his nervousness faded and he allowed her to rub his head and scratch under his chin.

"You like that, hmmm?"

* * * *

The woman's inane chatter as she stroked and cooed over Brandon finally drove Adam to interfere.

She jumped when Adam stuck his nose in her lap, snuffling for crumbs. His warm tongue caught pieces of muffin that slid into the seam of her crotch. She gently moved him away.

"Not on the first date." She scratched him on the head, laughing. "I'm not that kind of girl."

Adam barked at Brandon when the pup got too comfortable and tried to climb on the lounger with her. Adam nosed at the pup to take some of the sting out of his rebuke, and to get him out from under the lounger where he'd taken cover.

Adam kept his post, patiently waiting for her to pick up on petting him again. If he could get her to get that spot behind the ear again … he bumped her hand with his head once more.

She laughed again at their antics and fussed at the big one.

"Oh, I get it. You can't stick your nose where it doesn't belong so he can't sit up here."

The big guy looked so affronted that she grinned and leaned over to place an impulsive kiss on his nose. He went very still.

"It's all right," she stage whispered in his attentive ears. "I don't think the lounger would hold all of us anyway."

She felt a warm tongue slowly glide from her collarbone to the sensitive area behind her ear. He moved back, watching her so intently that she forgot not to stare into his eyes. Her entire body tingled. She placed a hand over the damp kiss and watched the two race across her backyard. The pale alpha paused, a break in his graceful stride, and barked over his shoulder in her direction.

I'll be back, he seemed to say.

Chapter Seven

Adam set down his hammer to put an end to the incessant chirping coming from his belt.

"Adam Weis?"

Wary? Yep. That would be one way to explain his sudden craving for a bottle of antacid. Or two.

What had Mark done now?

The sharp shards of the woman's voice lodged at the base of his neck.

"This is Ms. Whitmire. Mark's history and language teacher."

Adam sighed. Ms. Whitmire, his arch-nemesis. So far the score tallied, Adam Weis, supernatural bad-ass: zero. Ms. Whitmire, sixth grade History and Language instructor: Ten parent/teacher conferences and three phone calls a week.

"Yes?"

"You need to come to the school and meet with the principal."

Of course he did, Adam thought sourly. He had his own chair and everything in Mr. Lang's office.

"Why don't you tell me what's happened this time, Ms. Whitmire?"

"Skateboarding stunts. Sliding down the banister. Back flips and cartwheels, Mr. Weis. Unsafe acts that could get him and others hurt."

Damn. She had him there. Adam knew he should have confiscated that board when he saw it going out the door this morning.

"Are you aware Mr. Weis, that skateboards are not allowed on school property?

"I understand, Ms. Whitmire."

Ms. Whitmire's voice sneered back at him. He imagined her looking down her nose at him. The cold pinpoints of her eyes. He shuddered. That was one *scary* lady.

Adam placated the woman. He'd buy Mark a helmet. He hung up and thought about going to the school to pick up the confiscated skateboard and then realized the lesson value in letting Mark stew over the loss of his prized possession.

* * * *

Call 911!"

Shouting and the scent of burnt skin and ozone jolted Adam out of his funk over the call. He ran to the commotion and shouldered past the small crowd of six men hovering over two on the concrete floor. One man kneeled over the one stretched out prone.

"What happened?"

Adam crouched down beside his electrician Barry, unconscious on the ground. The man was the source of the burnt smell. Mack, the foreman, checked Barry's vital signs. Adam looked for, but didn't see Barry take a breath. Not even a faint shallow one. He didn't dare interrupt whatever Mack was doing for the man. Adam's medical knowledge was suited to his own kind. Humans were too fragile for him to bumble one.

Calm and professional, Mack had gotten his first aid training while fighting in dangerous places Adam had never heard of. In the wall in front of them, the electrical box smoldered. Its blackened remains testified to the cause of the accident.

Adam heard one of the men give directions to the nine-one-one operator via a cell phone while the other men looked on. Without a word, Mack cleared Barry's airway, took a deep breath, and started CPR. Adam scrambled back out of the way.

He felt helpless watching Mack take turns breathing into Barry, then shove on the man's chest to get his heart started again. Mack's movements flowed in a strong and sure pattern. Breathe first, make the heart beat, then breathe again.

Please God, let him live. Adam looked on and prayed. He breathed in time to Mack's movements, willing life into Barry.

"One minute Barry was hooking up the two-twenty for the stove and dryer, the next he was getting shocked. I thought Mack had gone crazy, knocking him down with that board ... *the ambulance.*"

T. J., one of the framing guys, hammer still in hand, fell silent and stared at Barry. The downed man twitched and made a protesting sound. Mack backed off his ministrations to check Barry's weak vitals.

A sigh of relief escaped every man.

"Oh. *Thank God.*"

T. J.'s pronouncement was seconded by everyone of the men, whatever his faith, then, he turned and hurried to the entrance to show the paramedics the way. Another of the men shuffled his feet, and then hurried after his fellow crewman.

There wasn't anything anyone but Mack and the paramedics could do for Barry right now.

* * * *

"What happened?"

Barry Miller's wife, Candace, stopped Adam as he came out of the emergency examining area. Standing a few inches over five feet, she met his eyes with a forced calm that made him want to squirm.

"He was electrocuted."

Adam pushed on through to the examining area.

"You go and take care of your husband. I'll take care of the rest."

She'd be okay, he knew, with her human pack, her family, to take care of her.

What was going on? Who was messing around his job site? Questions raced around Adam's mind. Something he was forgetting niggled in the back of his mind. He shook his head and finished filling out hospital forms. Whatever it was would come to him.

Adam's phone chirped at his waist. He unclipped it and checked the number. Since it was his work phone, he wasn't surprised at the unfamiliar number.

"Adam Weis, here."

"Adam, it's Bradley."

Adam paced to the window, putting his back to the Miller clan for privacy. Out the window, past visitors and family sneaking a smoke by the emergency doors, he watched cars drive through the parking lot.

"Everything all right?"

"I picked up Rick and Seth from the library."

Damn! He *knew* there was something he was supposed to be doing.

"I forgot. One of my crew had an accident. I'm at the hospital."

The incriminating silence on the other end pricked at Adam's conscience. He was the alpha and he'd forgotten all about the pack.

He was supposed to pick the boys up from the library and take Seth to some after school function. He didn't remember what. PTA maybe?

"I'm sorry. Thanks for picking up the slack."

"Yeah. Well, I need to drop Rick off at the house and get Seth back to the school for his presentation."

Presentation? Not PTA then. God, he was a horrible parent figure. He didn't have a clue.

"Are you going to make it?" Bradley's voice was neutral.

"What time does it start?"

Bradley made a sound, a derisive wuff into the phone. "Don't worry about it. I've got it covered."

Adam bristled. "Cool it, kid. I apologized and I meant it. I've got to run back to the job site. Do you have time to meet me there?"

"Yeah. I guess so."

"Fine. Let me talk to Seth."

There were some bumping sounds while the phone passed hands.

"Hey, Adam." Seth was upbeat through the slightly static sound of the cell phone. "Are you going to make it to the Science Bazaar?"

The science fair thing! Adam grimaced. "No, buddy. I had an emergency come up."

"Are you okay?" Seth's voice raised in alarm and fear.

"I'm okay. I'm sorry I can't make it. I've got to take care of a couple of things before I'm done for the day. But I want a complete rundown of your presentation when I get home."

Adam pulled up to the job site in time to see Bradley drive out. The older boy looked aggravated. Adam was glad that there would be no confrontation right now. He had too much to deal with.

Seth stared at Adam for a moment out of the back window of the little red Ranger truck then grinned and waved, on his way to present his science project to the judges. As much for the kid's self esteem as for his grades, Adam hoped the volcano took first place.

Everyone else was gone for the day. The lights were out. He didn't know yet if the reason was because the breaker box was fried or because Mack had conscientiously locked everything up.

He walked around the side of the house, following a familiar scent. The backyard was smoothed over dirt, with the fresh new growth of grass and weeds facing over a hundred acres of untamed forest. A boy stood at the edge of the yard, staring into the forest, his small frame silhouetted against the fading light of day.

"Rick."

The boy kept his gaze on the forest. Adam walked up behind him and set a hand on the kid's shoulder. He didn't see what kept Rick's interest. A few squirrels in the trees. A raccoon. A herd of deer that came to nibble on the new grass in the yard. And a few other things that had been nosing around his property.

"Do you smell them?"

Rick's question was soft. His dark brown eyes were worried when he looked up at his alpha.

"Yeah. But this is our territory. The wolven pack always dominates a territory. The coyotes will have to move on."

"They won't see it that way."

Adam gave the pup's shoulder a reassuring squeeze.

"Doesn't matter. We're at the top of the supernatural pecking order. Wolven do not share territory with other supernaturals."

"Why?"

Adam blinked, a little surprised at the boy's question. "Because, that is the way it is."

"What about sharing? Isn't there enough room for everyone?"

He laughed at the pup's naiveté and reached out to ruffle his hair. Rick shied away from the touch, only a step, but enough to evade Adam's hand. He respected the boy's wish and dropped his hand, hiding the little prick to his pride that the withdrawal caused.

"No, there's not enough room for everyone. Just us wolves. Now let's head to the house. I bet you have a ton of homework."

He still had to rattle some sense into Mark for the skateboard incident. But first he wanted to double check the house in progress for coyote scent, which he doubted he would find. Only an idiot would antagonize a wolven in his own territory.

Barry Miller was an excellent electrician. It wasn't like the man to make a stupid mistake that would jeopardize his life. Had someone else other than Barry done any work on the breaker box? Adam tried to remember anything odd about this morning. He frowned, aggravated. He had been so caught up in his other problems that he couldn't recall whether there'd been anything or not.

After determining that there was no electricity in the house Adam decided to check out the breaker box in the morning. His colorblind wolven night vision wouldn't tell him much. The smell of charred plastic and the faint linger of burned flesh covered up any other suspicious scents.

* * * *

By six o'clock the next evening Adam was ready to call it quits. He positioned a nail and drove it into the wood with one swing. He would have liked to have gone back to the hospital today to intimidate more information out of the staff on Barry's condition, instead of the meeting with the Middle School principal for a castigation on how Mark Cargill wasn't living up to his potential.

He pulled another nail from the canvas pouch tied around his waist. Instead of the hospital, he'd made do with a phone call to the electrician's wife.

Candace Miller's report was good. Barry would be out of the hospital tomorrow afternoon and under doctor's orders to take it easy for a little while. No one really knew how long *a little while* was. The doctor was concerned about damage the jolt may have done to Barry's heart.

Adam slammed the nail home.

Last night, while doing a little sleepless web surfing, Adam had come across a posting on the wolven website about a couple of unsanctioned stray killings in California. Executions done with a silver knife reminiscent of The Tracker, a self-styled werewolf hunter.

The Tracker hadn't only hunted wolven. The human had claimed various weres, bogies, vampires, and at least one dragon to his kills. The human monster had finally gone down under three hundred pounds of pissed wolven teeth and claws, proud to the end of his holy quest to rid the world of supernaturals.

Time. Now that was a joke. For him, time was money. Not to borrow trouble, but besides his frustrations with kids and his raging libido where a certain female psychic was concerned, there were quite a few little on the job screw-ups, besides the murdered female in his dumpster.

Two brand new nail guns had to be taken in for repairs. He'd had listen to a lecture on how not to operate on his tools anymore or mess up the inner workings again. *As if.* That voided the warranty on some stuff. An air hose mysteriously sprang enough small leaks that it had to be replaced. A chewed cord on the air compressor. Then there was Benjamin Gates' lawsuit protesting Adam's purchase of the property he was subdividing. A series of building permit issues that cropped up.

And now Barry's accident. Adam didn't believe for a minute that Barry Miller had been negligent in his work. No. Someone was after Adam, upping the stakes on a personal level. A move that pissed off every territorial issue bred into him. There was too much coincidence for him to ignore.

Adam paused to cut and measure a two-by-four for bracing under the stairwell. Working with his hands and the soothing scent of wood always helped him to think better.

Benjamin Gates bothered Adam. His instincts made him leery of the guy. He'd done a little checking up on the man, found out he was a major business owner in town. For now, Adam's brother, Dominick Sheppard was using his lawyerly skills to untangle the legal side of that snarl. Adam wasn't worried. Dom always came through, and it would give him an excuse to slip over to the Tarrant Pack and see his brother's new pup when it came.

With his wolven constitution, Adam could work steady all night if he called out for pizza to refuel. Wolven metabolism needed, no demanded, a steady high calorie and protein diet, especially if he expended a lot of physical or metaphysical energy.

* * * *

Adam positioned another nail, driving it flush into wood with one satisfying hit.

"Damn it, Adam! Watch out!" Mack snapped. "You're going to split the studs if you keep hitting those nails so hard."

Adam had been so deep in his problems that he hadn't heard Mack come back. He shot Mack a glare, aggravated that the human was able to sneak up on him.

"I know how to hammer a nail. Why aren't you at home? Everyone left hours ago." Mack included. So why was the psychic back, bothering him while he needed to think?

"Yeah? Well, I came back. So watch what you're doing." Mack shot back with his own grumpy look. "I don't want to have to buy more lumber because you need to get laid."

Adam snarled at his foreman. He brought the hammer down, missing the nail, but not his thumb. He yelped and dropped the hammer. Adam cussed, long and loud. He stuck the bloody digit in his mouth and leveled his angry gaze on the human.

With an otherworldly calm, Mack Spencer bent and retrieved the hammer. He slid it into the loop of his own tool belt and rocked back on his heels while Adam nursed his injury.

Some days Mack had serious doubts about the Fate's reasoning for his blood tie to the werewolf. Oh, he knew they liked the term wolven, not werewolf. He used the term out of the same stubborn pride Adam used for not finishing what he started. For a psychic to be bound by blood to a supernatural as strong as a wolven was a very personal thing. It was like prepping a surface for painting or texture, then not finishing the job.

When Mack had decided against reenlistment and caught that plane to Dallas, Texas, Mack had known he would never see his family again. He'd chosen the supernaturals over his twin sister and younger brother. To the psychic communities, he would be dead.

But there had really been no choice at all with the visions riding him. Adam Weis dying and the boys ...

No, Mack didn't go there, those visions were worse than the dead and dying. He could ignore some of the visions and keep his sanity, but not that. The Fates knew that and wanted him here. So here he was.

When the thumb came out, the werewolf's injury actually looked better, probably due to his supernatural ability to heal super fast. It really was all in the blood. Mack spoke again before common sense overrode what he sensed the wolf needed.

"You want to go to Jillie's? Get a beer? Chill for a bit?"

The receding anger lashed out, a burning pain in Mack's mind. As a sensitive-psychic his abilities were like a receiver for Adam's powerful barrage. Combine that with the extra sensitivity he got from the blood bond and that made for a powerful punch from the wolf.

As an Ex-Special Forces, Mack had endured worse physical pain than an alpha werewolf's anger. Psychically, Mack was a major player, even if the majority of his gifts were receptive. He was one of the few of his kind who could take the powerful onslaught.

Psychic, magic, whatever. It was all the same crap. Supernaturals and humans alike treated a psychic's abilities as a rare, weird human mental skill that cropped up periodically. That way the humans could sleep at night in their safe little world and the supernaturals could still classify psychics as human cattle, like they'd done since before the beginning of time.

They were wrong about a great many things concerning his people. Mack wasn't about to enlighten Adam or any other supernatural either. He might have burned all his bridges with his people, would likely become one of the wolven in reality in the not-too-distant future, but he'd take the psychics secrets to his grave as he'd sworn when he left the community.

Adam's light blue eyes shimmered red. The aggressive alpha wolf part of his nature ran close to the surface. Mack considered himself a pretty tough guy, and a smart one, too. He had known the suggestion would probably tick Adam off.

The wolf hated bars. Adam had once confessed that the close confines, the alcohol and cigarette smoke, and mixed body odors of such places overloaded his senses. For a guy with almost no modesty, Adam Weis had definite moral issues about paying for anything remotely related to sex.

Mack lifted his head to study a beam overhead. The move left his throat vulnerable to attack, as he planned, and kept his eyes out of range of the roused werewolf's. It was an apology of sorts.

If you ran with werewolves, the least you should do was learn to show the proper respect. Adam Weis was as territorial and possessive as any supernatural Mack had ever met. He'd kill, and had, to protect his pack and any he considered his from danger. The thing with Barry Miller had Adam ready to explode. Mack needed to control the blast area.

Jiggley Jillies? No," Adam's voice growled, deep and dangerous. The wolf was riding him hard. Feral frustration rolled off of him in waves. He didn't want to go to a goddamn tittie bar.

Diana Ridley juggling his milk in the store flashed through his brain. His blood burned hot with power, triggered by his desire. His eyes gleamed red.

"Don't you have a female already? You need to go trolling for leftovers?" Adam sneered.

"Sorry man, I didn't mean it." Mack took a step back. He held his hands out to the side. His tone was conciliatory. He never once looked into Adam's face. He might have prodded this beast with a sharp stick, but he intended to stay until the end. "Whatever her name is, she's got a hold on you like nothin' else. When that happens you might as well hang it up. It's fate. You're caught."

Adam curled a lip. He might be horny, but he wasn't tamed. No one caged him. Especially, not a little bit of a human female. He would decide when and where he had Diana Ridley. And he'd be the one to decide when he was finished with her. He, Adam J. Weis, was alpha wolf in this county.

He shook his head to clear his thoughts. He thrust a hand through his hair. Grime coated his fingers.

"No. I'm the one who should be apologizing. I've been an ass all day." Adam sighed and shrugged. "A beer sounds good. But no bar." He made a face. "They smell bad." That is, the females who tried to pick him up, smelled like stale cigarettes, alcohol and sexual interest. He liked a lighter lemon and vanilla scent, like Diana Ridley's scent.

Mac laughed. "You're the only guy I know that complains about the way a bar smells. Besides, I was only yanking your chain about going to Jillie's. I know you don't like places like that."

Mack gave Adam a friendly smack on the shoulder. Adam tensed but let it go, taking a small comfort in the brief contact with someone he considered his. Wolven needed the touch of their pack. His pack doled out contact in such small quantities that each small touch was a hard won treasure.

"We could pick up something to eat and toss the football."

Adam snorted. "We'd have to find the football first."

"Yeah. I think those boys of yours eat footballs for dessert."

Adam went to put away his tools. Mack followed, unbuckling his tool belt. Dust settled in the house. The peaceful silence made more acute by the absence of hammering, sawing, and air compressors humming.

* * * *

"You need to go to her." Mack's insight was as eerie as it was accurate.

Adam jerked around. The look in his eyes would have paralyzed a lesser man.

"You need to mind your own business." He didn't *want* a mate.

Mack continued to stare over Adam's shoulder, his eyes unfocused as the otherworldly quality in his presence deepened.

Damn.

Adam forgot his temper as the familiar tingle and scent of his friend's particular brand of magic washed over him.

Only other beings firmly lodged in the supernatural world would have scented or sensed Mack's gift. Humans were fragile creatures. And yet, the fates or gods occasionally bestowed on their number a measure of power and made them something more than human. Psychics with magic as real as any other supernaturals.

This made a great reason for those like Mack or Diana to keep their special abilities secret. Some of those supernatural beings would have the ex-special forces soldier on their grocery list in a heartbeat. Some would want the human for other reasons, some of them very dark. Human scientists would want to poke and prod, to find out what made the gifted different. To the wolven, those like Mack were potential pack members, or Diana Ridley, a breedable mate.

Mack knew all of this and still trusted Adam. For his part, Adam intended keep that trust, to protect that rare friendship and the human's humanity.

Mack returned to the present with a slump. Adam barely caught his limp as a noodle friend.

"What do you see?" he asked.

Mack's laugh was depreciating and a little wild at the edges. Adam was glad he'd been born wolven. He'd never have, and didn't want, gifts like the human's. He'd make Mack wolven to get rid of the visions if it weren't changing one set of problems for another. Neither did he want to jeopardize the man's humanity.

"What I always see. Shadows. Spreading darkness. Danger. *Death*. A Hunt." He rubbed a hand over his face. "Man, I hate when I see that one. He's a bastard to shake."

Adam frowned as the most important phrase pricked at his over-sensitized instincts.

"A Hunt? Is someone poaching in my territory?"

Besides all of the weres he'd yet to evict.

Mack's visions could be so damn vague. Part of him wanted to interrogate his friend about the hunt. Worry over Mack's health won out. Adam slipped an arm under the bigger man's shoulder and hauled him out to the truck.

"How about that beer? Leave your truck. I'll drive." He settled Mack into the passenger side. The foreman stretched out as much as possible and leaned his head back against the rest. His skin looked gray. He grabbed Adam's arm before he could move away.

"Give me a little while to sort it all out. If it has anything to do with Barry, maybe I can come up with something useful."

"Don't worry about it." Adam laid his own hand, for comfort, on the restraining hand. He moved it away before making the human uncomfortable with the contact. "You told me once that your visions aren't always about us, that the Fates mess around in your head sometimes."

Adam rolled the window half way down to help combat Mack's after-vision shakes. He shut the door with a slam.

"I'll get your belt and toss it in the tool box on your truck. Then we'll grab that beer and order some pizza at the house." His house, where he could keep an eye on Mack's recovery.

He paused and unclipped the cell phone from his waist, handing it through the window. Adam had learned from dealing with the boys' phobias that normalcy, *whatever that was*, was best for combating unnerving situations.

"Go ahead and call the order in. Six pepperoni and a couple of meat-lover specials for us."

"Do you think that's enough?"

Mack chuckled when Adam paused to think over the sarcasm. Teenagers were hard to fill up. Wolven teens were more like, well, a pack of starving wolves.

"Yeah, probably. If it's not, the boys can finish filling up on sandwiches."

Adam went back inside the house under construction, picking up with half a mind on the task.

He hadn't blown off the she-wolf poisoning incident as much as he'd portrayed to Mack. He'd looked into the matter.

God bless technology. On the Canis website a pack had access to nearly every Wolven community with a computer. There were chatrooms on topics varying from recipes to the best way to take down an elk. There were links to personalized sites for different packs. He could easily find out who'd been declared rogue. That is, if anyone felt inclined to answer the new guy's queries.

As a new alpha, Adam was starting over. His reputation as Tarrant Beta was good. Better than good. But no one knew if they wanted to take a chance on the new Pater Canis over Anderson County, Texas.

He'd lucked out. Her name had been Lynn Garner. Lynn had been declared rogue a year ago by her pack alpha in conservative Maine and formally cast out from her pack. There was no reason given and no one would ask. Wolven were medieval that way.

When an alpha declared a wolf rogue, it was law. Blacklisted. Other alphas respected that. No one wanted someone else's trash corrupting the pack's balance. Hell, applying for pack membership was like applying for an exclusive job. You needed references. Preferably, of the well connected variety.

The process of finding a mate went much the same way. Usually Canis decided it was time to pair up before instinct kicked in, demanding a mate. The alpha contacted his contacts. Contracts and treaties were drawn up. Nothing so important as a life-pairing was given away freely. And *voila*! A match was made with the final consent of both packs' alpha females. Moving and marriage were political. Without the proper references, forget it.

Could Lynn Garner have heard about the inquiries he'd made for new pack applicants? Or the insanity that had him post his interest for an alpha pairing? A brief lived insanity. He'd taken the posting down less than a month after putting it up.

Amanda was dead. Adam desperately needed a power base. Five teenagers did not cut it in the muscle department. An alpha female would have contacts to draw other females. Which would draw unsettled males looking for mates in another pack. All in all it seemed a simple solution to his problem.

Until he ran up against the issue of Garrick's reputation. No female wanted to be the first anything in the bastard's old pack. Adam hoped that Lynn hadn't wanted to join his group. He would've hated to have to turn her away.

What was worse was the knowledge that only a human would have killed her in that manner. A wolven would have ripped her to shreds.

Why put the murdered wolven female in *Adam's* trash pile? That had the feeling of a wolven challenge. A warning?

The sabotaged equipment and electrical box could be a warning that someone wanted more than to hurt Adam financially. Perhaps it was his position, like a stray wolven looking to settle down. No one on the council would say anything if Adam lost his pack, or his life, in a Challenge. His pack was too small, their reputation less than nothing, for anyone to care, except maybe the Tarrant Pack.

Mack's vision took on a more immediate concern. The psychic had seen a death coming. Well, it wasn't his death. Not this time. He had Mack to thank for that.

Adam's lip curled, showing teeth as a growl escaped from deep in his chest.

Bring it on.

He'd be damned if he let some piece of shit rogue out of a B rated werewolf movie invade *his* territory.

Chapter Eight

Diana let herself into the house with a sigh. She leaned against the door and closed her eyes, feeling alone and weary. Her traitorous thoughts drifted to Adam Weis.

Any woman the focus of attention that primal shouldn't be lonely. The fantasy alone was enough to get her hormones humming.

No. She did not need a man that powerful trying to control her. An overbearing human Richard had been hard enough to get out from under. Better to be lonely. She wouldn't survive a creature like Adam.

The sound of low volume arguing roused Diana to action.

Guests. Oh, joy. Karen's new study group. Or more aptly put, Karen's excuse to bring Bradley and the other boys back into her immediate circle.

Diana shook her head. No. She'd had a hard day was all. She wasn't lonely. She needed a break, to get out. She didn't need a man to make her happy.

She was *happy*, drat it!

She would take her happy self to the kitchen, where she'd make a healthy dinner. Then, she'd make that call to just plain vanilla human Bob Benedict for a dinner date tomorrow night. She'd have her break and some conversation that didn't involve pep rallies, college SATs, or werewolves.

Diana Ridley, that was her, *happy, happy, happy*. She squared her shoulders, pasted on a smile, and marched to the kitchen to meet her troops.

"Hi Mom!"

She stopped at the floral outside edge of the dining room carpet. Her smile faltered a second before Karen's pointed stare and bright *don't embarrass me in front of my friends* smile helped her to recover. Diana tried to digest the strangeness sitting at her dining table.

Surrounding her buoyant cheerleader daughter were all five fidgety and feral Weis boys and two geeky overachievers. Both poor kids watched the other inhabitants of the dining room warily.

"Hello everyone."

The Weis bunch was full of ma'ams. Diana had to admit the werewolves were polite.

Karen gestured to the two geeks.

"Mom, this is Marilyn and Doug"

"Douglas." The boy corrected. He checked the time on his watch. The thing might have been smuggled out of a NASA lab.

Marilyn nodded politely and pushed up her glasses.

To his credit, Bradley shifted slightly away from Karen when Diana's eyebrows rose. A slight flush stained his cheeks at her regard. Mark grinned like a loon and dropped his pencil under the table.

Interesting. Apparently, teen werewolf hormones were as active as a regular human teenager's. Probably more. Yes, she was definitely having a talk with the young, brooding, and hunky Bradley Starr.

Her gaze shifted to the other Weis boys. They looked both nervous and earnest for approval, except for Mark who'd disappeared. Marilyn squealed. Under the table came a bump and a small yelp.

"Ahem." The little egghead, Douglas, gave Diana a pointed look while addressing the rest of the group at the table. "We *are* on a timetable here people."

Whatever she'd been about to say was lost when a low rumbling came from Bradley's end of the table. Diana wondered if she was about to have a repeat of her introduction of Werewolf 101.

"Did you just *growl* at me?"

Bradley's white smile grew wider and hungrier as the boy's arrogance faded, replaced by white-faced unease.

Catching her daughter's panicked *help me* look, Diana interrupted, thinking to diffuse the situation. "Anyone up for a snack before dinner?" Instead of snacking on Douglas.

The hearty, *yes,* turned into the shuffling of papers and books. Mark got cuffed on the head and pulled out a few crumpled sheets from the middle of a book.

* * * *

The office phone trilled. Adam set aside the contract bid he was hurrying to finish working on to reach for the portable. He didn't want to be ate for the dinner date to interview a pack applicant.

"Hello?"

"You the head werewolf?"

The voice on the other end was gravelly and coughed a couple of dry smoker's coughs.

Adam went still, his hunter's instincts surfacing. Adam kept his voice light and very polite.

"Excuse me?"

"You heard me." The man sneered. "You're either the alpha fuzzy or not. Which is it?"

A red haze filmed over Adam's eyes. Fury rolled under his skin. No one disrespected the alpha. He snarled into the phone and hung up. He set the phone down before he flung it across the room.

A few minutes later the phone trilled again. He waited five rings before he picked up.

"What do you want?" There was real menace in his voice.

"Hey, don't get your tail in a knot. I want to trade information." It was Adam's turn to sneer.

"What makes you think I want anything from you, two-foot."

The man on the other end laughed, a raspy sound that ended in another smoker's cough.

"Two-foot, eh? I haven't heard that one. Meet me at The Blue Dolphin for a beer. You'll want this bone."

"I don't think so."

He started to hang up.

"Don't hang up." The desperation in the rough voice made Adam pause. "Please. Just don't hang up, man. You got some bad-asses talking shit about you. That's your bone. Okay?"

Adam rubbed the bridge of his nose with one finger.

"I don't care what *people* say about me."

"You'll care about this. My name is Grady. Grady Dobbs. *Please.*"

The last please got to him. And Grady Dobbs earnest waiting. The problem with befriending too many humans was that eventually you went soft on them. You let yourself be dragged into their problems.

"Look, I don't have time to meet with you. Tel me what you want. Maybe we can deal."

Maybe.

Grady coughed. Adam could hear the flick of a lighter and the sound of the man inhaling on his cigarette.

"All right. There's this girl I'm looking for."

This wasn't starting out good. "I don't think ...."

"Wait a minute. Okay?" Grady took another drag from his cigarette. "This girl. My woman. She went missing a few weeks back."

Adam's hackles rose.

"Why don't you call the police? I'm not going to track your runaway girlfriend."

"Lynn didn't run away from me. She's different."

Please, God, don't let it be her. He tunneled his fingers through his hair. He really, really did not want to be involved in this.

"I'll be honest. We're just a couple of strays passing through. I'm not even your kind. But Lynn is. She said, if we ever got separated, she'd leave a message with the local Canis where to find her."

Adam had a message all right. Not the one Grady Dobbs wanted to hear. He sighed.

"Is your girlfriend's name Lynn Garner?"

"Yeah. She left me a message?" Excitement lit the man's ravaged voice. "Where is she?"

"I'm sorry. Lynn Garner is dead."

The phone fell silent. It dragged out long enough that Adam thought the connection had been lost.

"Grady?"

A coughing fit answered. A breath shuddered as the man inhaled air. The line clicked dead.

* * * *

By the time Adam arrived at the restaurant, he had a raging headache. His nose flared at the mingling scents of food, exhaust, and people. A petite blond female, smelling of wolf, bounced excitedly in front of the door. She looked away, exposing her neck for his greeting when he came near.

He drew back, surprised when the female cuddled close, rubbing her nose over his chest.

"Tamara Linden?"

The scent of her nervous excitement made him smile. "Relax, I'm not going to bite. Everyone calls me Adam."

"Okay, Adam."

Tamara rushed the words together. Her big china blue eyes made him think, *young*. Another noncombatant to protect. Opening the door with one hand, he urged her inside with the other.

"They grill a good steak here. Let's order before we get down to business."

* * * *

Once she placed the chicken in the oven, Diana gathered her courage and picked up the phone. Jittery fingers smoothed the front of her dress as she dialed the number in the phonebook. The phone rang once. Twice. A third time. The receiver picked up and a masculine voice answered.

"Hello?"

"Hi, Bob. This is Diana."

"So, what can I do for you?"

Diana's stomach clenched. There was nothing to be nervous about. She was only asking a friend out to dinner. That was all.

"Ah, um, actually, Bob, I wanted to know if you were busy for dinner tomorrow night?"

The other end of the line lapsed into silence.

"Bob?"

He chuckled.

"I was listening for the ice crackling."

Confused, she wrinkled her brow.

"What?"

"The sound of Hell freezing over?"

"Oh. I didn't mean …."

Bob's warm laugh filled her ear.

"I didn't mean to embarrass you. Of course I'll have dinner with you tomorrow, pretty lady. I never believed you'd actually go out with me."

For an accountant named Bob, he sounded wonderfully gallant over the phone. Diana forced her suspicious nature to be quiet.

"Okay. Tomorrow night then. What do you like?"

How did a girl go about this?

He chuckled again in her ear.

"I like you."

Oh. What a nice thing to say, she thought.

"I, ah, like you too." I think.

"Why don't you wear something nice and I'll surprise you. I'll make reservations and pick up at about seven."

"Okay." She was certainly surprised all right. Surprised that she had actually followed through with this crazy plan.

Reservations? What was she going to wear?

"I'll meet you at seven then. Bye." Diana hung up and fanned herself.

She opened the refrigerator door and stuck her head inside to cool. While she was there she decided on the merits of a salad.

She'd bet money that only Karen and the geek twins would eat anything green and leafy.

Shake-and-bake chicken, salad, and rolls. What a gourmet accomplishment. A sense of defeat hovered around her. She rubbed her forehead.

Who was she kidding? Forget healthy. These kids weren't going to eat this.

"If you serve it, they will eat."

Diana hadn't realized she'd spoke out loud. She turned to face the teasing voice.

Brandon stood in the middle of the kitchen with his hands shoved in his back pockets, offering a shy smile.

"They will, will they?"

He nodded. The smile grew mischievous. "Oh, yeah. Shake it. Bake it. Burn it. Smother it in ketchup."

She laughed. "The salad, too?"

He drifted closer to look over her shoulder into the refrigerator. Diana could feel the warmth radiating from the boy soaking into her back. She'd bet werewolves made nice electric blankets in the winter.

"Well," he drew the word out as if thinking over the merits of ketchup on salad. "I'd bet that with enough ketchup, the most discriminating teenager will swallow veggies."

He reached around her to grab a bottle out of the door shelf. He flipped the bottle into the air and caught it.

"But me, I like Ranch."

"Shouldn't you be studying?" Finals were in a few weeks.

Brandon shook his head. "Nah. I already know that stuff. I came with Bradley." He swiftly refolded napkins into perfect triangles, placing the correct silverware beside each plate.

"So your brother is the one in need of tutoring?" She was shamelessly fishing for information and both of them knew it.

Brandon grinned and brushed by her, opening upper cabinet doors until he found her good glassware. The warmth of the boy's passing seemed to reach out and absorb into her skin with a tingle. The contact felt nice. Comfortable.

It was her natural empathic gifts, amplified. The difference was between black and white TV with tinny speakers and 3D with stereo surround sound. She pushed the disconcerting feeling into the background.

"Nah. Bradley's really good in school. He's making sure the others don't get mad and tear the twerp's arms and legs off before their grades come up."

Diana surveyed the table. Perfect. Formal dining, only with paper plates and napkins.

"I'm missing something here," she muttered. "Something important."

"Missing?" Brandon looked over her shoulder at the table. She imagined that could feel the concern radiating with the warmth from his body. "What did I forget?"

"Yo. Some-ting sure smells good."

Rick sauntered in swinging his arms. "What's wrong bro?"

Diana noticed that Rick didn't take his gaze from the table and still picked up on the undercurrents in the kitchen.

"I forgot something for the table."

Brandon's dejection cut her to the quick. Diana began to speak when Rick beat her to the punch.

"Oh, man. That's gotta suck. Looks good anyway. Smells good, too."

The short Hispanic teen sidled up close Brandon. Close enough that Diana felt sandwiched between the fevered heat that the werewolves emitted. Rick's hot fingers brushed Diana's back before making contact to lay a comforting hand on Brandon's shoulder. The strange connection she'd felt with Brandon jumped to encompass Rick.

She felt weirded out by the whole experience, disorientated when Brandon yelped and jerked away. The connection she'd formed with the older boy earlier slammed shut. Rick's confusion echoed within her.

"Don't touch me! Ever!" Brandon backed up until he bumped against the counter.

It took a moment to realize that he wasn't yelling at her.

On Diana's other side, Rick snarled.

Uh-oh. Diana had a flashback to the bloody kitchen fight.

"You better back down bro." Rick started around her.

"Fuck off!" Brandon crouched. Either to run or fight, she didn't know.

Rick growled, a real animal growl.

"Oh yeah? Wait till I really get my hands on you."

Diana reacted without thinking. She put a hand out, taking a fist full of Rick's tee shirt. The kid was shorter than she, slighter built, but strong. Very, very strong. She began to drag behind him as he stalked Brandon. She felt his fear as much as she felt Rick's anger. The need to assert his dominance in pack order.

Enough was enough.

"Not in my house!"

She yanked hard, tipping her captive's balance to gain his attention. Rick grasped her wrist in a painful hold. Thick reddish brown hair covered the back of the boy's hand. Normal nails curved into wicked claws that encircled her wrist.

Rick turned, his fanged snarl now for her.

Diana met the dark feral gaze with her own anger. She reached out with the connection she felt to all of the boys, tapping back into Brandon, as well, and absorbed their anger, frustration, and a great deal of humiliation. Following the link of hurt and pain, she gathered it to herself, trying desperately to ignore the horrible images that came attached to the emotions.

Diana reached for her own anger. No one does anger like a divorced woman. Anger at her ex's resentment. Discontent with her job. Life. Lost dreams. Sacrifices made for her children. Not just angry now, but *pissed*, Diana lashed out with the lava heat to punish.

Seconds after the confrontation began it was over.

Rick seemed to collapse upon himself. He barely stood, his head tilted at an odd angle, leaving him vulnerable. She realized it was his version of a submissive pose. Rick had given over to her.

He gulped air, shaking off the afterburn of adrenaline. The claws and hair receded as fast as they'd appeared.

Diana's hand raised on its own accord. Lightly she ran her fingers up the side of the boy's neck and into the thick silkiness of his hair, acknowledging the honor and respect she'd been given. She pulled his head down and placed a kiss on his forehead.

"It's all right," she whispered. "Everything's going to be all right."

Diana let Rick go. Dimly, in the outer workings of her brain, she knew there were others in the room. They weren't important right now. The danger wasn't quite past.

Brandon crouched into a ball in the corner of the cabinets. Murmuring, she eased up to him. He stared at her out of a furry face with wide, unfocused eyes. The previously shy boy snarled a mouth full of sharp teeth in her direction before hiding his head in his arms and knees.

"It's okay, sweetie. It's safe."

Diana held out a hand.

"Shhh. Its okay."

He snarled and curled into a tighter ball. A cornered animal will fight its way free.

She'd tried gentleness and failed. On to Plan B. As if she had any kind of plan A for werewolves freaking out in the kitchen.

"*Brandon.* Cut it out and come here."

He looked up. Dark familiar eyes watched her warily.

"*Now.* Get a grip and move your furry butt over here." Be strong. Be dominant. She pointed to the spot in front of her, hoping her bluff worked.

It did. Brandon crawled to her feet, practically sitting on the top of her bare toes. He looked up at her, neck bent to the side in obeisance. She bent down, ignoring the slide of her dress to mid-thigh. He tensed when the touch on his neck turned into an embrace.

A second ticked by as Diana waited for a repeat of his outburst. Brandon relaxed into her, shaking as hard as Rick had been a moment ago. Smoothing his hair back, she let go.

Dear God. The thought hit her hard. They were just children. Very needy, very powerful children. Adam Weis had his job cut out for him and she didn't envy him it.

Diana stood and faced the crowd in her kitchen.

Rick slouched exhausted into a chair. Mark appeared. His arm dropped over Rick's shoulder.

"Bradley took the normals home. The Nazi Nerd had an asthma attack. Says he's allergic to dogs."

Reality had a surreal drunken quality. Getting upset was too much effort.

She'd actually come between two fighting werewolves and come out the acknowledged alpha. Wow.

Her thoughts were as fuzzy as Brandon's face. And scattered, too.

"I need to sit down."

A chair materialized behind her. Solicitous hands guided her down into it. A glass was pressed into her hands.

Brandon curled his body around her legs and laid his head in her lap. She could feel the points of his claws wrapped around her bare ankles, secure and unbreakable. Like the ties she felt forming, binding her to the pack whether she wanted to be a part of them or not.

Diana reached down to rub his back. He snuggled closer, a puppy rooting for reassurance. She took a big drink, thankful that someone had found the wine.

"I'm tellin' ya, something's gotta be done. He freaks all the time," Rick said. His voice rose with an edge of hysteria. "What's Adam gonna do when he finds out Brandon flipped out here."

"Shut up, Fuckface," Mark snapped. "You know you're not supposed to touch him."

"Watch your language." Diana interrupted. "At least be creative if you're going to insult each other."

Barely noting the 'Yes, Ma'ams', she sorted through the overload of emotion. The horrible things she'd seen from the boys memories! She *knew* why no one touched Brandon and was glad the one who'd done *that* was dead.

Now, more than ever, she knew that she had no business with Adam or these kids. She didn't have the training to help someone through that kind of devastating abuse.

Power, psychic power and werewolf magic rolled through her. She felt the ferocity of a monsoon, feeling like her dreams of meeting Adam that first night in the park. Monsoons overwhelmed. They devastated. People drowned in all that raw power.

Diana gripped the thick hair under her fingers, wanting to be gone when the storm arrived. Diana was no coward. She'd survived marriage to Richard Ridley. She'd weather this storm.

"Brandon, change back if you can. The rest of you eat." Her words were barely more than a murmur, lost in the power headed her way.

Diana waited, and in the meantime, she stroked the soft fur under her hand and tried to send reassurance out to the boys while they ate chicken, rolls, and salad with lots of Ranch dressing.

* * * *

Adam steered much of the conversation around Tamara's chosen profession as a dental hygienist. He let her chatter about office gossip, her friends, and the wolven boyfriend who had broken their pairing contract in favor of one that brought a multiplex mall into their town.

She pushed away her dessert plate and wiped delicately at her mouth. The cloth napkin twisted tight between her hands.

"Thank you, at least, for seeing me." Her smile strained at the edges. "I know I'm not big business. But I'd really like a fresh start."

Adam liked that Tamara was twenty-six and smart enough to have already lined up a couple of job interviews in the area. She didn't have alpha potential, but he wasn't looking for that.

The power flared in him, igniting his tenuous hold to his pack. He felt their individual presences and reached out instinctively to check on them.

Another presence, strong willed and dominant, met him partway. Not Tamara. *Her.* He didn't understand how a human, even a psychic, could travel the fabric and paths of his pack. He reached out, curious.

Power flared brighter as he touched, met, and merged with a member of the pack. With *Diana Ridley*. Shock jolted him into a temporary retreat..

No. It couldn't be. He hadn't marked her like Mack. *This* could not happen. Not with a human female.

He blinked and came back to reality. Only seconds had passed.

Tamara's sad eyes said that she knew she'd botched the interview. She hadn't, and he liked the girl, so Adam tried to smile past the rush in his veins. The wolf howled in his head, ready for the hunt. He didn't realize that he'd bared his teeth instead. He threw down his napkin and stood.

"Welcome to Anderson Pack, Tamara. I'll take care of the details for your move later. Call me if you need anything."

Adam turned his back, missing the absolute confusion and dawning delight on his newest member.

Chapter Nine

Adam drove blindly, daring the police to stop him. Fury warred with the wolf's howls of triumph. He was not an animal to react solely on instinct. He was not a man to ignore what instinct told him. He was *the* dominant male. How had the human female invaded his pack bond? Such a thing was impossible. She was human.

Adam's mother was a formidable psychic and she'd never developed a link to Paul's pack. Paul had chosen Mara, a good strong, *wolven* female, to be his mate. Mara was the glue that held the Tarrant pack together, while Paul was the discipline that kept the pack strong.

As Alpha Canis, Adam would be the one to pick the Matra Canis. He would choose his own mate, even if the female had to carry out the binding ritual.

It was far past time he put Diana Ridley in her place.

The wolf leapt under his skin, excited. He was going to *her*. Yes, it was time she knew her place.

He pulled into the driveway, noting the beat up red Ranger pickup with the lettering, *Born to be Wild,* stenciled across the back window. Not very original, but what could you expect from a teenager who sprouted fur and howled at the moon?

Bradley had left out the small detail about where the study group was meeting tonight.

Adam jumped out of his truck, slamming the door behind him loud enough for satisfaction, but not hard enough to damage the vehicle.

He strode through the green front yard to the front door. He felt like ripping the door off the hinges, making his demands known. He pressed the doorbell and took a breath to calm down, listening to the chimes announce his presence.

What were his demands?

He counted them off in his head.

Number one, he was in charge.

Number two, as a member of this pack she would learn ....

The door opened, breaking Adam's concentration.

Diana Ridley stood in the doorway, clad in a soft bare armed shirtdress. The dress should have been modest. His eyes skimmed over her full breasts and hips, noting how material clung to her curves. Her bare toes were tipped in feminine pink polish. Arousal added to is irritation. She held a large glass of—he sniffed—berry wine.

He reached out and took the glass, dumping the contents in the flowers beside the door. "Alcohol impairs your judgment."

She raised her eyebrows, her expression overly patient, as if he were the one lacking judgment. He pushed past her into the house, shoving the glass back into her hands. A shiver ran down his spine at her touch. His skin tingled with electric power that surged in her presence.

"Do please come in."

Diana shut the door and followed the bristling man into the kitchen. She should have been surprised that he knew exactly where to go, but wasn't. Forget the werewolf thing. He was a man. He was probably sniffing out food.

Now that he was here, her nervousness dissipated. She didn't feel calm. She felt secure. She felt powerful. And best of all, she knew what he felt. Literally. Entwined into his little group, she felt all of their emotions.

She imagined the sensations would eventually grow maddening if they didn't go away. But for now, she had an advantage, a key insight to how he felt.

He stopped suddenly in the kitchen. Diana moved around him. He reached out, grabbing her arm. Power pulsed between them. Hot molten lava that swamped her limbs.

"Hi, Mr. Weis!" Karen's bright voice cut through the sensation. Adam dropped Diana's arm. He muttered something low in return. Perhaps he'd finally registered the burn between them. She felt every scorching wave of fury that rolled off of him.

The boys looked on with guilty, stricken faces.

Diana took the long way to her seat. She made brief contact with each boy, touching a shoulder, ruffling Rick's hair, asserting her place in her home.

"I'm so glad you could make it for dinner. Would you like tea, milk, or juice?" She watched him, waiting for the right response—that of a civilized being in her home.

Adam watched Diana touch Brandon through a red haze, proclaiming the boy under her protection. He wanted to shake the woman until her teeth rattled.

What? Did she think to protect them from the monster?

How dare she take a stand for his boys against him! He reached out with his power, intending to do some rattling from a psychic standpoint. If she wanted to play in his pool, *then by damn she'd get wet.*

His power met a wall of cool, calm confidence. A grim smile bloomed inside him. An Alpha, bred by wolven and psychic, he could play power games with the big boys. Psychics might have finesse that his kind lacked, but he was all punch. He pushed at her wall and found that it gave. He pushed harder, shoved his way past her flimsy defense.

Diana felt his arrogant attack. He was strong. Letting instinct take over, she accepted the intrusion and swamped him with her own power. She soaked his essence with her own. In her mind, she heard a wolf howl in triumph. Whatever she'd done was in the wolf's favor.

Startled, Diana tried to pull back. The wolf would have none of it, claiming her as his own. Diana struggled to free herself from his psychic grip. He hung on, wild, elemental, *powerful.*

Too late, Diana recognized the wolf was true essence of Adam Weis not the psychic power he wielded. His essence held tight to hers. Too easily, the wolf pinned her. Feral, gleaming eyes held her still while his power soaked into her, a psychic mating, finishing what she had unwittingly began, marking her as his.

Unbelievable pleasure shuddered through her mind, then her body. The world tilted on its axis.

Mortification swamped her and the realization that only seconds had passed instead of the hours it seemed her tête-à-tête with Adam had taken. She flushed in embarrassment, sucked in an unsteady breath while she straightened, barely hearing the room clear out. The boys murmured their appreciation as they scattered for the door.

"We've got school tomorrow. I guess me and the guys will head on out." Bradley turned to Diana, full of deference. "Thank you for dinner. It was good."

Vaguely, she heard Karen say her goodnights. Outside, she heard the stubborn r-r-r of an engine before it finally turned over.

Karen poked her head back into the kitchen.

"Hey, maybe you guys should escape next time. Go to a decent restaurant or something while we hot dog it."

Diana eyed her daughter's over bright eyes while tapping into her excited emotions. Maybe Karen's psychic abilities had picked up more than Diana had thought.

Super. Now, everyone knew she was a psychic slut.

"Good night, Karen." Diana couldn't believe her daughter was trying to set her up. She so did not need this.

"Maybe we will." Adam let his eyes roam over Diana before flashing Karen a warm smile. "Dinner sounds like a great idea."

"Now wait just a minute …," Diana began.

"Super." Karen steamrolled right over her mother's objection. "Because she never gets out. Or dates."

"I do too date!" Diana gasped, indignant. Her mouth and her brain took a vacation from one another. "I have one tomorrow night."

Adam's flare of emotion was as hot--hotter than his gaze. She reinforced her wall, trying to keep him firmly on the other side. So there, both of you, Diana thought. The attitude was childish, but there it was.

"Night all!" Karen called, waving breezily before disappearing to her room.

"You do not have a date." Adam's voice was hard. His silvery blue gaze piercing.

"It's none of your business."

"Oh, yes. It is my business." Adam leaned over the table. His hot fury erupted once more, battering down her defenses. "It is time we talked."

Talk? Ha! They needed space—the next state kind of space.

Diana jumped up, intending to get some of that space, when Adam's hand shot out. He latched on to her wrist, forestalling her escape.

Upstairs, the loud blast of music heralded Karen's bath time preparations.

"Come here." Adam started around the table.

Diana pulled away easily, because he allowed her. She backed up, out of reach as he stalked her. The hunter and his prey.

Diana wasn't afraid. She supposed she should be. Werewolves were supposed to be crazy monsters. She did feel threatened, though in a very feminine way. He was so very big. Her flight ended as she bumped into the refrigerator. His arms came up. He laid his palms on the door, caging her in. She had to crane her neck to look up into his face.

Diana's mouth went dry. Her heart pumped out an erratic beat. Her limbs felt heavy. Breathing was an effort. But not with fear, with desire as she'd never felt it before. She had to get away.

"Look ... I ... I was probably out of line." She gulped a breath as his blond head descended. His gaze held her mesmerized. "I didn't understand what …."

Adam's mouth settling over hers, stopped her words.

He growled low in his throat, reveling in his possession. Palming one full breast, he kneaded through the soft material of her dress. The hard bud of her nipple made his mouth water in anticipation. Her moan elicited another growl and a tiny nip at her lip before he laved the sting away.

She thought to escape him, but he would not allow that. This female was his. Kissing her was the only thing left to do. He pressed close, crowding her into the cool metal behind her, letting her feel what she did to his body.

His cock throbbed in time to their heartbeats. He literally ached for her. He needed to finish what they'd started. He'd bound her to his pack. The psychic joining only lacked physical completion to make her complete the mate's bond. She belonged to him.

The wolf in him, the beast, roared with demand. Take her. Take your mate.

A date? She wanted to taunt him with another male? No male in his right mind would dare show an interest in the alpha's female.

Adam plunged his tongue deep inside her mouth, tasting the unique flavor that was Diana. He memorized her, demanded that she respond, that she only remember him. Mentally, he reached out, merging their essences even as he ground his body against hers.

Diana's whole body was swept up into a storm. Her mind, her being, was not her own. She felt both her own desire and Adam's feeding hers to greater frenzy. When his other hand closed over her breast, Diana shuddered.

She had to touch bare skin, needed to feel the overheated warmth of his skin next to hers. Struggling with the buttons on his shirt, she finally ripped it free of his jeans. Diana tunneled her hands under the material. She reveled in the sheer tactile delight of ridges and valleys of his work hard body. Sliding her hands around and up the trunk of his body, she dragged her nails back down the ridge of Adam's back.

Groaning, he arched his back against the second draw of her nails. He straightened, wild, animal eyes fixed on her. He pulled her hands out from under his shirt and sucked in a breath.

"I want to see you."

With dizzying speed, Adam whipped the dress over her head. It fell unnoticed to the floor as he stared in wonder at the soft curves he'd unwrapped. An unexpected gift dressed in the barest of blue satin undergarments. Her brown eyes watched him with a hesitancy that he felt through their connection.

"Beautiful." Adam let out a breath as he went to his knees. Drawing her close, hands sliding over the sexy bounty of her hips, he buried his face against the softness of her stomach. He inhaled the scent of her sex—hot, musky, ripe for him.

Diana lost herself in sensation, threading her fingers through his hair. Rough whiskered stubble tickled across her belly. She felt hot, sexy, everything a woman should be as his hands grasped her behind and held her still.

The second pass of his cheek rasping across her skin, wrenched a whimper loose. She grasped his hair tighter, trying for some control of the moment. He would not let her have it.

Somewhere in the haze of sensation, she felt the tug before her panties wisped down her legs. Obediently she stepped out. The hot warmth of Adam's palm pressing against her damp entrance made her cling to his shoulders.

The work rough pads of his fingers rubbed back and forth against the wet slit of her opening. Back and forth, she rocked against the sensation, working the building ache deep inside.

"I need …." Diana gasped at the soft bite on her hip. Wet kisses followed a path of nibbles down the crease of her thigh.

The pressure, the slide of his fingers, increased, penetrating her core. Pushing deep inside. Diana whimpered with the vibration Adam's growl made against her sensitive skin. Hot breath and the hotter feel of his mouth closed over her.

Adam growled, lost in the taste of his woman. *His.*

She writhed against him, held in place by one hand across her perfect ass. Scenting, tasting her orgasm building, he had the faintest wish that it were his cock buried in her softness. He'd never been so turned on in his life. Her inner muscles tightened over him, milking him. He nearly came in his jeans.

Adam groaned again, laving his tongue across the delicious swollen bud before sucking it between his lips. His fingers pumped deep, finding that particular spot that made her jerk and moan. Her fingers twisted in his hair. He rubbed over and over, in and out.

His demand for possession of her both body and soul brushed away any reservations. Diana shattered, screaming, into a billion stars.

Still, the pleasure did not abate. She rode him, his hand and his mouth, feeling the build of another orgasm. She crumbled. Pleasure washed over her in waves. Clinging to him as they slid to the cool floor, she rocked against the sensations at her center, chasing a never before second orgasm.

The hot wet heat of his mouth left her bud and lips but the steady thrust of his hand remained. She shuddered against the flick of sensation as his hand took over his mouth's job.

The restricting fabric at her breast was pushed aside to be covered by the heat of his mouth. Tugging and rolling her nipple between his lips.

"Take it off." Diana reached for him, grasping a handful of fabric. Wanting the barrier gone. "I want ...."

He growled, possessive. Dominant. Switching breasts he increased the teasing brush of his thumb against her bud, deepened the strokes of his hand.

Sensing her second orgasm, he smiled against the plump softness of her breast. He pressed his hand deep even as he rode his cock against her thigh. The second spasm and gasp against him forced the shuddering orgasm he'd denied himself.

The world came into hazy focus. A warm comfortable weight lay half sprawled across her.

"You didn't come." Diana's breath was a shaky whisper. She wondered what she didn't do right.

With heavy effort, Adam lifted and shook his head. The pale blond strands sliding silkily against her cheek, elicited another shiver down her spine. He leaned his forehead against hers. The tension in him was monumental. "It's not you, love. I will next time. In a bed. *Naked.*" His smile was grim.

She wriggled until he let go and climbed to her feet. Adam let out a groan and pulled her close. Muzzy with satisfaction, she pulled away to gather her clothes and dress. Out of the corner of her eye, she saw him straighten the wrinkled mess she'd made of his shirt. A tell tale stain barely covered in time, told her that he had indeed been satisfied. Sort of.

Her breath caught as reality intruded. He was such a sexy creature. Wild, untamable. Too dominant by far.

The glow diminished as Diana realized that there wasn't going to be a next time. She couldn't let herself be overrun by a domineering man again.

How do you tell a werewolf that you didn't want to date him?

Very, very carefully, of course.

Diana turned away, wrapping her arms around herself, suddenly feeling the loss of his body heat. All of them had hot, feverish body temperatures. Must be a werewolf thing. She'd bet that their metabolism was super high, too.

What a new diet trend that would be! Get a werewolf to bite you, lose about twenty pounds. Or more, Adam didn't feel like he had an ounce of extra on him.

Gah. Diana shook her head, attempting to clear it.

"Adam. I … ah … well, this has certainly been interesting."

He shifted to lean against the refrigerator. His arms crossed over his chest as he watched her. Alert, intent. Satisfied. He was the perfect predator waiting to spring. And she was the prey.

"And you're right," she continued, pacing the length of the kitchen. "We do need to talk."

His delicious mouth quirked up into an arrogant male grin. Delicious? No. No, not delicious. She must have meant something else.

Like *scrumptious*, her traitorous libido whispered. She could go another two rounds with him and not be finished. But she wouldn't. Couldn't. And she needed to figure out how to make him understand.

"Babe, it's about time you realized that." He came off of the refrigerator, closing the distance between them.

"Realized what?" She squeaked, surfacing from her thoughts.

Diana licked her suddenly dry lips.

Adam followed the movement with his eyes, a growl escaping from his chest. "That I'm right. Always."

She felt swamped by his intense desire, no longer herself. She *needed* to be herself. She wouldn't let a man strip her of her identity again. Diana moved back as he reached for her.

"And right now, I say we go somewhere and finish this."

The front door slammed, the sound echoing like a shot through the house. Diana gasped. Adam whirled, his features twisted into a snarl.

"Hey, I'm back!" A male voice called.

Diana stared at Adam's hands, her heart caught in her throat. His beautiful long fingered hands transformed into vicious weapons tipped with sharp claws inches long, perfect for rending and tearing.

"Hello? Anyone home?" Slow footsteps echoed on the hallway parquet flooring.

Diana grabbed at Adam's shirt, unmindful of any danger he might pose to herself. By God, if he harmed her baby, she'd kill him.

"Adam!" She hissed, holding tight to the fabric. Was he bulkier? Did werewolves gain more muscle when they changed?

"It's my *son*. Matthew." She pleaded, glancing around for a handy weapon. "Don't you dare touch my son."

The footsteps stopped and headed away from the kitchen, back towards the living area.

"Mom?"

She took a breath, intending to call out for Matthew to run, when her words finally seemed to sink into the werewolf in her hands. A full body shudder worked down his spine. He glanced back at her. Upper and lower fangs filled his mouth, giving him a slight snout look. The teeth receded, leaving only the wild look in his eyes behind.

"Shhh. Be calm, sweet." Adam passed a hand over her hair. "I will not hurt your little one." He bent and possessed her mouth in a hard, hungry kiss.

"We'll have that talk later. And finish *other* things," he whispered against her mouth. He let her go and moved to the door. He pinned her with a hot look.

"No dates. You are mine."

He closed the door behind him. Soon Diana could hear the truck's engine turn over, then back up and drive away. His frustration was a live thing that stayed with her through the link.

Chapter Ten

Diana didn't know how long she'd been staring at the door when Matthew's voice startled her from behind.

"Who was that? Why didn't you answer?"

He looked suspicious and uncertain as his eyes roamed over her disheveled appearance. She knew she must look a wreck. Automatically, she smoothed back her hair.

"Uh …." She smiled. "That was Adam Weis." Werewolf and stud extraordinaire. "His kids are in Karen's study group."

Lame, she thought. Lame, lame, lame.

Diana turned around to the sink, intending to do the dishes. The best defense was a good offense. She changed the subject, keeping her tone light and interested.

"So, how was your dinner with Laina and Sherry?"

"Oh, fine. They just dropped me off." Matthew paused. "You didn't hear me come in?"

"Hmmm?" Diana paid special attention to arranging the glasses on the top shelf of the dishwasher.

"Oh, we must have been talking. Did you have fun?"

"Yeah. It was great. They've moved into a bigger place near UT."

Diana looked over her shoulder. She sent her son a bland smile. "Sounds nice."

"Uh-huh. They've got this huge two story place." Matthew's youthful enthusiasm lit his face. "A monster pool, with a deck, grill and everything. A mini-bar too. Sherry made steak and potatoes with cut up pepper things in it." He cooled down and shrugged a shoulder. "You should see it."

"Wow."

Diana's tone was neutral. She'd learned early to never compete with Richard or Laina income-wise. He made good money in the company he worked for and from personal experience Diana knew Laina was a very good divorce lawyer. She didn't plan to start a competition this late in the game with Laina and Sherry.

As a woman who'd been dumped for another woman, Diana naturally had the desire to keep her kids away from the jerk who'd hurt her and the woman who'd stolen her husband.

At the same time, she wanted a healthy atmosphere for her children to grow up in. She'd encouraged visitation and mediated when they were angry with their father or stepmother. Diana kept her resentment compartmentalized carefully away from the kids.

Early on in their relationship Diana had come to a truce of sorts with Laina, maintaining a cool, friendly face for her ex-husband's successful, model thin, and glamorous looking wife. Still, there were undercurrents of tension between them. How could there not be?

Diana and Richard's divorce had been an ugly emotional affair, at least out of the courtroom. Especially, since he'd been sleeping with his lawyer.

To Diana's surprise, Laina had risen to the challenge of being a part time parent. She'd been a wonderful stepmother to Karen and Matthew and the kids loved her in return. Laina's recent divorce from their father had been upsetting, but because of all the effort and love she'd given them, the kids took a stand on maintaining a relationship with their stepmother.

Matthew shuffled his feet uncertainly. He cleared his throat.

"Maybe we could go by on Saturday and say hi. Grab a burger or something." His tone was cautious. And rightly so. He knew he was treading dangerous ground.

"I don't think that would be a good idea," Diana said in a flat tone. She slammed a plate into the dishwasher.

"She wanted me to invite you to dinner then." Matthew flushed, and hurried on. "Sherry's going to be there. But they're committed, so you don't really have to worry about … ah ... well …"

Diana barked a short derisive sound and dumped the silverware into the little basket in the dishwasher.

"Good grief. I'm not worried about either woman making a move on me."

"Oh." Matthew seemed at a loss.

Diana turned back to loading the dishwasher. She reached under the sink for the detergent and squirted a liberal amount in each of the compartments before closing the appliance.

Since he was still standing there without having said anything, Diana turned to face her son. Matthew's hands were buried deep in his pockets. He rocked back on his heels, chest puffed out.

"So. You planning on dating him or something?"

"What?"

Diana blinked in shock that one of her children, for the second time this evening, would broach this subject. Did she have Hard

Up written on her forehead in neon letters? Was it national Pick on Mom Day?

Red flooded Matthew's face anew.

"Well," he stuttered. "Mr. Weis, is like, a *guy's* guy"

"He's gay?" She was way sure he was straight.

"No!" It shouldn't have been possible for the boy to get redder, but he did. "What I mean, is that he's out of your league."

"My *what?*"

All right, the conversation was getting a little repetitive, but the boy didn't say what she thought he said? Had he?

Never mind that she was just thinking the same thing before Adam left.

Of all the nerve. Just see if she saved his butt from getting shredded by a werewolf next time!

"I don't want you getting hurt when he moves on." Matthew gave her that sage look teenagers acquired with the revelation of how inept and stupid their parents were. "I hear things. You know *guy* things."

Locker room things, more like.

Matthew rushed on with his explanation. "Anyway, he's from the city. He used to live in Dallas. And he's been around the block a few times."

"You know what I think?" Diana's eyes sparked her anger. "I think that you should mind your own business."

She felt pulled in different directions emotionally. She was tired of everyone believing her some inept bumpkin. Frost coated her words. "Goodnight, Matthew."

He backed down, out of habit and a lingering respect for her status as his mother, if not for her capability to enter into an adult relationship. "Sorry, Mom. I …"

"Better quit while you're ahead," she warned.

"Yeah." Matthew backed up a couple of steps, indecision filling his posture with the words he still wanted to speak. "Mom?"

"What?"

"What about dinner Saturday?"

"You are welcome to go."

"But …."

Her hands bunched on her hips. Diana clenched her jaw as she fought the urge to scream, or throw anything, out of sheer exasperation at the male species in general.

"I. Am. Not. Going. To. That. Woman's. House. Is that clear?"

"But, Mom," Matthew's voice rose in a whine.

"And that is final." She slapped the counter hard enough to leave stinging prickles in her palm.

Matthew turned, leaving the kitchen with lagging, disappointed steps.

* * * *

Adam shoved a piece of toast into his mouth. *Alone at last.* Everyone was at school and out of his hair. No more questions about Diana Ridley. No more bickering.

There was only a man, his newspaper, and blessed peace and quiet.

He flipped the page of his morning paper. A gulp of scalding coffee made him juggle both the cup and the paper. He nearly had the cup on the table when the phone rang, jolting him into sloshing the burning liquid on his hand.

Cursing, Adam rose to answer the damned thing. He shook his hand to cool the burning sensation as he picked up the handset.

"Hello?"

"Mr. Weis, this is Jared Morgan."

The dorky cowboy?

"I'm from Animal Control. We met the other day at the house your people are building."

"Yeah?"

He wondered if the guy was calling to have his office space wallpapered in genuine nyogahyde and longhorns mounted on the computer monitor to go with his dorky cowboy image.

"I have something here that the county Pater Canis should have a look at."

That got his attention.

"What have you got human?"

Morgan's laugh was biting.

"I don't know if I've been insulted or not, wolf. What I do have, is another dead, and I want to know if it's one of yours."

Adam glanced at his watch. He was late for work. Very late.

"Where do you want to meet?" Adam's voice lowered into a growl. "And remember, if you betray me, I'll have you for lunch."

It was a scary threat to make to a human, but an unrealistic one. Wolven didn't eat the meat of anything that walked upright and carried on a conversation. But he would, and could, rip out the throat of his enemy and enjoy the taste of the blood filling his mouth. Every last rich drop.

"I'm not stupid, wolf. Meet me at the old Drury place on county road four-twenty."

"Which place would be the old Drury place?" Adam wanted to know.

Morgan laughed.

"I forget you aren't a local. It's a rock house with shutters that sits back in a pasture. The gate is open, so drive on up. You can't miss it. It's the only rock house on four-twenty."

Adam hung up and dialed Mack's number. He quickly relayed the conversation, wondering all the while why he felt compelled to do so. He really needed to stop involving Mack in pack business if he wasn't going to change him.

"I've got you covered." Mack replied. "Holler if you need me. I'll keep my cell handy."

On a whim, Adam swung by the high school. His pack sense told him that everyone was safe, if a little bored. Except for Diana Ridley. His psychic female was agitated, but not in danger. Her inner turmoil, he suspected, had to do with them and their … relationship?

He hoped it was him. She needed her safe little world shook up. And he was just the one to do it.

The old Drury place was further down the county road than Adam figured. The road, like most in the area, twisted and turned back on itself so many times that he felt certain a normal human would have been hopelessly lost. The mailbox said Lamott.

Adam bumped his way over the cattle guard. Huge brown cows with liquid eyes watched him drive up to the house then bent to graze. They looked tasty rather than intimidating, though he'd never seen one so close. Morgan had been right in naming him a city boy.

Adam parked under a tree shading the bare area designated for vehicles. A white truck with a cage mounted in the back and a dark blue dually with six wheel openings were pulled in close together. Two tires in the front and four pair in the back.

A restored cherry-red, nineteen sixty-nine Ford sat in all its regal glory a little apart from the two trucks. Adam chose a space on the far side of the red Ford, giving the vehicle the space it was due. He eyeballed the truck, nearly having to wipe drool from his chin, as he walked up the path to the porch.

Two black men ambled out of the house. Despite the warmth of the day, they'd dressed in western hats, long sleeves, worn blue jeans and boots, worn. The screen door banged shut behind them.

They eyed Adam up and down, taking in his hair pulled back into a short ponytail, the Carhart work shirt, faded jeans, and lace up work boots that was his usual uniform for work.

He must have passed judgment since the men relaxed into the rolling gait of cattlemen and horsemen. They met him halfway.

"Hey."

The first man, taller and heavier than his partner, turned his head to spit a long brown stream into the grass beside the path. His shirt was a blue plaid. Pearl snaps gleamed in the sunshine.

The other man, all angles, nodded his greeting. He wore blue denim, the monochrome color broken by a gold and silver palm sized belt buckle featuring a steer head inside the state of Texas.

"You the one Morgan called 'bout the wolf?" The first man extended his hand.

Hard work had taken a toll. Small pink-and-white scars scattered over the back of his hand, blemishes in dark leather. Dry skin gave the man's knuckles a grayish color.

"Name's Cherif. This here's my brother Yule.

Adam nodded accepting the hand for the due it was. All over the country, men shook hands in greeting, women, too. But where men worked hard, depending on the land to survive, the handshake became more. Around here it was a meeting of equals and respect. The worst insult a man could dole out was a refusal to shake hands.

"You sure it's a wolf?" Adam asked.

Cherif grinned around the wad tucked into his cheek. Yule's black eyes seemed to twinkle with laughter without him making a sound.

"Yeah. We're sure. Critter's too big for a coyote. An' Yule looked it up on the Internet. 'Sides that, his girlfriend is a vet. C'mon. We'll walk you around back to Morgan. That way you can meet T without him trying to chew your leg off."

The two cowboys led the way around the rock house and past several large prefabricated, padlocked storage buildings.

A large Rottweiler bounded up like a small tank, barking and snarling. T, Adam guessed, stood for Terminator. The dog stopped suddenly, getting a good whiff of Adam's scent, then trotted up to his feet. He bent and extended a hand for the dog to sniff, which it did in slobbery dog fashion. The dog gave Adam's hand a last lick before rolling onto his back.

"Never seen 'im do that before."

Yule scratched the short mat of hair under his hat while Adam crouched to give the dog a belly scratch in reward. When finished, the dog rolled back to his feet and gave a full body shake powerful enough to unsteady his feet.

Adam was impressed. It looked like it felt good. Sometimes you needed a good shake.

The dog led the way to a stand of trees far behind the house.

"It was the buzzards that clued us in," Cherif began as if there had been no break in their conversation. "Didn't want T getting into anything dead and causing another vet bill."

Both men were of the quiet sort, not needing to break the silence with conversation until warranted. Adam liked that in a man. It was a rare thing and spoke of confidence that few had.

Jared Morgan strode out of the trees. He had his hat in his hand, allowing the wind to blow his hair into a light brown haystack.

"Hey." Morgan stuck out his hand in greeting. "I thought you would never get here."

Adam shook hands. He let go to give a short wave to Cherif and Yule as the humans turned around to head back to the house. A piercing whistle from Yule called T, the dog, to his side. Adam fell into step behind Morgan, following him through the field that served as a backyard, to a stand of trees.

The mangled body of the wolf was difficult to see until he was nearly upon it. The smell however, he'd caught as soon as he'd left his truck, faint, under the scents of cow, feed, motor oils and fuels, dog, chicken, and the thousands of other scents from a working ranch or farm.

His nose efficiently caught them all while his brain automatically catalogued them for reference. As they'd walked around the house to the trees, the scent became stronger until it was overpowering. Death. Violent death. And the ghastly decomposition.

The body was ripped and torn where buzzards had feasted. The heat was already starting to cook the carcass, despite the shade. Ants made a trail back to their hill, carrying food for their queen.

Whoever the wolf had been, he'd died hog-tied, his throat slashed wide open with a knife. There'd been no dignity, no fight, just an execution and a place to dump the remains.

Adam wished he'd known the wolf. No, he amended that. He didn't want the responsibility that knowing the dead wolf would entail. He had plenty of responsibility for two or three people already.

He walked away from the carnage, hoping to find the killer's trail before the odor burned into his sensitive nose. He imagined that he'd be catching whiffs of road kill until the sensory image faded.

He sneezed a couple times to clear his nose and walked away, following a couple of trails that led away from the dead wolf. The first was a plain rabbit trail that doubled back. He inhaled, filling his nose with another, clean, live scent.

The next was human. He found several human scent trails around the area. He followed each one until he was satisfied, then walked back to Morgan, who'd opted to take his own breather from the stench of death.

"What do you want done with the body?" Morgan's tone was respectful. With Adam's nose on overdrive he took notice of the other man's scent and moved closer. Its mystery prodded him to investigate.

"What did you do with the other one?"

There was definitely something *other* about the man, but in a different way than the psychic humans he was used to dealing with.

"Cremated her and buried the ashes in a holy place." A glint of amusement shone in Morgan's eyes.

"You're subtle, wolf. But not enough." He lifted his arm under Adam's nose. "Here. But if you get too friendly, I'm out of here."

Adam took the man's arm and pressed his nose to the fabric of his shirt. He breathed deep. He would have liked to lick the salt from the skin to see if the taste matched up to what he smelled, but figured that might fall under the too friendly rule.

There it was, elusive, wild, *exotic*. A scent that made his blood tingle with possibility. He let Morgan's arm go, feeling as though the answer was barely out of reach.

"What are you?"

Morgan watched him, still amused. Adam was too curious to be aggravated. He should probably be focusing on the wolf, but the sucker was dead and Morgan was a live mystery.

"An American. As mixed blood as any other."

The answer didn't satisfy his question, but no other appeared to be forthcoming, so Adam let it drop. He had the scent memorized for later reference. If he came across it again, he'd identify it and solve Morgan's mystery heritage.

"Did I tell you that Cherif and Yule are my cousins?" There was laughter in Morgan's tone.

Adam stared, startled. Pale skinned Morgan was not human.

Morgan grinned, pleased at thoroughly confusing Adam.

"Very distant cousins. But the connection is there."

"Do Cherif and Yule know?"

"Very good, wolf." Morgan's grin faded a bit. "I didn't expect you to pick up on that. I think we'll stop my game for now and focus on the one that guy lost." He nodded in the direction of the dead wolf.

"You said you buried the other one in a holy place. A cemetery?" The answer was too obvious and Morgan shook his head as expected.

"No. But the spot is sacred and protected. You don't have to worry about wizards and their ilk digging her up for spell components."

Something told Adam that in this, Morgan could be trusted.

"Do the same with this one then." Adam glanced at the heavy toolbox that sat nearby and the black plastic folded square sitting atop. "I'll help you bag him up."

In the end, Morgan refused his help to bag up the stray, or haul him out. Morgan mentioned cleansing the area. Since Adam sensed that the cleansing could only be done with him out of the way, he left.

There were other things he could do for the dead mystery wolf and Lynn Garner.

Adam phoned Mack and called it a sick day--on account of someone very sick messing around in his territory.

In his office, he logged on to the Canis website and researched missing wolven. He paid special attention to any wolven thinking of relocating, say to Anderson County.

Other than Tamara Linden, there were no inquiries. He finished the last of the negotiations with the Canis of Tamara's pack. She'd be arriving as soon as she found a job assisting one of the local dentists.

He picked up a telephone with caller ID. Then, Adam decided to track down his one live connection to the dead wolves. Grady Dobbs.

Chapter Eleven

At eight-thirty, Adam began the search for Grady Dobbs in Old
Towne, next to the downtown area. The area was a quaint couple
of blocks that gave the illusion of an isolated old western saloon
and mercantile.

Across the street there was a steakhouse and a series of shops
so decked out in plants that the natural camouflage made the
coffee, antique, and souvenir shops nearly invisible.

Adam's destination was the old saloon style bar and game
room. Country and western music played, loud enough to be
pleasing to the two-stepping cowboys and girls, but not loud
enough to disturb the houses a few blocks over.

He got out of the truck and inhaled deeply, sorting through the
night air. He didn't have Grady Dobbs' scent, but he had to start
somewhere. Plus, Adam wanted a head start on any trouble.
Like, say, a stray with delusions of becoming Canis.

With the background noise from the man's phone call, Adam
guessed that he'd been in a bar. Western music narrowed down
his list. He didn't think that this place would be where he found
Grady. Maybe he was prejudiced, but the guy sounded like
scum.

The wolf rose, bringing his body to full alert, as one scent
brought him up short. The saloon wasn't too upscale for one
particular human female psychic. The wolf growled. *His female.*

Adam went inside, his work boots making no sound on the
wooden steps. Inside the music assaulted his ears. The bright
light of the entry temporarily blinded him. Beyond the interior
door, the bar was dim.

Scents of smoke, liquor, sweat, and arousal permeated the
place, though not as bad as some places he'd been in. Adam
usually avoided congested places like this because of the sensory
overload. He barely suppressed the urge to sneeze.

"Do you have a membership?" A cute twenty-something
cowgirl in a cutout western blouse asked. She grinned and leaned
on the window ledge so that the cutout over her bosom offered
him a view of firm, young breasts.

Adam dug in his back pocket for his wallet. He pulled out a
bright orange card and handed it to the girl.

Bouncing in time to the song, her tiny ass punctuated the beats. She handed him back the card with a sassy smile. He could smell cowgirl on the make.

"You want to renew your membership? It expires in a couple of weeks."

Adam shook his head. He'd waste the money the next time he let Mack drag him inside.

"Okay. It's a good thing you got here early. After the band starts at nine, it's five dollars to get in. That's when I get off."

She added the last with a flutter of homecoming queen eyelashes and handed the card back.

He replaced the card and his wallet and homed in on the one scent that mattered.

Inside the bar, Adam let his eyes adjust. He ignored the lingering looks of the bar bunnies and scanned the tables, the bar, and the dance floor, where he found his quarry.

Diana Ridley looked out of place in her sexy black dress and high heels among the boot-clad crowd. Men stopped to stare at her. Adam growled.

The short filmy black dress seemed to float around her over her short, but oh so, curvy legs. Little sparkles like trapped stars shone under the mirror ball. The black strapped on high heels also glittered, their height adding inches to her legs.

The man touching her wore a suit, minus the jacket. He danced well enough to the music, leading Adam's woman across the dance floor. Yes, they were both out of place, but while he stuck out like a sore thumb, Diana shone.

Adam walked to the dance floor, ignoring the hopeful glances of some of the women. He tapped the man holding her on the shoulder.

"Excuse me."

Adam slipped in, spinning her into his arms and leaving the bemused man behind.

Diana squeaked.

"What do you think you are doing?"

"Dancing. I don't have a commitment to you."

Matthew had been right. Adam Weis was out of her league. But it had been a nice fantasy for one night.

Adam pressed her close, resting his cheek against hers so that he could smell her hair. He wanted her to feel the effects of his body through the sheer material of her dress.

"I like this dress."

He rubbed his hands over her shoulders and down her waist. He wouldn't be so crass as to cup her butt in public. But he wanted to, badly.

He wanted to prove that she belonged to him. Instead, he held her close, letting that make his statement.

To his happy surprise, she leaned into him, allowing the closeness when he'd expected her to pull away. She was full of contradictions, his little human psychic.

"I told you not to date."

"You just had to spoil it." She bristled in his arms and tried to pull away from his tight hold. "Mind your own business and leave me alone."

He chuckled and kept moving, forcing her to move with him.

"Can't do that. You belong to me, not that schmuck," he rumbled, the growl vibrating though them both. "He has no right to have his hands on you."

"Schmuck?" Diana slapped at his chest with one hand. He captured it underneath his own, trapping her hand over his heart.

"Bob happens to be a very respectable man. *And*," she added for emphasis. "He is my date. So don't get any ideas."

His voice was deadly soft in her ear. Sending shivers down her body. "Bob is a shmuck. And you are not leaving with him. You are mine."

Diana had never let anyone intimidate her before. Richard's and Laina's money and influence meant nothing to her. She was determined that Adam Weis with his teeth and claws would not bother her, either. She was her own woman.

"No, Adam. I belong to myself. You're not my boyfriend or anything else."

She tried to extricate herself for a dignified exit and failed dismally. Other than causing a scene, which she was loath to do. Damn him, Adam knew she didn't know how to escape.

"I'm no boy, darling."

He pressed his groin tight against her belly. Proving that, yes indeed, he was all man. Her hormones cheered in relief.

Bob had been fabulous company, but there'd been no spark. He knew it and so did she. After a very nice dinner at the Coffee Landing in Coffee City they'd driven back to Palestine. The company had been pleasant enough, but there was no attraction.

Bob wasn't broad shouldered enough. He didn't gaze at her with hunger in his eyes. She felt cold in his presence. He couldn't compete with the hot hunk of werewolf, Adam Weis.

Bob and Diana had stopped in town for a beer and more chitchat rather than going home. Both knew without saying that they wouldn't be going out again.

She wasn't about to stroke Adam's ego with the knowledge. He was the type of alpha male that could run a woman over. The type that men like her ex, The Dick, only wished they could be. "Adam, no. You are making this hard."

He chuckled in her ear. His hand drifted up and down her back following the shivers he put there.

"No, you're the one making it hard."

He pressed the noticeable bulge in his jeans against her, pointing out his double entendre.

"Arrrgh." The man was sooo frustrating. So dense. "You are such a *man*."

He laughed again. "It's about time you noticed. Let's go and I'll show you exactly how much." He waggled his eyebrows suggestively.

"Dammit." The man was a jerk, bringing out the worst in her. She hardly ever cursed, yet every time she got around him she ended up loosing it. "I am not going anywhere with you. Especially, after what you did last night. I'm very upset at you."

He peered into her face, one eyebrow raised in question. "Mad at me? For giving you the best orgasm you've ever had? Honey, let me tell you, that wasn't even my best."

She turned bright red, her face and chest mottling under the fractured light of the mirror ball. "No." she hissed. "For almost attacking Matthew." Her voice rose to lecture quality. "Anyone who messes with my kids, messes with me. I don't take kindly to violence of any kind, Rover."

"Rover?" His booming laugh drew the envious gazes of several of the two-stepping cowgirls.

"Yeah, as in, *all men are dogs*. And you're the worst."

"Babe, for the record. I'm always in control. In no way was your son in any danger." He danced them in a tight circle. "I've never raised hand, paw, or claw, to an innocent. I don't plan to start." He flashed a roguish dimpled grin. "Besides, my dad would come loaded for bigger game than bear. And believe me, he's a damn good shot."

Diana let that bit of information digest, then tried to wriggle away. She spotted Bob watching them, concern darkening his face.

Diana panicked as Bob set down his beer and started their way. Belatedly, she realized that she and Adam had been out on the floor for several songs.

She pushed at his chest.

"Let go. I have to go to the restroom." And she did too. He watched her, suspicion in his wild blue eyes. Diana ducked through the crowd, avoiding Bob.

She needed a moment to figure out how to deal with this situation. She passed under the neon sign blinking the word, Cowgirls, in hot pink and darted into a stall. Alone at last.

Tottering forward on her three-inch heels, she steadied a hand against the stall in an *eeek* moment. She'd left Bob, an accountant, to deal with a possessive werewolf. Now that was smart.

A grumbling line outside drove Diana from her sanctuary. Washing her hands, she stalled, using the damp paper towel to cool her cheeks. She prayed for some sanity.

Well, there really was nothing to do about it. She wasn't going to be rude and leave Bob in the lurch. It had been a nice date and she'd end it that way. She'd march out there, collect Bob, and go home. Easy, right?

Right.

Hopefully, the bouncers were paid up on their health insurance policies. Heck, in this area, the poor men were lucky if they *had* health insurance.

Anyway, she wasn't going to let some howling at the moon son of a gun order her around.

Good grief, she was beginning to sound like a country and western song.

Diana squared her shoulders. She took a deep, fortifying breath. She pasted on a smile and exited the ladies, er, cowgirl-room.

Underneath the blow-up beer bottle, Adam and Bob stood side by side. Both men's arms were crossed over their chests, though, Adam's stance was the more impressive of the two. He wore a smug expression, while Bob looked pained and upset.

Lovely, she thought, *abso-frigging lovely.* Diana crossed her arms, as well, and faced Adam with a pointed stare, using the same tone of voice reserved for stubborn children. "Goodnight."

He had the audacity to smirk. Diana began to fume.

"I'm not really sure what's going on here." Bob cleared his throat and shot a glance at Adam. "But I don't like feeling used."

"What?" Diana wrinkled her brow? What had he done now?

"What I mean is, that I don't think its right for you to be going out with one man while you're engaged to another."

Diana gasped. "Engaged?"

On the heels of shock came full-blown fury.

Her fingers curled around the forty-dollar manicure she'd splurged for her date with Bob. She raised them in Adam's direction, unconsciously mimicking claws.

"Engaged?"

Her voice rose. She didn't care who heard. Maybe the bouncers would throw Adam out on his big fat hairy backside.

"You!" She jabbed one silvery tipped finger in the troublemaker's direction. "So help me God I'm going to make a rug out of your hide."

Make a rug out of him? Adam grinned, just to piss her off more. When they were mated properly, he'd have a fine of a time teasing her.

Their pups would be a living terror. He grinned wider, imagining a house full of loud rambunctious youngsters, both two and four footed, and a pack that laughed and loved.

Diana's angry growls amused the hell out of him. Wielding her painted nails as if they were claws that could rip through metal was cute.

"Laugh it up while you have the chance, Fuzzball."

Peripherally, Adam kept tabs on the bouncers, who were edging closer, attracted by the scene they were making. Or rather the scene his quiet proper, mate-to-be, was making.

"I ... uh ... don't want to get in the middle of some lover's quarrel," Bob began, trying for a soothing voice to calm Diana.

It didn't work.

"Then don't." Adam didn't bother looking at the human.

"Lovers!" Diana burst out.

"But, she came with me, so I'll take her home." The edge in Bob's tone made Adam glance over.

He'd dismissed the schmuck as a minor irritation. But now, apparently ol' Bob wanted to play in the big league. Adam was a fair man. But he didn't plan to tolerate any other male making moves on his chosen female. The instinct to protect her was paramount, especially now, before the mating ceremony was complete.

Until she used her psychic abilities to finish the mate-bond, the possibility of another male claiming her attentions was very real.

She could complete the bond with a normal like Bob or another psychic.

"Back off while you still have the chance, little man." Adam curled his lip into a sneer. "She belongs to me."

Bob pulled himself up straight, reaching for one of his shirt cuffs. Finding it already folded up to his forearm, he twitched it straight and crossed his arms again.

"Well, since she came in my car, I'd say she's my date."

One of the bouncers discreetly moved into Adam's vision. The warning was clear. Another bouncer drifted closer, alert for any real trouble they might cause.

The first bouncer, a decent sized human, dressed in long sleeves despite the heat both outside and from the press of bodies inside the bar, offered a good ol'boy smile.

"Why don't you guys cool down or take it outside?"

Diana shot a glare at her date. "I think we need to leave, Bob."

"Good idea, *Bob*," Adam drawled. "Go home, Bob, before you get hurt."

He knew he shouldn't egg the guy on. But damn, she wasn't supposed to be looking at the other man that way. She should be tucked under *his* arm, her sultry brown gaze staring up into *his* face with admiration.

Bob's chest puffed under his button down dress shirt. Anger rolled of the human in waves.

"I'll show you hurt." He headed for the door, pausing to look over his shoulder at Adam. "You coming or not?"

"Wouldn't miss it." Adam sauntered after him, the bouncers providing a discreet escort.

"Wait!"

Remembering the night before, Diana rushed to catch up. She grasped the back of Adam's shirt and was pulled along.

"Don't you dare hurt him. I mean it."

Ever so carefully, Adam detached the female. His strong hands gripped her shoulder. He gave her a feral smile, dark, dangerous, and all the more sinister for his pale coloring.

"It's too late for that, Darlin'. Wait here while I deal with your knight in a starched shirt."

With that, he exited the saloon. Diana could feel the other patrons' eyes boring into her back.

She flushed, mortified. She *never* drew attention to herself. Drat that werewolf!

Well, she wasn't going to stand in the middle of a smoke filled bar while everyone listened to second rate country music and speculated about her personal life. Diana marched to the exit and pushed the door open enough to slip through to see the fight.

Outside, her eyes widened. The spotlight provided by the parking lot floodlight illuminated the accountant and the werewolf.

Who knew Bob could move like that? Huh. An accountant with a black belt. It even made sense, in a Clark Kent/Superman kind of way.

Too bad Bob didn't have the super speed and stuff he'd need against a werewolf.

Adam was predatory grace, toying with his prey. He avoided Bob's well placed punches, easily sidestepping each attack.

In a blur, Adam's fist shot out, connecting with Bob's shoulder with a solid sound. Bob stumbled back. He shifted his feet and moved into a smooth defensive stance.

Diana released a breath. She should have known that Adam wouldn't kill a human. With his supernatural speed and strength, he could have already ripped Bob's arm's off and beat him with them.

Reaching out to Adam through the pack bond, Diana found a solid stonewall. No emotion. He was all calm control, centered completely on the task at hand.

She shook her head in an effort to clear her own mixed emotions.

Since, there was no more danger to Bob than his ego being trounced, both of them could do the testosterone tango together. Bob was as guilty as Adam. She wasn't some damsel to wait in the wings for the winner to carry her off to his cave.

Ugh. Neanderthal jerks.

Chapter Twelve

Disgusted, Diana used the distraction of the fight to slip away into the shadows of the trees. Behind the saloon, she crossed a picturesque little bridge and headed for the street.

She realized that Adam was going to come after her when he was finished humiliating Bob. Right now she was so furious that she didn't want to speak with either of them. What she needed was a way to hide from Adam's super senses.

Well, she was a psychic wasn't she? Maybe she could do more than feel other people's emotional garbage. She'd never tried. Mostly, Diana focused her attention on suppressing her abilities, not exploring them. Now seemed like as good time as any to try something new.

Diana thought about the witch that had come to place protection spells around her house. She had paid special attention to making Diana unnoticed to supernaturals while at home.

Think, think, think.

Diana tapped her fingernails against her forehead in the effort to drag the information to the front of her brain. What had the witch said about how they detect psychics?

Ah-ha*! Scent.* This should have been a no-brainer considering she was trying to avoid a werewolf.

Diana took a deep breath and went through her mind clearing exercises. She envisioned a bank of mist surrounding her, flowing from her chi, using the natural energies of her body to erase the evidence of her passing.

Doubts whispered the impossibility of what she tried. No one could erase her scent. She squished the thought. Doubt ensured failure.

Using her body as a starting point, and working outward, she dissipated the molecules that connected to her into nothing.

Diana held the images in her mind while she dug out her phone, intending to call home. She'd get Karen to pick her up in the car. She stared at the phone in amazement. She pushed the On button again. The screen stayed blank. The stupid thing was dead!

Diana disdained cell phones. She paid a couple of hundred dollars to keep one of those pay as you go thingies active for a year. She didn't waste the time on it for trivial things, like calling to find out what kind of ice cream the kids wanted from the store. She didn't really have a use for it, except for emergencies, where she kept it stowed away in the car with its charger.

Lovely. So much for the emergency cell phone.

Diana sucked in a calming breath. No problem. She'd walk over to the supermarket and use the pay phone. Then, Karen would come and get her.

She double stepped over the iron and wood footbridge and across the lawn to the buckled sidewalk as fast as the three-inch torture devices on her feet would allow.

At the corner, Diana took a breath. She lifted her hand to the stop sign for support.

Note to self: Never ever wear three-inch heals while taking a midnight run.

It wasn't actually midnight, but without streetlights it was dark enough not to quibble over semantics.

The roaring engine of a motorcycle caught the breath in her throat. The blending of more of its brethren made her gut clench.

"Damn," she whispered.

Frantically, Diana looked around. Should she hide?

To an average small town bred and raised girl, the sound of a motorcycle meant one of two things. Number one, Elvis, James Dean, and every other sexy bad boy to come across a movie screen. Number two, the villains out of a low budget seventies movie. Your basic pirates on wheels, doing the raping and pillaging thing before the small town sheriff takes care of things.

Diana sucked in another breath and decided to go for it. The supermarket was only a block away. She hopped off of the curb and darted to cross the road, tripped and sprawled on the pavement.

Three headlights found her. She tried to stand, only to have her ankle give way beneath.

"Owww."

The motorcycles stopped in a loose circle around her.

"Well, what do we have here?"

Diana blinked in the bright glare of the headlights. She couldn't see, save for the dark silhouettes of some very large men straddling their motorcycles.

A mix of danger and curiosity emanated from the trio.

Diana swallowed, hating the way her voice squeaked out.

"Sorry, I tripped. I'll move out of your way."

Another of the bikers laughed, a hoarse choking sound that skittered down her spine.

Diana felt like a trapped animal while she struggled to her feet, staring at the hunter. Only one leg supported her weight.

"Dog. Looks like you pegged a lady." One of the silhouettes said to the first biker who'd spoken to her.

"Need a lift?" Asked the one named Dog.

She choked on exhaust while her senses filled with the tainted flavors of lust and hunger. The need to hunt.

Either because of her psychic abilities or familiarity with the species, Diana knew that raw, vivid full-color emotions she was picking up were from weres. Maybe werecoyotes, maybe werewolves.

Don't run. Don't run. Diana repeated to herself. That would trigger their instincts to chase, like what had happened in Dogwood Park.

At the park she'd felt both the coyotes' then the werewolves' need to hunt. Her own fear and adrenaline had done the rest. The boys had only been playing a game, a weird game of tag. The coyotes had been after more than the thrill of the chase.

The dark emotions from these men chilled her, made her ill to her stomach. These were not playful boys out for a run. They were grown men, looking for trouble, and they'd found *her*.

Since Adam hadn't found her yet, and he no doubt would come looking, thanks to his possessive nature, Diana assumed that her hide the scent trick had worked. Good news, and not so good news, since she was going to have to deal with these guys on her own.

Diana pushed her fear back and locked it away. She didn't need to smell like food as well as look like it. Her ankle throbbed, sharp jabbing pains that radiated up her leg. She wobbled but didn't fall.

"Ah. No thank you. I'm, ah, making a run to the store. Ran out of milk."

Milk? She wanted to slap her forehead. Polite, yet stupid. That was her. She gestured at the back of the supermarket, where the parking lot lights glowed invitingly. So close, yet so far.

What idiot city planner decided against streetlights on this corner anyway?

She blinked and raised her hand, covering her eyes, as two more motorcycles, roared into hearing. The newcomers pulled around, completing the circle.

Calm, Diana thought, trying to quiet the rapid beat of hr heart. Fear, would only antagonize them. And she was positive she couldn't walk, much less run.

Like that was a smart idea anyway on her swelling ankle. Neither could the dratted shoe come off while she stood in the middle of the street waiting to become road kill.

She thought about calling Adam through the pack bond, dismissing that idea as soon as it filtered through her brain. Since she'd never tried that trick before, she didn't want to expend her energy on what might be a wasted effort. That energy might be needed to save herself.

She ignored the little sneering voice that was her conscience taunting her. *Pride goeth before the fall.*

Besides, Adam Weis might be like these guys, but there was only one of him and five of the bikers. There would be no one for the boys if anything happened to him. She couldn't leave the boys unprotected because of her mistake.

Her best bet was to bluff her way out. Diana suddenly wished she knew how to play poker. She couldn't even beat one of those stupid handheld video casino games.

God, she was so screwed.

"Um, don't let me keep you. I'm sure you guys have somewhere you're going." She gave a weak wave that wouldn't topple her precarious balance.

"Goin' huntin' girlie. Heard there was plenty of game here," said Dog.

Sex and innuendo filled the biker's words. Dark emotions of the same ilk clung to her like slime. Laughter and the rev of engines gave the situation the perfect evil punctuation.

When the racing motors died back down to an idle, Diana heard a sound from behind. Or a lack of one as an engine shut off. She didn't want to take her eyes from the leader, but also couldn't bear the thought of being caught from behind.

A deft kick brought down a kickstand. The hardy rider canted his bike, dismounting with fluid ease. His partner pulled in close and followed suit.

Wolf, she decided, watching their movements. Whatever monsters the other three bikers were, these two were all wolf.

"Yo, Dog," The deep voice was friendly. "We can't hunt this one."

"Shut up, Chase. I'm pack leader here," Dog snapped. "Unless you want to Challenge."

Chase's snort was full of derision.

"You've got to have a real pack for a real Challenge. Besides," Chase's companion added. His voice was surprisingly melodious and full of soul searching charisma. "The female is a psychic, and I for one do not intend to have my death warrant posted."

The wolfman with the lovely voice finished his dismount and practically glided into the circle with her. He stopped behind her, close enough she could feel the feverish heat from his body.

She blinked and stepped away, more of a bobble than an actual step that didn't take her any further from him.

The first of her would-be rescuers, Chase, was a god clad in simple leather pants that hugged his body. The shadows defined every muscle. A leather jacket emphasized the breadth of his shoulders, while his height towered over her. A long braid slithered over his shoulder as he leaned forward to sniff her hair.

Even in the dark, his eyes gleamed gold, a reflection of the light from the motorcycles' headlamps.

He sneezed, and then shared a covert look with his companion. She felt the heat from beside and behind, but did nothing. What could she do anyway? Scream like an idiot?

She felt curiosity from them, the need to hunt, but not the dark lust that oozed from the others, especially Dog.

Her heart pounded like it was trying to escape her chest. She swallowed, trying not to break the uneasy quiet and stared at the patch on his, Chase's, jacket of vicious snarling dog surrounded by flames. Its nose was too square to be a wolf. She wasn't sure of the colors but it looked evil enough for a bunch of werewolf bikers.

"You think you can lead the Hell Hounds, *bitten*?"

Chase shrugged. The movement flowed into a grip on her elbow that she didn't see coming. She jerked, stifling a scream, but he held her still, as if purposely steadying her.

Screw it all, Diana thought. This was the second time tonight she felt like the meaty bone in the middle of a dogfight. She was scared, but now she was getting ticked off.

"Let go. Leave me alone."

She added a psychic push to her words, throwing a mental jab at the man. She tried to pull away. He jumped a little at the unexpected assault, but held tight.

"Well, well, well."

Surprise and pleasure coated Dog's voice like sewage. Uh-oh. Diana felt the group's interest go up several notches.

"Nothing like a piece of tail with a bite. Tank bring the bitch here. Chase never could get it up when things got interesting. Even for a challenge."

The dark hunger and lust, not only for sex, but also for other foul deeds, left her feeling dirty in places a bath would never clean. Dog scented the air, obviously enjoying the fear she radiated.

"Be quick Tank and I'll even share. You ain't had nothing until you've had a psychic."

Tank, of the sexy voice, laughed. The deep silky sound that wrapped around her.

"That's not a good idea either." His tone was perfectly reasonable. Who wouldn't want to agree with that low voice?

"The female's been pack marked, Dog. If she goes missing, not only will the local Canis place a werewolf posting on the Internet. He'll come after her himself. Personally, I'd rather not have Weis on my tail after what he did to Garrick Moser and every adult in that pack."

The hair on Diana's neck rose. She wondered exactly what Adam had done to be old pack leader. Then again, some of the images she'd gotten from boys were pretty bad.

The purring of the motorcycles' engines filled the silence while Dog considered the argument. Tank had her vote, even without the psychic persuasion she felt threaded into his voice.

Dog was made of sterner stuff though. He growled. The sound ended in a vicious bark. The motorcycle canted as the biker leader slid off and started across the circle.

"Bitten bastard. I'll teach you to use mind tricks on me."

One moment Diana was standing in the middle of the coming confrontation. The next she was whisked off of her feet from behind and dumped near the chromed tires of the motorcycles. So much for gentlemanly manners. Then again, being dumped out of the way was better than being in Dog's way.

She huddled beside the tire. The oil and gas engine smells drifted around her, a bit of distraction from the tiny rocks biting into her hands and knees.

Out of the blinding light, Diana could see Dog's ugly, already disproportioned face contort. His jaws stretched demonically into a toothy muzzle designed for tearing. His hands grew claws worthy of knives, perfect for ripping and shredding tough werewolf hide.

Chase discarded his leather jacket. Out of the glare of the headlights, she could now see that his hair was a dark gold.

His change was more graceful. The curve of his man's ear flowed upward into points. His jaw elongated. Fur the same color as his hair ran along his skin.

Both of them bulked up, easily half again or more than their respective human size. Muscles developed that were not there before. The added body mass tore their clothes.

The dull rip of leather and denim sounded to her like what the shedding of human skin should be. What remnants of fabric still clung, they shrugged off, flinging away the last bit of humanity.

They were terrifying monsters. They were beautiful killing machines.

The werewolves moved with the same light agility, still managing to ram together with the power of a freight train. Roars and growls filled the night. Each tried to rip the other's throat out while claws tore at their sides and backs.

Diana cringed backward, taking in the fight. Tank, she could see, also slipped the skin of humanity. His huge dark form was a shadow of muscle, fur, and claws waiting on the sidelines close to Dog's changed companions.

She struggled with the straps of her shoes. Yanking the heels off of her feet, she forgot her ankle. Tears sprang to her eyes when she jerked on it. A three-inch weapon in each hand now, Diana scooted back from the fight.

She looked around. How long before one of the nearby houses heard the inhuman racket and called the police? Were any of them foolish enough to come check out the noise? The thought of a concerned neighbor or policeman getting hurt doing his duty sickened her.

Diana's mist trick had obviously worked or Adam would have shown up by now. She decided to try something a little more difficult.

She envisioned a circle ten feet beyond the motorcycles. A bubble to camouflage the sight, sound, scents of the fight. Diana channeled what energy she had left into the bubble.

The fight ranged closer to where she hid behind the bikes. Tank moved, a graceful watchdog, keeping his big body between the combatants and her. For a brief moment he turned and looked down, his black eyes meeting hers. He was ink black. His dark,

African American heritage and the black wolfman fur seemed to swallow the light.

She realized with a start that her eyes had roamed. Nude werewolf males were just as male as human males, more so. The fight, the scent of blood, would have excited the animal part of him.

That part of him was certainly excited, jutting full and proud while his muscles tensed under the fur. The sharp ebony claws opened and closed with the need to fight.

"Why?" She forced her focus up. Embarrassed heat burned her cheeks. Her voice was a breath. "Why go against your pack?"

Tank shook his head. The movement was an odd rounded gesture, like the start of one of those full-bodied shakes a dog, or wolf, will make. Diana refused to follow the shake down the muscled body.

"Shhh, little sister. Do not be afraid." The timbre of his voice was still beautiful, if a lot deeper coming from the wolfman.

"I'm not afraid." And she wasn't, not of him. No more than she would be of Adam or the boys.

He canted his head and nodded at the truth of her words. The sound of his voice was gravelly, but like the pleasant sound of polished rocks sliding against one another. Not the coarse sound that Dog had made. She realized that the leader's ugliness had more to do with staying partially changed than genetics. Maybe his real human form was even uglier?

"This is no pack," came Tank's answer. "Only a gathering of strays that no one will have."

A howl drew their attention back to the fight. Chase had his golden head at Dog's throat, teeth locked in the scruff. His jaws were dark with blood as he worried the other werewolf's neck.

Dog's buddies decided to get in on the action. Tank growled and leapt to intercept them.

The leap could have been choreographed for a ballet in grace and form. The deadly power of the movement impressed her as much as Chase's savage grace as he tore Dog apart. No one leapt ten feet in the air, or covered twice that distance without a pole vault, a spring board, something. Tank dropped down on top of the advancing werewolves in a blur of fur, flashing claws, and flying blood.

Dear God, Diana shuddered at the damage, *please let the bubble hold.*

She wanted to crawl away, but fear that without her presence the bubble would disappear, held her to her gory sideshow seat.

Please, don't let a car come this way.

Dog fell, the road underneath his body pooled with dark liquid. He twitched, claws scraping on the pavement.

Diana stuffed the back of her hand into her mouth to hold back the scream and the bile that threatened to follow.

Chase turned to help Tank with the remaining two wolfmen.

She stared while blows that would break a normal man in bloody halves, made the werewolves grunt and stumble back.

Not that they didn't suffer any damage. All of them wore gaping bloody furrows on their backs, shoulders, and chests where claws had torn their skin.

Diana Ridley was no Helen of Troy and she knew it. This fight must have been building for a while, because there was no way she could have incited this. She was pretty if you liked plump, knew a few nifty psychic tricks, and her empathy was more of a hindrance than a gift.

Diana felt more than saw movement. Her eyes slid to where Dog had fallen. The pavement was empty save for the wet smear of blood.

Oh God! She glanced around, flinching away from the evil hunger that suddenly bombarded her. Hunger that twisted lust and food into a single foul emotion.

A claw wrapped around her ankle. She screamed at the crushing strength that pulled, no jerked, her to Dog's maw. Pink bloody saliva foamed around sharp deadly wolf teeth. Except no wolf was ever that big.

She kicked while he crawled up her body. She felt his hot body temperature, the bristly fur, and the slick blood from his wounds. Even worse, the hard-on that the monster was getting from her fear and the fight.

"No!"

She wrestled, bucked, and tried to slam the heels into him. One claw caught and pinned her left arm. The right shoe hit hard. She felt the heel drive into the meat of the werewolf's shoulder with a sickening give.

He laughed. His fetid breath washed over her face and shoulders.

"Too bad I've got to eat and run." He pushed his heavy, too big erection into her lower abdomen and ground hard, pressing her legs apart. "Cause the whole ride would be a lot more fun."

Diana aimed for the temple, glancing off a blow, while his head slowly descended, even as his body slid lower on to hers. Oh, God, he was going to rape her and eat her at the same time.

He pressed against her, the member catching in her undergarments. Only the thin barriers of her pantyhose and the satin of her panties kept the huge length of him out, but not by much.

A claw reached between and caught the front of her dress pulling it and her bra away, baring her breasts. The too big head of the monster's penis stretched out a small space in the protective fabric between her legs. She bucked and beat with the shoe.

The claw groped at a bare breast. His teeth found her shoulder and bit. The huge jaws clamped down, feeling as if he was going to take her shoulder off in one bite.

Diana screamed, slammed down the heel on his head one more time. Dog yelped, his claws going to his eye, scrabbling where the shoe still dangled from the socket.

She tried to crawl away. She scrambled on knees and one arm because where his teeth had imbedded in her shoulder the arm wouldn't work right.

"Bitch!"

Dog lunged, his claws raking down her leg, catching and pulling her backward. Her fingernails broke on the pavement.

"No!"

A clawed hand shoved her face down, grinding her cheek into the pavement. Diana whimpered. She tried to wiggle away. The monster held her easily, while he aligned himself behind her.

Vaguely, she heard the sounds of the other werewolves fighting in the circle of motorcycles. If she turned her head she would be able to see for sure if both of her werewolves still fought.

"Uppity bitch."

While she struggled, the thin fabric of her pantyhose and underwear ripped away with the scratch of claw on the delicate skin of her hip. The hand and attached claws slapped her bare cheeks. Hot lines of pain burned her buttocks.

"I'm going to enjoy this. You're too much trouble for a fuck and food."

The claws lifted her hips, but before the thing could ram inside her, Dog was shoved away. The force of the attacking werewolves threw Dog outside of the bubble.

Diana felt the *pop* as the breached bubble disappeared.

Automatically, she reset the bubble a second time, this time adding a compulsion to avoid the area. She tried to figure a way to set the bubble so that it wouldn't pop if breached, or she passed out.

That was a very real possibility as her energy level drained. Her vision blurred.

She watched the pale werewolf, dark streaks marred his coat, and the pitch black werewolf tear Dog's more traditional gray body apart. Literally.

The two were not about making the kill pretty. Not all of the meat fell to the ground either. Some of those huge bites would be missing, never to be found, the only evidence the blood on the victors' muzzles.

She emptied her stomach, and then watched the werewolves finish their kill. Diana found that she wasn't upset at all. The bad guys were all dead, and that was what mattered.

She was bleary and fuzzy feeling when her protectors came to stand before her. Their hair was slick with blood, more blood and adrenaline racing through their systems, making the very male werewolves, very male indeed.

But they wouldn't hurt her, Diana knew. She was tired, and her stomach heaved again at the carnage around her. She looked up at the dark and the pale beasts standing over her and knew she was safe. Safe enough to let the darkness take her away from her body's pain and exhaustion.

Chapter Thirteen

Adam was frantic. There was no trace of Diana anywhere.

He followed her scent to the trees behind the saloon bar where it vanished as if she'd blinked out of existence.

He tried reaching her through the pack connection. A metaphysical wall shut him out the same as he'd done during the confrontation with her date.

Stubborn woman. His Diana was a quick study. The constant blank space where her presence should be shook him to his core.

For the first time in his life Adam J. Weis knew fear. She was probably just pissed at him.

A year and a half ago, Amanda had left, mad at his excuses for waiting to mate-bond. The next time he'd seen her, she'd been a trophy, her pelt nailed to the wall beside Garrick Moser's other victims.

Adam's fear for Diana was a live thing. The feeling gnawed at his insides while he trotted up and down the streets looking for signs of his intended mate.

Something was wrong. The danger burned in his gut.

Not again.

Most wolven believed nature as Divine. Adam's parents were God fearing humans. While Adam respected the beliefs of his biological father, he fell back on his raising.

Please God. He prayed as hard as he ever had. *Don't let me be too late again. Not like Amanda.*

Adam didn't want a fling, anymore. He wanted Diana Ridley for himself, not only because nature said it was time to take a mate.

He didn't know how things would be worked out with her human children, but with every part of him, wolf and man, he intended to have Diana Ridley. For his mate, as Matra Canis for his pack, however she would have him.

At one point Adam thought he caught a whiff of her perfume. He hunted the area and found no sign of her. He turned and left, fighting the wolf that once having scented his chosen mate, did not want to leave.

Adam moved to a different street, searching backyards.

Hell, he even went back and searched the supermarket parking lot. The faint scent of blood made him go back and look behind the store. He decided that the blood scent was from road kill, a dead dog or some other unfortunate animal. Adam left to meet back up with Bob.

How far could one human female go in those stilt-high heels anyway?

Pretty far if she found a ride. And a ride would effectively end her scent track too.

When he finally caught up with her, he was going to set the record straight. She needed to realize that he was the alpha male. He made the rules. No more of this running off nonsense.

Adam headed back to his truck. He imagined her kicked back in front of the TV, safe at home while he roamed the streets looking for her. That jacked up his irritation.

A black Mercedes pulled up alongside him. The exhaust trashed his olfactory.

The window glided down, exposing Bob's bruised face and dirty shirt.

The human hesitated a moment, then pulled a card from a holder on his dash.

"I think she went home."

Adam's suspicious look made the man smile, a little sad, a little depreciating.

"We wouldn't have gone out again, anyway. There wasn't any attraction between us." Bob's smile turned to a look of warning. "But Diana is a good friend, and I do care what happens to her."

Adam got the hint. He took the card and nodded. "I'll call when I find her."

* * * *

"Mom's not here." Karen's pretty brown eyes widened with feigned innocence. Feigned, because Adam could smell the guilt. "She went out with a girlfriend to see a movie."

There was the tiniest bit of hesitation on the word girlfriend. The way her pulse sped up, the faint scent of perspiration as she uttered the lie.

Adam noticed that since Bradley was openly dating her, how difficult it was to maintain any irritation at the girl. Her charm was innate, a gift, but hardly a psychic one.

She was popular in school, smart, and a member of several scholastic committees. The girl was a damn good cheerleader with a perpetual perky attitude, loved by probably everyone she knew. The boys were head over heels gaga with the girl.

Before the park incident with Diana, Adam didn't know she or her daughter existed. Now, every other sentence out of the boys' mouths was either about Diana or Karen Ridley.

Which was why Adam wasn't overly surprised to catch the twins' scents.

"May I come in?" He asked as polite as possible with his dark mood.

Karen flushed again, a pretty pink hue that lightened Adams foul emotions.

"I don't think …," she began.

Adam ended her cute indecision with a bark, "Bradley! Brandon!"

Bradley appeared from behind the door, not surprising since he already knew the boy was there. Adam shut the door behind him, sensing a building confrontation.

The teenager pulled Karen behind him. Brandon shuffled, full of nervous energy, into the living room entryway.

"I called them, Mr. Weis." Karen pulled away from Bradley. Her little chin rose in defiance as she defended her friends. "I heard a noise outside."

Bradley put a hand out to her.

"It's all right, Karen."

She shook the hand off and rushed on. Her eyes locked on to Adam's, willing him to believe. "There were coyotes in the backyard. They tried to get in."

Bradley wrapped his own arms around her. Karen buried her face in Bradley's chest.

The boy looked over her head, his fierce protective instincts on alert. Bradley's eyes glimmered red. His voice was low and rough. Adam knew how close the boy's emotions had him to changing.

"Coyotes came and knocked all the trash cans down, dragged trash all over the yard. There's marks on the doors and windows where they tried to get in."

Brandon's quiet voice filled in where Bradley stopped. He halted at his brother's dark look but gathered his lanky body and spoke anyway.

"The coyotes shouldn't have been able to enter the yard because Miz Ridley had both the yard and the house warded a few years ago by a witch. She also had the grounds blessed by a priest."

Karen's babbling drew Adam's attention again. She spoke over Bradley's attempts to comfort her, rubbing wide circles on her back and low shhh's.

"They were trying to get in. I'm not making it up."

She shivered again and Adam smelled the brief burst of psychic, covered quickly by the flat scent of a normal human null.

Adam met Bradley's hard eyes while he considered. She wasn't the normal human he'd believed her to be. He'd never heard of a psychic who could camouflage the psychic magical scent they emitted, especially when they used their gifts.

While Adam took everything in, quietly processing everything he'd learned in the short time he'd been standing in the entry, Karen pulled away from Bradley to pace.

She glared at Adam.

"You don't believe me." She accused.

Adam put a hand on the doorknob and tried to placate the girl.

"I *do* believe you Karen. But I want to check outside for signs."

Her laugh was a half sob. Tears glittered in her eyes.

"You won't find any. We cleaned up the trash. I tried to call Mom. Her cell phone keeps saying unavailable."

Adam squashed the knot that tried to grip his stomach. He attempted his best reassuring smile, but failed at that. The thought of werecoyotes marking the Ridley house made him feel feral. With Diana's disappearance, he'd have the next were that trespassed for dinner.

His dangerous gleam of teeth seemed to calm her. Karen nodded. She took a breath and went to stand by Brandon, her small hand seeking the boy's larger one.

"Bradley."

Adam motioned for the boy to follow him out. He glanced back at the other two kids. Karen huddled up to Brandon much in the same way that wolven do when seeking or giving comfort.

"Stay here."

Outside, the cool night breeze blew. Adam inhaled deep, confused when the air yielded almost no scent to his sensitive nose. The scent of fresh cut grass. Oil and gasoline rose from the driveway. The flowers in the haphazard flowerbed surrounding the house were sweet.

He realized that he was missing the scents of animals and human, old scents that layered over one another and whispered their tales to his nose. He had been in such turmoil every time he came to the Ridley home, that he'd missed the absence.

Adam walked into the street, noticing as he did that the air returned to its normal collage of scents once he stepped off of the curb.

The stench of coyote assaulted his nose. He remembered that he'd driven over in his truck, specially designed with an air filter in the a/c to keep the motor scents to a minimum in the cab. Whatever Diana had done effectively obliterated the coyote's scents in the yard.

"I'd bet they scent marked every mailbox on the block," Bradley said with disgust as he trotted up from a quick check of the neighbor's yard.

"How long have you known about them?"

Truthfully, Adam had wanted to talk to the boy more than check for werecoyote stink. His territorial instincts made him want to find and kill them all. The haunting memory of Amanda's pelt made Diana's absence worry him more.

The question took Bradley off guard. He glanced back at the house. Bradley finally shrugged.

Adam's snarl was swift and sure. "Answer the question." He'd tolerate a lot, but not disrespect. "How long have you known that a whole family of psychics lived here?"

Bradley watched him, his face a mask of stone.

You can do anything you want to me, but I won't talk.

Adam hated it when the boys closed off like he was the intruder. They took their cues from Bradley, closing him out when they needed to work as a pack the most.

Adam could see that one day Bradley Starr would be a powerful leader, a Canis in his own territory. Just not today.

Adam had paid for the right to alpha this pack in flesh and blood. He'd lost a potential mate. So lead he would.

"Eventually, you are going to have to trust me with what's best for the pack, son."

"I'm not you're son." Regret at the words, for the punishment he assumed he'd get, flashed in Bradley's eyes. The boy stood his ground.

Frustration ate at Adam. This wasn't the time or place for this confrontation. He searched his brain for something to say.

What did he know about raising kids anyway? Nothing. He'd been an only child, thinking he was human until his wolven genes kicked in.

"No, you're not my son. But I am you're legal guardian according to the state of Texas and Pack Council. You *will* respect that."

Bradley met his gaze with unflinching eyes, and then averted them to look elsewhere, proving that he wasn't the alpha he pretended.

Adam had a killer targeting strays. No telling when the murderer would decide to start on the local wolven population. And now, the werecoyotes were stalking the Ridley home. His pack was lousy with psychics and noncombatants. He didn't have enough muscle to protect everyone.

"We'll talk about respect later. Right now, though, I need yours *and the pack's* cooperation."

"I'm not leaving until Miz Ridley gets home."

Not for the first time, Adam thought he was handling the situation wrong. Maybe what the kid needed was *more* responsibility, not less.

Adam wanted Bradley concentrate on school, pack bonding, and doing things with his own age group. He wanted to give the boys back the childhood they didn't get to have.

"Bradley, I'm not going to hurt you. I don't understand why you guys keep thinking I'm going to go 'American Werewolf' all over everyone." He took a breath and let it out on a weary sigh. "Yes, I do. And I'm going to say it again. And again, until you finally listen. I. Am. Not. Garrick. Moser."

"I know ...."

He relayed the news of the wolven murders, watching with satisfaction as the reality of the danger sunk home. Bradley looked skeptical at first. He nodded solemnly.

"What do you need me to do?"

Adam thought about how to phrase what he thought the boy needed.

"Exactly, what you always do. Keep an eye out for your pack brothers."

Bradley raised his eyebrows half up his forehead. Adam set a hand on the boy's shoulder, stepped in close and met the boy's eyes.

"*And* I need you to keep me informed. Not ratting anyone out, but keep me apprised of what's going on."

Being the outsider was hell. Seeing Bradley's wince as he grasped the problem, helped Adam's pride some.

"Lets' go back inside. But first, you need to know that Ms. Ridley isn't out at the movies with a girlfriend."

"Uh … I know." Bradley nearly squirmed under his hand.

Adam nodded, understanding. "She's not on her date with Bob Benedict either." He wanted to snort at the name.

"Well? Where is she then?" Anxiety colored Bradley's voice, a little high, a little desperate, making him sound more like the child he was. Bradley recovered, but the slip was already out there.

"You sure have gotten attached to Ms. Ridley. You and Karen have only been dating a couple of weeks now? Right?"

"What happened to Mr. Benedict?" Bradley narrowed his eyes at Adam, his behavior all bristly and full of distrust. "You didn't have anything to do with that, did you?"

Yep, Adam thought, kind of smug and proud, the kid would make a first-rate alpha … if he survived being trained as beta.

Chapter Fourteen

Diana's head hurt. As she became more aware, her body began to catalogue more complaints. Her right shoulder ached with a raw soreness. Underneath the soreness, her joint and muscle burned, the pain radiating out.

There were more burning lines, the pain of lacerations, across her butt and thigh. Her ankle throbbed, pulsating with each beat of her heart.

"How do you feel, little sister?"

The beautiful, melodious voice distracted her. Diana shifted. Her stomach lurched.

Taking a handful of the soft, fuzzy blanket beneath to steady herself, she opened her eyes, focusing on the shadowed face of the man, no *werewolf,* bent over her. Behind him the night stretched out in a field of grass. The faint odor of cattle rode the breeze.

He was a study in shadows. Black eyes, dark velvety skin stretched over swells of muscle. A multitude of tiny braids made up his hair, sliding over the ridges and plains that made up his shoulders.

"Tank."

"Yes." His cultured voice made no demands. But Diana wanted up. What had she gotten herself into this time?

Heat radiated from both sides of her, pinpointing both werewolves without having to look. Her stomach protested again and Diana made a face. The sharp concern from both of them made her smile, wan, but still enough to offer reassurance.

"I'm okay, I think. I think I bit my tongue. All I can taste is blood and my tummy doesn't like it."

God. Caught talking like a mommy. She wanted to bite said tongue for uttering the words.

Tank passed a significant look over her head. She followed his gaze. Her eyes landed on the golden half of the duo.

Chase rested against the trunk of the tree sheltering them, his long body stretched out in all his bare-chested glory. The tail of the braid tickled one male nipple. She imagined that it kept his hair tamed while riding his motorcycle.

His eyes gleamed gold, then red in the moonlight. A predatory smile flashed across his face, exposing white, perfect teeth.

It seemed to her that every werewolf she'd met so far had excellent orthodontia. A predator of that magnitude would have to, she supposed. The nervous flush that his intensity caused made Diana blink furiously and look away. She'd probably go blind or faint from testosterone overdose.

"Want me to kiss your tummy and make it all better, Diana Ridley?"

She glanced back and caught the teasing light in Chase's eyes. It looked and felt like the prelude to a hunt, reminding her of Adam's intense gaze. She missed the macho jerk and his blue eyes, too.

Tank growled. Chase laughed with the ease that spoke of true friendship. But, he took the warning. The call of the hunt inside him leashed for the moment.

Being the intense focus of two such powerful creatures unnerved her. Not all of it was sexual. The intensity brought back all the warnings about supernaturals she'd been using to keep Adam at bay.

"I need to stand." She needed space.

With the help of Tank's long, elegant, and ever so careful hand, Diana stood. She smoothed down the extra-extra large tee shirt that hung mid-thigh. It smelled of man and musk.

Trying desperately not to think of the reason why she was wearing borrowed clothes, she wobbled a couple of steps away.

"Diana Ridley, are you well?"

Tank had some pretty powerful mojo in that voice of his. She realized that he had gifts other than being a werewolf. It made her suspicious.

"How do you know my name?"

"Driver's license." Chase's soft breath of a chuckle on the back of her neck made her jump. She hadn't sensed his approach. Her heart sped up with a jolt of fear as he buried his face against the fringe of hair on her neck.

"I thought it was taboo for a woman to reveal her true weight." He whispered.

The warmth of his body soaked through the tee shirt. A big hand slid around her waist, snuggling her against Chase's firm body. Her breath caught and her heart sped up another notch.

"I, ahhh ... honesty's the best policy?" She nearly whimpered.

She was in serious danger of becoming a werewolf groupie slut.

"Enough. Let her go, Chase. You do not toy with another's possessions."

The arm loosened and cool air replaced the heat behind her. "True. But she's irresistible."

"Well, resist. The blood lowers her inhibitions. I need to reassess her injuries before we return her to her pack."

Huh? Blood? Possessions? Diana didn't think she liked those implications. In fact, her temperature cooled and she made an effort to shut down whatever psychic connection she had inadvertently developed with these two strangers. She felt a sense of familiarity usually felt around people you knew and trusted for awhile. "Excuse me?"

The fog that seemed to be hazing her thinking lifted with the first spark of anger.

"With your permission, Miss Ridley, I would like to examine your injuries."

"I'm sure you would Mr. Spock."

Diana crossed arms under her full breasts, noticing that the tee shirt rode up as she did. Their gazes followed the movement that exposed more thigh.

So far, all the werewolves she'd met were a pushy bunch. She wasn't about to give any more ground to them. She ignored the amusement, *and other things*, that her psyche picked up from Chase.

"Mr. Spock?"

"Yeah, Doc. You remind the lady of that pointy-eared guy on TV. Man, has she got you pegged."

"I want you to explain that possessions bit." Diana held up a hand. "Then again, I don't think I want to know."

Diana half turned and pinned her narrowed eyes on the blond werewolf. "Is he really a doctor?"

"Yeah, he's a pretty good one, too." He waggled his eyebrows suggestively. "You gonna let us play doctor?"

She made an exasperated sound and rounded on Tank.

"So where's your license, degree, or whatever doctors hang in their office?"

She'd never really looked at the ones hanging in her family physician's office. Other than being official looking and encased in expensive frames, they could have been printed up anywhere. But Doctor Anderson had been treating her family for years.

Doctor Tank hadn't. She didn't trust all the warm fuzzies she'd been getting from supernaturals lately.

"And another thing. How do I know you really are a doctor? Except for the word of your smart mouth friend."

Up until now, Tank, had been calm, making his intimidating largess unthreatening. While his voice was captivating and his interest intense, he'd been tame, chaste, compared to Chase.

"And you expect me to hang my degrees, where?"

He arched an eyebrow, showing only mild irritation. The heat of his anger flared along her senses, making Diana gasp. She realized she'd pushed him too far. Still she didn't feel in any real danger from him. Just perhaps in ticking him off.

"I'm sorry." She rubbed at her temples and tried to move away. "I think I'm getting overwhelmed by too many werewolves in too short a time. Maybe I need to switch gears, take on vampires, or dragons, or something."

The switch that had tripped Tank's anger flipped the opposite and he was suddenly calm again, but she could feel the effort behind the emotion.

"Two things, little sister."

Tank held out a careful, elegant hand using the other to guide her back to the blanket where he proceeded to run light hands over her bare ankle. It didn't seem as sprained as it had before. At the time she'd wrenched it, she knew she'd be off her feet for a couple of weeks.

"We are *wolven*. Werewolves are the degenerates of society."

"Oh. I didn't mean to offend you."

"I know."

"And the other thing?"

Tank looked a little distracted, so Diana prompted him.

"You said two things. That was one."

"Hmmm."

He carefully, very circumspectly, looked at the claw marks on her thigh. There was no way she was letting him check out her butt.

"Doctor Tank?"

"Hmmm?"

Very gently he pulled the sleeve up over her shoulder. She thought about telling him that she really felt better. Unaccountably so.

Her stomach hardly twinged, despite the fact that she'd swallowed a decent amount of blood. The bites, claw marks, and wrenched ankle felt pretty good considering she'd only been banged up and chewed on a few hours ago.

Her Weird-O-Meter was tapped out. She might be able to put two and two together, but she wasn't ready to accept the answer. Or dwell on what had happened earlier. Not tonight.

"Tank?"

She touched a hand to his shoulder, finding out that his skin really was a smooth and velvety as it looked. And warm, feverishly warm.

It wasn't until she noticed the flare of his nostrils, or the dilated look in his nearly black eyes that Diana realized that he might have the same lusty feelings Chase had. Tank was just better at hiding what he felt.

God, she missed her underwear! A woman could be dressed in a snowsuit and a parka, and without her bra and panties, she was naked. Without the snowsuit and parka, she simply wished the bra and panties matched.

"What was the other thing?"

His smile was a white gleam in his face. More dangerous for standing out against the darkness of his skin, making her breath catch again with a little dart of fear. His intense focus settled on her mouth.

"Dragons," he breathed.

Diana felt the trembling hold he kept on the calm and didn't move a muscle.

"You wouldn't want to meet a dragon, *little sister*."

"Why not?"

He let her scoot away. Diana watched him gather his control back. Tank turned his head slightly away and inhaled, clearing his nose of her scent.

"Because psychics are considered a great delicacy among dragonkind."

Diana shuddered. "Oh."

Though Tank had stood and stepped away, she noticed that he clenched and unclenched his fists, like he'd done when resisting the urge to join the fight.

She really needed to convince them to take her home. But here was the opportunity to get some of her werewolf questions answered. The only one that jumped into her head, popped out of her mouth before she could censor the words. "So, what do psychics smell like?"

She'd forgotten about Chase with Tank hovering over her. But the gleam in his golden eyes said that he hadn't forgotten *her*.

"Delicious. You, in particular, are tasty enough to nibble."

"Sorry, been there done that. I don't think the last one had his rabies shots."

Chase's soft laugh was wicked and wild. "I said nibble, not bite. You don't hurry fine dining."

It was Diana's turn to laugh, but she was unsure of herself. The sound wasn't merry. She didn't understand. Helen of Troy was beautiful. Diana Ridley was pretty if you liked plump.

But these two, three, no four if she counted Adam and Dog, acted like Diana was the goddess she was named for. She could see that a little bluntness was needed. "Look, I don't understand what's going on here. I'm not all that. *And,* I know for a fact that I look like I've been dragged through hell, because the demon-Dog was the one doing the dragging. Why all the sex appeal?"

If the two werewolves, *wolven*, hadn't been standing beside one another, their twin looks of surprise would have been less hilarious. All right, they would have been funny if the situation had been less charged.

"Not that I don't appreciate your jumping in to save me." The last bit she kind of tagged on, since she realized she'd never thanked them.

Diana swallowed, really, *really* aware of the lack of undies. And that she hadn't thanked them.

"Dear God, woman. Don't think thoughts like that or we'll never get you back without doing more than flirting."

Chase heaved a breath and turned away, his body visibly raging for release. Diana licked her lips, nervous. She shouldn't have looked and vowed not check out Tank to see if he was as aroused.

She looked. He was. Damn. A little thrill at being found attractive by two such males ran through her before she squelched it. Damn, damn, damn.

"You read my mind?"

"No." His voice was strangled. "Your face." He took a breath of air away from her direction, and winced. "And your smell."

"What's wrong with the way I smell?" she asked, indignant.

Okay, well she might not be daisy fresh. But she was pretty darn sure they hadn't found a shower handy to clean up by either.

The loose predatory roll of Tank's shoulders tensed and straightened into his more scholarly role. Diana could feel him latch onto the distance that answering her question provided. It was Chase's whine that truly broke the moment.

"I can't do this." He whirled and growled at his friend. Tank tensed back up, an answering growl rumbling from his chest. Chase pointed a finger at Diana.

"I can't just stand here, *doing nothing!* Not with her dressed like that, smelling like ... like …"

The blond werewolf jerked his body around, the only non-graceful move she'd seen from any of them. His breath was almost a pant. He practically glided to the bikes.

Tank rubbed a hand over his face and sighed.

"He's right. It is time to take you home." With that he moved to pick up the blanket, quickly folding the fabric into a tight square, brushing aside her offer of help with a turn of his shoulder and a mild rumble.

Fine. She didn't get it. They were hot one moment and antisocial the next. Besides, Diana told herself, ignoring the little pang at the sudden loss of attention. She had responsibilities. She needed to get home. She might not have to work tomorrow but there was always stuff around the house to do.

"Here, slide your arms inside." Warm breath on her neck made her shiver and look back at Chase's golden wolf eyes. He gestured with the coat in his hands. His face was serious for once, his mood as distant as Tank's.

"Wear this. You need more to cover you with the ride back."

She made out the expensive lines of a long coat. It smelled of leather of course.

"Thank you. Both of you. I mean it. For everything."

He nodded and dropped the leather coat over her shoulders and very deliberately stepped back. Surprisingly, it was light, the fabric soft as a chamois cloth under the hand she ran down it.

It wasn't a coat. It was a duster. Snaps, not buttons ran down the front of it and up the sides. The wind shifted the loose back panels.

He handed back her shoes, the strappy black heels she'd thought made her legs look longer, and sexy. There was only a twinge of discomfort as she slipped them on.

"Um, I know this sounds stupid. But, how did I heal so fast?"

"I told you Tank's a doc. He knows what to do."

He wasn't going to give her anymore than that about the miraculous healing. Besides, she could hazard a guess on that one, given the strange taste in her mouth. She desperately needed a toothbrush.

"Okay. Thanks again. Am I going to turn into a, *a wolven*?"

Chase choked out a laugh and slid down on his rump with a belly roll of mirth. She glanced over at Tank. His own hastily smothered grin made her narrow her eyes.

"What? He *bit* me!"

"Little sister, the only female wolven you will find are those who were born to the species."

"So, you can't contract lycanthropy from a bite?"

Tank shook his head, all the mirth bled from his face. At her feet, Chase sobered and looked up at her.

"Naw. We can catch it fine. It's females who don't."

"Why?"

Chase ignored Tank's warning growl. He stood and dusted off the back of his leather pants. The mischievous light in his eye gleamed once more.

"Because you already have something more terrifying that lycanthropy can't compete with."

Okay, she'd bite. She foolishly asked what it was. Chase grinned and reached out. He snagged her hand, and tugged her toward the bikes.

"PMS."

A motorcycle roared, making her jump and scaring what little wits she had left. She turned to face Tank, unreadable in everyway. He nodded in her direction.

It was time to go. She carefully gathered the beautiful duster and climbed up behind him, not nearly so graceful as the werewolves, no *wolven*.

Slipping her arms around his waist, she settled closer. The man could been a heated lava rock for all the rigidity in his body. He might have been unaffected, but the ride back was a wild one.

The heat of the man in front of her, the motorcycle vibrating *there,* the wind in her face made Diana feel more alive, freer than ever. She didn't want it to end. And then, anticlimactically, Tank leaned left, and pulled into the driveway.

* * * *

Chase aided her dismount. Faster than she could move, his hands wrapped around her waist and lifted her from the machine.

When she looked up, the teasing was gone. His eyes were a serious whisky amber.

"What is it?" She whispered, caught up in the moment. The warmth of the engine and the men enveloped her more securely than the coat.

He reached up with one finer, the rough pad of his finger smoothing away the frown while something heavier weighted down her pocket.

"Shhh." The finger touched her lips stopping the question. "It's not registered or traceable. Learn to use it with one shot."

He was giving her a gun? What happened to old fashioned flowers and candy?

The finger pressed firmly against her lips and he leaned in close. His scent and Tank's were suddenly strong in her nose, clear, identifiable as a fingerprint.

"Regular ammo hurts like a bitch and slows anything supernatural down. Were-anything, vamps, and the like, use silver and aim to kill. 'Cause once they get over the regular stuff, they are coming after you. Got it?"

She blinked trying to absorb why anyone would try to come after her. Chase shook her. His voice was a harsh growl.

"Got it?"

She nodded and opened her mouth to ask why. The door slammed open.

"Mom!"

Diana felt the blast of fear and urgency as Karen bolted toward her. She hesitated because of the men. They moved aside, but only a couple of steps for the girl to pass. Karen threw her arms around her mother.

Diana felt awful to be the cause of her daughter's misery.

"Shhh." She soothed, rubbing big circles on Karen's back. "It's all right."

"No. It's not."

The rest of Karen's answer garbled into the coat as Diana's attention focused on the man approaching from the house. The twins followed like two bristling hounds.

"Dad came after Adam left. He, Dad, said you were ... were ..." Karen stuttered without finishing. "He and Bradley fought."

Diana noted, with satisfaction, the bruise on her ex's face. Too bad she couldn't praise Bradley's effort on her behalf.

Karen's hands tightened on Diana as she noticed the big bikers.

On cue, Bradley snarled at the intruders. Usually mild Brandon mirrored his brother.

"It's about time you showed up." The Dick gave the boys room while raking his eyes over her rumpled appearance.

"Why are you here Richard?"

All the other males present growled inaudibly. The rumble of the air was no more than a sound. She didn't know if they were picking up on her irritation or posing for each other's benefit.

Diana reached out through the pack link to enfold all of the children in a blanket of comfort and peace. Tank's sharp jerk, and Chase's more audible growl, told her she'd spilled over to the other wolven.

"My daughter called with a crazy story about a stray dog breaking into the house and you being kidnapped."

Richard always did like to exaggerate, to put down others and make himself look better. He sneered at Diana, spreading his hands to encompass everything.

"And here it is five AM. Apparently the only thing I need to worry about is the example you are setting for my children."

That was a lie. Richard never cared much about what happened to the children so long as he wasn't bothered and they were available for holidays.

Matthew, her son, shifted uncomfortably at the back of the group, close to his father. He glared at Tank and Chase with as much hostility as the twins, adding a large dose of fire for his mother, as well. Eerily, she was reminded of a much younger Richard. Judgmental and angry, like his father had been when he'd walked out on her.

She tried for gracious, as much as she could muster, without underwear, and covered in a borrowed leather duster in the warm early summer night.

It was pretty obvious what she was or wasn't wearing underneath. It made that lack of underwear thing a little more embarrassing.

Richard was beginning to seriously piss her off. How had she stood his smug attitude all these years? By playing nice to keep the peace. God she was a wimp.

Before she could castigate herself more, the freight train of emotion that was Adam slammed through her barriers. She thought she was pissed, Adam was a red fury. He was on his way. He *knew* where she was through the strange magical tie that bound the pack together. And her to them.

She smiled at Tank then Chase. "You guys better go. I can handle this."

"You sure?"

Cocky again, Chase stared over Richard, dismissing the twins and Matthew with a flick of his eyes.

Oh. Yes. She was sure. She didn't need this much supernatural testosterone in her driveway at five o'clock in the morning.

They'd all kill one another when Adam got here.

Her rescuers stared past her to Richard, their eyes catching the porch light with the feral intensity of wolves.

"Yes. Thank you again. Go," she urged at the men's obvious reluctance.

Chase's amber eyes flared with amber light as he looked down at Karen, quiet and still between them. He traced a finger down the wide-eyed girl's face. His voice was low and intimate.

"Stay safe Diana. Remember, you're on the menu."

He turned abruptly for his bike. The action caused Bradley to snap. He darted forward, faster than a blink, barreling into the blond biker.

"Bradley!" Karen screamed.

"No!" Diana echoed, reflexively trying to hold on to Karen as she twisted free, athletic as any gymnast, to go to her boyfriend.

The two rolled over in the yard, sounding like a couple of junkyard dogs.

In the dim light Diana could see Bradley's handsome face distorted. She saw a hint of fang and claw as he tried to reach Chase's jugular.

Older and stronger, he easily held the boy's head away and dodged Karen's kick.

"Oh, no you don't." Diana grabbed at Brandon before he joined the free for all.

For a change, he looked like a thinner version of his brother. Danger radiated from him. He didn't resist as she pulled him close.

For all the potential Brandon carried hidden inside to be a dangerous predator, more violence would harm his gentle soul.

"No, stay with me." Dina held tight, frantically trying to think of a way to end the fight. The water hose? Brandon's body strained to go to his brother's aid, but he didn't fight Diana's restraining hand.

"God, you are so incompetent Diana. This is just like you."

Diana started. She'd forgotten about Richard. Matthew stood behind his father, trembling with emotion.

"Oh, I don't think so. Go home Richard. This is none of your business."

Diana split her attention between the combatants rolling mere feet from them and her ex. Richard reached out a hand snagging Karen when she bounced too close.

"Hey!"

"Anything that involves my children is my business." He gave Karen a little shake to get her attention, speaking first to his daughter then to Diana. "Matthew, take your sister and get in the car. Now you're bringing home weirdoes. You need a professional. "

Dark vicious emotions rolled off of Richard. The need to hurt jabbed at Diana sharp as a knife.

With a last snarl, Chase pinned Bradley the ground. Not a scratch marred the boy, other than what he'd picked up rolling across the grass. Chase ground a knee in the boy's stomach, forcing a whine as Bradley reluctantly submitted.

Tank stepped in front of Richard, stopping him. The very real danger to Richard pressed in on her from all sources as all the wolven focused on him.

Brandon gripped Diana's hand. She squeezed reassuringly and let go, reaching out to lay a hand on Tank's dark velvety skin.

"Tank."

His black eyes, gleaming with power, focused down on her.

"I will not hurt the man, little sister." He sounded barely human.

Richard raked over the multitude of tiny braids spread over Tank's massive shoulders, leather vest, pants, and oversized boots.

"I see you've sunk to an all time low, Diana. Can't even stick to your own kind."

For a brief amazed moment Diana thought that Richard was talking about Tank's species, not his color. She shook her head, holding Tank's arm as if that would keep him from ripping Richard into itty-bitty pieces.

"Sooo, you're a bigot as well as an asshole? I didn't realize you were multi-talented." She couldn't resist one last jab. It wasn't big of her, but she'd had enough. She bared teeth at him, wishing her smile was as toothy and sharp as a wolven's. "I'll tell Laina and her *girlfriend* you said hi."

He jerked as if slapped. He turned dull red in the low light.

"Matthew. Karen. Get in the car."

Diana tamped down the urge to sic all of the guys on him. Or tear into Richard herself. Karen sat, safe in the circle of Bradley's arms.

"I'm not going." She lifted her chin, wrapped her arms over Bradley's.

Diana pointed at the Lexus in the driveway.

"Leave Richard. Before I call the police and slap a restraining order on you."

Multiple low growls from the wolven males underscored her threat.

"Fine." His gaze arrogant gaze narrowed on Karen. "But I wash my hands of whoever stays with the freak show. Permanently."

Karen stayed in Bradley's embrace. Matthew followed on his father's retreating heels.

"Matthew?"

"Don't hold me back Mom."

Her son's voice was a cold flashback to the day Richard had walked out. His eyes just as hard and unforgiving. For a second time in her life, her heart ripped in two by a man that she loved.

Warm, familiar hands slid around Diana. She turned into the comfort of Brandon's scent. He rubbed her back in the same soothing motions she'd used on her daughter.

The betrayal flooded past the numbness.

She'd known he was leaving. Soon. But like this ...

"Little Sister."

"Go." She told Tank.

She was at the end of her energy. Her body ached horribly, she was filthy, dressed in a borrowed tee shirt and coat. Her heart lay shattered at her feet.

"Just go."

Chapter Fifteen

Adam stared at the pack piled in the bed curled protectively around their chosen, *what? Den mother?*

How the hell had she bonded herself into his pack anyway? And how was he going to convince her to stay?

They watched him warily, waiting for an explosion. Several heartbeats passed, then one by one the group slid off the bed and out of the room.

Karen paused in the doorway. Her steady gaze and tilted head was very wolven for a human.

"She trusts you. We all do."

The girl left him, slipped away downstairs before he could form an answer.

Diana Ridley was the answer. His answer.

The dull ache of her pain called to him even in her sleep. Adam couldn't help but offer the only comfort he could. Shutting the door, he stripped out of his clothes and slipped between the sheets.

Gently, he curled his body around her battered one and inhaled the scent that was unique to her. Other scents that raised his hackles clung to her body, but he set that aside to concentrate on his almost-mate.

She whimpered in her sleep and curled closer. The press of her body to his skin set him on fire. Her hands smoothed across his chest before she buried her nose there and sighed.

"Safe. Missed you." Her mumbled whisper made him groan.

God, how he wanted her. His body was hard with need, but that, too, he would ignore for her sake. As much as he wanted sex, needed to complete the mate-bond with her, now was not the time.

Adam allowed himself to caress her hair before pressing a chaste kiss on her crown. He'd hold her tonight and prove that he wasn't like that jerk she'd divorced. Adam J. Weis was faithful, honorable, and yeah, damn horny.

* * * *

The rich aroma of coffee seduced her from the comfy spot. Her body was a mass of aches and pains.

Sliding off the edge of the bed, she nearly tripped over a full sleeping bag. Only a swatch of reddish brown hair peeked out the end. The bag gently rose and fell, matching the soft breath snores of the occupant. She stepped over carefully, spying Rick's innocent sleeping face. Another pallet sprawled at the end of the bed contained Mark and Seth, huddled together like sleeping puppies.

Seth whimpered and twitched in his sleep. Immediately, the other boy scooted closer, flinging an arm over his sleeping companion.

Diana smiled. There was nothing sexual or perverse about the action, as a matter of fact, she was sure either boy would viciously defend himself on that score. It was just one pack brother offering comfort and safety. She imagined that if the need arose, Rick would abandon his pallet to plop down on the other side, adding his support to the group.

She considered the rumpled bed, remembering Karen crawling in beside her. Obviously, others had followed suit.

Rather than getting upset, Diana decided to accept the gift for what it was. She was hurt and the boys had taken her into their circle. The gesture left a warm feeling in the region of her heart.

Too bad she couldn't have woken up in Adam's arms. That would have been comfortable. Diana frowned. She liked them all. To be honest, she was far more involved than a mere promise to bake Mark's birthday cake. She didn't want to be this involved.

She made a quick run through her drawers, grabbing underwear, the sturdy grandma kind, and a stretchy sports bra. She found another oversize tee shirt and a pair of cutoffs. Sexy, the outfit was not. For comfort and a feeling of blah camouflage, it was perfect.

* * * *

He'd nearly lost her, just like Amanda.

The strays had given her their blood.

Adam poured himself a cup of coffee and struggled to get a grip on his erratic emotions. Otherwise he was going to owe her more than the shattered birdbath in the backyard. He hoped she wasn't too attached to that one.

First Adam was relieved. Then, the self-recriminations had set in, followed by jealousy. That was the point where the birdbath had lost its cutesy concrete existence in the backyard. It was now a pile of rubble and he was still agitated. Only, now he owed her a birdbath.

What kind of injuries had she sustained, that she needed wolven blood to heal? He owed those strays for protecting what was his.

Then again, they could be the ones moving in on his territory. By creating a blood bond with Diana, taking Adam's position as Canis Pater would be smoother.

He bared his teeth at the thought. They'd have to take him out first, and Adam didn't plan on making his death an easy one.

He ran a hand through his hair and sighed. His hands were raw from the battle with the birdbath, but he didn't notice.

He didn't really think that the strays were after his position. They wouldn't have brought Diana home. She would be the perfect bait to ensure Adam agreed to a formal challenge. Plus, she wouldn't have needed the strays' protection if he hadn't goaded her in the first place.

Diana's footsteps above alerted Adam that she was up. He'd know her movements anywhere. His breath caught in his chest. He wanted desperately to go up to her again, but decided to give her privacy.

Coward.

To prove that he wasn't, Adam closed his eyes and followed the pack bond to Diana. Even without the mate-bond, every time they touched, physically or psychically, it seemed their connection became stronger.

Her flimsy barrier did nothing to hide her fragile emotions. The pain and vulnerability triggered Adam's own volatile emotions.

A psychic vision invaded his mind. His first. A brief flash of the monster and her rescuers shone in raw horror movie style. Rage boiled up in him.

Now he knew the whole story.

Adam did the only thing he could. He retreated from the connection before she realized his trespass.

* * * *

In the shower, Diana scrubbed viciously, fighting the horror of Dog's attack. Each event after she left the bar flashed vividly behind closed eyes.

The moment that the motorcycles first drove up. Diana shuddered.

The sensory memories were both emotional and physical. She could still feel the sick hunger of lust. The heavy hairy weight of the werewolf getting more excited by the scent of her fear.

Diana scrambled out of the shower, threw up, and then brushed her teeth. Her fresh minty breath allowed the coffee smell to be appealing once again. Diana followed its lure downstairs. She hoped the kitchen was empty so that she could use it to fortify her defenses in peace.

It wasn't. Adam's drawn face looked up from her morning paper. Lines pinched around the chiseled slash of his mouth. A banked fire glowed behind the blue ice chips that made up his eyes. His white blond hair hung loose around his shoulders, obviously finger combed many times.

The work shirt he wore was as wrinkled as her bed sheets and his feet were bare. That she thought he was sexy after heaving her guts up less than twenty minutes ago told her something. The comfort she felt at his presence was something she didn't care to examine closely.

Adam's nostrils flared. Diana reinforced the shield around herself to keep out the mix of emotions from him and the rest of the house. Her own were too much for her to deal with.

She didn't need to find out if she could leak her trauma back through the pack bond. The boys, Brandon especially, might not be able to handle the reminder of past rapes.

She probably needed therapy. But any therapist that she told, "Hey, I'm having issues about being nearly raped by a werewolf," would probably heavily sedate her. She'd deal. Diana wasn't willing to go down that road again.

She paused and ignored Adam. She reached into the cabinet for a coffee cup. She was still unhappy with his macho act at the Saloon anyway.

If she tried hard enough, Diana could lay the series of catastrophes last night squarely on his broad shoulders. Sharing the blame made her feel better. Petty, but better.

Diana poured her coffee with deliberate precision, keeping her back to him. She felt, more than saw, Karen enter the kitchen with Bradley at her side. Brandon would no doubt soon follow. The boy was near inseparable from his brother.

Diana took a sip of coffee, waiting for her wolven king, no-*despot*, to explode. Thinking of Adam Weis as hers made her frown. She would not become attached to him.

"I told you to stay in the bar."

Yes, she decided, that was one ticked alpha male. She took another sip of coffee, pointedly ignored the waves of frustration and anger that poured out of him.

"You deliberately disobeyed my order."

Diana turned slowly and leaned back against the counter. She rested one arm under her breast, balancing the other to sip her coffee. Let the man stew.

"You kids eat yet?"

She watched Karen and Bradley watch Adam simmer. They looked concerned, as they ought when the pack leader was upset.

Adam drummed his fingers impatiently on the forgotten paper. Brandon answered, slipping past his brother and Karen.

The boy gave Adam a wide berth and stopped next to Diana. His voice was soft and polite while he reached into the cabinet for a coffee cup, filling it for himself.

"We ate the cereal. Karen made biscuits and ham."

Brandon cradled the cup between his hands and took a drink. His chocolate brown eyes half closed in pleasure.

Diana thought it a little odd that he wasn't hiding from the tension in the room.

Since emotional and psychological evaluations were beyond her this morning, she pushed the occurrence to the back of her mind and focused on his words.

She figured that all four boxes of cereal and the three-pound hunk of ham were long gone. Matthew could eat ... she sighed silently and shied away from the thought.

Diana gave Brandon a quick hug, ruffling his hair. A twinge in her shoulder protested the movement but she pushed away the memory with a false, bright smile. Brandon's shy answering smile made the movement worth the pain.

"Would you kids mind running out to the garage freezer and getting the brisket out for dinner?"

She sensed, not through any special gift, but through plain old intuition, that Adam had finally reached the end of his temper holding abilities.

Not that she'd experienced his temper holding ability to be all that vast before. But he seemed to be doing a better than usual job of it this morning, er, afternoon.

"Pull out anything else you want to add to the menu." Take your time, she added silently, because when he blows, it's going to be a doozy.

The kids fled through the adjoining door leading into the laundry room and garage that served as a storage area to more than the freezer. The car lived in the driveway.

His explosion was swift and silent. Diana found her back pinned to the refrigerator, two hundred plus pounds of wolven in her face.

"I told you to stay inside the bar," he repeated in a low growl.

He wasn't hurting her. His grip was gentle, yet immovable. Under normal circumstances, Diana would have given him some leeway. She could feel the fear that had finally rattled his cage open leak through her shield. Instincts that drove him to protect what he perceived as his.

She was still angry that he'd butted in to her business last night. Her ego was bruised and she was still hurting from her son's rejection. Angry that she'd let 'the Dick' find a way to rip her heart out a second time, through their son. And through it all, she felt sick and violated by Dog's attack.

She felt guilty that maybe Adam had been right. Maybe she'd brought it all on herself by leaving.

Deprived of any of the true objects of her fury, Diana rounded on Adam.

"And I told you--you're not my anything. Get over yourself."

Diana embraced the fury and pain twisting in her gut and threw it at him like a fireball, a weapon. Dealing with the horror by lashing out at the safest target.

Adam flinched. He let her go and backed up a step.

Diana continued, empowered and on the offensive.

"I know exactly what you are. And I'm not impressed."

She poked a broken silver nail in his chest, forcing him back yet another step. She embraced the power she'd buried all her life. She'd wasted so much time by hiding and still the monsters had caught up with her last night. The seductive magic of her power flared under her skin, feeding the maelstrom inside.

It felt good. Strong.

"You think you're so god-damn above the rest of us. That you say jump and the rest of us do it." She poked at him again. He backed away, a bemused look on his face. "Not. Me. I'm a grown woman. I will do what I want, when I want. And you can take your macho shit and choke on it."

Adam stopped and held his ground. Diana took a breath, her fury and power driving her on.

"Or I'll drive a stake through your chest."

"That would be vampires, sweet, not wolven."

His low careful voice contrasted with her yelling. She blinked and lowered her tone.

"Vampires, wolven, whatever. You want to try me Fido?"

She still wanted to fight, to hurt. Picking at him might not be smart, but she knew she was safe with him.

Adam grabbed hold of her arms and gave her a quick, hard shake. His eyes glowed with suppressed emotion and power. The mingled scents of her angry passion and the aphrodisiac scent of psychic power rolling off of her heightened his own needs, making it hard for him to hold himself in check.

Diana snarled and attacked. She screeched with frustration as he held her firmly away from him.

Adam was surprised at the strength of her fury. It threatened to consume him through the bond. The sweet human female that had entranced him was gone, replaced by a mad she-wolf bent on tearing him apart. *If* he let go long enough for her to do so.

Last night his territorial nature had spurred him to displace Bob Benedict in Diana's affections. He wanted her for himself. He accepted that now.

Even when Amanda, his fiancée, had disappeared, Adam had been angry, more interested in justice than grief stricken. His pride might have been damaged, but his heart had survived intact.

Finding out Diana was missing had frightened him, threatened to carve a hole in his heart. It was a new experience that confused him, making a dangerous predator even more dangerous while he searched the streets for her.

He felt her pain though the pack bond. Like with the boys, it made him feel ineffectual. That riled him as much as the stray's blood scent on her skin, knowing that strange males had a link to her.

"I'm sorry."

She didn't hear and kept trying to get at him. Adam repeated the words with more force.

"*Diana.* I am sorry."

She stilled and blinked at him, unaware of the tears tracking down her lovely face, even with the alarming red splotches. She heaved a breath.

"Why? *Why?*"

It was a general *why*. He understood that. He didn't have an answer for her, hated that he didn't, and offered up the only comfort he could.

"I would kill to keep the hurt from you if I could."

She shook her head, unaware of the audience they had drawn from both doorways.

"Really? Or just a way to use me for your own gain?"

Adam frowned.

"I don't understand."

Diana laughed, harsh and disillusioned. She had a feeling Doc Tank had left out a lot of details in his explanation about dragon delicacies. Otherwise, why would Chase have warned her about being *on the menu*. No one had ever mentioned *why* she should avoid other supernaturals. Just to stay far away from them. Why were the wolven so interested in *her*?

"Oh, I'll bet."

"Mom?"

Diana blinked and looked into the doorway where Karen stood clutching Bradley's arm. Her daughter's face was pale.

Diana sucked in another breath to calm her skittering emotions. She ran a hand through her drying hair. It always dried in a half straight, half waved mess, like a rumpled haystack.

She needed to get a grip.

Diana cleared her throat, aware of all the eyes centered on her.

"I … I apologize for my outburst," she said to the room at large.

Every eye seemed to judge her and she thought she came up lacking. Maybe not true, but it was how she felt. The crowd closed in on her without taking a step closer. The sensory memory of Dog looming behind her made Diana catch her breath. The kitchen pressed in on her.

"Excuse me. I have to get dressed."

She was dressed. She needed to get away. To hide. Diana angled for the doorway when Adam reached out. To capture her. She didn't want to be captured. Held down. Forced against her will. Diana slapped the hand away.

"Don't," she hissed, missing the hurt her rejection caused. "Don't touch me again."

Diana spun on her toes and shoved past the two boys in the kitchen entry, cringing at the contact. She prayed her room was empty as she fled up the stairs. Wrapped up in her own pain, Diana missed the confusion she left behind. And in one case, too much understanding.

* * * *

Adam waited until he couldn't sit still any longer. The sound of the shower barely muffled a sob. Steam filled the bathroom with hot moisture.

Stepping over the pile of clothes, he eased the curtain aside. Wide startled brown eyes met his. His libido reacted instantly to the wet naked curves on display. He pulled the scrubber thing out of her hand and tossed it behind him.

"You're going to hurt yourself like that."

"I …"

Adam shook his head. With one finger, he traced the path of a stray drop of water down her cheek. Or was it a tear? A wry smile tugged at one corner of his mouth.

"Sweetheart. You are killing me."

Diana shook her head. She squeezed her eyes shut. Wrapping her arms around her body, she began to shake.

Caught up in the pain, she lost track of time. One moment she was denying him, the next he was in the shower with her. Naked and holding her close.

He felt familiar. Right.

Diana buried her face against his god's body and absorbed the comfort of his presence. Her hands traveled over the ridges and valleys of his terrain. She felt the jut of his desire against her hip. Warm water cascaded down her back and buttocks.

Diana didn't want to remember the horror from last night. She raised her face.

"Make me forget."

"You're not ready."

The unsure squint in his eyes made her grip the swells of his biceps and press against the slick wetness of his body. Sliding her breasts against his torso, she repeated the demand.

Adam's head descended. The water darkened his hair. Slicked back, his features looked chiseled from marble. Hard and graceful, a work of art. His lips were perfect.

Diana melted into the kiss, taking strength from him like a draught on tap. She wanted this. To feel wanted. To be cared for. To belong forever.

She pulled back with a gasp. The emotions were his, not hers.

Shaking her head, she tried to pull away. She needed distance or she'd be doomed.

"I don't want a commitment. I just want …."

His finger against her lips stopped her words.

"I know. I'll give you a new memory."

Taking the digit into her mouth, she teased the rough pad with her tongue. She sucked him hard before letting go. The heavy digit at her hip jumped in response.

"No commitment."

Adam's answer was to cover her mouth with his. His tongue delved deep. His hands traveled down the line of her back to grasp her full buttocks. Reveling in the slide of their bodies, she looped her arms around his neck as he pulled her up in an easy movement.

Holding her tightly against his body, Adam began to slide his thick shaft against the folds of her pubis.

Diana gasped. Adam growled into her neck. The rasp of his whiskers left a tingling trail.

Growing wetter by the stroke, her grasp on his neck tightened. She rocked back over him, trying to ease the thickness inside. He eluded her movements, torturing her into clenching her abdomen with each almost entry until she whimpered for mercy.

Adam had none to give. He'd waited too long for this moment. Both the wolf and the man wanted to mate.

Letting her slide down his body, he turned her around so that she faced the shower wall. His little human she-wolf half turned, but he would have none of that. Grasping her hands, he placed them on the wall tiles before covering her with his body.

Trailing small bites across her shoulders, he thrust against the crease between her legs. Diana arched backward and he took the opportunity to palm one full breast. His other hand traveled down the front of her body to bury in the auburn curls of her sex.

She was his. Words were meaningless. She could deny him with words all she wanted. He'd stake his claim now, with his body.

Diana gasped and pressed backward, riding his shaft, wanting more. Her breasts ached. Her nipples were tight and hard, sensitive to every touch he gave them. Every thought evaporated as his fingers found and teased the bud between her nether lips.

Adam rumbled in satisfaction as she squirmed against him. He scented her climax was close. This time he wanted to feel the clench of her as she came on his cock.

He entered her in one stroke, tearing a strangled cry of sheer pleasure from both their throats. Pausing, he regained control. He was in charge. A nip of encouragement on her made her writhe again. Pulling almost out, he drove his next stroke back in, setting a steady pace.

Diana found that she could use the wall for leverage against each thrust that filled her completely. She met his rhythm stroke for stroke, slowly building toward her climax. His hands settled on her hips, urging her on, keeping her balanced.

Then he changed his angle, the head of his penis pressing against *that* spot inside her channel. Diana groaned. She panted.

Both of his hands covered her breasts, teasing her nipples with light tugs. Adam's hips kept pace.

She wanted ... Diana gasped, her fingers curling against the wall. Her body shattered and locked around his. Adam heaved a groan and pulled free of her body, spending his release into empty space.

Cooling water cascaded onto their still-huddled bodies. He turned off the water before the spray turned ice cold.

Feeling her gaze on him, Adam dared to look at the sexy woman he'd just made love to. She lounged against the tiles, a sated smile on her face.

Just one more kiss, he told himself. Then he would leave her with her memory and give her time to adjust to the idea of them together.

Her sex swollen lips tasted faintly of blood. His tongue teased against the marks her teeth made as she'd held back her cries of pleasure. Sweeping once more inside her mouth, tangling with her tongue in an imitation of the act they'd just completed, made him ready for more.

Adam pulled back and dove for one more quick kiss. Another round and he'd press her for the commitment she wasn't willing to give. Yet.

He made good his escape while his ragged honor was still intact.

Chapter Sixteen

Adam's cell phone rang, breaking into his musing. He pulled it out and checked the ID.

Mack. Damn. He'd hoped to get at least a little rest. Finish another cup of coffee. Figure out a way to get in Diana's bed for good. God he was pathetic.

"Yeah?"

"Hey, Buddy. You need to get your hairy ass down here."

Dread loomed over Adam's already shot day. Mack was more than a good foreman who wanted to keep his job. Hell, he was an investor. If he said Adam needed to get his ass there, then well, Adam was about to haul ass.

"What's up?"

"That inspector, that's what. God-damn house is miswired to fuck and back. An A-1 fucking fire hazard, that's what." Like most guys, when the shit hit the fan, Mack's language deteriorated to gutter quality. "Inspector *Cleuso* will be back tomorrow. I didn't want to push him too far."

Translation: Mack the psychic had mind-screwed the building inspector into thinking the inspection was tomorrow.

Adam rubbed a hand over his face. He didn't need this. He needed a shave, a bath, a bed, and food. While he was wishing, he decided to add sex with the soft and curvy female upstairs. Having his pack trust him was on that wish list too.

"Fuck. Re-dos cost money."

"Yep. Me and Jase will be here waiting." Mack sounded tired. Adam remembered how much energy Mack's powers required. All that on top of working all day had to drain the foreman.

"Okay. Give me a few. I'll pick us up something to eat on the way."

Adam flipped the cell phone shut and headed back to the kitchen to inform everyone of his plans. He'd give Diana a little space to work through her problems. Not that he intended to give up his suit. He was more determined now for a permanent mate-bonding.

Bradley sat at the kitchen table mooning over the cute and bouncy Karen while she started dinner. In a move much like her mother, the girl shooed Brandon out of her way and into a chair.

She leaned against him for a moment, touching like wolven do to offer companionship, a move that most humans would consider a sexual invitation. For wolven, it was non-sexual, the equivalent of a pat on the shoulder or an upper torso hug.

Adam had noticed that little miss cheerleader was comfortable enough with wolven touches even before last night's puppy pile incident. She seemed awfully trusting for a human, more so considering she was a psychic. He wondered again what her abilities were and shook his head.

Adam had an idea. He smiled, letting it creep over his face. Yeah, that might be exactly what he needed to do.

"Brandon." The boy jumped, his eyes wide and startled to suddenly be in the alpha's radar. "You're with me."

Adam couldn't stand the dull-sick wave of fear that rolled off of the boy. But Brandon nodded dutifully, as expected. Nor did Adam like the brother's sharp look of protest. Karen came to rest a supportive, and protective, hand on Brandon's shoulder.

She smiled cheerfully at Adam.

Adam gestured for Brandon to get a move on. He killed Bradley's protest with a look.

"I've got to head back out to the job site. Keep an eye on things here. Call if you need me. And," he pointed a finger at the floor, "everyone stays close. Got it?"

* * * *

"So."

Mack gestured with a jerk of his chin after Brandon. Loaded down with fast food bags, the boy headed to the kitchen where Jase was setting out the drinks.

Adam and Mack followed at a much slower pace, presumably to talk about the miswiring sabotage. "Why'd you bring that one?"

Then again, maybe not. Adam frowned, resisting the urge to rub the ache between his eyes.

"What? Do you have a problem with him?"

"Nah. I just wondered why you brought the pack nothing instead of one of the others."

Adam stopped. He reminded himself that Mack was his friend. Because right now all he wanted to do was deck the bastard. He planted himself in front of the foreman.

"Let me tell you something," Adam growled. His tone was soft and deadly. "He's not a nothing. He's part of the pack. He's mine."

Mack held up his hands in surrender.

"No offense, partner." Mack's tone was also soft, but careful, and smart for pointing out the relationship between them. "Just a question. I've been reading up on wolves on the Internet. I'm trying to see how it applies. From what I read, it seemed like the alpha wolf wouldn't take the omega out on a hunt. Hell, it seemed to me, that guy was lucky he got anything to eat."

Adam cocked his head. Mack went still as he met the eerie husky blue eyes that looked nothing like a human's. As Adam sized him up, Mack wondered if he'd pushed the wolven pack leader too hard this time.

Mack was good in a fight. He'd taken out wolven rejects, real werewolves, before and wondered if he'd have to protect himself from his friend. The friend he'd given up his life, literally and figuratively, for.

There was no going back for Mack Spencer. For the sin of choosing tying himself to the supernaturals, for choosing them over his family, Mack was dead to the psychic community.

Adam smiled. Not the smile of a friend. A dominant predator's baring of teeth.

"We're not animals. We're people."

Adam walked away, leaving Mack in the hall to call himself all kinds of stupid for forgetting the eye contact thing. One of these days, Mack realized, that wolf was going wind up biting his dumb ass for being his aggravating self.

He didn't have to use any of his psychic sensitive abilities to figure that one out. Mack was counting on it.

* * * *

"Geez, it's late." Mack yawned and pulled a long cylinder tube out of his shirt pocket.

"Nah. It's early."

Exhaustion dimmed Adam's usual appreciation for the sunrise. Jase was long gone, mumbling a half English/ half Spanish reminder to pick up diapers.

"Why don't you take off and get some rest? That inspector isn't going to be here for a few hours," Adam said.

He kept one eye on the yard light pole at the far corner of the back yard. More accurately, on Brandon balanced on the ladder, also balanced against the light pole.

Adam stretched at a kink in his back, and then leaned back against the wall.

"He's just about done. Then we're outta here."

Mack grunted.

Adam glanced over. Being up for two solid days made him think he was exhausted, but in reality, with his wolven constitution, Adam was just very tired. And selfish.

As a human, being up the same amount of time, and a psychic who'd expended energy to make the building inspector come back later today, Mack looked ready to fall over.

"Mack. Go home. Get some rest." He tried to frame the order in his gentlest tone.

Mack straightened and gave a full body shake similar to what the wolves often did. Unbuttoning the pocket of his work shirt, the foreman retrieved a capped silver cylinder and pulled off the lid. He upended a cigar between his fingers.

"Nah. I want to see the kid finish."

Adam wanted to argue, but the exhausted human would only fight any suggestion he made. Besides, Mack had already clamped the cigar between his teeth and lit the noxious package. He puffed and exhaled bluish smoke that drifted Adam's way.

Adam stifled back a cough and ended up sneezing instead.

"You do that on purpose, don't you?"

"What?" Mack was all offended innocence.

"Light those damn sticks so that I'll sneeze half the day."

"Now why would I do that?"

"Because you're a prick."

Mack settled back against the outside wall with a grin.

"Hey! I'm finished!"

Brandon jumped the ten-foot drop to the ground and jogged back to the men.

"Well, turn it on." Adam thumbed in the direction of the sliding glass door, waiting while Brandon slipped through.

After a couple of minutes of nothing happening, the boy stuck his head back out the door.

Adam waited while Brandon walked back out to the yard, thinking. He wanted the kid to figure it out himself. The boy climbed back up the ladder and checked his electrical connections. Brandon smacked a palm against his forehead.

"Duh!" He jumped back off the ladder and ran into the house. The light blinked on with a warm yellow glow.

"I wondered how long it'd take for him to figure out to flip that breaker." Mack laughed. He pulled out another cylinder from his pocket and offered it to Adam. "Cigar?"

"God, no. Why?"

"'Cause you got the look of a proud papa. By the way, I'll get that motion sensor installed in a couple of days."

Adam chuffed, a canine sound between a cough and a laugh from deep in his chest.

"I'm no one's papa. But he is a smart kid."

Adam's sensitive ears picked up Brandon's soft tread on the bare concrete floor and he shut up. The boy spilled back out onto the patio area with a look of amazement. The light winked out.

Brandon walked forward a few steps and waved his arms. The light blinked back on. Adam shot Mack a smug look. The foreman responded by tossing him the cigar.

"Yep, you're right. He is a smart one at that."

* * * *

From the cab of his truck, Adam watched Mack drive off with a wave. He'd nearly had to arm wrestle the man into letting him lock up. Brandon quietly caressed the leather tool belt and basic tool set Adam had given him earlier.

He reached behind the seat and grabbed one of the Lobos Luna Construction caps. He dropped it in Brandon's lap, then cranked the truck and started back to Diana's house to round up the rest of his pack and plan on his next move.

Out of the corner of his eye Adam could see the boy trace the sunshades of the Lobos Luna wolf on the front of the cap.

"Every one of the crew got a cap. That one's yours. You earned it."

Brandon touched the wolf logo once more before settling the cap over his head. After a few moments of driving in silence, the kid spoke up.

"Could we get something to eat? Breakfast?"

A growl rose from Brandon's stomach that made Adam grin.

"You bet. Sounds like you're stomach's ready to go hunting without you."

"Not rabbits."

"Hell, I mean, heck no. That's the sound of a big game hunt."

"Like deer?"

"Nah. More like the whole cow."

"Or an elephant." Brandon's grin was brief, but reached his eyes.

"You think you could eat a whole elephant?" Adam asked, deadpan.

Brandon appeared to consider the question.

"Maybe, it all depends."

"On what?"

"How big the hole is."

Both of them laughed at the stupid joke. Adam didn't know if it was really funny or if he was that tired. Maybe, it was relief that he'd managed a small crack in the wall that surrounded the pack's inner circle.

Chapter Seventeen

Brandon Starr leaned against the track fence and waited. It wasn't such a hard duty, watching the cheerleaders practice.

Athletic girls bouncing up and down was an uplifting way to pass the time. On the other side of the field, football practice was in full swing.

He watched Karen execute a double back flip and bounce back up into place. He flashed her a grin and a double thumbs up sign. He noted, but ignored, the hoo-has in the stands behind him, yelling their guts out, hoping one of the cheerleaders would notice them.

As if.

Brandon, unlike the hormone driven jerks behind him, wasn't here to letch all over the girls' practice.

Though, a suppressed part of him appreciated the girls efforts in an elemental way. The monster inside him stayed in a cage deep inside, far apart from his own impulses.

Brandon tried to push his confusion about Adam aside to focus on the cheerleader training. Karen always asked him for his opinion afterward. She valued his input. That's what friends were for.

His mind kept turning back to last weekend and helping Adam with the wiring and that yard light. Sunday, they started finishing out the house. That's what Adam called putting in all the final touches like flooring, cabinets, and painting.

Mostly all Brandon had done was carry out trash and use a pole sander to smooth down the sheetrock seams until he was white as snow with the dust. The fifty bucks the alpha had handed him had shocked and made him suspicious.

"An honest wage for honest work," Adam told him. He'd never expected to be paid for his efforts.

Brandon pulled the Los Lobos cap from the cargo pocket of his new jeans. Both were more unexpected surprises from the alpha. He put the cap on to shade his eyes.

All the guys had gotten new clothes that fit, but none of them had one of Adam's construction caps. Not even Bradley. It gave Brandon a little thrill, a feeling that he was special. Special to the pack leader in a good way. That scared him, too.

It reminded him of the day Adam had called him to his office. Instead of hurting him there had been some kind of blood bonding ceremony.

Garrick had never done anything like that. The only special feelings Garrick Moser had given where those of the special torment he'd liked to inflict.

"Hey!"

Brandon jumped and blinked at the hand waving in front of his face. Karen smiled the smile she reserved just for him and slipped her arm through his.

"You were a million miles away. What's up?"

Brandon shrugged, embarrassed. He'd missed her big finish.

"I'm sorry. You always do perfect cartwheels anyway. I liked the back flips, but you might want to involve the other girls more. I got a whiff of anger when you started off on your own."

Karen sighed.

"Oh. I get on a roll and you know. ..." She shrugged.

Brandon smiled. The other girls wouldn't stay mad at her for long. No one could.

"I know, Tigger. You should start gymnastics again. You miss the solo competitions."

Karen made a face at the nickname. He'd called her that since third grade, but only in private.

"It's the individuality I miss."

She sighed, then paused to send a bright smile and wave at one of her fellow cheerleaders leaving the field. Karen turned back to her friend.

"But Bradley would have a fit."

"He only spazzes like that when he can't keep tabs on everyone. Things are changing."

"Really. *Ya think?*" Karen smiled past her sarcasm and bumped Brandon with her hip. "I think the biggest change so far is Adam, chasing his tail, trying to figure out how to make up with Mom."

Brandon frowned. He wasn't sure how he felt about Adam and Ms. Ridley together.

"Oh good grief. I think he's good for her."

"Maybe," Brandon conceded. "I just don't want her hurt. None of us do."

Karen let him take her book bag as they started off of the field. She bumped him again. She knew Brandon and the pack better than anyone else.

"Hey, Brandon!"

One of the other cheerleaders called and waved. He sent a polite wave, smiled back her way, and shifted Karen's heavy bag. He never understood why she insisted on carrying every book home every night.

Of course, he had his work planned out in the first six weeks. His electives were always something not cool. Who wanted to hang out with a guy who took Home Ec?

"Sooo, what do you think of Heather?"

Brandon remembered the girl who had waved at him. He shrugged. Heather had only a fraction of Karen's charisma and sensitivity. It was like comparing a tiny star to the warmth of the sun.

"She's nice, I suppose."

Karen snorted.

"Oh, *come on*. She *likes* you." Karen's tone turned cajoling. "She thinks you're sweet."

Brandon ignored the comment. Karen had otherworldly charisma, but he could ignore it. Bradley couldn't. His brother took one look at Karen's pretty brown eyes and turned into a puppy.

"She wants me to see if you'd meet us after school for tacos."

He was really out of his comfort zone.

"Look. Bradley said that it's not safe to go wandering around right now." Actually, it was Adam who said it first, Brandon knew.

"Oh, pffft." Karen waved a hand. "Bradley's got issues. And Adam needs to learn how to find the florist. That apology sucked the other day."

Her laugh was like music in the air.

"Mom's so PO'd. If you mention Adam's name, she goes off on a rant. I've never seen her like that. Not even over my dad." She paused as her mood dimmed a bit. "But that's probably not saying a lot, huh?"

In Brandon's opinion, it did. Her dad was a major jerk off and her brother was following his dad's footsteps.

"I'm sorry about Matthew." He offered

Karen nodded, momentarily subdued, and then she brightened.

"Oh, come on. Please go with us?" She batted her eyelashes. "*Please?* She thought you didn't like her until I told her you were really just shy. Please?"

Brandon sighed. Okay, so he fell for her charisma, too. He just held out longer than Bradley would have.

"Do I have to sit by her?" He felt embarrassed by the whiny tone.

Karen stopped and looked up at him. A look, pity he guessed, flickered behind her pretty eyes. That bothered him. Brandon didn't want Karen to pity him. Everyone else either pitied or looked down on him.

"Have you ever thought about talking to someone? A counselor?"

Brandon pulled away from her. He stared as if she'd grown another head.

Suddenly, there was a shortage of air. He felt sucker punched by his best friend. Staring down at the puzzle like pieces of broken curb by his feet, Brandon tried to calm the swirling emotion.

Bradley was close. Close enough to keep an eye on his girlfriend. Brandon tuned and took off across the parking lot.

"Brandon? Wait! I'm sorry!"

Karen ran after him. She wasn't supposed to do that. Brandon turned to tell her to leave him alone, to go with Bradley, when he saw the four guys move in behind her from the parking lot.

Apparently, the guys didn't notice Bradley or see him change directions for the parking lot. The wind came from the wrong direction for his brother's scent to carry.

Brandon let Karen catch up, and then pushed her behind him. She squawked but stayed when she saw the four football goons.

Brandon's nose flared at the stink of coyote that the breeze blew off of them. It wasn't a big school. Coyotes and the wolves knew who was who without the smell.

The four boys spread out in a wide loose circle around them. Coyotes were, as a general rule, bullies and cowards. Other weres weren't as strong and didn't heal as fast as the wolven.

Bradley had proved on the playground that he'd retaliate against any were that messed with his pack brothers. There was a kind of truce among the younger set of shape-shifters. The only exception had been when Garrick was involved. Garrick was a whole other set of rules.

"Well, well, well. What have we got here?"

The leader, Nick McRay with orange, spiked hair, was stocky with the sort of permanent tan that mixed race human offspring often had. Like most of the were-coyote young, they had similar coloring, but were shorter than Brandon and heavier. All of them were on the football team and proud of the privilege.

Nick stuck his hands in his jeans pockets and sauntered up to them.

Brandon kept a hand on Karen, trying to keep them all in his sight. His lip curled and a snarl escaped. Bradley was walking casually, nearly to the curb of the parking lot. All he had to do was hold out until his brother arrived.

"Watch your place. We know what you are." One of the coyotes sneered at him.

"You've got no rights over me."

Brandon voice was much calmer than he felt. He had good practice at hiding his scent emotions from monsters scarier than these bozos. Garrick was dead, he reminded himself. A fine tremor started under his skin, urging him to action.

"That's not what we heard." Campy McRay sniggered.

Not funny at all, but then the coyotes were an inbred lot. Brandon knew that for a fact. Just like he knew that he'd die before he let any of their pack touch him again.

He growled low, warning them off. The tremor in his body turned into an itching, signaling that the Change wasn't far off. Only his loyalty to Karen kept him from running, or maybe fighting if he had to.

"What are you after?" Brandon's voice was gravelly. He was close to the change. He growled again when Nick tried to look past him at Karen. "Well?"

Nick shrugged and winked at Karen. Brandon felt her disgust. The coyote leaned in toward Brandon.

"I'm delivering a message. You guys trespassed on our hunting grounds. Benj says that he wants com … compen … payment for every acre of our woods you stole."

Nick looked proud of his delivery despite his illiteracy.

Brandon didn't like Nick or any of the coyotes. Their opinion didn't matter one bit to him. Having Karen believe that he was pathetic spurred him to do something he wouldn't have done otherwise. He antagonized them.

"We didn't steal anything of yours so back the fuck off."

One of the coyotes lost his temper and jumped at Brandon.

"I'll take it up now!"

Brandon crouched in front of Karen, letting himself change enough for claws and fangs to defend with.

Nick caught his coyote brother mid-jump and gave him a short shake.

"Chill, we're not here to fight." Nick eyed Brandon. "Yet."

"You butt-sniffers going to back away from my brother? Or am I going to have to make rugs out of your mangy hides?"

The werecoyotes started and turned to look at Bradley lounged against a brand new blue Camaro. Bradley smiled his trademark, bad to the bone, sharp-toothed smile.

"I *know* none of you are stupid enough to try anything with my girl. Hmmm? Nick?"

Nick paused. His hand went to his chest and rubbed absently where Bradley had once laid open the coyote's chest in a playground fight. The bully had had enough sense to stay away from the wolven pack brothers. Until today.

Nick backed down, his aggression folded away until Brandon was sure the coyote was about to hit the ground and grovel like a dog. All of the coyotes watched Bradley warily, with the respect due him. His brother was going to be alpha one day.

"We were just passing on a message." Nick said.

"Yeah? Spit it out so I don't have to play fortune cookie with your jaw and rip out your tongue to read it."

Nick started to growl but remembered himself and cleared his throat. He nodded.

"Benj wants the coyote hunting grounds back. Tell your new leader to cut his losses and turn what's ours over. He wants to be paid for the trouble too. Or else."

Nick looked uncomfortable giving out the ultimatum to Bradley. He then looked meaningfully in Brandon's direction.

"Benj said he'd take the same arrangements he made with Garrick."

Bradley lunged faster than any human or were. His hands became claws that wrapped around Nick's thick neck. Bradley slammed the coyote onto the hood of a compact car. He shoved his face into Nick's.

"Here's a message for you, Nick. Anyone touches my brothers, or what's mine, and I'll rip out your intestines."

He released the coyote and let them disperse. Luckily the class bell had already rung. There weren't more than a couple of bystanders, both students who walked away rather than get involved.

Brandon shivered uncontrollably while his brother looked him over. When he finished, Karen fled to her boyfriend's arms.

A pain made Brandon look at his fisted hands where claws had pierced his palms. Blood ran over his hands and dripped on the pavement. He concentrated, shifting back into a fully human state.

Bradley reached out and laid a hand on his brother's shoulder. Concern reached out to him through the pack bond. Karen watched Brandon, her worry added to Bradley's.

"We're not going to let them do anything. Adam wants to protect the pack." She glanced at Bradley. "Right?"

His brother looked in the direction the coyotes had gone. Bradley nodded.

"Yeah. No one's gonna touch you. I'll make sure."

Brandon shook off his brother's hand, and their pitiful attempt at comfort. There wasn't anything that could be done anyway. Not if Adam wanted to make a deal with Benjamin Gates.

Brandon's chest tightened painfully. There was something *he* could do.

He ran.

Chapter Eighteen

"Hi, Mom."

Diana looked up from her papers to see her daughter standing in front of her desk. She glanced at the clock.

School was definitely out, but her daughter didn't often come to the insurance agency where Diana worked. School practice and hanging out usually took up Karen's free time before Diana insisted she be home.

Karen drifted over to the chair across from the desk and fell into it. Her book bag thunked onto the floor beside her. Despondency radiated from Karen in waves.

"Did you and the girls have another disagreement over the routines?"

Karen shook her head.

"You and Bradley have a fight?"

Karen shook her head again. She stared at her two toned Nikes.

"You are going to have to help me out here, hon."

Karen sighed and rubbed her red-rimmed eyes with one hand. She'd been crying recently.

"It's been a rough afternoon."

Diana waited for her to elaborate, but Karen slumped back in the seat and chewed on a thumbnail. Diana heard the rustle of plastic as Karen toed the wastebasket, lost in her misery.

Diana made up her mind. Reaching under the desk, she flipped the computer tower off and picked up her purse. The papers she shoved aside for tomorrow.

"Come on. Let's go get something to eat."

All afternoon Diana had been plagued with an uneasiness that made her want to snatch up all the kids and tuck them somewhere safe.

She reminded herself again that the wolven pack was not her business. Adam, pushy aggravating male that he was, had the boys' welfare taken care of.

"Carol, I'm leaving early," Diana called out.

She slid her purse over her shoulder and headed for the coat rack, where Chase's beautiful duster hung, minus the gun. Diana couldn't make herself handle the thing, even to practice. It sat safe in her lock box. Guns gave her the heebie-jeebies.

After prying the story about werecoyotes out of Brandon later, Diana felt more secure knowing the gun was there.

Perversely, she didn't think she could actually use it against anyone. She needed to give it back before someone got hurt messing with the thing. Like her.

Werewolves or wolven, now werecoyotes, she didn't know what was next. Her whole world had been shaken up. Oh, after meeting Jax, the gnome, she'd known there were other things out there. But it wasn't real to her. Now she *knew.*

She wondered how she'd managed isolate herself from supernatural creatures for so long. She'd known the boys from the pack for years without realizing what they were.

Chase and Tank had said her scent gave her away. Apparently, the boys had been in on her secret for years while keeping their own.

Diana wasn't stupid. Blind maybe. Karen and the boys contributed to that. She was a little hurt that none of them trusted her with the truth.

After experiencing a little of Garrick Moser's evilness through Brandon, Diana could see how the boys would be careful of who they let know of their secret.

Carol called out a goodbye and Diana gathered up her daughter and herded Karen out to the car. What she needed was a night free of wolven and other bogies.

Diana was beginning to worry about her daughter. Karen had such a bright personality. She never held a bad or sad mood for long. They were nearly to Athens when Karen finally focused on her surroundings.

"I thought we were going home." Karen said the statement like a question and looked around the car with worry on her face.

"No. We are eating Italian tonight."

"But there's an Italian place in Palestine."

Diana nodded and turned toward her second favorite eatery.

"There are also shape-shifting wolves and coyotes. I'd have gone all the way to Tyler, but a gnome and a witch lives there. A hereditary witch, *not* a theological one. There's a difference," she clarified.

Ignoring Karen's goggled look, she rambled on. "Athens is closer. If there are any vampires, rabid fairies, or dragons looking to barbeque the local psychic, I haven't heard. *So*, we are going to Athens."

"Okay." Karen's face brightened for the first time since she slouched in Diana's office chair. "Is there really a gnome in Tyler?"

Diana nodded.

"And you know it? Personally?"

Diana smiled.

"Yes. *His* name is Jaxeramilix."

"What do gnomes do?"

"Jax sells used computers and designs custom visual basic databases for small businesses."

"Wow."

Diana pulled into the small parking area of the restaurant and killed the engine.

"Wow is right. But I think that's a new hobby. Jax makes his real money from the stock market. He's been around for a while and can spot trends." Diana reached for the door handle. "No more weird stuff for now. Let's eat."

She and Karen needed to get away from all of the strangeness in Palestine. They never really talked much anymore.

Diana finally broached the taboo subject of Matthew. Richard had made good on his promise to disown his daughter, going so far as to stop child support.

Lately Diana and her daughter were more like two residents of the same house, rather than a family.

Karen frowned and looked up from her dessert. She stared around the dim restaurant before returning to her apple pie *a' la mode*.

"Is something wrong?" Diana asked the next time her daughter began searching the shadows.

"Huh?" Karen jerked, absently rubbing at goose bumps on her arms. "Nothing. Maybe talking about Matthew and Dad is making me jumpy."

Karen leaned forward, a conspiratorial smile on her face. "Did you know that Laina is pregnant?"

Wow. Diana stared at her daughter, her fork raised halfway to her mouth.

Karen smirked and took a sip of her soda.

"Dad refused to claim the baby, so she and Sherry are going to raise it together."

Double wow. Speaking of odd families. It was time to deal with her own. "Karen, its time you told me what's going on."

Diana aimed the Mom-Knows-All smile with deadly accuracy. "You can't lie worth a flip. So spill it."

Karen looked down at her empty dessert plate, looking a little green around the gills. She took a sip of her soda and finally heaved a sigh.

"I'm a terrible person."

Used to the dramatics, Diana reserved judgment for after the confession.

"I hurt my best friend and now I don't know how to find him because there's a psycho killer after the wolven."

"He? *What psycho killer?*"

Karen took another shaky drink of her soda.

"Brandon ran away right before last period today."

"I thought Bradley was your boyfriend." The feeling of uneasiness that had plagued her came back with a vengeance, making her slightly nauseous. *"What psycho killer?"*

"The one that is killing strays that come into the pack's, uh, Adam's territory."

"Does he know about this?"

Karen nodded, looking pretty sick herself.

"And Brandon?"

Karen shrugged and grabbed her cloth napkin to wipe at her red watery eyes. "Bradley dropped me off at your office and went to look for him."

"Are you sure that you're the one he's upset at? Maybe something else is bothering him."

"I told him that he needed to see a counselor."

Karen told her about the confrontation with the teenage werecoyotes. Her stranglehold on the poor cloth napkin would have shredded the cheap paper kind.

The world had a nice faraway feeling. Diana wasn't drunk, but the two glasses of wine and the information overload had definitely done a number on her. "I think I may need a counselor," Diana mumbled and rubbed her forehead. "Let's go home. There's a certain fuzzy backside I need to chew out."

Karen gave a faint smile at the weak joke as they got up to pay the bill and leave. Outside, Diana settled the duster around her shoulders, inhaling the smell of it.

"It sure did get dark fast." Karen plucked at the duster. "This is great. But isn't it hot?"

"A little." Diana admitted. She opened her purse to dig for her keys. "I'm kind of hoping to see Chase and Tank again."

Karen gave her a funny look. She rubbed her arms again, glancing around the shadowy parking lot.

"But what about Adam?"

"What about him?" Diana looked up from her purse. "Oh! I don't know." She fished out the keys and gave a general wave in the air. "Everything is just so … crazy. It's like I'm connected to them all. But then again, I'm just some busybody lady who's the mom of Bradley's girlfriend."

And she'd had sex with him twice. Sort of.

Diana sighed and slumped.

"And Adam makes me *so* … *so* ... did you know he's enlisted Bob Benedict in his cause for me to date him? He's insane."

"Is that a good insane or a bad insane?" Karen looked hopeful.

Was her daughter looking for a surrogate father?

Adam's sexy, bossy image flashed through her mind. For some strange reason she could see him taking Karen to the annual Father-Daughter dance. She laughed the image away and answered honestly.

"I truly don't know. Don't tell him, but I think the hairball is growing on me."

"You know Mom? I don't think anyone but you could call Adam Weis Fido, fuzzy, or a hairball and get away with it."

"You think so?"

Karen nodded. Her features were soft and thoughtful in the dim lighting. They reached Diana's Cavalier and parted to get in on each side. Karen paused at the end of the trunk to share a smile with her mother.

"I'd bet the bank on it, Mom."

"Think you'd bet your life on it?" A gravelly voice cut into their conversation. The dark form of a tall man grabbed Karen from behind. She jerked up straight, her eyes wide with fear.

The silver teeth of a hunting knife glinted in the dim parking lot light. The blade pressed at Karen's throat.

Diana lunged forward, not thinking of anything but getting to her daughter. The knife flicked forward at her face.

"Ah-ah-ah," the man sing-songed. He was a dirty specimen of a biker. The kind that lived in old Mad Max movies. His greasy hair hung around a long, thin face covered in a patchy beard. He bared teeth that Diana expected to be broken and rotten, but were movie star straight, if dingy. His breath was soured beer and old cigarettes.

Dog, the werewolf who'd tried to rape her, breathed a nauseating, ghostly shudder down her spine.

"Hands up bitch, or I'll go ahead and skin your pup now."

Fear and rage coiled into a fierce ball in Diana's middle. Strength rushed through her.

He wasn't going to let Karen go. Diana felt his determination to kill. The hate that lived in him, reached out to touch her with slimy tentacles.

The knife was still closer to her than to Karen, if only by inches. He held her daughter against him. His hand gripped her hair.

Diana lunged while he was still spread thin, stretched between them.

Her hand closed around the wrist holding the knife, forcing him to relinquish control of either Karen or the knife.

He let go of her daughter, just as she figured he would. The attacker bore down on Diana. She hit the gravel hard. Rocks pierced her knees. She fought with both hands to get the knife in her possession.

"Run!" Diana screamed. Or tried to when the sound cut short as his fist collided with her jaw.

Her head swam in a splotchy underwater. She felt her grip loosen.

"Nnnn," she groaned.

Burning fire slid into the top of her breast.

"Mommy!"

"Get the keys." The gravely voice coughed in Diana's ear. "Stupid bitch."

Pain radiated through her body pounding in the beat of a drum. The world spun as she was jerked upright by one arm and shoved against the side of the car. She had to stay conscious for Karen's sake.

Keep Karen safe. That was her mantra.

"Get in and drive or I'll finish her off now."

Karen got into the front seat while the man shoved Diana into the back.

She tried to pay attention as the car vibrated to life, but mostly conserved her strength while trying to figure a way out of this mess.

The sensation of her lung filling with something other than air, began to intrude on the throbbing burning pain in her chest. Diana choked and coughed.

"Where are we going?" The sound of Karen's high thready voice gave Diana something to focus on.

"Shut up. I'll tell you were to go," the man rasped, coughing a dry smoker's cough. A rustle, a brief flare, and the rancid odor of cheap cigarettes wafted in the car.

Diana prayed to God that someone had seen them in the parking lot and called nine-one-one. Her next hope was Adam.

She tried to concentrate, to send a message, the feeling of danger to her wolves. A pothole jarred the car, sending pain throughout her body. Her concentration scattered. She choked again, and sputtered, and coughed again.

Chapter Nineteen

Adam walked to the back of the house, entering through the kitchen and dropped his load on the table.

"Hey! Anybody home?"

He didn't' see Bradley's truck or sense anyone, but called out anyway. It seemed the thing to do since he was late getting in.

Probably everyone was at the Ridley house. He'd thought about going out there while at the grocery store, the feeling that he needed to check up on his females ate at him.

He thought about the migraine that had sent Mack home and to bed. A bloody migraine, his friend called it. The kind the psychic occasionally got when he had a bad premonition, seeing, or whatever the hell the man called it.

Whatever the images, they were bad enough that they had to be pieced together, instead of viewed as a whole.

One of the reasons Mack wasn't in active service anymore was that sometimes he randomly experienced someone's death before it happened. Sometimes the psychic was able to track down the designated dying in time. Sometimes not.

Seeing Mack go through that much suffering on someone else's behalf made Adam respect the man like no one else. It also put him on edge.

Who was the target? Him?

Not so far fetched an idea with everything that was going on.

Mack assured him that it was no one the psychic knew.

What was it like to know someone was about to die? That you might be able save them if you could find them in time?

How did you choose who to save? Should you try? Or was it messing with the natural order of things?

Adam ditched the philosophy since he was one of the saved.

He paced across the kitchen.

Where was everyone? He checked the fridge for notes and found none. He concentrated on Diana Ridley, his biggest frustration.

He imagined they were at Diana's enjoying homemade lasagna. She was having Italian food tonight, planned specially to exclude him. It was either a feeling he gathered from her, or he was being particularly paranoid because of Mack.

Either way, he picked up the phone and dialed her number. After four rings, the answering machine picked up.

"Diana? You know, using caller ID to avoid me is cowardly." He took a calming breath. No sense in *totally* pissing her off. Again.

"Look, I'm just trying to locate the boys. It's a school night and no one's here." He felt so stupid rambling on like an idiot to her answering machine. "Are you sure you're not there? Because-- *Beep!*"

His time was up. Briefly, he debated calling back, but decided against it. If she were there, one of the boys would have interceded to let him know where they were.

The wolf inside him strained, unhappy with his conflicted feelings. He needed to pace, to run, to find the answer. Mara, Paul's mate, always said that he needed to embrace being two halves of a whole. He was both wolf and man.

Instinct told him there was trouble in the air. The man, having female troubles, second-guessed his feelings. He took a deep breath and reached deep inside himself to find that he was still conflicted.

Trying to follow the threads of his pack was useless. He ran into walls everywhere. Bradley, Brandon, and Diana, his touchstones had blocked him out again. Thin, faint ghost trails mixed in the personalities that made up his pack.

Not for the first time, Adam wondered if one of Garrick's wardens still lived to cause him trouble. Would they still be connected enough to the boys to be part of the pack fabric?

Sometimes, if there was a strong enough attachment to someone when a wolf transferred, a ghost thread, a faint bond formed in the pack fabric to the loved one left behind.

Could the blood shared with Diana create a pack link to the strays? Dozens of questions with no answers circled his brain.

Forget it. He was Wolven. Head alpha. Canis Pater of his own pack. He'd follow instinct and hunt down his pack, every last member, be they supernatural or human. Those bound by blood to the pack would *have* to answer his Call.

Adam shoved the gallon of milk in the fridge. His cell phone rang, making him jump and bang his head. He scowled, a little embarrassed and thankful no one was around to see his blunder.

He grabbed the offending gadget from his belt and looked at the ID and blinked.

He shouldn't be surprised. Why shouldn't the very psychic he'd just planned to aggravate call him? Adam pressed the answer key with his thumb.

"Hey, Mack. Feeling any better?"

"Hey, yourself. I'm better."

Adam felt a little better about almost Calling the pack with Mack's health improved. Not that Mack had anything but unofficial ties to the pack. Ties bound in blood one dark night, when he tried to trade his human life in place of Adam's on Garrick's claws. Mack survived the massive damage done by the werewolf attack, barely.

For distracting Garrick and saving his life, Adam shared his blood with the psychic. Considering the severity of the injuries, wolven blood was the only medicine that would have worked.

Mack Spencer would have been dead before an ambulance arrived. Even then, the psychic had been restricted to bed rest for two weeks.

The careful tone of Mack's voice alerted Adam that something wasn't quite right.

"Anyway, I had this urge to run back out to the job and make sure our vandals didn't show back up."

Urge. The fine hairs on the back of Adam's neck stirred. Psychics don't get urges, Mack once said, unless it's about food or sex. They get premonitions.

"Did our hot wiring hounds show back up?"

"Not the hot wiring kind. A couple of the bike riding variety. They want to talk to the Canis."

"I'm on my way."

"Good. Because, I finally put together that puzzle."

Positive that middle-schoolers on bicycles weren't waiting for him, Adam slammed the door behind him, already on his way to the truck.

He remembered Diana's injuries and the type of medicine used to heal them. A territorial growl rumbled from his chest. If those strays so much as laid a paw on another one of his people, he'd rip their throats out.

He knew the strays dispatched with the other members of the gang. That much he'd gotten from a brief handwritten message found in the mailbox. The strays promised no trouble while they were in the area. The scents around the box and on the note matched those Diana had carried that night.

Despite the promise, Adam didn't feel comfortable with the remaining two members of the Hell Hounds running around his territory.

The Hellhounds weren't a pack. They weren't a single gang. They were nomadic animals with no loyalty to any pack, forming small groups simply because hunting with a group was easier than hunting alone.

He was about to find out if he could hold a territory and his choice of mate without any wardens.

Adam tried to reach out to his pack members without using the call. Everywhere he searched, he met a blocked tension that heightened his anxiety.

A pain lanced through his chest. Adam gasped and nearly plowed into the back of the car in front of him. Fear and determination flowed from Diana as the shield around her emotions weakened and dissolved. The sensations he received from her weren't overpowering. They were surprising and muffled.

Adam pushed down the panic that threatened to overwhelm him. She was in danger. Hurt. She needed him.

Think. Where would she have gone?

He dialed her home number again and got the answering machine.

"Diana, call me on my cell as soon as you get this message. It's important."

He pushed the end button, spying the red Ranger truck Bradley drove. Sure enough the teen was at the wheel, his pack brothers crammed inside the cab with him.

Adam flashed his lights and laid on the horn. He didn't care who he annoyed on the street.

Adam slowed while Bradley made a U-turn and pulled in behind him. With a hand wave out the window, he signaled for them to follow.

Did he just get a truckload of teenagers for backup? A sixteen-year-old with a brand new license was the oldest of the lot.

There was no help for the cramp in his abdomen, or the situation. He consoled himself with the knowledge that at least he knew where the boys were. He could send them off with Mack if things got too rough.

Adam sped down the rutted, unpaved subdivision road to the end, where two motorcycles gleamed under the yellow yard lights mounted in the front yard. After the break in and vandalism, Adam was making it a policy to have his properties well lit at all times. The red Ranger pulled in beside him.

Four teens spilled out of the truck as Mack and the two leather clad strays stepped out of the house. One of the strays was dark-skinned, often called African American by humans, or simply black. Supernaturals didn't make racial distinctions. Their prejudices were species orientated.

The other male was as golden as his companion was dark. The coppery scent of old blood hung in the air. Even injured, both wolven strays would be formidable in a fight.

In the moment it took for Adam to size up the males, Bradley went for full attack mode. The teen's claws ran out to full dueling claws. His face contorted, lengthening into a muzzle full of sharp predator's teeth before he hit the blond biker. The shit was about to hit the fan.

Chapter Twenty

"Bradley!" Adam yelled. "Down!"

Everyone moved back, the dark biker included. Soon Adam had the pup pulled off the man. The blond biker's eyes gleamed red in the lights, but he was calm. Adam noted the blond male held Bradley off with human hands.

Adam shook his pup hard by the scruff of the neck, rattling teeth, and then let the boy's feet touch the ground. His hand remained on Bradley's neck.

Emotion ran high in his little pack. The other three boys took their cue from the eldest, shuffling their feet and shooting angry glances in the strays' direction.

"All of you calm down."

Adam turned an authoritative eye on the two outsiders.

"Now. What are you still doing in my territory?"

His fingers gripped reflexively when Bradley lunged again. The boy didn't get to lean more than a few inches forward.

Really, the kid was going to have to cut this alpha wanna-be shit out until he had more muscle to back the attitude. A faint smile twitched around Adam's mouth at boy's tenacity. He arched an eyebrow at the strays, waiting for an answer.

The dark one responded with a nod, an autocratic mien that made the hackles rise on the back Adam's neck. He narrowed his gaze on the male. Mack took the opportunity to move closer to the younger boys.

"Show 'em, Tank," the blond male said.

Tank responded by pulling his tee shirt out of the leather jeans. A white bandage marred the dark definition of his exposed belly.

Several were pink and fading, or darkening to his normal skin tone, healing wounds. Obvious claw marks, scraped the length of his body from his armpits to his waist. Dueling wounds received from the teeth and claws of other supernaturals and silver healed at a slower rate than normal injuries.

Tank peeled away the white square, revealing a raw ragged wound, still red and weeping around the clotted blood. Neat, even stitches kept the five-inch opening in his belly closed. Someone or something had twisted and yanked on the weapon, doing as much damage as possible. A human in Tank's place would likely have been dead.

"Man! Don't that hurt?" Rick's accented voice was laced with awe, despite the pup's bored drawling of words.

"Course it hurts you idiot." Seth gave his pack brother a light shove, but the boy's tone was neutral. His dark brown eyes were fixed on Adam as they waited for the alpha's decision.

He felt Bradley's focus also shift from the strays to himself.

"Tank got that when we stopped to help a human on the highway. A psychic."

The blond male looked Adam full in the eyes. He seemed to come to a decision within himself. He dropped his gaze to a more neutral, less aggressive, spot, giving the local Canis the respect of his station.

"The name's Chase. This pin cushion--" he pointed a thumb at the darker male--"is Tank."

Both males kept a close eye on the pack and Mack while managing relaxed, unthreatening, postures. Which Adam knew from past experience, was more difficult than it looked. Quite a feat for a couple of strays, bitten ones at that.

"Anyway, we were at some dive, on our way out of the territory. We stopped for a beer and to shoot the breeze about where to head to next. This guy came up needing a hand with his bike. The dude reeked of psychic, so we decided help out."

"And being the helpful kind of guys you are, you just jump up to go fix it, huh?" Mack's expression said he thought otherwise.

Chase shrugged.

"He was pretty rank looking. But hey, we've been on the other side. So what the hell?"

Chase smirked as he confirmed his bitten status. Being bitten was the wolven equivalent of being born out of wedlock. There wasn't the stigma there once was, but it still raised a few eyebrows from the old school.

"Besides, there's nothin' more pitiful than a broke down biker that can't fix his own ride."

The blond male grinned, obviously more impressed with his humor than anyone present.

Adam shook his head, disgusted. His hand dropped away from Bradley as he turned toward his truck.

"I don't have time for this." He turned to Mack and the boys. "It's time to hunt. If anyone's got a clue where to look for Diana, spill it."

He didn't want the strays in on his pack problems, but he felt her fading. He wasn't going to lose her like Amanda. This time if he failed, he'd lose a lot more than his pride. He'd probably loose a good chunk of his heart.

"Adam, wait. Let's hear them out." Mack looked at the strays, but through them, as well. His voice was distant, caught between here and wherever his gifts took him.

"No. We've got to go." He too was torn between places. The line he associated with the female psychic was unraveling, slowly but surely.

"Adam!"

"Canis!" Mack and the dark stray called at Adam's retreating back.

He didn't know where to find her. If he'd been more persistent, convinced her to accept him as a bonded mate, then he'd be able to track her now using the mate's bond.

"Canis! The human who stabbed me knew what he was dealing with. He thought to surprise me while my brother was occupied with repairs."

"Adam, it's your girlfriend. She's in a car with the killer."

Adam turned, suddenly furious at Mack.

"You knew. You've been seeing her," he accused. His fists balled as he walked back to the psychic. "Where is she? So help me God ...."

The psychic should have been afraid of the angry wolven approaching him. Instead, he looked sympathetic. Damn the irritating, *human*, bastard.

"I've never met her. You were courting her, so I've kept my distance."

"Kept your distance?" He snarled. Jealousy and impotence fueled the fires of his rage. "How the hell do you keep your distance from someone you've never met?"

Mack was calm.

"I know how to find my own kind, Adam."

The two strays growled. Mack glanced their way. Some kind of undercurrent passed between them, then the psychic focused back on Adam.

"She's not dead yet. While there is life, there is hope."

"What the hell does that mean? I need details to find her, not platitudes," Adam growled.

"Heads up, Canis. You're about to get more company."

Chase nodded at three sets of approaching headlights turning into the subdivision, bouncing down the road toward them. The thump-thump of their speakers beat the air before the sound reached their ears.

Neon lights glowed under the vehicles, outlining two low-rider trucks and a car.

"It appears you could use some assistance, Canis."

Tank moved to stand beside Adam. A protective growl trickled from Bradley.

"It's that coyote Nick and the rest of his werejackasses." The boy slipped in front of Adam directing his comment to his alpha.

Despite Bradley's unexpected defense, Adam moved the boy aside to confront the stray himself. Again he was struck at the incongruity of the leather-clad biker with highbrow speech and manners.

"Thanks for the offer, but no." His pack, his business.

A chorus of high-pitched howls rose in the tree line behind the house. From the road, the stenciling, *Bite the Hand that Feeds You*, of the first truck became clear. Appropriate for coyotes.

Beside him, Bradley, and the other boys, froze. Wary nervousness rolled from them. Not outright fear, not yet, but soon.

"Oh, shit," muttered Rick, "it's Benj."

Now, Adam smelled fear. And he didn't like that this Benj brought it to his pack. A growl slipped from his throat.

"Where's Brandon?"

He hadn't had a chance to ask before and hadn't been too worried since Bradley didn't appear to be. Brandon tended to disappear when he felt pressed and Adam had been more concerned with Diana's disappearance.

"I was looking for him when we passed you."

Bradley stared into the dark behind the house, as glued to the imminent approaching coyotes as his pack brothers.

Benj. The werecoyote leader Adam had been putting off meeting. Most likely, the coyote was another friend of Garrick Moser. Trust that sick individual to make a deal with weres. Adam had a real good guess who this Benj was.

"If they wish to fight, Pater Canis," Tank said, ever so carefully. "The coyote pack stands to gain your human ally for their own. Then how will you find your injured female? The young ones ...."

"Will fight," Bradley interrupted. Fire and venom laced his words. "Those bastards won't touch what's ours."

Adam was outnumbered. The approaching vehicles braked in the drive, spitting dirt and gravel everywhere. The coyotes hidden in the dark had the wind with them. By the sound of them, they outnumbered a good-sized wolven pack of twenty.

"What do you want?" The time for negotiations was gone, wasted on petty jealousy.

"A place in your pack, Pater Canis." Tank used the formal title again, pointing out Adam's responsibility as Pack Father. The honorary felt weighted, more significant to him, as the boys' guardian.

"Now wait a minute," Chase's voice rose with indignation. Tank waved his companion to silence. Adam hushed Bradley with a hand on his shoulder. The boy's jaws snapped together with an audible click.

"Quiet, brother. It is time we belonged."

Chase scowled and crossed his arms. He nodded once, put out, but not about to let Tank enter into an agreement without him.

"You are in dire need of wardens. Consider the coming confrontation our interview."

"Done."

Adam gave his back to the vehicles. He turned to face the coyotes he scented coming from the woods. The youngsters sitting in their vehicles held no threat for him.

Shadows slunk into the next cleared lot. The little bit of light was enough to see coyotes. Smaller than wolven in animal form, half the size of Adam's animal form, the coyotes were still larger than their true animal cousins.

They stopped about a hundred feet away.

The biggest of them changed first. Bones shifted, popped and moved under the half-coyote form. Fur receded like water into a vaguely human physique. The elongated muzzle shrank. Claws became hands. Normal hair returned onto the man's perfectly average body, toned without being muscular.

As a human, the coyote leader was unassuming. At least a couple of decades older than himself, Adam guessed. The coyote had medium length hair, probably reddish brown with a sprinkling of premature gray, considering the werecoyote's longevity. Wolven night vision, while excellent, did not pick up color very well.

The coyote seemed to be waiting for something. His followers ranged around him in animal form, looking to their leader for guidance. He spread his hands out in a gesture of peace, a conciliatory smile gracing his plain features.

Adam felt the shift from fear to guilt in his pack. Whatever the boys failed to tell him, it was too late now. Finding out at the last minute seemed to be a trend with the boys.

"I am Benjamin Gates." The coyote's voice was his one distinguishing feature, a rich deep baritone. "You must be Adam Weis. My friends call me Benj."

Adam crossed his arms over his chest and waited, his demeanor as icy as his pale coloring. After a few moments of Adam's silence, the coyote faltered.

"I've heard of *you*, Weis. Garrick and his wardens were no small feat to defeat."

Bradley moved from his place behind Adam to where his pack brothers closed ranks. The older males moved in a protective circle around the boys, yet not so close that they'd be tripped up in a fight.

"However," Benjamin continued, recovering his earlier confidence, "You are new to the area, so I understand that you don't quite understand how things work around here."

Adam cocked an eyebrow.

"Or perhaps," he said with fake surprise, "you didn't receive my message. You see, these are *my* running grounds you are trespassing on."

Adam's tone was bored. His expression was unimpressed in the face of the twenty some-odd werecoyotes. "And here I thought my name was on the deed. I'm sure my lawyer notified you. He's very thorough."

"No!"

The werecoyote's eyes gleamed red in the night. His anger rolled across the field, the scent bitter, triggering a rush of territorial heat in the wolven. Adam kept his features bored, though he wanted to run the intruders off of his property. The irrational coyote leader headed the top of his list.

"This place is mine! These woods have been in my pack for over two hundred years!"

"Then you should have paid your taxes."

Adam had bought the land for a song by paying off the back taxes. He'd also thought the property would be good to run, but the proximity of two hospitals and a funeral home was too close.

It never failed to surprise him what humans tolerated.

For most supernaturals, especially the more long-lived ones, death was abhorrence. Sickness, triggered latent instincts used for pruning the weak and the sick from the herd.

In the end, Adam decided to break the land up for subdivisions and use the profit for the boys' college. He'd buy cleaner running grounds later. For now, he alternated between using the forested Dogwood Park and about a hundred and fifty acres owned by an out of town businessman.

It was too bad for the coyotes that their leader had mismanaged their inheritance. The coyote's loss turned into a good financial move for the wolven pack.

Gates snarled. His average features twisted into a more sinister visage.

"You are the interloper here, wolf. I've tolerated your kind long enough already. Time to pay up. On my terms."

Adam sensed the boys freeze behind him. There was a silent expectancy in the fabric of the pack while they waited for his answer.

"You were the one defaulted on your taxes. I've got the receipts and the deed of transfer. I don't owe you a thing."

Curiously, the coyotes didn't attack. In Adam's place, with the superior numbers, he would have gone on the offensive.

He didn't know what to expect from werecoyotes. He'd never dealt with them before, as wolven didn't allow the presence of other shape shifting supernaturals in their territory. Another mark in Garrick's offense.

Gates stalked closer, anger and frustration palpable. His coyotes shifted, tuned into their leader's agitation, but stayed where they were. Low growls filled the night.

Gates stopped out of Adam's immediate reach.

"I could have you torn to bits, boy. I've got this town wrapped up from city board members all the way down to dealers." Spittle flew in Adam's direction.

"You think you're a builder? Your high dollar Dallas references don't mean squat. All I need is to say the word and your piddley little business dries up." Adam's smile was grim. "Get off my property *were*. Better yet, out of my territory."

The werecoyote lunged, changing back into his coyote form. He was fast and clever. Adam was quicker.

Gates' forward motion ended in an abrupt drop on his butt. Adam stood over him, three inches of lethal dueling claws extended. Four red lines gaped across Gates' chest. The aroma of fresh blood scented the air as rich rivulets ran down his torso.

Adam snarled at the coyotes, daring them to intercede. He backed away, allowing Gates to stand. Inside, the wolf snapped and snarled, wanting the kill.

As bad an idea it was, Adam didn't have the heart to kill him, especially in front of the boys. He held a tight leash on thousands of years of instinct bred to defend what belonged to him.

Magic, power leaked around his control, spilling into the air. Someone, he didn't know who, wolf or coyote, whimpered in response.

"Get off my property." Adam repeated. "Unless, anyone else wants to dispute me?"

His question was a statement, a challenge to the werecoyotes. All eyes stared past him to his pack. Behind him, the two strays had changed for dueling. Mack held a couple of very sleek handguns.

Gates gave a bark toward the low rider vehicles. The group of coyote teens, having left the safety of their vehicles, scrambled back inside.

"Guns aren't allowed in a challenge duel."

Gates had the audacity to look affronted. Adam nearly laughed. Instead he curled his lip, exposing the sharp length of his canines.

"Duel? You are not wolven."

The click of Mack's guns, readying for a confrontation drove home Adam's point. Wolven did not extend the privilege of their laws to other weres.

"We had an agreement with the old wolf leader." Benjamin Gates sounded desperate. He needed something from the wolves. "I'll tell you what, we share the territory and I'll share the profits from my businesses. I'm diversified, you could say."

"I'll tell you what *were*." It had changed so much, Adam's voice was a deep growly bass. "In case you missed the obvious, I'm not Garrick Moser. And I don't share …" Adam flashed his canines. His clawed hands flexed with restrained power, "… *Anything*."

Chapter Twenty-One

The world drifted in a surreal haze of pain. Diana was no doctor, but she knew that something was wrong. She shivered with a cold awareness that cold was a bad thing.

Her front and hands were covered in sticky cooling liquid. Blood. Her blood. Alarm skittered through the haze.

Think calm. Don't panic. Got to help Karen. Make sure the bad guy doesn't hurt her.

Breathing hurt. Diana tried to take a breath around the pain in her chest, but couldn't get air in right.

Thinking was hard. A plan. Diana needed a plan. A simple one.

She knew she might have one chance for Karen to get away. All she had to do was save her strength and hold out long enough until they stopped.

She eyed the sagging seat belt that the man shrugged behind him.

Karen complained constantly that the high riding seatbelt choked her. The belt caught over the narrow top of the Cavalier's passenger bucket seat. The man settled sideways to keep an eye on Karen.

"Turn here," he directed in a raspy voice.

Diana eased up, carefully, thankful for the dark interior.

Shallow breaths, she reminded herself when she nearly choked.

"Why are you doing this?" The angry thunk of Karen's fist against the steering wheel sounded loud in the car.

Good girl. Diana cheered silently. Don't show him any fear. That's what he wants.

"Fucking werewolf whelp. Shut up!"

Please, please, please don't set him off. Diana pleaded silently with her daughter. She was too weak to shield herself. The man's anger and madness were knives that beat inside her brain.

"You werewolves think you're so special."

The man fumbled a bit, one handed, producing a cigarette lighter that flared briefly. Diana glimpsed the shine off of the tip of the serrated hunting knife he held at Karen. The blade was dark with her blood.

Smoke curled in the interior, acrid, making Diana cough.

"Mom?"

Karen's voice rose and hitched.

"Shut up and drive."

"What did we ever do to you?"

He laughed. It was an awful sound, like a rusty saw blade, all sharp, jagged, and filthy evil.

"Animals. You dress up in human clothes and pretend you're not an animal. But I know. Grady Dobbs sees the beast inside."

He gestured with the bloody knife.

"Turn here. You and your mom thought you could trick me. But I saw it in you anyway."

"I know this place." Karen's voice was a whisper. "Not here."

"Yeah. Fitting ain't it? Does your mom know? I bet she does. Animal."

"Stop in front of the waterfall. That way when you Change, you'll already be in place for your *boyfriends.*" He spat the last word at Karen. "Both of them, to find you. I guess horny teenagers are all the same, whatever the breed."

"But I didn't--"

"Shut up and get out wolf slut. And don't try running off. I'm a tracker. The Dobbs are all trackers. Big game hunting runs in the family."

He laughed that evil sound again.

"How do you think I found your cozy little den in the first place?"

Karen's fear and worry spurred Diana's adrenaline, giving her a boost of strength.

Karen opened her door, bringing in the smell of cool water. The overhead dome light was bright. Diana lowered her eyelids, trying to look out from under her lashes.

She only had one chance to help her daughter escape. No re-dos.

Karen looked over the seat and gasped. Horrified.

"Mom."

Run baby, please run, she urged.

"Get out, bitch. Or I'll finish her now."

Diana slapped the door lock down with one hand. She grabbed the seat belt, slipped it over the man's head with the other. She pulled the slack tight with her failing strength.

"Run!"

Her scream was a garbled croak. The emotional, psychic, scream she slammed at her daughter made Karen stumble back.

Grady Dobbs bucked and fought the seatbelt. He stabbed backward, over his shoulder, with the knife, missing Diana by scant fractions. The spiked studs on his wristband scraped her cheek.

Diana held on as tight as she could, twisting it around her wrist until the circulation stopped. The seatbelt became a noose.

She grabbed the man's greasy ponytail. She wrapped that into her trembling fist. The seat rocked, slamming against her. The knife flailed blindly, knocking against the car ceiling.

She was dying anyway. Karen said she knew these woods. Her daughter could still get away.

Karen screamed. Loud and long.

Run, Karen, run. Run. Run. Run. Diana chanted the words in her head, a mantra to pace herself by as the darkness crowded back in.

An explosion burst the glass inward, showering both their attacker and Diana. She jerked forward, and then slumped down, into Hell, where the tormented screamed for mercy and received none. The screaming followed her into the darkness.

Chapter Twenty-Two

Brandon blinked awake and froze, attuned to the nuances of his surroundings. He turned an ear toward the mouth of his cave and listened for the sound that disturbed him.

He was a coward and a sorry excuse for a wolf. The fact that he was hiding from not just the coyotes, but also his own pack, proved the point.

He didn't want to find out Adam's price for peace and he wouldn't let himself be sold to the coyotes as fresh meat again. The coyote pack was bigger than the wolven and a lot inbred. Their females were mean bitches, especially in their first heat.

Brandon knew that personally. He definitely didn't want a repeat with two of Benj's females coming in season. The idea of breeding with the coyote females made him sick at his stomach.

God. What if he got one of them pregnant? He shuddered, glad he hadn't eaten or he might throw up. Would he be forced to stay with the coyotes for a moon? Or longer this time?

No. It wasn't happening. They'd have to find him first, and he'd leave before they found him. He might be a coward and an omega, but he wasn't going to be coyote meat.

The shine of headlights and scent of exhaust fumes shook him from the memory. Brandon crept forward and peered out the bushes concealing his cave above the waterfall.

He'd come here because it was safe. He had safe holes all over the territory, but only Bradley and Karen knew about the waterfall cave. The comforting scents of his brother and friend lingered here.

He considered taking off for one of the other safe holes when the engine shut off and the door opened. The scents of fresh blood and familiarity rose on the wind followed by the stink of an unwashed stranger.

"Run!"

Brandon's supernatural hearing picked up the choked out word.

If there was anything Brandon Starr was familiar with, it was the combined scents of blood, fear, and madness. He froze. Nightmares of Garrick's basement and the blood moon of a coyote hunt swam before his eyes. His bowls quivered in reaction.

Karen's scream shattered the nightmare. Brandon spurred into action. He didn't think about the danger, or being afraid. The monster buried inside of him rattled the bars of its cage.

The girl screamed again. The monster lifted its nose, scented the air for blood and found a bleeding hunter near his lair. The creature inside roared, shattering the cage.

Brandon changed for battle, shifting into the half man-half wolf movie monster and rushed out of the cave. The twenty-foot drop was nothing for an enraged wolven defending its territory. He leapt, landing light on his feet.

Karen screamed again. Brandon howled. He bounded four times, landing to run around the front of the car.

Inside, the knife stabbed downward toward Diana Ridley. The female held particular memories that flashed through the monster. Baking cookies. A hand on the boy's forehead while her face creased with worry over his temperature.

The scent of her blood pounded in his veins. Fury overrode all other thoughts.

With one more snarl, Brandon smashed his claws through the window's flimsy barrier. He ignored the crumbled glass and went for the insane hunter inside, snagging him in a claw. He pulled the screaming man free of the restraint.

"Watch out!"

Brandon caught a glimpse of the knife as it arced down, toward him. The bite of the knife sliced into the meat of his shoulder sharply. Instinct took over.

He went for the kill, burying his fangs wide around the creature's neck. His powerful wolven jaws closed, crushing the fragile human throat. Fresh blood, warm salty, life giving, flowed over his tongue. He swallowed then pressed the carcass of the kill down to feed.

A sound intruded before he could begin his feast. He turned and snarled at the female. Not his mate. He wouldn't share. The predator, finally unleashed from its cage, did not want to give up the prize.

"Brandon?"

The angel's tears penetrated the red haze. He licked his lips, considering what the angel meant.

"Karen."

The wolf's jaw wasn't meant for human words, but he managed. The angel's name brought understanding. His angel knew everything and still cared.

"Karen."

She threw her arms around the breadth of his bloody, furry torso. Brandon bent to wipe his tongue over her cheek. He tasted salt, female sweat, and friend.

"Oh, Brandon! Thank God. You saved us!"

She pushed away from him. He watched, a little confused, as she rushed to the car and climbed over the broken glass in the seat.

"Mom?" Karen sniffed.

Brandon followed, drawn by the scent of blood, vanilla, and citrus. He heard her sob quietly while she crawled into the backseat.

"Oh, God. Brandon. Help me. I think she's dead."

Brandon went around to the other side, the urge to kill and eat gone. The driver's seat folded down and he climbed in. He studied the crumpled form Karen was trying to extricate from the tangle of the seatbelt and move from the floorboard into the back seat. Something he was pretty sure she shouldn't be doing.

"No." He said around his wolfy muzzle. "Not dead. Not yet."

But death was near. He heard the faint struggle of her heart, the choked gurgle as she slowly drowned on her own blood. He'd heard the sound before. Brandon pulled Diana Ridley into his own lap.

"Are you going to …?"

He shook his head. He forced himself to look into Karen's eyes.

"Might not work."

"Try anyway. Try sharing blood in both the wound and making her drink."

"She's already drowning on her blood."

It didn't matter. Brandon tore at his wrist with his teeth. It hurt badly, but he'd had worse. The magic that lived in his wolven blood was stronger in this form, maybe that would be enough for Diana Ridley to live.

"Brandon, are you sure this won't hurt her more? I mean, she's already had blood once from those strays. Would too much hurt her?"

He concentrated on his task, carefully tending to the gaping chest wound first, then trying to get Diana Ridley to swallow the rivulets he dribbled into her mouth.

He spoke slowly around his muzzle so that Karen understood everything.

"You are my friend. I would die rather than hurt you."

He reopened the wound on his wrist and switched from feeding to the wound. He hoped that his blood directly in her bloodstream would speed the process of healing.

Or it might throw her body into some kind toxic shock and kill her.

"She dies, Karen. The hospital is forty-five minutes away. Maybe my blood will heal her enough to stay alive."

"Will it change her?"

He shook his head a tiny bit. "No more than already done by werewolf bite."

Brandon remembered the night the strays brought Ms. Ridley home. Bradley had been furious. The females were under their protection, ever since they met Karen. She was special, so was her mom.

They'd kept Garrick away from the psychics for years, only to have Diana leave with a human date and come back werewolf bit and smelling of the blood of strays. Bradley had nearly been insane over it. Adam, too.

He started to feel the effects of his own blood loss and stopped. She'd had enough to replace what was lost, and more.

"I think it's beginning to work."

Karen's worried gaze met his.

"She feels warmer."

Karen's hands fluttered over her mother's face. She checked the chest wound before tearing off her blouse for a compress. This would work, she told herself. She'd seen it done before wolven injuries. She'd heard of one human, near dead, stabilized with wolven blood.

It would work.

"Now what?"

Bradley wadded the stray's coat up into a pillow and situated Ms. Ridley so that she wouldn't choke any more than necessary when she started coughing out the blood in her lung.

Mack had had a hell of a time with the coughing, but the man's lungs had only received minimal damage, Brandon remembered. Garrick's claws had ripped open Mack's abdomen, then he had nearly chewed his arm off at the shoulder.

The man's total recovery was due to Adam sharing his blood as soon as he saw the man lived. Then Adam continued treatment over the next couple of days because he couldn't afford to give the psychic too much of his blood in case any of Garrick's followers had escaped to regroup.

"I've got to deal with … *him*." With his muzzle, Brandon indicated the dead man outside the car. "Won't take long. Then we go."

Chapter Twenty-Three

Adam allowed Gates the dignity to regain his feet and walk back to his coyotes.

Another wolven would have finished the coyote leader and been done with it. He wanted to resolve this without his boys witnessing any more violence than necessary.

Gates retreated behind his coyotes. He turned and smiled. Sharp predatory teeth gleamed in the night. Then he lifted his head and howled.

The coyotes leapt up and rushed *en masse* at Adam. Gates hung back, howling while the coyotes attacked.

Two gunshots rang out. Yelps of pain proved Mack's marksmanship.

Two coyotes, in animal form, darted in low at the human's legs.

Tank spun around backward, putting his back to the psychic's. The huge wolven kicked out, knocking one of the coyotes back.

The second coyote, deprived of his first target, jumped. The coyote's aim was aborted with a handful of claws in his belly. Tank wrapped an arm over and around the animal's neck.

The coyote howl was cut off sharply with a crack. It fell in a quivering, dying heap on Tank's boots.

Adam flung himself toward the coyote leader, carving a path through the few coyotes who mustered enough power to half change and stupid enough to step between the charging alpha and his quarry.

A wolven roar of challenge bellowed behind Adam. Scent identified the stray at his back. Two more shots rang out, dropping coyotes.

Adam followed the movement at the edge of his vision. He reacted, but he wouldn't be fast enough.

Rick changed and lunged after a coyote. The coyote turned and snarled, spooking the boy enough to make him falter.

Adam roared. Chase turned and leapt the six feet, landing on top of both the coyote and the boy. He dropped and imbedded his claws and fangs into the coyote's back. He used his teeth to tear out the throat of his prey.

Chase stood, lifting the bleeding, dead carcass over his head. He tossed the useless hunk of meat aside and reached down to grab the boy in one claw.

The blond wolfman glanced in Adam's direction and nodded once. He tucked the squirming protesting boy under one hairy arm. He walked back to the wolven group and dropped his load.

The coyotes' attempted attack fell apart as fast as it started. Benjamin Gates turned tail, literally. He turned, changing and running back into the woods.

One last coyote flung himself at Adam, only to be slapped aside like an annoying gnat, only larger and more persistent. The distraction slowed him down enough for Gates to finish his escape.

The sounds of car doors slamming, and engines turning over, caught Adam's attention. He turned in time to see the coyote young make their escape. The ridiculous overpriced speakers drummed out their retreat.

Bradley and the boys gave a halfhearted chase. They stopped in the middle of the road.

Rick gave a two handed finger salute at the retreating cars. "Yeah! An' don't you be coming' back unless you want some o' dis!"

"Yellow tailed bastards!" Mark yelled. "Run!"

After a few more colorful taunts and threats, the boys trotted back up the drive.

Adam watched the last coyote limp into the darkness. Only a couple had been killed. Those hit by Mack's gunshots wouldn't die. The lead shot was extremely painful, but not life threatening unless one happened to be the fairy type of supernatural.

Adam threw back his head and howled. His silvery fur practically glowed in the moonlight like a ghostly wolf man. The others watched him then joined their voices to his in victory song.

"You howl pretty good for a human," Chase said.

Mack grinned like the devil. Adrenaline still charged through his body. He held up the handguns, one in each hand, and simultaneously flicked the safeties on with ease. Ambidexterity was a good thing in any fight.

"Finally got to shoot someone, eh, Mack?" Adam asked. He resumed his human state.

"Just like old times. Only this time I got to use these babies."

"Yeah, it was weeks before you'd use a nail gun again," Adam jibed. "Too bad framing nails aren't made of silver."

"Yeah. I thought about that the whole time I was laid up after you shoved my guts back in."

Mack tucked the guns in the waistband of his jeans, one in front and one behind his back. His expression turned serious.

"I think I'll pull the silver ammo out until all this blows over."

"Good idea."

The heat of battle was over and the sick dread returned to his stomach. Adam reached for his cell phone, intending to try Diana home number again.

"Do any of you guys know Diana's cell phone number?"

He remembered that someone had mentioned the night she was attacked, her cell phone batteries were dead.

"No. Miz Ridley doesn't like to carry a cell phone. It usually stays turned off in the car." Bradley volunteered. "Karen has one, too, for emergencies."

He gave Adam the number. His brown eyes met Adam's and held.

"Mack said Miz Ridley was with the killer. Karen's with her mom. After I dropped her off, she called me and said they were going out to dinner."

Adam's brows bunched together.

"You've got a phone?"

Bradley shrugged, just the small rise and drop of one shoulder.

"Pay as you go. In case one of the guys or Karen needs me."

Adam nodded. That fit with Bradley's protective instincts. He imagined the boy had gotten the phone long before he had arrived on the scene. Once they were through this, he was going to issue each one of them a cell phone.

Adam dialed Karen's number. After the fifth ring he left a message on her voice mail for her to get back with him ASAP. He left his number in case she didn't remember it. He dialed Diana's home number again with little hope she'd answer.

"I don't suppose you have your brother stashed in a safe place, do you? Studying at the library, maybe?"

He hung up when the answering machine came back on. He'd left enough messages there.

Bradley's vague uncomfortable mutter of, "I'm sure he's okay," snapped Adam's self control. He grabbed the front of the boy's shirt and dragged him up, face to face.

"What do you mean, *I'm sure he's okay?*"

Bradley's eyes flared, angry as he struggled futilely in his alpha's grip.

"What I said! I don't *know* where he is. He ran off."

His voice was hot. Not challenging, but angry, and scared, Adam noted. The fear calmed Adam somewhat, but he still gave the boy a shake for good measure, enough to get the kid's attention, not a teeth rattling one. He set Bradley down.

"I told you to keep an eye on everyone. I *trusted* you to keep them together."

"Adam," Mack interrupted. His voice was calm. Adam could feel the psychic trying to project that calm onto him.

He growled a warning at Mack's interference. Yeah. He knew he sounded harsh to his own ears. Brandon had fewer survival instincts than the humans and the killer was already out there with the females.

Bradley's confession came out in a rush.

"Nick and his brothers stopped Brandon and Karen at school today. She and Brandon had an argument right before that. I don't know what about. She wouldn't tell me." He sounded a bit sullen. "Then the coyotes showed up shooting their mouths off. After I ran them off, we told him that he'd be safe."

Bradley finally took a breath. "He ran anyway."

"God-*damn* it, Bradley." Adam pushed the boy away before he hurt someone.

He dragged in a breath. Held it and let it out slowly. Nope, didn't help. He growled and spoke slowly and succinctly.

"Why did Brandon run off? What was the message you *forgot* to mention to me?"

Bradley swallowed and looked away from Adam's palpable fury.

"The coyotes wanted to cut the old deal with you. No matter what," the boy warned. "I won't let it happen. Sending the message through Brandon was just a way to hurt him more."

Bradley looked back at Adam and something broke inside the boy. The strong twin's grief and pain for his brother, a vulnerability Bradley didn't usually show, touched inside Adam.

The boy was overwhelmed, but determined to carry on.

"What did they want?" Adam prodded.

"They wanted … wanted …." Bradley flushed red. He looked sick to his stomach.

"Good God. Spit it out. What did they want?" Adam's impatience spilled over. He needed to get out of here. Not play catch up.

It was Mark who came to stand beside Bradley. The happy go lucky kid, always on the go in his bright shorts, loud shirt, and surfer haircut laid a hand on his older pack brother's shoulder, in solidarity and comfort. His innocent face hardened with disgust. "Sex."

Mark continued in the adult's stunned silence. Tank and Chase stared. Adam felt he and Mack were beyond any kind of surprise.

"Benj's pack has a couple of females coming into season."

Since none of the adults seemed to be picking up on the revelation, he rolled his eyes, obviously amazed at the collective stupidity on their part.

"*And* they can't just bite someone and make them a werecoyote. *And* Benj's pack has been here for a long time." Mark huffed a sigh. "Damn you people are slow. *And--*"

"They're inbred." Rick finished. He took Bradley's other side. Seth added his support to the group.

Rick's usual accent faded, sounding closer to the other boys'.

"Benj's pack don't breed with nuthin' that ain't supernatural. So, he paid Garrick a percentage of his profits for a wolf to … you know, when a female came into heat."

Rick shrugged. "Didn't happen that often and none of the old pack wouldn't do it without Garrick beating the shit out of them first."

Mark's fair skin burned under the scrutiny. All of the boys fidgeted.

"Last time Benj called in his marker was two and a half years ago."

Adam had trouble breathing. He worked his jaw.

"He's breeding out."

All eyes turned to Chase. He shot a look at Tank.

"Right?"

Tank nodded, a single dip of his aristocratic chin.

"Yes. That would explain his belief that Adam would grant him challenge rights, or give him wolven rights."

Everyone's ears pricked at the dark wolf's logic.

"When a pack acquires a territory, the first move is to clear out all other potential predators. Especially, other shapeshifters. The werecoyotes may be breeding out for protection."

"Basically, the old, *you wouldn't kick out cousin Benj would you?"* Chase clarified. He made a face. "That's just sick."

Tank gave another dip of his chin. Acknowledging both Chase's statements. Wolven did not cross breed with other animals.

Adam watched the boys. More pieces of the puzzle that was his pack, clicked into place.

Rick, physically the smallest and the youngest of the pack sidled closer to Bradley. Seth closed the distance, putting a hand on the smaller boy.

Adam's eyes flicked back to Bradley, whose embarrassment stemmed more from the boy's inability to stop what had happened.

"How long has this been going on?"

"Does it matter?" Mack's question hung in the air until Adam shook his head.

"No." Adam took a breath. He found his center and let it out slowly. The flash of his teeth was grim. "What matters is that I'm going to kill the bastard."

Other things mattered, too. Things he would not voice. That anyone thought him capable of pimping out his kids turned him inside out.

The trust issue was his personal hell. He didn't claim to understand what these boys had survived, but he was tired of paying for Garrick's, and now this Benjamin Gates, crimes.

Cheryl, Adam's mother, had given him a decent semi-normal childhood. After he changed for the first time, she'd come clean about his biological father. Adam still remained in public school at home with the only parents he knew and spent summers with his new wolven family.

With his biological father, Paul, Adam had seen death. He'd handed it out in challenges and territory disputes. He'd had a hunt for Amanda, and killed those who'd killed her. But each atrocity he uncovered of Garrick's left the taste of rotted meat in his mouth and belly.

His head knew why these kids gave trust so sparingly. But his heart and pride had taken one too many hits today.

Adam turned away to collect his thoughts. He needed to find the females. They weren't dead, at least Diana wasn't, not yet. He felt that.

Her weakness pulled at him, verifying that she still lived. He prayed that Karen lived too.

He startled and growled, when the phone in his hand vibrated and trilled a stupid song. He glanced at the ID. The number was unknown.

"Hello." He answered in a flat tone.

"Adam?"

"Brandon! Where the hell are you? I told you to stay close. There's a killer out there."

"Uhhh, not anymore."

"What do you mean, *not anymore*?"

Adam had died and gone to Hell. Because he was sure in his own personalized version, he was doomed to repeat everything that was said to him while his gut clenched alternately in fear and relief.

He stood stunned as Brandon haltingly told him about Diana and Karen's abduction and his own part in the killer's demise.

"We're on our way to her house now. You've got to hurry. I did what I could, but she's hurt bad."

"How bad?"

"Knife in the chest. Lot of blood loss." Brandon paused a moment. His voice was soft. "I gave her some of my blood. She'd bled for a while before I got there. Then before we left I had to clean things up. I couldn't give her anymore or I'd pass out. I might've been too late. I don't know."

What little confidence Brandon had in his actions wavered. He hung up abruptly.

"Well?" Mack asked.

As the only human, he was in the dark, both literally and figuratively. All the sensitive wolven ears had picked up the cell phone conversation.

"Let's go. Someone will explain on the way."

Chapter Twenty-Four

In the corner of the room, as unobtrusively as possible, Brandon watched the stray named Tank tend to Diana Ridley's injuries. Adam frequently came and watched.

The alpha insisted that his own blood be used for her healing until Tank decided that too much supernatural blood might do her harm. Then Adam came in to watch and wait.

Brandon might not have been as disturbed at the whole process if everyone wasn't so *aware* of him. Miz Ridley was the one laid up on the bed with a hole in her chest.

Tank said she'd be all right. Once she finished coughing up the blood in her flooded lung, she'd stop scaring them with those horrible fits.

Adam drifted into the room, again, and watched the bed. Like he had other times, the alpha wandered over to where Brandon sat, back to the corner, with his knees drawn up to his chest.

Adam set his hand on Brandon's head. He felt the alpha finger the strands of his hair before patting his head a couple of times. Then he finally drifted away.

Mack came in a couple of times and stood beside him. The human didn't say anything. He stood there, waiting, watching Miz Ridley's pale form under her pretty blue flowered blanket. Mack left after he began to fidget.

Chase walked in and crouched in front of Brandon. Past experience made him wary. He was beginning to wonder what the older males were up to.

"Hey, kid. Hungry?"

Brandon shook his head no and the stray left. He came back with a Dagwood sandwich, a bag of chips, and a liter soda. The guy didn't go away until Brandon ate the sandwich, the chips, and drank at least half the soda.

The blond man stood, gave him another pat on the head and left with the dishes.

It was freaky. Freaky bothered him enough that he didn't worry as much about the monster being let out of its cage. Freaky alpha type adults made him consider his options.

He knew he had enough supplies stashed for when he made a break for it. Only this time, he wouldn't stick around.

Adam was adding the strays to the pack tonight. Brandon had heard Tank and Chase arguing about that. Chase didn't want to be bound to a pack.

Tank had all kinds of logical reasons why the two strays should stay. Brandon didn't trust the strays and he was just beginning to get used to Adam. Now Adam was making changes, adding others to the pack.

The huge dark skinned man nodded, silently acknowledging the boy's interest in the patient. He moved slowly and deliberately, allowing Brandon see what was done each time he checked the chest wound, or looked into Miz Ridley's eyes with that pencil sized flashlight. Freaky.

The guys were avoiding him. Seth glanced in the room for the third time, obviously intrigued with the wolven doctor. He glanced at Brandon and ducked back out fast. The others had pretty much done the same. Bradley avoided him completely.

It occurred to Brandon that maybe they knew what was up and decided to make a clean break. Besides, what was the loss of the omega wolf anyway?

Brandon got up and eased out of the room, head down in case he ran into someone in the overcrowded house. In his mind he mapped the course and calculated the odds of his escape.

Chapter Twenty-Five

Adam was going insane.

He paced the house and made another check on Diana and Brandon. The kid looked okay. But Brandon had made his first real kill without any guidance. Not an animal, a live sentient creature. A human.

The boy needed to go out for a run. A good long run and hunt for rabbit or some other small game, something right and natural. Killing humans, any two-footed creature, could leave a foul taste on your conscience, a dark smear on your soul. That too was the proper order of things, otherwise everyone, humans and supernaturals alike, would become unremorseful monsters like the one Brandon had killed.

There were a lot of other more pressing needs than a hunt. Unfortunately, Brandon would have to deal with that particular horror a little while longer.

Diana's injury and the safety of the pack came first. For that he left Brandon to his beside vigil, the place Adam would rather stay if his responsibilities had allowed. He finally had everyone under one roof. He wanted to keep them there until he'd bound Tank and Chase to the pack.

His instincts told him to go after the coyotes before they had time to regroup. He was loosing his edge. Here he was pacing the house like some lovesick sad sack and new father, worrying over a new pup. He should be out, *doing something* to secure his territory.

Adam stopped beating himself up to watch Brandon slink down the stairs. He followed the boy into the kitchen. Mark and Rick mumbled in the teenager's general direction and scatted without making eye contact.

"How's it going up there?"

Brandon jumped. His eyes touched on Adam then focused on the linoleum.

"Okay."

"Come sit down. I want to talk."

Brandon froze. He struggled with something inside and glanced at the back door. He looked like a cornered animal.

"I was going to get a breath of air. I'll be back in a few minutes."

Adam smelled the lie and moved to close the distance between them. Brandon erupted into motion. Panic and fear rolled off of the teen. The kid dodged for the patio door, intending to go through the glass. Adam was faster.

He launched into a tackle, rolling to take the brunt of the fall. Brandon changed quickly and smoothly, under his hands and lit into Adam. The boy was a flurry of dark fur and teeth, fighting to get away. Survival at any cost.

Adam growled at the pain and took the damage.

"Cut it out!"

The boy landed a vicious bite on his arm. Adam moved fast to pin Brandon both wrist and neck.

"Damn it! That hurt. What's got into you?"

Underneath him, the boy writhed and growled, trying to escape. Sharp teeth snapped a few inches from Adam's face. He switched his neck pin to include the jaw.

"Stop it. Now." All the authority of the Canis Pater went into the command.

Brandon's attacks ceased. The wolven boy strained against the confinement. Desperation was a bitter aroma in Adam's nose.

He settled his weight solidly. Underneath, the rise and fall of the kid's chest panted out harsh breaths. The boy's furred ears laid flat against his head.

"Shhh. Easy. No one's going to hurt you," Adam crooned and feathered his thumb over the pinned wrist. "Shhh. Don't bite. Look at me, son. Shhh."

"I won't do it." Brandon's voice was muffled. "Lemme up, *please*."

The *please* tore Adam up.

"First tell me what's got you so upset."

"I won't do it. The coyotes. I won't go."

That was the last thing Adam expected. All right, maybe it should have been the first, but for some strange reason he kept assuming his pack would recognize the difference between him and his predecessor.

He let go and sat up. The silent stares of the rest of the pack, the strays included bored into Adam from the doorway. Their lack of trust hurt. The constant waiting for him to screw up hurt more.

He stood up and looked down at Brandon. The boy poised to flee. Adam sighed and shook his head.

"No. You're not going. I'll kill Benjamin Gates for what he's done. But you're free Brandon." Adam waved a hand at the patio door. "Go if you want. I'm not keeping you or anyone else against his will."

Adam ran a hand through his hair. He rested his hand on the back of his neck and looked around the kitchen. The area was trashed. Diana would probably skin him alive for busting up her table.

He turned to walk out. The others moved aside.

"Where are you going?"

Brandon's small voice stopped him. Adam didn't turn around.

"I'm going to find a place to crash for a couple of hours. I'm tired."

Chapter Twenty-Six

Diana blinked awake. She carefully turned her head to look at the light filtering in around the curtains. Apparently, she'd finally mastered the fine art of passing out in her own room and waking up there again.

Sitting up proved exhausting. For her next trick, she was going to try not to pass out again.

How long had she been out?

Snatches of blurred memory came to her. The man at the restaurant parking lot kidnapping them. Wrestling to keep him in the car while Karen escaped.

Karen had to have gotten away and come back. Diana rubbed her fingers against her forehead. She thought one of the boys might have been there but she could be imprinting her time here over their escape.

She pulled down the loose neck of her nightgown. Diana saw the healing wound above her right breast. It had the look of days, maybe even weeks of healing.

The last time she'd woke up remarkably healed, she'd had the same foul taste in her mouth. Like--

No, she really didn't want to make a simile. Anyone who'd bitten her tongue would know what the flavor was. The thought churned her stomach.

The clock said six fifty-eight and the little dot for pm was lit. Diana figured that the way things had been going lately, she should probably spring for one that displayed the date too, for the next time she passed out.

She tried to think of that fairy tale about the guy who slept for so long, maybe a hundred years, but kept mixing it up with Rumplestilskin and the princess who spun gold from hay. Jax, the gnome, would know for certain.

Maybe she would send him an email or something when all this was over.

Diana made a face. Stupid, stupid, stupid. She had enough problems with werewolves, pardon, *wolven*, and assorted fringe psychotics, ah, psychics. She didn't need to drag the fairie realm into the mix, too.

Besides, the gnome expected certain strings if she asked for favors, even knowledge. Diana had reservations enough about dating a werewolf, er, wolven to think about gnomes. She pressed down a shudder. She wasn't prejudiced. She happened to like her men *a lot* taller than gnome sized. Jax made a perfectly sized friend.

She gingerly moved to the side of the bed. Deep in her chest, a warning tickle made her pause so as not to trigger a coughing fit. That would hurt. A lot.

The room spun a little when she stood. She steadied herself on the bed and listened. Were her senses getting better?

Chase, the biker wolf guy, had said females didn't contract lycanthropy because of PMS. Beneficial hormonal surges? Go figure.

She heard something and shuffled to the door to investigate. The hall was no biggie to navigate. Just hold onto the wall and do the geriatric slide to the stairs.

At the stairs, Diana looked down the long bumpy tunnel. It was going to be a bitch. She was already winded.

By holding her breath, she ascertained that people were indeed in the house.

Karen's happy laugh floated up the stairwell, unclenching the painful knot around her heart. She should go down and see with her own eyes that her daughter had made it out all right.

All Diana had to do was make her way down the looong flight stairs and across eternity in the hall to the living room.

In the past few weeks Diana had been chased down by a pack of werecoyotes. She knew that first incident for what it was. She'd been attacked by a gang of biker werewolves, and kidnapped and stabbed by a killer after the werewolves. In each instance one of the supernatural wolves had come to her rescue. And Karen's.

Oh, yeah. And Matthew had taken up with his asshole father for college tuition. But that was on a more personal, sucky, note. Diana decided to shuffle back to the bathroom instead, where she could wallow in private.

Tank materialized in front of her. She sucked in a sharp breath of surprise.

Her eyes watered, her chest itched deep inside. Diana held her breath, hoping not to embarrass herself by hacking up a lung. Finally, she gave in to the cough, grabbing a fistful of the shirt in front of her for support.

Afterward she realized what, *who*, she was hanging onto and couldn't quite seem to let go.

The dark velvety swells and plains of Tank's muscles were tense under her hands. The glorious stretch of too small sweatpants announced his untapped potential as an underwear model. Billions of women everywhere were deprived of this sight. And thankfully so, she thought, with more than a little possessiveness on her part.

Diana wondered if she was becoming a slut. Psychic wolven groupie slut, that was her.

"What are you doing out of bed, little sister."

"I'm not your little sister," she grumbled and pushed away, her pride pricked. "I've got to go to the bathroom. You scared me. Don't swoop out like that."

She glared up at him, feeling childish. Simply because he wasn't interested didn't give her cause to throw a guilt trip at him, but she didn't feel like exercising any self-restraint.

"I apologize for the fright." He was so serious. A professor on steroids. Tank unclenched a fist and raised his hand to brush his knuckles down her cheek.

"And for the physical complications our *blood donations*, mine and Chase's, have caused you. The addition of more supernatural blood will cause your hormone levels to shift while your body readjusts."

Huh? The reason she was so worked up was because of all the wolven blood she'd ingested lately?

Tank ducked his head. The thin braids slid over his shoulders and swung free. Unfortunately, whatever subtle cologne he wore made her feel even more childish. She opened the bathroom door and slammed it behind her.

Too bad he didn't feel like apologizing for anything else. Like being a man and blaming her mood on hormones.

Diana sighed. God, she was being a bitch. She knew it and that made it worse. She felt hypersensitive physically and emotionally. She wanted to cry and laugh at the same time at how absurd her life had become. Memories of the near rape by Dog blurred with the kidnapping.

Suddenly, she wanted to see that Karen was all right, not just feel the happy tug that was her daughter in the back of her head.

But first she needed to wash away the nightmares that danced behind her eyelids. She turned the shower on. The need to scrub the nastiness away before she was too exhausted to crawl back to the bed was more imperative than drawing her next breath.

Chapter Twenty-Seven

"Diana!"

The thumping on the door made her drop the purple squishy scrubber. Diana clambered out of the tub in defense of the bathroom door. She snatched her towel from the rack and held it to her chest, letting it drape down to cover the important parts.

"Hold on. I'm coming."

"Diana, open up or I'm going to break this door down!"

"Good God. Don't get your tail in a twist."

She jerked open the door. Adam stood in front of her, fist raised to pound her poor door in. A muscle ticked in his whiskered jaw. His facial hair was a couple of shades darker than the straggled mane on his head. The pale husky colored eyes were blood shot.

He looked exhausted and still ready to take on an invasion. Behind him more huge males ranged out. She heard the boys rather than saw them.

"What are you all? Thor and his pals from Valhalla?"

Someone behind the men sniggered. He stared. The men stared. Diana held her chin up, held tight to her towel, and stared right back.

Adam swept her up. She squealed and sucked in a breath. Her chest might be healing super fast but didn't like being jarred.

Adam froze. He carefully finished scooping her up, one arm under her knees and cradled her close to his chest.

"Adam! Don't!" She tried to readjust the towel and failed miserably. She knew she flashed everyone in visible range. Thank God the boys were behind the men.

"Are you okay? Did I hurt you?"

The man looked and felt so worried she couldn't help but grin.

"I'm fine. Can I *please* have some clothes?"

He nodded, shouldering past the crowd to her bedroom door.

"Everyone back downstairs. I'll holler when you can come back up."

"But, I want to see my mom."

Karen's voice was somewhere in the back with the boys.

"Is she okay? I want to see she's okay."

Their protests lightened some of the sadness in her heart. She felt … *needed*.

Adam set her on her bed like a fragile treasure and went back to shut the door. Diana started to get off the bed. She really wanted her clothes. The towel clamped to her chest just wasn't enough.

Adam waved her back down and went to her nightgown drawer. He pawed around before pulling out a long blue nightgown she'd treated herself to a few years ago at a pricey boutique in Tyler. It managed to be both conservative and sexy at the same time.

"Turn around." Diana circled the air with one finger. "Look for the robe on the back of the closet door." She told him while she slipped the gown on, and then stood for a moment to smooth the silky fabric down.

Turning back, his facial expression said how sorry he was that he'd missed the show. The robe had been buried behind several other, less appealing, robes of terrycloth, cotton, and flannel. Too bad.

She rubbed her nose. He smelled different, stronger, as if he'd been drenched in male pheromones. Like Tank had in the hall. Of course the hall had smelled like a testosterone factory.

"So. What's up?" She asked, taking the robe and belting it around her waist. As if it was a normal day and he'd come by to pay a visit. Chit-chat.

Adam rounded the bed and pulled back the fresh sheets someone had changed in her brief absence. He picked her back up, tucking her under the covers.

"Hey! I'm not crippled."

His face set in stone. Concrete male determination filled him.

Diana laid a hand over his. She wasn't sure what emotions she was receiving from him and what were her own.

"You don't have to do this. I'm fine."

He cocked his head to one side and stared at her with the wolfy expression his permanently furry cousins in the wild reserved for scientists and the like.

"Of course I do."

She gripped his hand on impulse, pulling him down to sit beside her.

"We need to talk. And shut up before you say something stupid, like I need to rest."

She still didn't know what had happened after she passed out. She felt her mouth opening, heard the words pouring out, and couldn't stop them.

"What's wrong? Is it about the werecoyotes? Did you find Brandon?"

Adam blinked at her like he'd been blindsided. His lips curved into a sensual grin.

"You're not all soft and sweet, are you, Diana Ridley?"

She narrowed her eyes and gave his shoulder a smack.

"I'm not a dessert."

He grinned. She smacked him again.

"Seriously." She took a breath, and then grimaced as a cough took over. Adam dove for the tissue box and shoved a handful into her hands.

"Ummm. Look, I know you want me to be your girlfriend."

"Mate." The sound of his voice vibrated through her. "Wolven mate for life. I want you for my mate."

"Like regular wolves."

He made a sound that thrummed through his chest, lulling her.

Do not become derailed by the sexy guy proposing. Focus. Did she really want to go through the whole marriage thing again? Diana pushed away from the comforting circle of his arms.

"I'm just not ready for m … ma … commitment." She was so pathetic she couldn't even say the word. "I was burned so badly last time. I'm just not ready. Maybe never."

Yeah. An excuse. At least Richard was good for something.

The intense stare never wavered, making her search for something else to say.

Excuses, excuses, excuses, her conscience taunted. *Chicken.*

"I mean, I only started dating again. And look how that turned out."

"I told you …." Adam was eerily patient. He reached to pull her into his embrace. She stopped him, pushing against his chest. She couldn't help but feel how nice it was under her hands.

Slut! Her conscience screamed. *Every man in the house was not fair game.*

Yes they are! Her hormones rallied.

"No. Keep your hands to yourself. You didn't want me to date anyone."

"No, not anyone. Just me."

She huffed a breath and told her hormones to shut up. She'd been stabbed. She didn't need to roll around on the mattress.

"You are so aggravating. Why me? I don't want to be involved. Why not find a nice wolven girl to bother?"

Adam tried to process what Diana was saying. He wanted her trust so that she'd agree to do the mate's bond. She probably wouldn't appreciate him doing Richard Ridley bodily harm, or rapping some sense into that kid of hers either.

It was getting idiotic to claim that neither she nor Mack were pack. Or Karen. The boys worshipped the ground the Ridley females walked on. And whether she admitted it or not, Diana doted on the boys. She loved them. Adam saw and felt that plainly though the pack bond.

Adam rubbed at his breastbone with the heel of one hand. He sucked in a breath of the thinning air in the room.

Trust. It all came down to trust. There was so little in his pack, he was falling victim to the effects. He hardened his resolve. Adam J. Weis was no victim.

"Adam?" Diana's soft question brought him back to the present.

Adam looked down and studied her pretty face for a moment. She had so much love to give. Selfish him, he wanted it all. He gave her a half smile before wiping his damp hands on his jeans.

"I haven't given you a chance. I've bullied and pushed at you to get what I want. Just as you haven't given me one."

He waved at her to let him finish, his nervous steps taking him back and forth across the room. He was going out on a limb, like he'd never done before.

"Hear me out. All right?" He took a breath.

"I came here last year, looking for my fiancée, Amanda. Garrick and his pack killed her." He held up a hand before she could interrupt. "Before you get upset, let me tell you that most wolven matings are arranged. It was all worked out long before Amanda and I met."

He looked at her for reassurance that she hadn't completely closed from him. Diana nodded again.

"Anyway, Garrick was a sick bastard. He did … bad things to the pack, to the boys."

"I know. Don't explain, *please*." Her voice held a combination of anger and sorrow.

"Someone here tipped off my pack in Tarrant. So I came to find her."

He stopped to look out the window, hands shoved in his back pockets.

"I did, eventually. Her skin was nailed to a wall, in his basement, the scent of violence and sex still on her fur."

Diana shuddered. So much of their short relationship involved violence.

There was a mix of anger, grief, and guilt that churned in him.

"They raped and killed your fiancée. What did you do?"

"I didn't love her. It was all arranged." He recovered old ground. Guilt swamped him, then anger. "I killed them. I was supposed to report back. But I killed them because they touched what was mine. And because I found out what was happening to the boys."

To Brandon, but he didn't want to go into that story. He'd pretended to be a stray so that Garrick would allow him close enough to snoop. He'd snooped all right and found both Amanda's pelt and the violated child in the same basement.

After that Garrick and the pack wardens were as good as dead. They just didn't know it. The sick bastards were supposed to be protecting the pack from harm, not causing it.

"Reporting back to Paul, my Pater Canis, was a technicality. I knew Paul would give the okay to clear them out. "

He looked back at the bed to gauge her reaction.

"Only he didn't. He called it a duel for ascendancy and wouldn't let me come back. Someone else was moved to the beta spot."

His half-brother Dom, the lawyer, got the beta spot. Adam's laugh was dry, humorless. Dom, who Adam had challenged and beat for the position, was back at Paul's side.

"A moving truck arrived a week later with my stuff."

"I knew from the first that you were an alpha."

"No." Adam shook his head. "I was Paul's beta warden. I protected the pack."

Diana smiled at the lost tone. He didn't realize how hurt he was that his old pack leader wouldn't let him go home.

"I think you are confusing rank with personal power. I'd bet that you were already an alpha at heart when you showed up here. You were more than ready to be on your own and your old leader knew it."

Adam considered her insight. A heaviness in his chest lightened. Maybe Paul had tossed him from the nest, so to speak, in the only way he knew how. Paul Sheppard was a sink or swim kind of guy.

"I thought that after I cleared out Garrick and his ilk, I'd take the boys back with me."

"Instead, he worked out a way so that you were obligated to stay here. I think your title fits you, Father Wolf. I'd bet he thought so, too."

"He's my father."

Her surprise prompted him to explain.

"He didn't raise me. My mother married a man, a psychic, named William Weis. Will's my dad. Paul Sheppard is ..." Adam made a loopy gesture with one hand.

He crossed back to the bed and sat on the edge. If he didn't finish this he'd go insane.

"As proposals go, I'm sure this one sucks." He took her hand.

"Listen before you say no again. You give us something that is missing. Hope, I think. The boys need someone who cares enough to make birthday cakes and cookies. To fuss at them when their clothes are wrinkled."

He was right, the proposal sucked.

"You want me to be den mother to your pack? To ride herd on a bunch of teenage werewolves? That's why you're proposing?"

She pulled her hand free. Not that she'd have said yes anyway. But, well…it sucked big time. A girl wanted to know that her man wanted, needed her for himself.

"Hello? I don't get furry. And I'm not likely to either any time soon. You might try *negotiating* for another of your kind."

"You're angry," he said.

Damn skippy she was angry. Diana narrowed her eyes. She kept her jaw locked before she told him what to do with his proposal. She did not want to marry him. Den mother indeed.

Adam sighed. He gave up trying to retake her hand and straddled her lap, one arm on each side of her legs, to capture her gaze.

"What you don't understand is that you *are* a part of the pack, Diana. You, and Karen, and Mack. Close your eyes."

He reached up and brushed his hand over her eyes, forcing her to close them. He leaned in to whisper in her ear. "Reach out. You have the pack alpha's awareness."

"I'm an empath. I'm aware of a lot of things."

"No. It's more than that. Close your eyes."

Adam placed his hand over her eyes. The warmth seeped into her skin.

"Close them. You are a part of the magic that weaves the pack together. Feel where everyone is, how they are. You can dispense comfort or pain as you choose."

Diana reached out with her senses to the fabric that made up the wolf pack. She felt the individual threads that made up each one. Knew the identity of each. They were hers. If she chose, she could follow each thread to its owner to find out what he was feeling.

She could communicate if she wished, not with words, but she could express a need or simple command. One strand, heavier than all the rest, glittered with power. She followed the thread back to the source. She opened her eyes, meeting his.

"Yes. I feel it."

Adam nodded.

"Even without choosing me as your mate, you are the Matra Canis." She didn't know what to make of his smile. "You are the Pack Mother of *their* choice."

Adam shook his head.

"It's not supposed to be that way. I don't know how the boys managed it. From that first night in the woods, when they brought you to me, they had made their choice. But I think that they needed to be able to choose. They need you to choose them back."

I need you to choose me. He didn't say the words. He was tired of begging for scraps of affection from his pack. She'd either choose them, *him*, or not.

"One more thing."

Okay, he wasn't quite through. He couldn't have her cutting all ties and walking away.

"Brandon doesn't defend himself, much less anyone else. Garrick damaged him so badly. But for you, he *changed*. He protected you from that man. He was running and afraid. He came back to make sure you would make it."

He sat back and watched her shoulders sag. Guilt was a wonderful motivator.

"I don't know. I need to think."

She did look tired. Wiped out. He'd laid a lot of responsibility at her feet and demanded she take it. He felt a tiny bit bad for her, but not so much that he wouldn't do everything in his power to keep her near. Not for the boys sake, for his own.

He got up and pulled the covers up.

"Get some sleep." He bent and rubbed his cheek along the sweet softness of hers while she was too tired to resist. "I'll hold them off as long as possible, but before long everyone will filter up here to keep you company."

Adam paused in the doorway to watch her drift off to sleep. Her short straight hair stood up in spikes against her pillow. He ached to uncover all the full womanly curves that taunted him under that nightgown.

"Have just a little more courage, for you. And faith, in me."

He quietly closed the door. There was more exhausting pack business waiting downstairs.

Chapter Twenty-Eight

Adam stood for a moment in the opening to the living room. Inside, everyone sat in a loose huddle. It amazed at him how comfortable the humans were.

His mother had never been so comfortable around wolven gatherings. That was why she moved halfway across the country, away from Paul Sheppard, to non-pack area, and married a man as human as she.

How human were psychics?

Mack laughed and play wrestled with Mark, knuckling the boy's blond chili bowl haircut, while Karen sat secure in her boyfriend's lap. Bradley's arms circled around the teenage girl.

She giggled and cringed when he buried his face in her neck. The rest of his pack, Tank and Chase included, chatted among themselves.

"There is a lot to do before tonight's hunt."

He walked to the center of the group and crouched in front of Karen. She met his stare with her own, unafraid, a touch uncertain for being singled out.

She was always in and around the boys, especially Bradley, so Adam had never singled her scent out before.

He'd been slow to realize that the boys had made Karen a part before his arrival. If she carried pack scent for another reason then the close association with the boys would hide that. Still, there were things he had to be sure of.

"You're a very pretty girl, Karen. It's no surprise that Bradley has taken to you." Adam gestured at the teenagers, together, as a couple.

"But, I have to wonder. What happens when it's time for college? I know I'm going to insist on it for Bradley. You know how young men are on the college scene."

Karen stared at him, her brow furrowed and her hands gripped at her boyfriend's until her knuckles whitened.

"No. I don't think I do," she lied.

"Adam."

He silenced Bradley's protest with a cut of his eyes. The weight of censure from the pack bored into his back.

"College is a happening place. Lots of other pretty girls. A guy's hormones are going to be playing hell. He's gonna slip up." Karen's face paled, as white as her knuckles. Adam went in for the kill.

"It makes me wonder. What's going to happen when he does slip up? He may get it on with another female."

Adam shrugged off Bradley's warning growl. The pup's uncomfortable noises didn't bother him.

"You know, at some point he's going to screw up big time. What are you going to do?"

Karen's white face pinked with anger. She struggled out of Bradley's grip and stood up with her hands on her hips looking down on Adam.

"You think I'm going to betray them? *Me?*"

She sputtered for a moment, obviously trying to find vile enough words without resorting to foul language. She looked so much like her mother that Adam had to suppress his smile under a scowl.

"Betray you? Let's get a few facts straight. I've been around far a lot longer than a year." She raised a little hand and started to tick off her fingers.

"I've helped hide the little boys from Garrick and his so-called warden scum. I've bandaged burns, learned enough first aid by the time I was eight to splint arms and legs. I've lied. And once drove the getaway car!"

By the time she finished her arms were waving wild enough for a plane to land by. Bradley grasped the hem of her tee shirt and tugged gently.

"Karen."

Off to the side, Brandon made a series of cutting motions across his neck for her to stop. Adam figured the rest of the boys were making similar cease and desist motions the girl did not heed.

"The getaway car?" Adam allowed himself to grin, finally. He couldn't have kept up the stern face much longer without choking. "Now that's a story I'd like to hear."

"Urp!"

Karen landed with a thud in Bradley's lap. The boy literally took matters in his own hands. He wrapped his hands around her waist and pulled her off her feet. He winced hard when she made contact and buried his face in the back of her neck.

He garbled something that sounded like, "Show some respect." But it was hard to make out through the whimper.

Adam stood and turned to face Mack. The ex-soldier was leaned back against the bottom of the sofa, arms crossed. He upended his hands in the air.

"Don't look at me. I'd shoot you myself before letting anyone else at your hide."

Adam shook his head at Mack's off the wall answer. Yet, he had no illusions that his friend wouldn't take him out if he deemed Adam a danger.

"Let's get down to business folks."

He crouched down, unlaced his work boots before toeing them off, and stowed the socks inside. Everyone else who wore shoes followed suit.

Adam whipped his tee shirt over his head. Karen gave a squeak of protest.

"Hey! Wait a minute!"

Adam turned back to the girl with a smile.

"Don't worry. It's important to be comfortable for this ceremony. Less restrictions on the body." Less mess too, he refrained from saying out loud. "If you want to change clothes, feel free to do so. Remember, there will be some touching of skin to skin."

He glanced a make to make sure the man understood he'd be included in this, too.

"Nothing perverse, I promise. Everyone keeps his, and her, hands and body parts contained appropriately."

Almost everyone in the circle nodded. Karen beat a hot retreat up the stairs to her room. Adam stepped over Seth's outstretched legs and crouched in front of Brandon. He kept his hands in plain sight on the tops of his jean covered thighs. His voice was low and careful.

"That okay with you, buddy?"

Brandon drew his knees up under his chin. He looked past Adam, trepidation oozing from him. Adam kept his body language non-threatening. He didn't need another outburst from the boy.

No, he didn't think he could *handle* another outburst like the kitchen incident.

"You're making Chase and Tank your wardens."

"Yes, I am. But they're not so much my wardens as the pack's. A warden's job is to protect the pack from harm. Any harm. Even if it's someone in the pack that's doing harm. And frankly, as is, we're not strong enough to hold our territory against other predators."

"What about the werecoyote pack?"

"Well," Adam felt as though he was walking a thin line. One wrong answer, and the kid might take him up on walking out. Brandon might make it alone, but he'd fare far better with his pack to buffer for him. "I'm going to order a purging."

"What's a purging?" Seth sidled closer. Serious curiosity lit his dark eyes. "Are you going to kill all the werecoyotes?"

Adam reached out and set a hand on the fuzzy dark curls. Chatter started up around him. He raised a hand in the air to quiet them.

"Good God, people. A purging is an evacuation of other predatory supernaturals. It's not a slaughter."

He didn't know if his kids were naturally a bloodthirsty lot, or they acted that way because of all they'd been through.

Though, truthfully, a purging was exactly that before the various supernatural leaders got together and hammered out a treaty.

"What sets wolven apart from weres is that we are an organized society. A strict society that protects itself. We can't do that if we let in the weres, vampires, and other predators, that do not follow our laws, run amok in our territories."

Adam stood. All eyes followed his movement.

"We are wolven. We keep what is ours safe and we don't share with outsiders."

"But are you going to kill them?"

Adam looked down at Brandon. He sighed and crouched back down to the boy's level.

"What do you think?"

He waited, feeling the weight o the boy's judgment.

"I think that you will try to be fair. Some are going to die because Benj won't want to leave his businesses behind. And he thinks we owe him."

A slow smile formed on Adam's face. Sharp, white teeth, pointed for tearing his prey, gleamed.

"Benjamin Gates will die."

Brandon nodded. His knees bumped his chin. His focus found and centered on the two strays they were about to adopt. He was okay with whatever plans were made. Soon, his tormentor would be unable to bother him again.

"I don't like to be touched." Brandon's protest was small, but harsh in the scheme of the pack. A rejection.

"All right." Adam agreed. He knew the statement was false. Brandon was in constant physical contact with those he trusted. Bradley, Karen, Diana, and to a lesser extent the other boys. Occasionally, the boy brushed up against Adam to fulfill the need to connect that all shape shifters shared, wolven and weres.

Adam slapped his palms together. It was time.

* * * *

Diana woke to the sense that something was about to happen. Something momentous, she should be a part of. A glance at the clock said that she'd been asleep for only a few minutes.

Like before, Diana used the wall for balance. At the head of the stairs, Adam's voice lured her on. She descended the stairs, careful to hold on to the handrail.

"The Welcoming is a ritual as old as time, going back to before memory, when our kind slipped away from the human tribe to run with our cousin the wolf."

Adam's story swirled in her mind, as half remembered images tried to surface. She felt herself slip into the pack bond.

"Eventually, curiosity lured the wolven ancestors back to the human realm. But, after living so long among the pack, they were no longer human. But neither were they completely wolf. We were Wolven.

"A pack is more than a group that hangs out together. It is comforting your pack brother. Helping with homework. Watching for other predators that could harm the whole. The pack is family."

"Tonight we welcome Tank and Chase into our family."

He turned to the strays.

"We offer you acceptance. The comfort and trust of the pack. Do you accept?"

Both males stepped forward. Tank took another half step, presenting himself to the alpha. He swept his hair off his shoulder, baring his neck in a formal gesture of submission and went to his knees.

"In return for your gift, I offer blood and meat to the pack. My muscle to protect and provide. My blood to bind and heal. My allegiance to the Pater Canis and to the well being of my Pack."

Adam drew a pale claw tipped hand delicately over the vulnerable dark skin covering Tank's artery.

The words beat a familiar cadence in Diana's head, as if she'd heard them before, taken them inside her to live. She made it as far as the entry to the living room, edging around the frame to slide down the wall and watch the mesmerizing ceremony.

Adam took one sharp claw and drew it up his forearm. Blood welled and ran in scarlet lines down his wrist. He offered the arm to the man kneeling before him. Tank took the offering, lapping up his chosen leader's life's blood. A sense of satisfaction eased from the dark warrior.

"Blood to Blood. Brother to Brother. Hunt to hunt." Once Tank released the arm, Adam placed both hands on the still kneeling man's shoulders. Red drops ran down his forearm, dropping onto Tank's chest in the region of his heart. "Now, we run as one, my brother. Heart-Hunt-Pack."

Adam lifted his arms and Tank rose in a single fluid motion. He stepped back gracefully, making room for Chase.

Diana was drawn by the power in the ceremony. The sizzle ran through her, the connection made. Her limited understanding glimpsed what it was to be *pack*.

She felt joined with every male and female, running through the woods in harmony together. All four of her paws were the wind, her fur the cloud the wind pushed along, and the woods were her sky.

Diana sucked in a breath as she came back to herself.

While she was out running metaphysically with the pack she missed some of the proceedings. Chase was now kneeling in Tank's place at Adam's feet.

Adam started the chant again. This time, the pack, *everyone*, joined in. The swell of power lifted her up into sky again. Howl-song surrounded her. When it was gone, run to its end, the pack, human and wolven, flopped in a satisfied half furry heap together.

Diana smiled from her place at the door. She was too tired to crawl into their cozy pile, but it looked right. None of the wolves were unaffected by Adam's call of power. He was an alpha all right.

He lay back against the bottom of the sofa like a pagan god. His pack lay scattered around him.

Silvery gold fur gilded the dense muscles of his body. He was bigger in his man-wolf form. A pale blonde mane fell over his pale blue eyes, half closed, sleepy and satiated, after the huge amount of power he'd shared and tied to his pack.

The peculiar pale blue of his eyes fastened on her and he smiled at her, a strange and still handsome movement of his muzzle that exposed white predator's teeth. In that moment Diana felt a connection with him, a oneness of purpose that she'd never felt before.

A shaggy golden wolf rose and stumbled over to her, breaking the intensity of the connection. Adam smiled again and turned to gently scratch the neck of the wolf boy curled up next to him. The boy made a wuffy giggle.

"Chase, right?"

The gold wolf bumped his head against her shoulder and settled down. He laid his head across her lap. Soon a lanky wolf, so dark a brown he was almost black, curled up on her other side.

Chase reached his snout over, snuffling at his new companion then after a couple of cursory licks relaxed back into Diana's lap.

Their coats were clean with the twin scents of musk and woods. From a distance their fur looked silky and soft. Up close, with her fingers dug in, Diana felt the stronger, wirier over-pelt. Underneath, the second layer of fur was soft as down.

Comforted by the soft warmth of their bodies, Diana drifted back to sleep tinged with the images of the forest beckoning to her.

Chapter Twenty-Nine

"I want to go with you."

Adam pushed in the clutch and brake, and shifted the truck into neutral to look at the boy framed in the open truck window.

He clutched the door like a lifeline, as if his will were anchored to the truck. The boy's washed out features looked even worse in the night.

Adam's wolven night vision leeched the color out of everything leaving behind the stark, strained tension in Brandon's face.

Hell, he could feel the kid's need as if it were his own. As Pater Canis of the pack, it was. Adam's need for retribution was a fire in his belly.

"Not this time, son" Adam shook his head. Death glittered in his eyes. He kept his gaze on the house instead of the boy. No sense scaring the crap out of the kid again tonight.

He tried to keep his tone mild, for Brandon, but he was already preparing himself for what had to be done tonight. Before Benjamin Gates discovered where he left his nuts and retaliated.

Adam had already let one night go concentrating on Diana's injuries. Another would undermine his authority.

"There's going to be violence tonight. People will die."

Brandon nodded, leaning into the door. The heady scent mix rolling from the boy was a combination of gut fear and determination. His voice was hoarse.

"I want to go, sir. *Please*." Brandon took a breath. Once he started talking, he couldn't stop. His dark eyes pinned Adam with a feverish intensity the alpha leader could feel in his soul. "You said you would kill him."

Adam looked up at Brandon, meeting the boy's eyes. God. He didn't want any of the kids tagging along on this hunt.

Brandon especially, didn't need more blood on his hands after losing it over that psychotic biker. The kid needed a clean hunt, a rabbit, something for food. Not another vengeance killing.

"I said I would. I will. Now, get in the house. I want everyone under wraps tonight."

Part of the light went out in him. Brandon sort of folded in on himself. His hands dropped away from the truck window as he stepped away to give Adam clearance.

Adam put the truck in reverse and pulled out into the street. The red taillights put a darkish cast over Brandon's form in the rear view mirror. The boy's image in the mirror shrank then vanished from lack of light as he started down the street. But he was still in the yard watching.

Would he wait there, in the driveway, until Adam returned with news that the last of the bastards that had tormented him was gone? Torment was such an understatement for what they'd done.

Adam slammed on the brakes. He threw the truck in reverse and backed up the way he came. He slammed the brakes again to stop in front of the yard. He leaned on the door, resting his elbow out the window.

"You stick like a burr or I'm going to rip you a new one."

"Yeah!"

He watched Brandon run around the front end like he'd been invited to Six Flags and scramble into the cab.

Brandon squirmed in the seat. He retrieved a folded baseball cap from his back pocket.

"Are you ready? *Seatbelt, son. Seatbelt*," Adam grumbled.

Brandon pulled the Lobos Luna cap over his head and reached for the seat belt, buckled it in place. He flashed Adam the first predatory expression the alpha had seen on the boy.

"Bloodthirsty whelp." Adam laughed and grinned back, then shifted gears.

Let the hunt begin.

* * * *

Adam drove to the job site, leaving the truck in plain view. He and Brandon walked to the back of the house. There, they quickly stripped down and stashed their clothes inside the tool shed. Adam relocked the shed and buried the key.

They changed. Bones and muscles reshaped in a pleasure/pain of sensation. Fur flowed like water over their bodies. Their faces elongated, teeth exploding into muzzles.

The larger wolf, pale cream and silver, nearly glowing in the moonlight, waited for the smaller wolf to finish the transition. By no means could either wolf could be termed *small*. The alpha snuffled over the smaller, almost black wolf.

Once assured his companion was all right, the pale wolf swiped a few affectionate swipes of his tongue across the smaller wolf's jowl. He barked and ran into the woods behind the house. Behind him, the other wolf was a dark shadow.

As a wolf, Adam's senses far outranked those of his human form. The information from the world around him was received and processed much more efficiently in his wolf form. His power was no less, but his senses were greater.

He picked up the scent trail he was looking for and followed it. The trail was as visible to his nose as the leaves on the ground, more so since the wolven were color blind.

Scents had a texture and flavor that no human understood. In his human form, Adam's nose was far stronger than a human's. But changing into his wolf form, even partially, it was like a shroud being pulled away from his face. Who needed color when the scent offered up so much more information? Like going from two dimensional, bypassing three dimensional, and going for ten dimensions.

Adam found the small clearing he was looking for and circled it, aware that his enemies could have laid a trap. He sniffed both the ground and the foliage above.

A resourceful supernatural trying to keep a wolven pack from taking an area might form an alliance with the local fairy population. A vampire or a witch would lay spells designed for maximum damage.

Wolven were more resistant to magic and psychic attacks, which often raised the question as to whether their precious psychics were another form of magic wielding supernaturals.

Adam didn't know about much about werecoyotes. Until recently, he'd always assumed they were intelligent enough to stay out of the way of the more powerful supernaturals. He didn't give them a lot of points in the smarts department. Yet, after all his years of watching Paul's back, Adam erred on the side of caution.

Finally satisfied that he wasn't about to be blasted into oblivion or set upon by a bunch of fleas in a fairy thrall Adam entered the clearing. He'd escaped that particularly nasty trick, but seen the flea thing done before.

Adam consequently had a deep respect for fairies, especially the little bitty winged ones.

He snuffled around inside the clearing, searching for more traps. You could never be too careful about fairies. All he found was a three quarter mushrooms circle, nothing to worry about. Finally, Adam sat down and wuffed the okay for Brandon to follow.

The smaller wolf trotted in. Brandon's gaze searched the clearing before he dropped down beside his alpha with a canine sigh.

Adam sensed their arrival before he scented them. He wasn't alarmed. Everything so far was going according to plan. He stopped panting, and waited, his attention on the direction they would enter.

As expected, two wolves slipped into the clearing. Perhaps not as overcautious as Adam, but they were still wary. The black led the way. Tank the wolf was dark as midnight on a moonless night. He respectfully touched noses with the alpha then sat, tall and dignified.

The second wolf, golden Chase trotted in with a hello wuff and flopped down beside Tank in a comfortable sprawl. His amber gaze roamed, alert, despite his lazy appearance.

Wolven enjoyed the best of three worlds. The superior form of the wolf form was ideal for travel, even better for recon missions. Their supernatural heritage gave them stupendous endurance and strength, and the bridge to connect both human and wolf forms.

The human base form gave wolven the ability to communicate complicated ideals that the wolf's form could not. Supernatural gifts gave Adam an insight to the emotional and physical well being of the members of his pack, but for real communication he needed to change.

Adam started the change first, Tank next, and then Chase. The three dominant wolves changed alternately to protect the shifter while he was in the vulnerable first stages. Once the wolven achieved the wolf man form he was able to defend himself.

Brandon stayed in wolf form. The omega, the lowest ranking wolf in the pack, the kid also had the least reserves to draw on for the Change. The boy was strictly a follower. During this planning stage he would save his energy to change later if needed.

Chase grinned, showing fangs. His eyes gleamed red in the darkness.

"We tracked the coyote to their night time lair. It's a bar down by the railroad tracks outside of town called The Diamond Back."

"I don't know it."

Adam's knowledge of Palestine nighttime hotspots relied heavily on Mack's periodic carousing adventures.

What he knew for certain could be found in the telephone book. He spent half his time on business and the other half at the school, juggling aggravated teachers and counselors.

He didn't have time for a nightlife that didn't include the boys.

Chase spared another trademark deadly wolven smile. Tank crossed his arms over his bare chest. A look of disgust twisted his dark autocratic features.

"It is a dung heap that reeks of were scent," Tank sneered.

"Yeah, I might even spring for some flea dip." The bite behind Chase's words belied his light attitude.

And Mack thought *he* was elitist, Adam thought. He had nothing on these guys.

"Guards?" he asked.

"He's got three coyotes doing bouncer duty," Chase said. "Butt-sniffers, not muscle. By the way boss, I'd watch my tail. He's got a few regulars, old trails, same scent, that overlap, and they're not just werecoyote.

"I caught a whiff of cat, probably panther or mountain lion. Loners like that usually hit the were-bars for company every now and then. Most of the rest is covered up by the tobacco smoke. Don't know how the bastards breathe in there."

Tank picked up where Chase left off. Adam had noticed that his newest pack members did that a lot, loyalty and companionship that had been in place for years.

"The local government no doubt lost the battle to close the place down. We did not go in. An experience for which I am eternally grateful to have missed.

"In that place Benjamin Gates is alpha. We acquired our information via one of Gates' human followers. According to our informant Gates' will be the one *covered in chicks*. His wording, not mine.

"Yeah. The place is disgusting. Can't say we've ever hit a worse dive. They're begging for us to work the place over, the security is so bad."

Adam was satisfied.

"Fine. Let's run."

Chapter Thirty

The men changed, staggering the order as before for safety. They lit out in a dead run. The smaller dark brown wolf that was Brandon, kept up easily.

Chase darted for point, leading the way and keeping guard for his alpha. Adam, a cream-and-silver splash of light, dropped back to flank Brandon. Tank, shadowed their tails, making sure that no attacker fast or foolish enough attacked from behind.

Adam barked with the sheer joy of the run. He bumped the smaller wolf's shoulder with his own. In this form he felt the closest connection with his pack, to the life force that connected all his kind. His will became their will.

He surged forward, outdistancing the gold wolf. His nose easily picked up the two wolves back trail. He was the leader of the pack.

Adam ran until he smelled were. An old path crossed theirs, smelling of cat. He growled low in throat.

The acrid stench of tobacco and the bitter sour smell of old alcohol filtered through the woods. Here and there the scent of sex teased his nostrils.

Adam thought he spied a used condom under a nearby bush, a paler shape against the forest floor, but he didn't dare investigate. He could be right. Behind him, the small wolf sneezed.

The hunting party stopped at the edge of the forest and changed. This time Brandon changed, as well. The boy's gaze focused on Adam, waiting for an order.

Adam eyeballed the building for himself. As a human, his vision was better. Some color gave the building definition, while the dingy dirty appearance of the place detracted.

Outside, the place was deserted. Discarded bottles and trash dotted the ground between the forest and the bar. He didn't need the extra sensitivity of his ears to hear the loud twangy jukebox country music or the raucous noise from the bar's customers.

"What we need is a distraction," he mused aloud. "We clear out the building and someone as greedy as Gates will stay long enough to secure his valuables before leaving."

Brandon's voice was the least expected. "There's a storage room on this side. It's got paint and stuff for the werecoyotes' picnics."

"They have picnics?" Chase beat everyone else to the question. The utter amazement summed up all their shock.

"Well, yeah. Every moon-hunt they start out throwing meat on the grill. Goat, I think."

The boy got another strange look. No one dared ask about barbequed goat.

"Actually, I hear goat's pretty good if you cook it right." Adam surprised the wolven with his comment. He shrugged. "I've got a worker, Jase Ramsey, who swears it beats beef hands down. He raises them, or something."

Adam turned back to Brandon. He didn't say aloud, but he didn't like the idea of coyotes so socially organized. The ideal went against everything he'd been taught about weres. Not to have group picnics and formal hunts during the full moon. That implied pack unity. The hairs on his neck crawled at the thought.

"Does this group have any contact with outside coyote *groups?*" He couldn't bear to say pack in conjunction with the coyotes.

Brandon shook his head and focused on the building instead of Adam. The pack leader thought the boy looked younger, more childlike than his sixteen years.

He was average height for his age and very lean. Not exactly starved, but the kid definitely didn't have the bulk and muscle definition of his twin brother.

The look in the kid's eyes was nothing innocent.

Of course, standing stark naked in the woods while planning to kill someone and toss the rest out of their homes probably wasn't the best frame of mind to judge others standing there naked beside him planning the very same thing.

Adam still wanted to shove a few hamburgers down the kid. Like eight or ten.

He forced himself out of the ridiculous nurturing funk that had come over him and focused on what Brandon said, instead of the boy himself.

"What Chase and Tank said before, about them breeding out is true. They don't mix with humans, even psychics. They think that anyone who can't shift forms is inferior." Brandon lost his train of thought. He caught a small, pained breath and finished. "They don't mix with other animals either. Just wolves, because we look alike."

The three adults growled as one. Hackles rose. Three pairs of eyes narrowed.

"No," Adam said. "We're not alike. We are *wolven*."

Adam gestured at the building.

"Show us what you've got. I'm right behind you."

Brandon slunk off into the expanse behind the bar. His pale form, bare of covering, blended into the night with eerie grace and stealth.

He picked through broken glass, sharp rocks, and patchy weeds. The petroleum scents of gasoline and paint thinner led the way, though there were enough motorcycles and beat up vehicles in the parking lot to account for the gasoline scent. Especially, if some idiot had spilled a can of it nearby.

Somewhere close, a part of Adam's brain noted, was a female in heat. A were female. It was a morbid kind of interest that he dismissed quickly.

Brandon went directly to the recessed shadow of a locked door where the twin odors of gas and paint supplies were strongest. He also sifted other scents, charcoal.

Strangely, the same brand his dad, Will, had used when Adam was growing up, before he knew what he was. The sour smell of old beer. The metallic tang of metal rusting in water.

He scented traces of the blood and the death of a creature, not goat. They were old scents that could never be covered up. Gates had probably used his storage room to store more than just his barbeque stuff and paint supplies.

The lock was a joke. A padlock attached to a hasp nailed to the door and frame. The whole assembly came off in Adam's hand with a quick twist. Adam tossed the trash around Brandon into the dark room beyond.

He pushed the boy behind him and ducked inside. The scents enveloped him, telling their stories. Adam scanned the room with his eyes, finishing up the picture his nose painted for him.

Adam reached for his hip pocket and encountered the skin of his hipbone. He remembered why he always thought missions like this were a pain in the butt. Unless you were a kangaroo or an opossum, naked meant no pockets.

He found what he was looking for. A box of painting rags that should have been discarded.

Heavy fumes from the evaporated thinner came from the bucket. The same half-assed cleaning job had been applied to the cheap plastic roller trays stacked together. He would have a fit if any of his men treated tools like that.

Adam caught the scent of what he wanted. He followed the barest bit of sulfur to the source above the barbeque grill. He found the box of matches between the lighter fluid and the not quite closed zip bag of mesquite chips.

He picked his way back to the door to check on Brandon and his newly appointed wardens.

Chase gave him a thumbs-up sign, while Tank kept scanning his corner of the building for trouble. Brandon stood silently by the storeroom door, watching Adam's every move.

"Go wait in the woods," he told the boy.

Adam pulled out a match. He closed his eyes against the sudden flare and stroked the match against the side, tossing the fire into the rags. He lit two more and tossed them before dropping the matches between the cans of thinner and the bucket of half cleaned brushes and rollers.

Maybe it would look accidental, but more than likely no one would care to investigate the fire very far. The place was a dump and a gathering place for degenerates.

He ducked out of the room and ran for the woods. Behind him, the fire caught quickly. Adam spared a bit of concern for the trees should the fire get out of hand. There *were* a lot of flammables in that room. And the place *was* a bar. Liquor was flammable, too.

Chapter Thirty-One

The wardens and the boy met Adam in the tree line brush, out of sight from the bar. Together they watched the fire consume the storeroom, growing brighter as it fed on the flammables inside. They flinched at the explosion of cans and bottles.

Adam got the distraction he wanted. Doors slammed at the front of the building. He heard yells back and forth between the bar personnel coming to investigate.

The fire spread fast, escaping the storeroom via the roof. He imagined that the explosions damaged the inside wall of the storeroom, bringing the fire inside the bar. What Adam didn't hear was a fire alarm.

There was one other exit other than the usual entrance at the front. The wolven hunting party believed that was where Benjamin Gates would try to make his escape.

They moved to a better vantage behind a foul dumpster, planning to catch their quarry escaping from what they believed to be his personal bolt hole. Since none of the other patrons appeared to use the door they were either right or the door was blocked.

Adam was betting the door was out of the line of sight from the rest of the bar and near Gates' own table.

Another blast. This one was big enough to take out a portion of the bar. Probably the inside storeroom for hard liquor, Adam thought.

"Go back to the trees. If the fire comes to the forest, outrun it. Don't stall or wait for us, change and head home fast," he told Brandon.

He met and held the boy's eyes. Seeing compliance, Adam turned his attention back to the task at hand. He changed fast.

Fur spread like water over his skin. He ignored the itchy crawly sensation and the wrench of muscle and of bone jerking into different formations that happened when he forced the Change. With power was choice. Adam could change as fast or as slow as he wanted.

The sound of motorcycles and cars leaving came from the parking area. Rats deserting the sinking ship. No one wanted to be around when the fire department and the county sheriff showed up.

Finally, Gates and another werecoyote, probably a guard, slipped out the side exit.

Adam jumped out of concealment. He lowered his head, bared teeth, and approached stiff legged. His wardens flanked him on either side, blocking Gates' path to safety.

The werecoyote leader froze. His expression looked strained, then panicked. Three huge wolves snarled at him. Fear rolled off of the coyote leader, mingling with the combined scents of tobacco, the chemicals off of the burning building, and alcohol.

His suit was a ruined mess, stained with soot and wet patches of alcohol. He threw his hands in the air. A fat bank bag, clutched in one fist, dangled in the air.

Adam sneered inside. One of the reasons he rarely drank more than the occasional beer was alcohol's ability to inhibit the change, or the shape shifter's control of his change. Sometimes the results were unpredictable.

The werecoyote was definitely impaired. He tried a smile. It came out a wide grimace.

Adam's plan was simple. Corner the werecoyote and tear him to pieces. Adam would pass the rest of the bad news on to the remaining coyotes after.

The smile became real as the coyote's eyes settled on the space beside the dumpster. Gates' brightened and dropped his hands, less threatened with his chosen quarry in sight.

"Decide to take me up on my offer after all?" He met Adam's eyes. "Burning down my bar, Weis. Tsk, tsk. That's going to come out of your cut."

Adam snarled and walked forward, angry that the bastard had spotted Brandon. That was one of the reasons he wanted the boy in the trees.

The lascivious gleam boiled Adam's fury over. He stalked forward, head still down, ears still flat. He snarled again, baring his sharp wolf teeth.

"Hey!" Gates' threw up his hands again. He cast a glance in the direction of the parking lot and sidled in that direction. "But, you know what? I'm insured. I can let the bar slide."

Adam changed to human, drawing the process out to slow painful proportions while tracking the coyote leader to show off his precise control.

Okay, he was stalking Benjamin Gates, drawing out the bastard's fear because it added spice to the hunt. And because Gates deserved every terror filled second.

Adam's wardens flanked him, covering his back as he changed to a mostly man form. He felt Brandon disobeying his orders, following the wardens at a discrete distance.

If the boy wanted to watch, fine. Adam would deal with the fallout later. He had rivals to purge from his territory.

Adam the predator smiled a hungry wolf smile at Gates. Adam kept his teeth and claws, the tools he'd need for this mission.

"Actually, Gates, I don't care for your business. I'm here to serve eviction notices."

At the edge of the parking lot now, the werecoyote stopped. His eyes flared with anger. His skin flushed dusky to Adam's monochromatic, but sharp, night vision. Frustration and anger rolled off the were-leader. He screeched at Adam.

"You can't evict me, you selfish bastard. My pack roamed these woods when the Indians still camped here."

Adam flexed his fighting claws, sharp deadly digits that were more daggers than claws, designed for destruction. His pale blond hair blew around his face in the night wind, partially covering his eyes. The firelight cast a hellish flickering light in their depths.

He was both terrifying and beautiful, drawing the remnants of the bar patrons, but keeping them at a distance.

Adam raised his voice. Growly, like water over gravel and full of supernatural power. Magic coursed in the air, pulsed around him. He snapped the power out at the crowd with his words.

"Do you hear? All supernatural predators, weres, vampires and the rest. You have until noon tomorrow to leave my territory. Anderson County belongs to me and mine."

Faint whimpers of protest escaped a few members of the crowd. Adam's eyes followed them to their source. Duly noted, he made an amendment. He wasn't a *complete* asshole.

He slashed the air in a silencing gesture with the claws. It worked fine.

"Those with young under the age of twelve have forty-eight hours to make arrangements."

"No!" Gates screamed at his followers. "There are only three of them. We can take them!

The werecoyote's eyes raked the crowd. He pointed a finger at the wolven.

"Chris! Dennis! Eli! *Attack!*"

The werecoyote who'd left the building with Gates and two from the crowd jumped at the wolven party. Apparently, Adam and his pack were threat enough to burn off some of the alcohol in their systems.

The coyotes changed for fighting. They were slow to change, minutes longer than the weakest of the wolven pack.

Adam could have set his wardens on them during the vulnerable period. Gates probably would have. To wait was a matter of honor among the upper hierarchy of supernaturals.

To strike now would be a human's equivalent of a backstab. Mouths became furry muzzles full of sharp teeth. Their claws were smaller than the wolven, but still sharp and made for tearing. They stopped changing in mid-form as coyotemen.

"Get them! Can't rely on your cheating human now, can you Weis? All of you-- *get them!*"

Adam let the coyotemen come to him. While avoiding the werecoyote's slicing claws, he slowed the point man with his own weapons. He opened the coyote from chest to belly.

The coyoteman howled and fell clutching at his belly, futilely trying to shove his escaping bowels back inside.

The two wardens leapt past Adam, each taking down a werecoyote from the crowd that was brave, or foolish, enough to join the fray.

Blood sprayed from a severed jugular. Chase stood. He dropped the dying coyote to the ground. He spit the missing piece of neck back at the downed coyoteman then snarled at another enemy.

Blood and gore washed down the front of his nude body, rained into his skin, head to foot. The advancing coyoteman shook his head and turned tail.

Tank flung his enemy off to the side, freeing his claws from the coyote's body. Less blood marred his body but was still visible, a black shine on his dark skin.

Behind him, a mustached human in a short sleeved western shirt and jeans pulled a knife that shone silver in the night. The cowboy flung the knife.

"Tank!" Brandon yelled. "Behind you!"

Adam turned, catching the silver along his ribs, and the human in his claws. He shook the man hard and quick. With a muted crack, the human's neck snapped like a dry stick.

Adam hadn't expected wholesale suicide of humans and coyotes alike. He slashed a hand, scythe style, across a woman bearing a silver knife. He could taste the woman's blood, spiced with adrenaline, and the bitterness of drugs.

The scent of the silver blade aggravated him. He ripped the weapon away and threw it into the burning bar, now a roaring inferno. He stepped over the dead female, the last of the resistance against his pack.

His sole quarry was now Benjamin Gates.

Adam searched the area for his escaped quarry. The hunt pounded in his veins. Blood, death, fire, fear, and all the other scents melded together in an exciting melody.

Tank and Chase rounded up the bare few who were left, a mere five that all the fight had gone out of. The werecoyote prisoners whimpered and whined, crouching submissively at the wolven wardens' feet.

"Adam!"

He turned toward Brandon's panicked scream. Claws raked the air where Adam's vulnerable bare back had been.

At last. He smiled in anticipation.

Gates eyes reflected madness in the flickering light of his burning bar, the same madness Adam had seen in Garrick Moser's eyes the night he died. The werewolf had died in the fire he set for Adam. Now, the bastard burned in Hell.

Soon, Garrick would have his old partner Benjamin Gates for company.

The werecoyote snarled, showing the fangs he was finally able to manage. The werecoyote slashed the air again, pressing his attack. Adam sucked in his belly to avoid being raked. The coyote's claws might be shorter, but they'd still hurt.

"You should have taken my deal, *werewolf*," Gates spat. "You're bodyguards are a little far away to save you."

The werecoyote's glance over Adam's shoulder was all the warning he got. He moved, but not fast enough. An arm slid around Adam's neck. The extra weight of a coyote female on his back was slight. She held fast.

Pain lanced under his shoulder blade. The agonizing burn of silver poisoning radiated from the wound. Agony from the poison sucked at Adam's strength.

He inhaled around the deadly blade in his body. Striking the attacker in front of him, his claws ripped down the werecoyote's torso.

Gates grappled with his own claws. Physically shorter, the werecoyote's teeth sank into the meat on Adam's bicep, an easy reach for Gates. He'd have to stretch to go higher.

Adam tried to rake a claw backwards, to shake the bitch off his back, only to return his claws to the werecoyote leader's ribs. All the while, he fought to keep Gates' snapping teeth away from his face.

The silver in his back robbed him of strength, while the female's vice of an arm gave his neck a measure of protection.

Adam dodged away from his attacker's sharp teeth only to have them latch onto his collarbone. He grunted and tried to twist away from the silver, the coyote on his back, and the one attached to his front. His collarbone broke under the pressure, almost as painful as the silver blade in his back.

Desperate, Adam let go of Gates. The coyote hooted with glee.

"You're going to die werewolf and *everything* of yours will be mine."

Adam dodged one way. His fist flew from the opposite direction. With his good arm, Adam's next shot turned into an opened handed grip on Gates' face. The werecoyote began gnawing the hand into dog meat.

Adam ignored the screaming in his ear, the pain in his back, and jerked his hand free. He bent his knees, set his stance, and slapped away Gates' claws one handed.

Inside the coyote's guard, Adam went for a snatch and grab of Gates' larynx. His claws closed around the werecoyote's neck and sank in with slight resistance. Warm blood washed over his hand. Adam jerked his fist back, taking half the coyote leader's neck with him.

The flea on his back fell off. Adam turned to face the female, his one good hand reached the handle of the silver blade and he pulled it out. He dropped it on the ground next to the sobbing female curled up at his feet.

The werecoyotes and their humans stopped, stared, shocked at the fall of their leader. Adam stood tall and straight. He gazed around at those still standing.

"Anyone else have a problem with my arrangements?"

"I do."

Chapter Thirty-Two

Adam couldn't believe his eyes. Two crouching female werecoyotes held Brandon stretched out between them, his arms pinned behind him. The boy looked ill. His eyes were closed. His breath was excited. So was the poor kid's body.

How many females did Gates have hiding out in the fringe? As one, Tank and Chase started for the females and their hostage.

"Stop!" one of the females cried. "Come closer and your wolf dies. He's no use to any of us dead," she said.

Neither of the females was overly pretty. With long brown hair that would probably be coyote red in the daylight and roman noses, the females still looked slightly canine in their human forms. They looked to be in their mid-twenties. But they were in heat and they were close. Rich pheromone perfume teased the air.

Adam found himself interested and disgusted, as well.

One of the females rested a hand on the boy's bare thigh. The other ran her fingers through Brandon's hair. She seemed mesmerized by the texture.

"You killed Benj," she stated. She didn't look overly distraught. Her dark eyes glittered, though, with some emotion. "You owe us."

"I don't owe you anything. You leader is dead. You have no running grounds. Let the boy go unharmed and you and your family can leave this territory without any trouble." Breathing shallowly helped both the pain from his wounds, and the obvious new pain that was beginning to irritate him from his traitorous hormones.

The dominant female laughed. Her full breasts were tight with the need from her heat and strained against the fabric of her too small tee shirt.

"You've killed everyone that matters to me already, besides my sister," she growled. "This one was promised to us already."

"He wasn't your leader's to promise. He belongs to me."

The female made a strangled sound in her throat. She stood, dragging both Brandon and her sister up with her.

"No. Garrick promised me a fertile mate. He promised me this one. We *know* he's capable. He's mine, and Dresilla's," she added her sister's name on when the female growled her protest.

Brandon shuddered.

"No," he said softly. "No, no, no."

Brandon's breath came in short pants that brought a fresh whiff of the females' scent with each intake. He didn't want to want this. This was his embarrassment and shame. Wolves didn't mix with coyotes, Adam said.

He concentrated on the acrid scent of the fire. The bitter scent of Sheila's hairspray as she bent close. Her hands in his hair made his skin crawl. The sick sweet smell of her perfume made him sick to his stomach. No, the female did that all on her own. Dresilla's sharp claws raked across his hip, leaving hot lines in their wake, marking him like she did during sex. Only then she drew blood.

"Garrick's promises died when he died." Adam's voice came through the haze of his fear and disgust. "Let him go."

Brandon struggled. He didn't want to disappoint Adam even more.

No. He wouldn't lie still and let them do it again. Dresilla smacked him on the butt, digging her claws in for extra punishment.

He heard Adam, only not the words. He felt the anger, felt his own. The heat of the emotion burned through him, drawing the supernatural power from the place hidden within him. Brandon wouldn't let them do this. Never. Again.

This time, Brandon didn't merely let the monster out of its cage. He embraced it. He changed. Adrenaline lent him speed and physical energy. His jaws found and closed on his tormentor's flesh.

The wolf didn't understand the shouts around him. Only escape. He snapped. He lunged. He bit. Finally, he slipped loose and found a bolthole, a place to stay out of the way while the alphas fought.

When the fighting stopped the only sounds were the cries and whimpers of the wounded and subdued coyotes. Crouched under a car amid the scents of fire, blood, death, and ready females, the smallest of the wolves hid and trembled. He watched it all.

He tried to think, to focus on what the lead alpha, a pale two-legged wolf whose magic tugged at him, said. The words were simply noises used by two-legged humans. He was afraid. He was a four-legged wolf now. He crawled deeper under his hiding space and whined, wanting the four-legged alpha wolf to come for him.

When the other two-legged wolves bent to reach for him, he snapped at their human paws and darted out from under the space that wasn't safe anymore.

The smallest wolf remembered that he was supposed to run to the trees. So he did. He ran and ran, all the way *home,* where he was safe.

Chapter Thirty-Three

"Brandon!"

Adam reined in the urge to find and comfort the fleeing wolf. There was still work to be done. Benjamin Gates lay dead by his hand, exactly as planned. As Adam expected, the trauma of the last few days was too much for the boy.

Before the boy changed, Adam had sensed a difference in him. The boy had exploded in a fury of fur and fire. It had been one of the fastest changes Adam had witnessed.

Once Brandon freed himself of the females' clutches, he'd hightailed it, literally, under a car. There the boy stayed until the wolven tried to coax him from under the car.

"Damn kid nearly took off my finger," Chase complained while dragging another body to the fire. The fight hadn't taken more than ten or fifteen minutes.

The flames were still burning bright and hot consuming more of the building. When it was done, there would be nothing left of the bar. Adam intended for the dead to be part of that nothing.

Adam flicked his eyes over the able bodied werecoyotes. It was cruel, but had to be done.

"Those of you that can move, get to work. The fire department may be slow, but they will be here soon."

He bent and grabbed Benjamin Gates' body to heft over his still good shoulder. Tank's dark hand covered his. The warden gently pulled the carcass from his alpha.

"Allow me, Canis. I will make sure he burns."

Adam nodded, biting back the nausea from his injuries and the silver poisoning.

"Move it people!" Chase urged the werecoyotes on with their grisly task. "Fire truck's coming! If you don't want to be here when it shows up, you'd better get moving."

Adam watched the last of the bodies tossed into the building. The flames covered enough of the front so that the last one was a difficult throw battling the heat and smoke. Chase took the body away from the were and chucked it inside.

This wasn't the first time Adam had to do something horrible to protect his pack. He looked around. Now the stakes were higher.

He watched the building burn and realized that whatever it took, whatever he had to do to keep his pack, all of them, safe, he would do it.

A deafening *boom* shook the ground. Everyone dropped, taking cover where they could. Adam looked up, seeking out his two wardens. His gut clenched.

"Tank! Chase!"

Damn, he couldn't hear past the ringing in his ears.

Ash and pieces of the bar rained down around him, catching in the dry brush and trees of the woods. He caught movement out of the corner of his eye.

Chase waved at him to come, then pointed down the road. Flashing lights were making their way slowly up the road. Adam chose the better part of valor and followed his warden into the trees. Here and there, small brushfires flared up.

The forest. Adam's gut clenched at the new danger. He glanced around, but he didn't even have a shirt to beat out flames with.

"I should have kept a closer eye on the boy. I thought they were surrendering. The female's scent …"

Tank's distress over Brandon made Adam pause and rest his good hand on the big man's shoulder for comfort.

"Just say it." Chase's eyes were hard amber bits. "They were a couple of sneaky bitches."

Adam started to shake his head and stopped short. His broken collarbone made movement almost impossible. He'd have to change soon to jump-start the healing process.

He prayed that the fire department would concentrate on the forest. Aside from the wildlife and the trees, there were human homes a few miles away. A fire could travel fast.

Adam's eyes blurred. He focused again on the small fires and watched it fizzle out in a small cloud of steam. Small multicolored sparkles flew around the extinguished fire and up into the trees.

He turned his attention back to his pack. Mentioning the sparkles or the extinguished fire might have Tank fussing more over the silver poisoning.

"Don't blame yourself. Either of you." Adam blamed himself enough for all of them. "Anything can happen in a fight. You do the best you can at the time."

They watched the fire truck from the safety of the trees. Tank fussed over Adam's wounds until he growled and snapped at the big man to leave off. The volunteer firemen made a big show spraying the surrounding area so that the fire wouldn't spread.

"You're lucky, wolf. Between the fire department and my people, the fire won't spread."

Tank and Chase closed ranks around their leader and faced the intruder with bared teeth. Fighting claws ran out like switchblades on the warden's hands.

Jarred Morgan held his hands out in the universal sign of peace. He looked very different without his dorky cowboy getup. A gauzy sheet wrapped around his body similar to a toga or ancient Greek style. He still wore the black-framed glasses.

Adam finally figured out what the scent was that eluded him.

"You're an elf," he accused. A fairie lord. Adam really didn't want to mess with fairies, anytime. Never mind when he was wounded.

Morgan smiled. He glanced up at the sparkles that coalesced over his head. Scent and closer inspection by the wolven revealed a humming mad swarm of fairies.

"Mostly an elf," Morgan corrected. "I told you I'm mixed. The purebreds in the courts hate it when we mongrels think we're good enough to associate with them."

Tank and Chase relaxed their stances a little. Enough not to offend a fairie lord, but not enough to jeopardize Adam's safety.

Adam wondered how long he'd have to chat before he could go curl up somewhere and tend to his wounds. Would it insult Morgan if he emptied his stomach in the bushes? The silver was making him *very* nauseous.

"Take your Pack Father home, gentlemen." Jarred Morgan stepped back into the trees and disappeared. Fairie folk were more at home in nature than wolven. "The fire will not spread any further. The county has been trying to shut down this place for a long time. They'll be happy it's gone."

Adam wanted to stay. He managed to wait until the fire was out. The water hoses made puddles that the volunteer men stomped through until the parking lot was a muddy mess.

The county sheriff showed up and made it a point to canvass the area by flashlight, looking for anything suspicious. Adam didn't care what the final verdict was, so long as the wolven were left out of it. While the sheriffs made notes in their notebooks and talked to the volunteer firemen, Tank finally pressed Adam to Change.

The wolven slowly headed for home, followed by a sprinkling of colored fairie light.

Chapter Thirty-Four

Diana stirred awake. In the dim lamplight, the gleam of wolven eyes watched from the corner of the room. Intent and hungry, she saw the visage of the predator that had hunted other predators earlier tonight. She wasn't afraid.

"You're back."

She didn't see any obvious injuries until he came closer, accepting the silent invitation to join her. Closer inspection revealed the weary strain in the lines around his eyes. His normally fluid movements dragged.

"You're hurt."

She'd prayed for him to come back alive and well. Oh yes, she'd fumed and vowed to rip Adam Weis a new one for taking Brandon into that mess. But he was back now and she couldn't wait to touch him to see for herself that he was okay.

Adam rolled one shoulder in answer before using that arm to pull off the tee shirt he'd donned after his shower.

He'd wanted to come to her immediately, but had to get rid of the stink of blood and death and vengeance first. He'd made do with a phone call, telling Diana the basics and assuring her over and over again that the kid wasn't hurt.

The sweatpants came off next.

She swallowed at the pink lines of shredded tissue healing on his torso. The mass of scar tissue on his collarbone was eerily similar to her shoulder bite, only much worse. Her mind blanked of everything but the thought of how she might have lost him.

"I stayed up and waited."

It was so late and even though she felt better, her own healing injuries dragged her energy level down. She'd fallen asleep listening for his truck.

Nude, he crawled into the bed careful of jostling her. Diana leaned back as he covered her gently with his body, settling between her legs. One armed, he held himself away from her chest. His other hand gently traced her features as she tried to decipher his feelings. He was shut down tight against intrusion.

"Adam."

"Shhh. No words."

His head descended. The clean mint of his toothpaste mixed with the flavor that was uniquely Adam filled her mouth. She matched him stroke for stroke, their tongues mimicking the act of lovemaking.

Heat filled her belly. Her breasts tightened, ached for his touch. She moaned, trying to pull him down so that they lay flush.

He slid down. His fingers made quick work of her pajama top buttons. Brushing a brief yet tender kiss near the healing chest wound, he buried his face between the full breasts that teased him constantly. Her wonderful tits played a major role in his dreams and fantasies.

Citrus and vanilla surrounded him with the feeling of peace, of homecoming.

All he could think of while getting his pack settled at home was getting here. To Diana, his haven. He *needed* her. His mate. Needed her so badly that he could not chance her glimpsing his emotions and pushing him away.

Diana moaned as he suckled her breast, threading her fingers through his hair. A direct line of heat shot from her breast to her womb, which contracted in sheer pleasure. A hot work roughed hand replaced his mouth when he switched breasts.

Adam didn't just suck her nipple. He feasted. Rolling the berry tip around with his tongue, he scraped her sensitive skin with his teeth. The opposite nipple, he plucked with his fingertips. She was the perfect dessert.

Diana keened in ecstasy, writhing upwards against him.

God, she needed this. Instinctively, she reached out with her gifts, to share the pleasure. A blank wall met her efforts. She was as blind as any normal human woman to her man's innermost feelings.

In a way, it was freeing. She only knew what he showed her with his body. And his body said that Diana Ridley was sexy and arousing. Her hands traced over the roadmap of the battle.

Thank God, they healed so fast. She was too attached to him by far.

Adam rolled over and her thoughts scattered. Her pajama bottoms had disappeared without her realizing it. Now, she sat straddled over her very own werewolf lover.

He stretched his arms over his head. In a tiny fantasy, she could imagine him bound, a slave to her whim.

She felt powerful. Bold. Desirable.

A smile tugged at her mouth for the delicious body on display. Wide muscular shoulders, defined pecs, and a six pack abdomen were perfect to drool over.

Diana danced her fingers over the valley that divided his body. Fine, pale hair made an almost invisible trail down. His staff nestled against the crack of her behind, teasing her. So close she ached for him.

Adam moved when she moved. His blue eyes grew darker by the moment. She teased him, just by moving up and down against him.

God he was so erect. So big. She couldn't stand it anymore. Raising to her knees, Diana speared herself on his thick sex. Shuddering as he slid inside.

With a growl, Adam grasped her thighs, striving to match her stroke for stroke.

God, the man knew how to work it. He swiveled his hips, gaining entrance to that special spot inside and rubbing over it again and again.

Diana's nipples tightened even more, her body a flame that grew in intensity. He was the fuel making her burn bright. She ground down on him as he ground up.

The pace shifted, faster. His fingers grazed her abdomen and his thumb found her clit, massaging the little nub. Diana's head fell back as the pressure below built. She felt him growing harder inside her body. His strokes delved deeper as she swelled around him.

Someone moaned. Someone growled. The world shattered into an explosion of stars and she locked up around him.

"Ahhh!" Adam's howl cut off as he strained and shuddered against his climax. "Mine!"

The word was a garbled growl, but she understood. Diana fell across him, sated. The possessive didn't even bother her.

He laid a hand over her behind, stroking her like a cat.

Finally, she managed to sit up. Her eyes felt crossed from all the pleasure. The faint trail of hair caught her attention and she followed it down. The dark curls of her sex mixed with the white blond of his.

She shoved away the half formed notion, already sliding into an exhausted healing stupor as she lay down beside him with a kiss on his chest.

When she woke, he was gone.

* * * *

One week and four days later, Adam stood at Diana Ridley's door, ready to settle in person what he'd only been able to hint at in snatches of conversation spoken in moments of stolen privacy.

Adam's parents, proving what wonderful psychic parents they were, showed up at his door in time to make breakfast the day after the coyote fight.

Cheryl and Will spent the next week and a half proving what wonderful grandparents they were, taking care of things while Adam and his wardens facilitated moving the weres out of Anderson County.

He'd helped pack up and send off the four remaining coyote families, a werepanther that treed Chase for twenty minutes out of sheer perversity, and a family, of all things, of *wereraccoons* that everyone thought were hilarious until they changed.

As Mark so succinctly put it, *Dude. That is one freaky family.*

Adam's parents took the boys and Karen to Six Flags. Cheryl stuffed them with cookies that made Adam miss Diana all the more.

Will took everyone fishing, something that Adam had forgotten how much he enjoyed. Growing up, Adam had had a lot of great times with his dad fishing.

Watching Chase gripe and bait all Tank's hooks because the snooty warden refused to touch something as disgusting as fish bait was priceless.

The boys loved their new grandparents and whined when they had to leave. Karen cried and hugged Cheryl like she'd never let go. Adam loved his parents all the more for the gift.

The only flies in the ointment, so to speak, were Brandon and Diana's absence.

After fleeing the burning bar, Brandon went directly to the Ridley house and stayed there. Diana had taken two weeks off work to stay with the traumatized wolf.

Now, Adam was here to make things right.

He knocked on the door, wishing he felt the same freedom the boys did, to barge right in. He frowned at the furious barking inside.

The door flung open. Karen smiled bright as a new penny up at him. She cocked a fist on her hip and frowned up at him prettily.

"Why are you waiting outside, silly?"

She snagged his hand and tugged him inside by the arm.

"Cut it out Brandon!" She called over her shoulder.

The barking stopped and Adam caught sight of the dark brown wolf in the living room.

Brandon peered over the back of the couch, ears laid back with suspicion as he watched Adam. The wolf whined and broke eye contact, ducking back out of sight. But not before Adam saw the red collar.

He frowned hard. A small growl of displeasure escaped him.

"Calm down, Adam. You're scaring him," Diana said.

The sight of her made his mouth water, or it could have been the meat and cheese smell of lasagna coming from the kitchen.

"He's not a dog," Adam protested.

His fantasy woman walked past him to the kitchen. Her hips sashayed an invitation for him to follow. The wolf ran from the living room and followed on her heels. Adam couldn't help but follow, too.

"You're right. He's not a dog," she threw back over her shoulder. He watched the sway of her ass instead of the irritating collar.

"But the city isn't goin to believe that he's really a sixteen-year-old kid who prefers being a wolf. I thought the collar was appropriate. He liked the red one."

Diana raised one delectable shoulder he'd like to nibble on.

"So, there you go. Tea?" She offered him a tall glass, already prepared and waiting for him. She'd known he was coming.

He cocked his head as he studied some indefinable change in her. She looked different. More serene, like the Mona Lisa. A woman with a secret.

"Did you cut your hair?" Adam threw out the question as he accepted the glass. When in doubt, it was always a safe bet that a woman had had her hair done.

Diana laughed. The poor man really didn't have a clue.

Karen, bless her, had kept Diana informed of all the goings-on while she tended to Brandon. She'd worried and fretted until he called each night to check on her and his missing wolf.

But she didn't dare leave Brandon alone at first. All the boy, wolf, did was hide under her bed.

Adam didn't understand yet how far the boy had retreated from the world. How much damage those monsters had done to him.

Selfishly, Diana welcomed the distraction from her own problems. Of course, Brandon had turned into another very delicate and odd situation to deal with.

Matthew, she finally decided, was a big boy, a man really. He was graduated from high school and starting college. His life. His choices. She had to let her son go.

Diana finally broke down and visited Laina, wolf in tow.

These days, Brandon didn't stray far from her side. After lunch and a rather emotional let-it-all-out girl talk, Diana's ex's ex handed her a small envelope with MOM scrawled over the front in Matthew's handwriting. The message inside was short and to the point.

I'm sorry, Mom. I love you. Matthew.

Diana clutched the letter to her breast and cried. Laina began to cry, then Sherry, Laina's girlfriend started to cry. Brandon became agitated. Diana finally had to calm down and reassure him, scratching behind his ears.

By the time lunch was finally over, the women weren't best friends, but they were amicable.

Diana felt good, better than good in fact. She gave Adam a small smile and decided to have mercy on him. She dished a portion of the lasagna she'd made for dinner and passed him the plate. She'd already enjoyed a share of the warm cheesy dish when it came out of the oven.

Who knew that wolven blood would speed up your metabolism? In the last week Diana had trimmed off nearly ten pounds without changing her eating habits. Okay, she'd sneaked some chocolate cake, but she deserved it with all she'd been through.

She cut Brandon a piece and took him out to the patio to eat it. There was already a bowl of iced tea on the lap tray she had set out earlier. Her neighbor was beginning to think she was weird.

Oh, well. At least Brandon was eating, instead of lost in the funk he'd started out in. Diana slid the glass door shut behind her and turned back to the wolf in a man's skin in her kitchen. Adam stared hard at Brandon, hunched over his tray, nibbling at the lasagna.

"He needs to come home."

Diana cocked her head. She realized where she'd picked up the mannerism and smiled to herself. Here we go, she told herself.

"He's not human, Diana. Don't pretend he is."

She blinked, and then looked out at the patio where Brandon had abandoned the food and was nosing a ball around, lost in a private game of fetch.

"You're kidding, right?"

She walked around the table to go nose to nose with the stubborn alpha male. "I know exactly what he is. And you, too." Diana took a breath and ventured a guess. "I think maybe it's you who are confused."

She felt the anger and frustration, a tight knot inside. Adam shot up out of his seat and pushed past her.

He stormed into the dining room and stopped, struggling with his own inadequacies. He set both palms down on the smooth finish of the dining room table, letting the cool texture seep into him.

Adam sensed her behind him. He took a deep breath and confessed. "You're right. I don't know what the hell I'm doing." Frustration knotted and rolled in his gut.

"Every day, I wake up. The school calls because Mark or Rick have flooded halls or they're charging ten bucks a peek through the glory hole they made in a locker into the girls changing room. I don't know what to do with them most of the time."

He took another breath and looked her in the face. "I don't know what to do for Brandon. I thought I was doing right, letting him face them."

Diana started to tell him it was okay. He kept on talking, laying his frustrations out.

"Half the time I want to deck, Chase. Then there's Tamara. I didn't realize anyone would be interested in her so soon. She's barely moved down here and ... then there is you and Karen, and Tank. That's a lot of psychics for one area."

"Who's Tamara?"

Diana set a fist on one hip and stared at him in the eye. She raised her eyebrows meaningfully, feeling the stirring of something she absolutely would not call jealousy.

Adam blithely continued unloading his problems. He ran his hands through his hair.

"A good alpha always knows what to do. The Canis Pater is supposed to have all the answers. I'm feeling my way blind in the dark hoping no one notices."

His turmoil stirred inside Diana. Giving a huff, she gave up on finding out who Tamara was and slid her arms around him, offering comfort. These wolven of hers always seemed to need comfort.

"Adam," she repeated his name when he didn't answer the first time. "That's what being a good parent is all about."

He blinked and looked down at his little female. He took her arms being around him as a good sign and turned around to reciprocate. She felt so good cuddled up next to him.

She smiled the little smile up at him while he tried to make sense of her words. She laughed. "That means you're doing a good job, you great hairy beast."

"But I haven't fixed anything. I might have broken some things big-time.'

Diana shook her head. Lord, but the man was dense.

"You can't fix everything. You love them through it. Brandon will get better," she assured him. "Maybe not today, or tomorrow, or even next month. But he will. And when he's ready, we will get him some real counseling."

She shrugged inside his embrace. "The rest? We take it one day at a time."

Adam grinned. She said *we*. A pair.

"One day at a time, huh?"

Diana nodded, noting the glint that came into his eyes.

Adam bent, taking advantage of her surprise. He swung his prize up into his arms, relishing the feel of her softness against his body. "Well, I have been feeling pretty frustrated lately. I was hoping you had a good answer for that, too."

His keen nose picked up the instant her libido caught up with his. His hands were already occupied, so he used his mouth to silence the inarticulate sounds she made while gathering her wits. He didn't want her to gather them yet.

Adam swept his tongue past her defenses and reveled in her taste. She melted against him, meeting him stroke for stroke, deepening the kiss before finally breaking away for a breath.

Diana's senses reeled. A stereo of sensation, his and hers, filled her as he scooped her up and started up the stairs. She draped an arm over his shoulder for balance, burying her nose in his neck to inhale his incredible scent.

Still, she wasn't going to make it easy.

"If you think you're getting any more sex without a first date. You've got another thing coming, Sparky."

"You know, I've always wondered what that other thing was."

Diana smiled into his neck. He decided that he could definitely learn to love that smile. The realization gave him a jolt, sharper than the nip she took out of his shoulder with her little teeth.

He stopped in front of her bedroom door. She felt what he felt. Did she feel the same about him?

"Adam?"

He leaned his forehead against hers and sighed. Well, no sense doing things halfway.

"Diana, I still want what I wanted before."

She stilled in his arms.

"A mate." She said the words carefully and wriggled to be let down. He loosened his grip, allowing her to slide to the floor.

"Yeah."

"For all the same reasons?"

He expelled a breath and moved to enclose her against the door with his body.

"I want you for all those reasons, yes. *Wait.*"

He stopped her from escaping under his arm. He ducked his head to meet her eyes.

"I want you for those reasons, yes. But, I want to for other reasons, too. I want to smell you, taste you, everyday. I miss you when you aren't with me." He touched his chest, pulling her trapped hand to his heart. "There is an emptiness here when you are gone."

Tears sparked in Diana's eyes. Adam panicked.

Oh, shit! He should have kept his stupid mouth shut! She sniffled. It was too much to hope she had a cold.

Diana nearly laughed at the panic on his face. She smiled through the tears. "That is the most beautiful thing anyone has ever told me. I missed you, too."

She caught his head, bringing him down for another toe curling kiss. She had to catch her breath afterward. She was blindsided by what she felt from him. Hope and ... love?

Diana bit her lip. Could she dash everything with her hang-ups?

"I tell you what, big guy. I'm not exactly sure what this thing is between us. I'm not saying no to the mate thing," she hurried to reassure him. Diana smoothed a hand over the hard planes of his chest, needing some comfort for herself.

"I don't know about love between two adults. I bombed out so bad the first time that I never let there be a chance for a second."

She wet her lips with the tip of her tongue and gathered the courage to look him in his beautiful blue eyes.

"I know that I care for you. A lot. *I need you.* Can we take it one day at a time?"

Adam grinned and bent to touch noses. He felt like he'd made a touchdown on Superbowl Sunday. She'd be his mate. Maybe not today, or next week. But soon. She was *his*.

"One day at a time, huh?"

"Yeah." Diana's voice was all soft and melty. She smelled ready to take up where they'd left off a moment ago.

"Then, I'm counting this as our second date. The next one can be the first."

Diana laughed as they tumbled onto her bed. "Oh, yeah. I insist."

The End

Printed in the United States
79786LV00001B/11